Zapocalypse:

Pathogen

To Renee,
In case of a zombie apocalypse,
I won't worry about Al with his
thick skin, the rest of us should
stock up on leathers - harder for their
teeth to bite through
- Carol Lynski

by
Carol Lynski

First published by Dog Ear Publishing
4010 W. 86th Street, Ste H
Indianapolis, IN 46268
www.dogearpublishing.net

dog ear PUBLISHING

ISBN: 978-1-4575-3435-5

Library of Congress Control Number: has been applied for

This book is printed on acid-free paper.

This book is a work of fiction. Places, events, and situations in this book are purely fictional and any resemblance to actual persons, living or dead, is coincidental.

Printed in the United States of America

Prologue

Maria rushed through the alley made by cages, wiping up all matter of debris where she sprayed, while the ill-appearing cats watched her with empty eyes. She hated double duty. Unlike Justo, Maria took her position seriously. There were bigger and better things coming than being a research assistant. Justo did what needed to be done and no more, leaving her this mess on his day off after her weekend. The cats with feline herpes, Justo's charges, would get the attention first today, and then she could concentrate on her babies, the genetically modified rats that would put her, Maria Castaneda, on the top of PhD program lists, maybe even get her into the United States and out of Mexico City. Maria already made the mistake of looking in on her charges; the rat dorm resembled a pigsty and would take some time to put right. Her jaw clenched thinking of the select words she'd have with Justo: *If you gave any of my rats your cat cooties, I will report you!*

Maria imagined herself pinning Justo with her words. She jumped at the rap on the cat dorm door.

"Hey!" Hugo yelled in. "One of your rats is loose!" He turned and left, message delivered.

"Shit!" Maria sprinted through the door, carefully removing her gloves and gown in the decontamination room the two animal labs shared and pulling on a fresh set before opening the door to the rat dorm. Sure enough, the sounds from the food bin made it clear where the wayward rat could be found. Any observer could see his tail from the window in the hall. Maria reached in and grabbed him as the little rat started struggling and shrieking. None of her charges acted this way before. The rat turned toward her sleeve and clamped its teeth down on her arm, tearing through the thin sterile material and to the flesh beneath. Maria screamed as it tried to burrow its head beneath the cloth without letting go.

Panic set in. She swung her arm, resulting in an even tighter grip as the blood flowed down her hand, starting to fill her glove. Coworkers from other labs punched in the emergency code to get to her. Antonio grabbed the rat's head, finally forcing the beast to disengage. It turned and bit the fresh meat on the man's hand. Antonio yelped and tore the rat away, flesh from the base of his thumb in its teeth, and threw it into an empty cage marked 142. Belinda maneuvered Maria to a chair, applying pressure to the free-flowing wound on her forearm.

"We'll get you to the hospital. What do these things have—some kind of rabies?" Antonio found a clean towel to wrap his hand and looked at the spreading stain with some concern.

Maria shook her head to clear it. "No, nothing contagious, —a genetic modification to fight disease. I can't give you more details than that."

Antonio let out a sigh. "That's why I don't eat anything genetically modified; you don't really know what it might do."

The rats were given a virion that could attach to any cell in the body. The virion contained a gene from stem cells that stimulated organs to replicate healthy cells and speed healing. Maria remembered the researchers cheering over their champagne, calculating the money they'd make. There would be no further need for transplants if a few healthy cells could regenerate the entire organ. The only cells the gene could not affect were the gray matter in the brain. The scientists did not factor in the virion's tendency to bind with foreign DNA, especially with DNA packaged in a naturally occurring virus.

Belinda shooed Antonio and Maria off to the clinic for stitches and any shots they may need while she sighed and began the job of cleaning. Belinda doubted that Maria would bring herself to say anything to Justo; she was just too young and Justo too entrenched. Belinda would make sure that the lab managers knew about the day's fiasco. However, with four labs to clean and four sets of animals to feed, there was little time for that. Belinda grabbed the scoop for the rat food bin and doled out the marked ration for each. Some of the rats, including the one in cage 142, stayed in the shadows in the backs of their cages, lunging and retreating when she approached. After feeding, she turned to a quick cleaning, finding gloves smeared with feces obviously not belonging to a rat—the proof of Justo's negligence.

Maria tried to call Dr. Anderson from the clinic to see if he wanted her to keep the aggressive rat from being transferred with the others the next day. The rats were being sent to secondary lab sites spread all over the world, sites that would verify the findings and make all those involved famous. His cell phone went to voice mail. Maria called the main lab in the States and was told that Dr. Anderson was on a plane to Beijing to get the lab ready. She left a message summarizing the events of the morning. The receptionist made sympathetic noises and promised to pass on the information when Dr. Anderson checked in.

Maria ended up in the hospital, after all, her fever an impossibly high 110 degrees, with Antonio arriving in a nearby hospital with similar symptoms.

The next morning, Justo received an earful from Belinda and then huffed as he organized the transfer of 280 rats, all screeching and straining against their cages, latching onto any finger that presented itself.

The baggage handlers always hated live cargo, even those in small cages. The supervisor marked off the packages—twenty to Beijing, thirty to Shanghai, twenty to San Antonio, Texas, twenty to Atlanta, twenty to Toronto, twenty to Berlin, twenty to London, thirty to Sydney, and so on until the shipments were accounted for. The rats shrieked when the covers came off their cages. The baggage handlers were in the process of transferring the live cargo to the appropriate flights when one man yelled and a pair of cages clanged to the ground, allowing the small doors to pop open and their contents to scuttle into the dark under the building. The handler stuck two fingers into his mouth as he chased after the escapees, but they were long gone. The man shrugged at the supervisor and went to pick up the next cage, careful not to let any body part get too close to the cover. The supervisor sighed. He'd need to explain why there were two fewer for the Atlanta contingent.

The rats smelled the meat from the restaurants and made their way through the ducts and vents, drawn by an incredible hunger. The few stray rats they met were either immediately killed and devoured or injured by the ravenous pair. Under the grating, they sensed their quarry, the dry-aging room in the "Best Airport Steakhouse in the World" where the prime cuts were spread on racks to age in their own juices. The two started to chew through the metal at the edge of the grate; they did not feel any pain from the jagged bits of steel. Once through the first barrier, the plaster was quick for rat teeth. They jumped to the first shelf a foot from the wall. The fat on the edges of the meat drew them from one cut to the next. After fifteen minutes of gustatory bliss, they were blinded by sudden light and shrieked from the pain. This brought on yelling by the humans that entered.

The rats tried to attack the humans by smell, running and leaping from tray to tray. When the people had them surrounded, one cook grabbed the first rat, which promptly sank its teeth through the mitt and into the cook's hand. The cook's scream ripped through the room as he smashed the rat's body against the wall, causing droplets of human and rat blood to spray the area. Two other kitchen staff grabbed at the writhing monster now embedded into the mitt, getting nipped and scratched before wringing its neck. A sous chef hacked through the other rat's body, covering a tray in its blood. Four employees in the kitchen displayed their bites after the creatures met their deaths.

The head chef surveyed the damage, thousands of dollars in product affected. Canned foods allowed a certain amount of rodent debris, so he surmised this would be no different. He ordered the workers to rinse the blood-sprayed steaks. The sous chefs cut away the obvious rat-chewed sections; those too damaged were ground into hamburger. All knew the cooking process would kill pathogenic bacteria; none realized that heat did not kill all contaminants.

The next morning, five restaurant workers' families called to inform the restaurant manager that the employee had been taken to the hospital with a very high fever. Five different hospitals throughout Mexico City now housed eight people, six with very high fevers, and although Maria's and Antonio's fevers had reduced to a more reasonable 101 degrees, they pulled against their restraints, lunging and biting at anyone drawing near. The eighteen travelers through Benito Juárez International Airport who'd eaten rat-blood-contaminated beef began showing signs of very high fever within twelve hours of their meals.

CHAPTER 1

April 10; Z Day 1

Busayo eyed the fare he'd picked up at La Guardia. The man was covered in sweat on a cool night, barely above fifty degrees. Initially, Busayo thought he'd been given a gift to drive the well-dressed man to a high-end Manhattan hotel near Central Park. What little he could get from the businessman was the name of his hotel and that one should never eat a steak at an airport. A few blocks from his Central Park hotel, the man began to seize.

"Hey!" Busayo pulled the cab into the edge of the park. The driver jumped out and yanked the back door open. Spittle and foam leached from the businessman's mouth, and with a last moan, his breath stopped. "Shit!" Busayo checked the man's pulse at the neck and wiped the slime and spittle onto his pants. The cab's medallion was contracted to his cousin. Busayo could not legally work, so his cousin loaned him the cab overnight for 70 percent of the fares and a full tank of gas. Even at 2:00 a.m., the traffic along Fifty-Ninth Street would begin to notice a parked cabbie swearing. Busayo shut the door and looked for a more secluded spot. A hospital would ask too many questions. He found a good place near the dumpster behind a restaurant. Busayo crossed himself and pulled the man from the car. It was unchristian to leave the body, but Busayo had done worse things in his former home for worse reasons. Someone would find the passenger in the morning. The cabbie made sure that all of the man's belongings were out of the car, wiping down what he could see. He couldn't have the body dump coming back to ruin things for his family.

Busayo drove away, hands trembling as he wiped his face and brow with an old towel. He forced himself to calm down. Coming to America had made him weak. A group of drunken twentysomethings stumbled out of a bar, waving and whistling at the cab. Busayo thought of the money he needed for his wife and daughters, forced a smile, and pulled over.

They slid across, laughing. He heard one say, "Gross!" as she smeared something from her hand onto the very short skirt. One of her companions laughed and pushed her.

"That's New York." The companion smiled and turned to the cabbie. "The Uptown Hotel."

Busayo smiled again and pulled back into traffic. *Just forget the man*, he thought. *The dead can do him no harm.*

Behind the dumpster, the dead man's body became the interest of the night scavengers. A starving mother coyote sniffed and danced around, finally biting into the soft flesh of his neck. When she was done, the rats began to converge, leaving little behind by dawn.

Damilola sighed and looked at Busayo's dirty clothes. She held the odd white smear up to her nose. It did not smell like a woman—no need to worry about him sleeping with someone else. It was likely just something from one of the passengers. The dirty pants joined the other clothes in her washbasin, scrubbed with her abraded and well-worn hands. Once satisfied that the stain was gone, she hung them out the window to dry. The clock showed 1:00 p.m.; Busayo was normally up by noon.

His skin felt warm, and he tossed in his sleep. Damilola picked up the bottle of children's ibuprofen from the cabinet and poured out three teaspoons, reasoning that it should be enough for an adult. Her husband woke with a start when she touched him.

"You are getting sick, my love. Here," she said, handing him the small cup of medicine and some water.

"Thank you" was his only response before he promptly returned to sleep.

Damilola pursed her lips. Busayo needed to be at work in two hours at the restaurant to bus tables. The owner frowned at those calling in sick, assuming that they slept off hangovers. Busayo had never been ill beyond a small cold. A touch of the forehead confirmed that she would have to make the call.

By the time the children came home from school, Damilola was terrified. She'd never touched skin so hot. Busayo needed to be at the hospital—there was no question. She called his cousin Femi, who had the contract for the cab. Once Femi stopped yelling about the mess in the back, he agreed to drive them to the hospital. The children stayed calm until they saw their mother weeping. Damilola was not one to normally bother with tears. In order to get Busayo out of the apartment, Femi needed to strap him onto a rolling chair since the family could not rouse him enough to walk.

The jaded triage nurse who thought she'd seen everything started calling for help as soon as she checked Busayo's temperature, immediately relaying the information to the emergency medicine resident.

"Why am I getting excited about a 100.9?" he asked as he strolled up. The nurse grabbed his hand and placed in on Busayo.

"Not 100.9—*109*," she said through her teeth. "Get the attending."

The resident ran while the nurse rushed Busayo back behind the doors and screens, leaving Damilola standing at the entrance, dumbfounded, holding two crying children. Femi heard the temperature and sped away. Eventually, someone showed Damilola a chair and began asking questions while checking off a form.

On the Upper East Side, a college girl who had been interviewing at NYU for graduate school was admitted for a high fever. At dusk, a family walking along Fifth Avenue was attacked by a "rabid coyote." and workers at a swanky Central Park restaurant were bitten by rats as they took out the trash. Around midnight, Damilola began to feel hot.

CHAPTER 2

April 12; Z Day 3

Dr. Emma O'Conner led the morning rounds. No one needed to ask her heritage—the auburn hair, green eyes, and name said it all. In the few remaining months of her family medicine residency, she was expected to be a team leader and act as the attending's right hand. Emma excelled, earning the respect of the other doctors at San Antonio General. Her third patient on rounds had the same odd symptoms as the first. Both Mr. Velez and Mr. Ortiz had arrived on a plane from Mexico two nights ago, after which each developed fevers of over 110 degrees. Mr. Ortiz had the expected outcome and lay in a coma on a ventilator, waiting for family members to arrive and say their good-byes before life support was stopped. The team put on masks and gloves as they approached Mr. Velez.

Mr. Velez growled and lunged, his hands tied to the railings on the bed. He tried to bite anyone coming near and curled away from the window, shrieking if the blinds allowed in light. The patient had successfully injured at least eight staff members before being restrained. One nurse had to get two layers of stitches in her hand and forearm. Emma tried to get close enough to shine a penlight in Mr. Velez's eyes, showing Dr. Brown, the attending, that the patient's pupils no longer reacted, accounting for his sensitivity to light.

"Go on. Get closer." Dr. Brown sounded irritated. "He's restrained."

Emma still felt reluctant. She'd seen the nurse being carried away with her arm pumping blood.

"Here, I'll hold him back." Dr. Brown stepped forward and placed his forearm against the patient's chest. The others on rounds looked to Emma, who sighed and came forward. The patient heaved and lunged, his mouth clamping onto Dr. Brown's jaw. Dr. Brown yelled and tried to pull away, but Mr. Velez's teeth tore through his mask and past the skin until he held bone. Emma forced the metal diaphragm of her stethoscope between Mr. Velez's teeth. The patient released his grip on Dr. Brown, but Emma could not retract in time before his mouth found her hand.

The yelling attracted her acquaintance Dr. Andrew Perdue. He opened the code cart and grabbed a paralytic, injecting it into the patient's neck. Velez's body went stiff as Emma drew her hand free. The medical students stood by numbly until the team's intern grabbed a towel and held it to Emma's hand and yelled, "Pull yourselves together! Help Dr. Brown!"

Emma and the attending were led to the ER, where they found a small available room in the already overcrowded department.

Dr. Cory Miller, an emergency medicine resident Emma had known since medical school, peeked in. A quick look at Dr. Brown made Cory shake his head.

"Sorry, but that's gonna need Plastics. They're already down here. I'm not quite sure what's going on. I've never seen so many bites in a single day – human, dog, rat, even a raccoon. You'd think the city was going cannibal." Cory tried not to grin as he took Emma's hand. "Not too bad. Let me get some iodine and we'll get a few stitches in you."

If her hand didn't hurt so much, Emma would have given one of her traditional rejoinders to continue their ongoing, mild flirtation. Anytime she had to admit a patient through the ER, the two spoke in double entendres and would have tongues wagging. Today, she allowed the doctor all the nurses fantasized about to continue his job. While Dr. Brown and Emma waited, an assistant administrator showed up with an on-the-job injury form.

"I have never done so many of these in a day. I can't seem to do anything else. Please let your treating physician know if you'd like to receive treatment for prophylaxis against HIV."

Emma thought about telling the administrator that she knew that Mr. Velez was HIV negative; it was one of the first tests run when he spiked such a high fever, but the woman was gone as soon as she had their signatures. Emma went home with six stitches, a prescription for antibiotics, and a note granting her two days off. A side note from Cory offered to take her to dinner and cut her meat if her hand hurt too much to do it herself.

President Paulson fidgeted with his pen as the secretary of state, Elisandra (a.k.a. Elsie) Hudson, finished her report on the trade talks with Japan. Paulson noted the fatigue, likely jet lag, on the active woman's face.

After her report, he summarized, "After three days of talks, they'll think about easing their restrictions on US corn imports. Great."

Elsie bristled at the half criticism. She had wrangled more concessions in these talks than any of her predecessors, but Paulson needed the Midwest for his reelection, and better corn prices helped the Midwest.

"Before we finish the daily briefing, Drs. Goodman and Graham from the CDC are here to give us an insight on that infection that's starting to hit the news," Chief of Staff Gehler announced. He nodded to the Secret Service agent at the door, who allowed in the two doctors and their laptop.

"A great pleasure to see you again, sir." Dr. Goodman whistled through his teeth and shook the president's hand.

Dr. Graham nodded and took his turn pumping the president's hand before sitting. They faced the computer toward the president.

"This is more Dr. Graham's area of expertise, so I will let him do the honors," said Dr. Goodman.

Paulson gave a silent prayer of thanks. Listening to high pitches from Dr. Goodman was already making his skin crawl.

Dr. Graham brought up a simple bar graph dated April 10 with the number eight on it. "Eight people who arrived in the United States through Mexico City two days ago are either dead or acting in a very unusual manner. One of the dead was found behind a New York City restaurant yesterday morning. Most of the others checked into US hospitals within a few hours of their arrival into the country, all sporting fevers of 110 degrees or more. All have been diagnosed with a previously unknown encephalovirus—a virus that attacks the brain."

The president suddenly sat forward.

"Of those hospitalized," Dr. Graham continued, "one is on life support, one is dead, and the rest are acting in strangely aggressive ways." Dr. Graham clicked to the next slide, which had a second bar a little over twice as high. "As of eight this morning, there are nineteen additional cases of people presenting with very high fevers of 110 degrees or more, not all of which can be directly linked to the arrivals from Mexico City."

"We have asked our colleagues in the INSP, and one spoke off the record," Dr. Goodman added. "He said they had two cases three days ago and several from the airport. His bosses are under political pressure not to say anything for fear of further damaging tourism."

President Paulson gripped his chair tighter.

"Wait, we've had an agreement with them since 2011 to share information on emerging infections." Elsie commented as she leaned in toward Dr. Goodman, not as bothered by the lisp.

"Yes, but as you know, that was at least two administrations ago. The current Mexican government has not been as forthcoming." Dr. Goodman answered and nodded to Dr. Graham to continue.

The next slide clicked on, showing the bars on the graph sharply spiking upward. "If it grows at this rate," Dr. Graham remarked, "by the end of the week, there will be over 175 cases across the country. Right now, we believe there must be direct contact to transfer the encephalovirus, but if it is able to spread in other ways or can use nonhuman vectors, that number may be higher."

"What about the run on the emergency departments the morning news has been showing? Is it another case of SARS or bird flu that has everyone in a panic over nothing? " Paulson asked.

"Like in many of these outbreaks, people with mild symptoms from any illness tend to flock to medical centers, concerned they have whatever serious infection of the day is being televised. The majority of those likely have a late season flu or other virus." Dr. Goodman reassured President Paulson.

The president nodded to the two scientists, who rose and shook hands again. "Keep me posted," he requested as the scientists left.

Press Secretary James Zimburg cleared his throat. "I can make a remark at today's press briefing that you have been apprised of a new infection and are monitoring the situation."

Paulson nodded. "Yes, we need to reassure the public and try to prevent mass panic. The CDC looks to have it in hand. Let's see what we have tomorrow."

With that, the daily briefing adjourned.

Emma spent most of her day puttering around the house and watching TV shows looking at houses around the world. She clicked through the news channels and watched Press Secretary Zimburg field questions that Emma knew the answers to better than he did. The national news showed footage from Los Angeles abuzz with a "zombie attack" when a plumber entered a basement and one of the owners came after him. There were also reports of aggressive rats in dark alleys and a spike in rabid dog cases. After dinner, she felt a little off and went to bed. A few hours later, Emma woke feeling very hot, followed by intense chills. A search through the bathroom drawers procured an old mercury thermometer. Her temperature was 105. She'd never run a fever like that, even as a child with pneumonia. Emma woke her roommate, Veronica, to take her to the hospital.

"God, Emma, you look like shit," Veronica said as she helped Emma to the car.

When they arrived, the area around the ER was packed with cars. There wasn't room to stop by the entrance, so Veronica drove Emma a couple of blocks away to the employee parking garage, which was also unusually crowded for the hour. Veronica left Emma by the sidewalk and went to park. Almost ten minutes later, Veronica found Emma shivering with teeth chattering, burning hot, and leaning against a pillar. Veronica took Emma through the back entrance and waved down a running nurse.

"Oh, another one." The nurse sounded exhausted through her N-95 mask but indicated for them to follow. The emergency department's walls were lined with stretchers. Some had growling people throwing themselves against restraints. Others held patients like Emma, burning with fever, though Emma was the only one with chattering teeth and chills. Everyone was wearing masks with shields and gloves. Even with the mask and yellow infection control cover, Emma recognized Cory, who jogged over to them.

"Wow, you're back too. Dr. Brown came in about an hour ago—continuous seizures." Cory grabbed a nurse with a digital vital-sign cart. "Your temp's not as bad, 105.4. I'll find you a spot upstairs. We've kept a few beds in the post-op floor open." A few minutes later, he brought a piece of paper and a mask for Veronica. "Head up to ten. The nurse will check you in there."

Veronica helped keep Emma upright through the journey in the elevator, dodging doctors running to codes. When they reached the tenth floor, a nurse with cool hands and a colder smile took Emma to a small room with a cot and let her lie down and started an IV on her. Emma quickly lost consciousness.

CHAPTER 3

April 13; Z Day 4

"I suspect the CDC docs underestimated how quickly this could spread," President Paulson said, staring at his TV. He had been getting calls since midnight and looked like a man with no sleep. An aide brought him a fresh shirt and jacket while he gave himself a quick shave in front of an Oval Office mirror.

"At this time, we've counted well over a thousand cases, most currently centered in New York, San Antonio, Dallas, Atlanta, and Chicago. A lot of health care workers. A nurse in San Antonio attacked her neighbors yesterday. It turns out she'd been bitten by a patient the day before. Dr. Goodman from the CDC is on his way." Gehler rolled his neck.

"Oh, God, the whistler? Why can't we get the other one?" Paulson wiped his face.

"Already in San Antonio," Gehler answered. Moments later, Dr. Goodman huffed and puffed into the room, carrying a large sketchpad.

"Spit it out," Paulson demanded. "Why so many, and why are we so unprepared?'

Goodman flipped up the pad and began to write. "We thought it was only human-to-human contact. Most infections work that way—they have a preferred species for a host." The whistles were fast and low with his breathing. "But this is worse, much worse." The black, green, and red lines diverged on the chart as he drew. Dr. Goodman pointed to the black line, which marched up ominously enough. "This is what we thought—two infections per infected individual by direct contact." The next line was green, which rose twice as quickly. "We now know absolutely that dogs carry the infection, which makes it faster." The doctor tapped the red line, which swooped into an almost vertical line. "But this is what we are seeing. It means that there is either another vector, such as rats or even mosquitoes, that can carry the infection, or there are more ways to spread the infection, such as by ingestion of contaminated food, water, or both."

The president stopped being annoyed by the sound of the man's voice and focused on the red line spiking into the sky. He slowly sat on the couch, eyes on the red line as a fixed spot in space. "How many?" was all he could ask.

"There could be over a million infected by the end of the week." Dr. Goodman let the graph drop. "We are already beyond our surge capacity, there is little we can do to slow this down, let alone stop it. I'm sorry. I—"

The president waved his hand abruptly for silence. "Mr. Gehler, get Vice President Solis on the next transport to Cheyenne. I need to be on the air in fifteen minutes. Get the cameras in here."

Charles Tremblay stood in front of the hotel TV, toothbrush half out of his mouth while transfixed by the chaos playing out around the world. The teaching conference in Philadelphia would end early due to the outbreak, but watching the news, he realized that unless a miracle happened, he had no way to get home. Getting out of everywhere appeared to be the plan. Those not succumbing to this new disease were creating even more panic. Charles had cousins with a farm, and the news showed little from Canada. Maybe it wasn't there yet. He picked up his room phone.

"Chantal, let's skip breakfast and go straight to the station. Were you able to get through to get tickets?" Charles' strong French accent marking his home from near Quebec.

The voice on the other end sounded like she'd been crying. "My husband got through, but I could only get two billets on the ten o'clock. I promised the other to Josette—she's married and has—"

Charles nodded. "*Bien sur*. I will see you to the station. Maybe I can get another when we get there." He dressed and met his fellow teachers in the lobby. Charles taught chemistry and physics, and the two women taught biology and environmental sciences at L'École Secondaire de Charlesbourg. The Philadelphia Conference on Education and Science in April provided their annual refuge from sulking teenagers. Charles thought a few sulking teenagers would be an improvement over the throngs at the station. The ticket lines led out and around the building, and every automated kiosk was closed. The women had printed their tickets at the hotel and were warned to keep the precious papers out of sight until a conductor took them on the train. Charles knew that he would be going nowhere until the panic eased, resigning himself to waiting out the infection in an expensive hotel room his teacher's salary would soon be unable to afford. He was an average-sized man, but he knew how to stand and look protective over his fellow teachers until their train was called. Only those with tickets could pass through to the tracks.

Chantal hugged him. "I am so sorry, I will let M. Barclay know you had to remain and why. Enjoy your few days of vacation without us."

Charles chose not to speak and ushered them to the gate, waving good-bye.

"Women and children first," he muttered to himself, heading back to the street. A grilled hot dog looked like a good idea for breakfast, and he passed the money over to the vendor. Walking and eating, Charles dodged people on cell phones, their voices filled with panic. He finally looked down at his almost completed breakfast. There were a set of small teeth marks along the edge of the wiener. Gagging, he tossed it into the first waste bin he could find. Despite the chaos around, littering still bothered him. Charles returned to the hotel and took advantage of the empty gym and steam room, followed by a few glasses of palatable Malbec in the bar, where the few other trapped denizens remained mesmerized by pictures of looting in all major cities.

"Well, aren't they gonna feel like idiots when it turns out like the bird flu?" a heavyset man wearing a cowboy hat and boots and with an appropriate accent commented to no one in particular. All in the bar agreed, but no one wanted to talk and went back to watching the TV, none feeling safe from the brewing chaos outside.

At dinner, Charles did not feel like eating. He retired to the privacy of his room and his own TV just before dark. He checked the room temperature, which said seventy-four, but it could not have been. It felt much hotter than that.

Peter Saitou felt crammed next to the wall of the coach. It seemed as though three were sitting in spaces for two on the train. He'd bought one of the last official seats for the southbound Colonial Express from Boston to Williamsburg. Last night's conversation with his father ran in a continuous loop in his head: "I am sure it is nothing, but can you come stay with your Sabo? She is so worried. I will be at the plant to do a temporary shutdown." That bothered Peter more than the news. The nuclear power plant at Surrey was never just "shut down." It was too essential for the power grid. Everyone seemed to be leaving the city, so he decided to be one of the masses. Besides, most of his work now revolved around drawing out the designs for his thesis, which could be done on the train. At every station, more people tried to cram in, and more with hopeful faces looked for seats. Peter started to chew a nail. He'd promised his adviser that he'd stop the habit before he had to do interviews. The chewed-up nails made him look nervous, but the old habit developed while his mother lay dying fifteen years ago reared back up. Before the next stop, two nails were down to nubs.

"I'll use all that Southern charm and my Platinum Plus. Don't worry, hon. I'll find a flight." Charlene listened to her husband, Al, on the phone. Despite his reassuring words, she could hear the tension in his voice. He was supposed to return from LA the following week. The video feed from one of the airports—LaGuardia, it said on the news—showed fights breaking out over tickets.

"I'll be waiting for you." The phone clicked dead. Charlene set it on the counter, half expecting it to ring back, but there weren't any bars. The reception in Marietta could be spotty at the best of times, she told herself. Her .45 held a full clip and one in the chamber. Both the gun and the Winchester rifle had plenty of ammo. She'd always been one to stock up, so there were cases of canned tuna and at least ten gallons of water. She stopped up the bathtubs, let them fill, and then added a few buckets from the garage, as well. The red cans held enough gas to run the generator for two days, so the food in the freezer could keep for a little while. Charlene dug through her recipe books and found the one she wanted. *Jerky, the Fun and Flavorful* read the title. She hoped so. She transferred the meat to the refrigerator to thaw through the day, and then she would slice it and cook it overnight. She knew doing all this was probably overreacting, but it was hard not to think the worst when watching the news.

"Now that we are obviously *in* the end times, let us read from the book of Revelation!" Reverend Curtis shouted from his Camden pulpit. He got a few nervous amens.

"Oh, hell, no!" The woman everyone knew as Auntie, to the point where no one remembered her real name, stood with her cane. "If it was the end times, don't you think I would be one of those called up? I ain't seen no one disappear, but I seen lots of fear."

"Amen, sister," responded the room.

"No, these is bad times," Auntie called out to the pews.

There were nods all around. The young reverend cleared his throat but was quickly stayed by Auntie's hand.

"I read a book once where some white man wrote 'These are the days that try men's souls.' Now I don't know about the time he was goin' through, but it could not—*could not*, I say—be worse than today!"

The room knew there was no stopping Auntie once she got going.

"No. We need the Lord today …"

"Amen!" cried the crowd, many on their feet.

"But as much as that, we need good men, strong men and women, to lead us through the darkness." Auntie turned and stared at Stokes, raising her cane to indicate him. "We need those with the strength, the ability, and the nerve to protect us. To help those who are weak."

Many turned to Stokes and his sister, Toya, sitting back in the pews. "Amen!" they shouted again.

"We live in deprivation," Auntie continued.

"You know it, sister!"

"But we do not lack in intelligence, in courage, or in love of our neighbor." Auntie's eyes drilled into Stokes. He fought to keep contact. Stokes had done things most would consider evil, rising in the ranks of his gang, the Shujaa, named in the 1970s from the Swahili word for *warrior*. Auntie had a power over all those in the Poynt, and even Stokes had to look away from the steel in her eyes.

Her voice softened. "This is a new day. This is a new beginning. What has gone before was before. If things get worse"—she shook her head, taking in the room—"and they look to get worse, we have only each other to rely on."

"Amen!"

"You have seen the news, you have seen the panic across the bridge. Even the white folks are hittin' the police trying to get onto buses and planes. We need to get food. We need to build a wall of protection to keep out those things that roamed the streets last night," Auntie continued.

"And weapons for those who know how to use them." Stokes stood, allowing all present to fully see him. He glanced to Toya, who'd forced him to come tonight. Stokes figured that Auntie must have waylaid his sister as soon as she'd arrived in town that afternoon. Auntie slowly walked up the aisle, leaning heavily on her cane.

"I did not live for seventy-two years, taking pills for high blood pressure and sugar diabetes and what all else the doctor said I had to be killed by some monster from hell itself." She stopped at Stokes's pew.

"My men have weapons. We'll take up positions on roofs at every block. There's not enough ammunition to do that for long," Stokes offered. He let his voice carry for all to hear.

"We'll go across the bridge tomorrow. In their panic, lots of supplies will have been abandoned," offered Burt, the motorcycle mechanic. "I can take my guys."

"The stockroom and the minibars in the rooms at the hotel." Saya stood. "I've been a maid there for years. It was almost empty this afternoon. We go room to room, clear it out."

"I'll go with you," Toya offered. "I know how to use a gun." She eyed her brother.

Stokes made certain that she'd stayed out of the gang, but it was impossible to avoid all of gang life when your brother was third in charge. Neither Duke nor Daniel had been seen since early the day before, leaving Stokes as Shujaa chief. He tilted his chin in agreement.

Auntie turned and walked back down the aisle and then smiled at Curtis. "Now, Reverend, lead us in a prayer of hope and maybe a hymn?"

Emma woke to a loud bang, like a door slamming but more hollow. Then there was yelling, loud, angry, and persistent. Her hands reached for the call button but stopped before their goal, tied with torn bed sheets. She heard another bang a little closer.

"They're infected! They all need to be put down!" The man's voice ripped through the door and walls like bullets. Emma's throat caught as she wondered what he'd do when he entered her room. Emma's fingers found the end knot, and she started pulling. Once the first one released, she started the next. The shots continued, and a woman started screaming. Emma worked faster. Her right hand came free as someone moved outside the door. She rolled off the bed to the floor, keeping the bed between her and the entrance. Emma's teeth and freed fingers tore at the knots on the left.

"She's different," a familiar voice pleaded. "Her fever never got as high." Emma was down to the last of the bindings when the door flew open. A man she'd never seen came in with gun drawn, Andy Perdue flying in behind him, taking him to the ground in a full tackle. The man saw Emma on the floor and tried to bring his weapon up.

"Please, don't shoot," Emma managed to say, not as loudly as she wanted.

The man paused, and Andy looked up.

"Please, please don't shoot me," Emma repeated a little louder through her cracked lips and hoarse throat, crying for water. She felt her eyes try to well up, but only a couple of tears could moisten them. "Please, don't shoot me," Emma said again.

The two men withdrew and stood.

"Check her eyes," the gunman said.

A moment later, Andy crept around the bed with a penlight.

"Hold still for a minute, OK?" Andy looked scared.

Emma nodded and held her eyes open as best she could against the bright light in the dim room. She forced herself not to blink.

"They reacted!" Andy realized he'd yelled too loud. "She's OK. Her pupils react." He came forward, tears in his own eyes. "I can't believe you're OK."

Andy hugged her. Emma wanted to cry but was too tired. As her adrenaline dropped, so did the desperate energy. Andy removed the last of her restraints. He turned to the man with the gun.

"We have to tell the CDC guys. They need to see this," he said.

The gunman turned, and Emma saw the flash of his gold detective's badge.

A moment later, they heard the gunman on the phone. "I'm serious—documented bite, but she's OK." He paused. "Yeah, getting too dark to try to go out now. We'll barricade here for the night. Get a roof evac in the morning."

The detective walked back in, warily watching Emma sitting on the edge of her bed. Andy brought a glass of water and left again.

"I'm Detective Williams of the SAPD. Governor Burton called a state of emergency with orders to kill all infected persons due to their immediate threat to the uninfected. I have not heard of anyone bitten that has recovered. A Dr. Goodman of the CDC said he'd heard a rumor that some people might get better, but it had not been confirmed."

The water loosened her throat up enough so that it no longer felt like her vocals cords rubbed on sandpaper. "I guess I'm the confirmation," Emma said, looking up at him. She was already exhausted from sitting for ten minutes.

Andy returned with a blood pressure cuff, thermometer, IV bag, and IV start kit.

"I know a nurse normally does this, but at the moment, she's busy throwing up after our friend the detective shot the other patients."

Emma lay back down as Andy checked her vitals. Her blood pressure was 90/50, pulse 115, temperature below normal at 96.9. Once Andy started her IV, he found some blankets.

"Just sleep," he said. "We may need to run tomorrow."

"Mr. President!" Dr. Goodman returned to the oval office. "We may have a survivor. A young doctor in San Antonio with a confirmed bite, fever above 105, woke normal with reactive pupils."

President Paulson's exhalation and look to heaven spoke volumes. "Thank you. Is she secure? Can we get her in front of the American people?"

Goodman shook his head. "She's on one of the top floors of San Antonio General. The place is overrun with Zs. The detective I spoke with sounded like they could secure the wing they're in now, wait until morning, and then try to run for it."

Paulson turned to General Duarte. "Make sure she's secure. Send in your best men—rangers. That one in the news last year—the one that saved the village in the Congo, with the name that sounds like a movie character …"

"McLeod." Elsie Hudson supplied the name.

"He's stateside, right?" Paulson asked.

"Yeah, teaching at the ranger school. Camp Merrill, I think." Duarte picked up the phone and began giving orders.

"Give me what you can on her." Press Secretary James Zimburg pulled out a notebook. He preferred his smartphone but was skeptical about being able to keep it charged. "I'll start drafting a statement. When will we be heading to Seattle?"

"Once the sun is full up," Burke, the head of the Secret Service spoke up. The vice president had been evacuated that morning to Cheyenne, but President Paulson wanted another day to try to restore calm. The Seattle location was more secret than Cheyenne, and little Z activity had been reported in the Emerald City.

Peter walked to the road from the train station about an hour past sunset. He'd outrun two Zs, and other passengers were screaming, trying to escape rats. No one was there to pick him up. He searched the abandoned cars along the Colonial Parkway, finding one with keys. Peter locked himself in the trunk since it appeared the safest place to be.

Paulina landed her chopper on the roof. The streets below were always filled with cars honking and barely moving, but now the horns were more insistent and louder, the shouts more desperate. She could not believe how fast this thing had spread. Her orders from Generale de Ala Pedroza were simple: land on the roof, pick up two men, and fly to a house between Cancun and Playa del Carmen. Instructions were not to ask any questions and not to take any detours. The second would not be an issue. There was just enough fuel to drop them at the house and get to Cancun to refuel for the trip back to Santa Lucia.

Once on the roof, her passengers—two men wearing suits and a woman in much too flimsy a dress for the wind that day—did not take long to present themselves. Paulina had been told two passengers. The second man was not too big and the woman thin. Overall, she calculated an extra seventy pounds. It might take a few more gallons of fuel, but they could still get to the destination. Once the three strapped in, she lifted off, her final coordinates memorized. Paulina felt a tap on her shoulder. She'd been trying not to make eye contact. The big one was not a man whom she wanted to know.

El Padre Palacios, "the Father," was a man who dropped out of the priesthood to become the head of the Palacios family cartel. Like all the crime bosses, he was evil to the core and felt himself to be above all. It galled Paulina, a lieutenant in the Mexican Air Force, to be shuttling around one of the worst of Mexico's civilian population. He must have had his own pilot and a dozen much nicer helicopters and planes.

El Padre smiled through his well-trimmed beard. "I need to make a stop."

"If we stop, we walk the last twenty miles, and it'll be getting dark soon," Paulina replied.

"You can refuel there." El Padre showed his small, even teeth. His companion pulled out a small pistol, a Walther PPK.

How very James Bond, Paulina thought to herself.

"He can fly, as well," Palacios said, nudging his companion. "Here are the new coordinates."

Eyeing the small gun, Paulina turned the Bell helicopter and eventually landed at a small abandoned airport south of the city.

They arrived an hour before sunset, and Paulina immediately began refueling, with the companion near her elbow and his pouting girlfriend in tow. As far as Paulina could tell, her name was Dulce, with a voice so high and annoying that Paulina wanted to turn the fuel hose and stick it in her mouth. She had to turn and cover her smile with the thought that it wouldn't be the worst thing the woman put between her teeth.

Since the age of eleven, the only heat Paulina was interested in was the heat from an airplane engine, the only vibration that of plane through her cockpit seat, the only thrust that of a fighter plane as it vaulted into the sky. Every moment of every hour of her life had been dedicated to becoming a pilot. At twenty-one, she could fly anything, in any conditions, anywhere anyone wanted to go. Paulina turned off the fuel pump and shoved it back into the holder. And here she was, the equivalent of a limousine driver. She forced the gall back down her throat before the idiot next to her pulled a trigger and blew them all up. Bells were great, practical machines for flying through any kind of weather condition, but if she'd had a Eurocopter or a Blackhawk, the present company could have been made to have an unexpected exit.

El Padre returned with another man carrying two small bags with something heavy enough to try to rip through the nylon bottom.

"Is he going too?" Paulina asked.

"Why do you need to know?" The companion pushed the gun farther out.

"Weight and balance, *pendejo*." She set her jaw and met the gunman's eyes.

"Ha!" Palacios guffawed. "You've met your match, my friend." He turned to Paulina, appraising her anew. "No, just the bags. About eighty pounds."

Paulina nodded. "Put them behind the woman or next to you with her in back."

"Dulce, in the back," El Padre commanded.

She complained for a moment, but with just the lift of the companion's finger, she shut up and climbed in. The growing whine from the engine drowned out the whine from the rear passenger the rest of the trip.

It was full dark when they touched down in the fortified compound. When they landed, El Padre tapped her again. "Stay the night. It is too dark to go on."

Paulina shook her head. "Orders."

Always a good military excuse. Facing a thousand Zs would be less dangerous than a night in the compound with one hundred of El Padre's men. Señor Palacios shrugged and got out, his companion grabbing the heavy bags, leaving Dulce to get out on her own. Those high heels that made her legs look so long did not look so great climbing around and out of the chopper. Before Dulce was clear, the gunman was back with pistol pointed straight at Paulina, cocked and ready.

"El Padre says he insists on you staying. He has a job for you tomorrow."

Paulina thought about risking it, taking off and banking away. Instead, she shut down the rotors. The gunman opened the door and took her elbow as soon as the seatbelt clicked open.

"By the way, my name is Raul Lara. I am sure we will become good friends."

CHAPTER 4

April 14; Z Day 5.

Emma woke before dawn to pounding. Not really pounding, more of a steady beating. She checked her pulse—seventy-eight; almost down to her normal. She felt the need to use the restroom, desperately. The waste bin held two empty bags of saline with the one still connected half-empty. *No wonder* Emma thought as she tested her feet, found that they would hold, and pushed the IV pole into the hall. Detective Williams sat with his back to one door, gun in his lap, and Andy at the other, holding a flimsy aluminum rod from an IV pole. Emma thought of all the zombie movies and shows that started with the hero waking in a hospital bed with the world around him forever changed. This had to be a dream or a fevered nightmare, but she was awake, watching her new friend without military training try to keep guard.

Emma peeked into the next patient room and saw the blood on the floor and the body on the bed. She stepped back into the hallway, caught Andy's eye, and then mouthed "bathroom." He jerked his head toward the nurse's station. Emma found the nurse with the cold voice under a desk, arms around her knees with her face tucked in. Emma could see the mascara tracks trailing down the side of her cheeks and onto the knees of the maroon scrubs. Emma wanted to stop but the call of nature was too urgent. Emma nodded and kept walking to the room with a woman's silhouette.

After relieving herself, she couldn't help but look in the mirror. Emma regarded her pale skin and sunken eyes and could only imagine what she'd looked like a few hours earlier. She splashed cold water on her face and head, then ran her fingers through the knotted tangles of her hair to made herself look as human as possible under the circumstances. Emma emerged and knelt beside the nurse under the desk, handing her a couple of damp paper towels and a dry one.

"Thanks" the nurse said, taking the towels and beginning to remove the worst of the black lines on her face. "So much for water-proof."

Emma smiled "More water resistant. Can I help you with anything?"

The nurse shook her head. "I'll be OK in a few minutes. I'm not ready to go back out there yet." Emma gave the nurse a reassuring smile, and stood to find the detective and Andy still at their posts. Emma shuffled over to Andy and sat next to him, tired from the exertion.

"What's it like out there?" Emma asked as she propped her back against the door to the stairwell. The beating came from the other side.

"You know all those end-of-the-world movies? Where we all scream and cheer as the heroes run around, risking life and limb to save the dude who turns into a zombie later?" Andy looked at the ceiling.

"Yeah, I was just thinking about that—the main character waking in the hospital." Emma caught his half grin.

"Hmm, that would make me the supporting character here to get you out." He nudged her shoulder to shoulder.

"Naw, that'd be him." Emma tilted her chin down the hall at Detective Williams. She blushed for a minute, looking at Andy sideways. "You could be the love interest."

Andy started to laugh and then tried to keep his voice down. "Hopefully Nurse Nightingale is a bad-ass champion kick boxer with mad skills." He started laughing so hard that he held his stomach and rolled.

"Hey, I'm glad the two of you found something funny in all of this!" Detective Williams did not sound amused.

Andy looked up from the floor and brought himself upright. He whispered back, "And once we make a break for it, we'll band together to find his family." Andy glanced down the hall at the long stare he received from the detective and started laughing again.

"You've been watching too much T.V. How long has it been since you slept?" Emma asked.

"Two days I think, maybe three?" He scratched his head. "The night before you got bit, I was home in bed, deciding if I was going to ask Dr. Castro in pediatrics out on a date."

"Eduardo Castro?" Emma's eyebrow cocked up.

"Yeah. He's pretty hot." Andy smiled and looked away.

"I'll agree with you there. I guess that changes your role to gay best friend?" Emma nudged him.

Andy started laughing again.

Emma thought his every nerve must be on edge. "Yeah, that one normally survives—unless he's too brave," Andy said as he collected himself after another scowl from down the hall. "Anyway, and then that guy bit you and Dr. Brown. I was on call last night when everything hit the fan and then trapped here today after Cory and I decided someone needed to run up and check on you before he got evac'd out to SAMMC."

"Cory's OK?" Emma perked up.

"Yeah." Andy rubbed the back of his neck. "The real love interest is alive and well." Andy's grin grew slightly wicked. "So, have the two of you ever …"

"No! He's too … I don't know … Grass is always greener, I guess." Emma couldn't hide her blush. It wasn't like she'd never thought of it. After all, he was the best-looking man in the hospital, and not like Cory hadn't tried.

"Yeah, well, it's more fun being the love interest than the sidekick," Andy commented.

"How do you know I'm not the sidekick?"

"You survived being bit. I already know how big a deal that is." Andy became serious and looked at Emma's hospital gown. "We'd better find you some clothes." He felt the pressure against the door. "OK, *you'd* better find some clothes. Don't look at the beds. The good detective over there made fairly efficient work of the bitten. They may have clothes in their closets. Just avoid anything with blood on it, and feces. It may be able to spread that way too."

Emma nodded. After finding a bandage and removing her IV, she explored the rooms. A T-shirt that showed the Alamo and a pair of shorts she could belt with the string from her gown would suffice, and at least she wouldn't have to keep people from seeing her butt. It was impossible not to look at the beds, but her attention was diverted by the growing glow of dawn.

"It's morning, almost," she told Andy and sat back down.

"Good. There are lots of windows in this building. If it's like yesterday, they'll be driven into the stairwells and dark rooms." Andy heard the scraping behind him. "They're not like the zombies in the movies. I mean, they eat everything, including people, but they're not dead. Once you flatline, you're gone and not coming back. They're brain dead—just the human parts killed off. I haven't decided if that's better or worse."

"On the bright side, cemeteries will be safe, and if we have to lock ourselves into a crypt, we won't need to worry about the bones coming back to life." Emma tried to find something positive in their situation.

"Sorry. I don't see myself running through any cemeteries. I plan to hole up anywhere the good detective and his buddies take me. Once the CDC gets all the Zs quarantined and the coast is clear, I'll come back out." Andy turned the aluminum pole in his hand. "I'm not much good with one of these."

"We're calling them Zs?" Emma raised an eyebrow.

"As I said, they're only part zombie, but it's the worst part." Andy flipped the pole again.

"When we make a run for it, I'll need some kind of weapon." Emma started to get up when she saw movement by the nurse's station. The nurse stood and straightened her scrubs and then picked up some small tubs from below the counter. As she approached, Emma saw her badge read "Melanie, LVN."

Melanie, LVN handed a tub and plastic spoon to each of them. "Not much, but pudding has a lot of sugar and may help us have enough energy to get out of here." Emma and Andy nodded their thanks, and Melanie headed toward Detective Williams with breakfast. Nurse Melanie proceeded to the rooms, opening the blinds, filling the area with the pink light of dawn.

Emma finished her pudding and looked for anything she could use as a weapon. One of the patients had a pocketknife; another had a bag of pennies. She cut away a shirtsleeve and tied one end, filled it with pennies, and knotted it closed. It would only last a few hits, but it was something solid. Emma saw Melanie test items as weapons in other rooms. Detective Williams turned on his phone and made a call.

"Yeah. Thirty minutes on the roof. We'll be there." Williams faced the group. "You heard. We can go ahead and start now or wait another fifteen minutes then go. It should be getting light enough on the roof to keep them at bay."

"There's only one window per floor in the stairwell. The Zs will be there," Andy reminded him.

"Why can't we take the elevator?" Nurse Melanie asked.

"The fire department shut the elevators down to keep the floors isolated. Besides, the elevators are the darkest spot in the entire hospital. They're crammed with them. When the doors open, Zs spill out. I drew almost the shortest straw coming to ten. There's a beat cop on eleven that hasn't checked in, and Detective Morales on twelve should be joining us with another pair of nurses and a surgeon."

Emma looked around and turned to Melanie. "Are there any antibiotics up here? Pain meds? Anything? If all the hospitals are being evacuated, then SAMMC will be in short supply."

"Yeah, I'll grab my bag. We can clear out the med cart. It's a hodgepodge, but I suppose even acetaminophen may be hard to find soon. There might be some flashlights as well." Melanie went into the small nurse's break room and grabbed her bag. Emma took the pocketknife and popped a few lockers open until she found a small backpack and dumped the contents, keeping only the hair scrunchie. She mentally apologized to the person in case she came back. They found a few penlights and a flashlight with weak light that briefly brightened with a few taps. Within five minutes, Melanie and Emma cleared the med cart and signaled that they were ready to go.

Williams took the lead and unbarricaded the main door. The floodlit hallway in front of the elevator was clear. He signaled them all out, and they lined up by the door to the stairs. The door opened onto the landing with the window, so it was clear, but the dimmer landings above and below held a dozen or more Zs, pushing away from the light. Williams raised his gun and aimed for the head, bringing down one after another. The sound reverberated through the stairwell, magnified by their close confines. The Zs groaned and shifted faster, smelling the blood. Some tried to descend but were stopped by light or bullets. Williams finished his first clip with three remaining above them. He reloaded and four bullets later dropped them, as well.

"Let's hope the next landings aren't as crowded," the detective said. "After this, I only have one full clip."

Williams looked down and gestured all to follow, carefully picking their way through the bodies. They turned through the helix and to the next window, already hearing movement above and then the sound of gunfire.

"That must be Morales. Once we get past this group, we can join him," said Williams.

Emma counted nine Zs waiting twelve steps up, shuffling and sniffing the air. One seemed more alert, watching them, making eye contact. What was in his eyes made Emma shrink back more than anything else she had seen. Those eyes contained pure hate, pure hunger. It wore nondescript gray-green scrubs, typical of both residents and students, and its face looked familiar. When Williams opened fire, it kept shifting behind the other Zs. When Williams stopped to reload, it ran down the steps toward them, teeth bared and shoulders down. Melanie screamed as the detective took the tackle straight into the wall, his gun flying down the steps and under the railing, falling a dizzying hundred feet and clattering at the bottom.

Emma wasn't sure why, but she found herself moving in. She brought down her sack of pennies at the base of the Z's neck. It grunted and turned, allowing Williams to pull his club, striking the Z on its head and forcing it back and then back another step with repeated blows, until sunlight streamed across its face. The Z tried to shield its eyes and backed into the balustrade. Andy rammed his aluminum pole through its neck. It arched back and fell, following the gun a hundred feet below, taking Andy's weapon with it. They heard some shots from above as the last three on the landing went down. A set of rapid steps followed, revealing a young, black-haired detective.

"Just checking to see what was keeping you. We have one more level to clear, and then we should be on the roof." Morales seemed overly chipper for the circumstances, but his bright mood lifted the spirits of their little group.

Williams inspected his arms—no broken skin; the thing hadn't been able to get a grip. The group glanced over the railing but couldn't see the bottom.

Williams looked at Emma. "That was another first. That one had intent."

"And a plan," Andy added.

Morales looked confused and shrugged. "So are you guys coming, or do I need to give you a written invitation?"

Without further comment, they followed the young detective up the stairs and joined the twelfth-floor group. They jogged up to the next gallery. Andy knew Dr. Broadwell. Lupita and Joanna greeted Melanie warmly.

Once introduced, the group moved on. The last landing held only a few Zs, none with that stare that Emma knew she'd never forget. Morales had enough bullets to finish them, and Williams still had his spare clip. They reached the roof door. The handle turned, but the door didn't budge, barricaded on the outside, they hoped, by other survivors.

Williams started banging. "This is Detectives Williams and Morales of the SAPD." They heard rapid talking on the other side.

Finally, a voice shouted through the door, "How do we know you're not bringing out a bunch of those *things*?"

Morales called through. "Because we're human, and we just killed about another thirty or more of them."

The voice came back, "How do we know you're not infected?"

"None of us have fevers!" Williams shouted. He looked at Emma. He couldn't say none had been bit. They heard the talking again.

"OK," the voice said. "Come through one at a time."

"Emma, stay behind me," Andy whispered. He grasped her bandaged hand. They streamed through, and a nurse with a thermometer checked each one as they passed the threshold. Andy did not let go of Emma until they both reached daylight. Close to twenty people sat in a circle in the sunlight. The positioning seemed odd until Emma saw the now-dim floodlight above them. Even if the Zs had made it to the roof, they would not have come within that circle of light. She wondered what the one with the evil eyes would have done.

Morales and Williams called in, informing SAMMC of the increase in numbers. They were assured that more helicopters would come. The detectives told the people on the roof about the evacuation plan and were cheered and hugged by most of the group. Some wept. Over 130 feet up, Emma could hear the shouts and screams on the street below. She didn't want to look. A few minutes later, they heard the blessed beating sound of the helicopters and even more cheers.

When the helicopters landed, a squad of camouflaged men with large rifles jumped out. They circled the first helicopter and waved the detectives forward.

The biggest one spoke. "Which one's the immune?"

Williams pointed to Emma, and she in turn came close, with Andy in tow; this time, she was not letting go. Emma looked up at the soldier, closer to seven feet tall than six, the blades whirling uncomfortably close for comfort.

"I'm Lieutenant Colonel Angus McLeod," he said. If he had followed with "*of the clan McLeod*" and "*There can be only one*," she would have believed it at that moment. He stooped and led her to the chopper, initially holding his hand up for Andy to stop.

"He goes with me." The expression on Emma's face left no room for argument, so Gus nodded. After Emma and Andy were secure, he led the surgeon, two nurses, and a few medical students who had escaped to the roof. Gus banged on the side of the chopper and stepped back, allowing liftoff. As they banked away, Emma saw another one coming in.

They flew over the city she'd come to love, the streets crowded with cars and people. Interstate 35 was bumper to bumper in both directions. Everyone was running—though where to was anyone's guess. The mob outside of Fort Sam Houston stretched for close to a mile, with tent after tent set up next to the entrance. They did not set down on the roof of SAMMC as Emma thought they might, landing instead on a strip about a half mile from the hospital, near a line of white tents. A man approached them wearing a hazmat suit and carrying a clipboard.

The voice that came through was distant and hollow. "Dr. O'Conner?"

She nodded, and he checked the paper.

"Do you have the medical records?"

Emma looked confused, but Andy pulled off his backpack.

"Here. I printed everything I could." Andy handed the man a stack of papers. "I couldn't find a file or envelope. Everything's electronic."

The man took the papers. "And you are?"

"Dr. Andrew Perdue, third-year anesthesia resident."

The man nodded and scribbled on his paper.

"Wait here, Dr. Perdue. I'll get to the rest of you in a minute to start decontamination and quarantine proceedings. Dr. O'Conner, please follow me."

He started walking down the row created by the tents. Emma gave Andy's hand a quick squeeze and then followed. At the third tent on the right, he opened a flap, and three more people in hazmat suits stood.

One stepped forward. Emma could discern that he was middle aged with a salt-and-pepper beard.

"I'm Dr. Thomas Graham of the CDC," the man said. "I'm hoping that what they say about you is true. My colleagues here are Drs. John Lowe and Cavita Mehra. I am going to review the medical file while they examine you, ask questions, and draw blood. I realize this will be awkward for you. Please understand that it is necessary."

She saw the small exam table at the back of the tent and followed the doctors as indicated.

Dr. Mehra was a small woman, little more than five feet tall, with a quiet voice difficult to hear through the hazmat mask. She had obviously realized this and did a lot of communicating with hand gestures. Dr. Lowe's booming baritone could cut through any mask or wall, so he asked the questions.

"How did you get infected?" was the first and obvious question.

Emma relayed the incident, trying to keep calm, though goose bumps ran up her arm, and she had a tight feeling in her stomach when she spoke of how the man latched onto her hand. She held it up for examination. They asked her about the onset of the fever, her symptoms, what she'd eaten and drank the prior day, bowel habits and if they'd changed, medical history and last pap, last intercourse, and other questions she felt uncomfortable answering. Normally, she was the one asking very personal questions. She did her best to reply to each question completely, no matter how much it made her squirm. When satisfied with her answers, Dr. Mehra drew over twelve vials of blood. Emma stripped, and the two examined every inch of her with a magnifying glass. She wanted to point out the bite they'd already seen but allowed the process to continue. This was followed by an oral exam with cheek swab, pelvic exam, and rectal exam.

Now feeling thoroughly violated, Emma was given a gown and led to the next tent, which was set up with a pair of showers— the liquid was not water, but smelled of disinfectant, and the second was cold saline. After decontamination, Dr. Mehra handed Emma a large cup of milky liquid and instructed Emma to drink the entire contents. From the smell, she knew that it was lactulose, a common prescription for constipation, in the hospital and out. Normally in fifteen- to thirty-milliliter doses, this was a full eight ounces, which translated to eight times the normal amount. She gave them a look. Dr. Mehra shrugged. Emma tilted the glass to drink when the door flap opened.

"Don't drink that yet." Dr. Graham entered holding a phone and a small bag, with two people in tow. One was Lieutenant Colonel McLeod, and the other was a tall, neat-appearing woman who looked familiar. As soon as she spoke, Emma recognized the woman as the night anchor on Channel Five.

"I've reviewed your file," said Dr. Graham. "There's no other explanation than you have immunity to the virus. Ms. Garcia here will help you get ready for the news conference. We'll do it on the steps of the hospital. All reporters who have passed quarantine and every camera we can muster will be there."

Emma opened her mouth for a moment, but nothing would come out.

"And the president would like to speak with you," Dr. Graham continued.

Emma realized that her hand shook as she took the phone. "Hello?"

"Dr. O'Conner, you cannot know how relieved I am to talk to you." The voice she'd heard so often talking about the budget and railing against the members of the other party sounded strained.

"Thank you. It's an honor, sir." Emma had no idea what else to say.

"I need you to know what the country needs of you right now. They need to know that there is hope. A week ago, the people were going about their normal days with their normal worries. Today, they wake in their worst horror-movie nightmares with some neighbors trying to eat them and the others trying to break in and steal their food. You can change that. Let them know that people will survive."

Emma felt odd, suddenly distant. Her heart calmed from the rapid fibrillation into a normal, steady beat. She had become a doctor to give aid to the sick and to comfort the dying. President Paulson was asking her to do this on a much grander scale. She knew he could not see her nod, but she did, anyway.

"Yes, sir. I can do that," she said, her voice now calm and firm.

"Thank you. Your country thanks you. I understand there is a colonel from the rangers with you," the president continued.

"Yes, sir. Lieutenant Colonel McLeod," Emma replied.

"Good. Put him on."

Emma handed the phone up to Gus. "The president would like to speak to you."

Gus stiffened to attention out of habit, taking the phone in one hand, his body rigid. "Sir!"

"I have an order for you; this is from me, your commander in chief, not to be countermanded by anyone but me."

"I understand, sir," Gus replied, but his face displayed consternation.

"You are to pick seven more men and women, whomever you need, with the only job of protecting Dr. O'Conner. Her survival is paramount. Do you understand?"

Gus could not help but look at the woman before him with dripping auburn hair, freckles, and keen green eyes.

"I understand, sir!" He started to hand back the phone and then stopped. "One question, sir."

"Yes?" President Paulson asked with some small amusement.

"Can I choose people from all armed services or just the army?"

"*Anyone* you need, Colonel," the president answered clearly.

"Thank you, sir." Gus paused and then spoke again. "I have no right to ask this, but I feel I must."

"Yes?" Paulson was curious.

"My family—my wife and two daughters. Is there any way ..."

"Yes, Colonel, I will see to it they are brought into a safe place. I am sure we have your address."

"Yes, sir. And thank you, sir." Gus handed the phone back to Dr. Graham.

"Let's get you cleaned up. We have a news flash for the world, and we want you looking as doctor-like as possible." Esmeralda Garcia took Emma by the hand and led her to the next tent.

Gus followed. Esmeralda raised her hand to stop him.

"I am her presidentially appointed bodyguard. Where she goes, I go." Gus lightly tapped the top of the newswoman's hand. She retracted it quickly as if slapped and then turned to Emma.

"I guess we'll have company," Esmeralda said.

Esmeralda led Emma into a tent partitioned into four rooms and took the first on the right. She dropped the bag onto a folding chair set in the middle and pulled out a simple gray dress, bra, black shoes, and a lab coat. Gus turned his back, and Emma pulled off her robe. The bra and shoes were too big, and the dress was OK, but the lab coat could cover most flaws. Once dressed, Esmeralda fussed with Emma's hair, drawing a comb through, toweling and combing again.

"No dryers," she explained. Once mostly dry, she combed Emma's hair back into a low ponytail and twisted it into a bun. She expertly applied makeup to Emma's fair skin. "You can thank all those summers I worked at a cosmetics counter for this."

Emma had no idea how she looked, but from Esmeralda's satisfied smile and the colonel's appraising look, she decided that it had to be pretty good.

"I think you'll do," Esmeralda commented with one last brush to Emma's cheek.

The calm that filled Emma when she spoke to the president began to drain away as her overly large shoes clomped down the concrete walkway between the tents and out into bright sunlight with a sudden onslaught of cameras and shouted questions. Emma smiled to them and waved, the blue stitches on her right hand standing out for the reporters to see and photograph. The brick wall that was Gus safely gave her passage as she climbed to the entrance of the SAMMC hospital. Under the eaves on the top of the steps was an occupied table where Dr. Graham took his seat. Emma caught Cory's quick grin as he waved her over to the chair between him and Dr. Graham.

Cory gave her a quick hug, keeping a protective hand on her upper back. "So you got the double showers?"

"Yeah, and the cavity search." Emma grimaced.

"Ooh, didn't have to do that. How about the purge?"

Emma assumed he meant the lactulose. "Not yet," she replied.

"Lucky. I got here yesterday. It was getting too crazy. I thought you'd be one of *them*. Andy wanted to check on you and got trapped upstairs. The nurse reported that your fevers weren't as high as any of the others. He wanted to make sure." Cory's eyes did a quick scan of the stairs.

"Andy arrived in a chopper with me. He's in quarantine right now." Emma felt better again talking to Cory.

Those at the table and those assembled before them settled down as Dr. Graham tapped his water glass.

"As most of you now know, I am Dr. Thomas Graham of the CDC's National Center for Emerging and Zoonotic Infectious Diseases. I have been in contact with other experts on this worldwide pandemic, and there have been reports of individuals who have survived bites and not"—he paused for a moment—"had a dramatic personality change."

The assembled reporters snorted at the understatement, but Dr. Graham continued without break.

"Dr. O'Conner, seated to my right, is the first verified case."

The reporters started shouting, and the camera flashes became almost blinding. Dr. Graham rapped for silence again.

"Dr. O'Conner was bitten by San Antonio case beta, a man admitted to San Antonio General Hospital five days ago after arriving from Mexico the night before. Another man arriving from Mexico earlier that day also had similar symptoms and died two days later from febrile seizures and brain death. Before communications with Mexico failed, we were able to ascertain that both men ate at a restaurant in the airport, and several employees from the airport also developed a fever within twenty-four hours of these two men's arrival. Now we will let Dr. O'Conner discuss how she came to be bitten."

There was more flashing. Emma saw the video cameras with all their green lights.

"I was on rounds with Dr. Brown, my attending, and was demonstrating an unusual finding in"—she glanced at Dr. Graham—"patient beta when he bit Dr. Brown. In attempting to force the patient to release Dr. Brown, I was bitten." Emma held up her hand. "I was taken to the emergency department for treatment, where Dr. Cory Miller placed these stitches in my hand."

"Dr. Miller, please continue," Dr. Graham prodded.

"When Dr. O'Conner arrived, we performed normal human-bite protocol, cleaned the wound with a hospital antiseptic cleaner, likely the same one they made us shower in"—he got a small laugh from the crowd—"and placed eight stitches using synthetic suture. The resident on the night shift did not arrive, so I continued caring for patients. Approximately twelve hours after their bites, Dr. Brown arrived in continuous clonic seizures and died shortly after having no response to multiple meds. Dr. O'Conner arrived with a lower fever of 105 and was sent to the tower where we had beds waiting for medical personnel. Since no physician could be spared to attend the upstairs patients, the nurse on duty called down with their vitals. Dr. O'Conner's temperature never topped 105.5, whereas most of the others reached above 109. The next afternoon, the hospital was overwhelmed with many infected patients loose in the halls. It was determined that the hospital must be evacuated to protect remaining medical and uninfected persons. Dr. Andrew Perdue volunteered to go to the tower to check on Dr. O'Conner but was trapped with so many of the infected in the stairwell and elevators."

"Since Dr. Perdue is still in quarantine, we will return to Dr. O'Conner," Dr. Graham prompted.

"I woke up feeling very weak with loud noises that turned out to be gunshots. Detective Williams was disposing of the infected." Emma had carefully thought of how to describe what he was doing. "My hands had been bound by torn bed sheets, and when I realized what the sounds were, I untied one enough to get to the floor. When Dr. Perdue and Detective Williams reached the room, I was able to speak, and my pupils reacted to light, so they confirmed that I was OK. Our ward was barricaded overnight, and in the morning, we retreated to the roof to be evacuated." She focused on a camera in the center, whose name bore one of the main networks. "I survived being bitten. Please, if you are infected, secure yourself so that if you change, you cannot hurt anyone, but if you recover, you can free yourself. Keep water nearby. The fever will make you very thirsty." Emma's head rang with her instructions from the president. Her job was to bring people hope. "Instead of fighting your neighbors, join forces and fight side by side to eliminate those who have turned. We will do best if we pool resources and talent. The faint line between chaos and order is based upon the faith you have in your fellow man. Rely upon that faith and any other you possess. Humanity has survived many trials, and we can survive this. Do not give up hope."

Mitchell swigged back the warm beer. The resort had thirty minutes of power twice a day to draw water, flush, shower, and cook. Technically, he was still a tourist, so after a quick shower, the four remaining employees cooked and did all the work. He and Beatrice, a middle-aged Englishwoman, were the only ones who stayed, because if the world was going to end, they'd rather end their lives in paradise. The bar TV was set to cable news, one of the few English stations the all-inclusive picked up. Both their heads jerked up at the change in scene.

An attractive woman wearing a white doctor's lab coat sat facing the camera. The crawl below stated, "Doctor confirmed to recover from encephalovirus." Beatrice raised the volume hearing the last part: "Do not give up hope."

"Some of us have not."

Mitchell and Beatrice turned to face a young man flanked by two older ones, all with rifles across their shoulders and swords strapped to their sides. None brought a weapon to bear, and the youngest one smiled in a friendly and familiar way. Beatrice recognized him first.

"Aren't you the young man from the riding tours? The one who played chess in his head with the German man?" Beatrice stood, her smile more nervous with guns in proximity.

Mitchell remembered the match, since he was on the biggest horse the stable had for his fat ass, and he heard the match clearly. The German, riding in front of him would suddenly state that his piece was someplace else, and the young man would pause and say, "Yes, of course." Mitchell hoped the blowhard had given the kid a big tip. At this moment, he was fairly glad his own had been generous.

"I am, and thank you for remembering me." The young man walked forward, extending his hand. "Since I doubt you will remember my name, I am Guillermo." He indicated the man to his left. "My brother, Rodrigo, and our friend Javier."

Mitchell and Beatrice introduced themselves.

"I am here, since this will be the ideal place for a compound," Guillermo said. "We went to the library yesterday, and in all of Playa Del Carmen, this resort and the ones on each side sustained the least damage in the last three hurricanes. They have independent wells and a pier for fishing boats. My people will be coming in soon, and then we will build our fortifications. You are welcome to stay."

Mitchell had the distinct impression of being dismissed. He and Beatrice found themselves wandering out to watch the procession of slow-moving cars winding down the paths to the rooms. Guillermo, who could not have been more than fourteen, spoke with the remaining manager, who was in the middle of preparing brunch. Scrapped cars were pulled in place to line the beachfront as Guillermo's men started digging to build the foundations of a wall. Guillermo's eyes and body looked about waiting for a challenge, but no one spoke. Everyone was thankful for direction and tasks. Mitchell picked up a shovel and started to help, already sweating in the humid morning air before he even started. He did not understand the banter in Spanish around him and knew some was directed at his size, but Mitchell was determined to pull his substantial weight. Thirty minutes later, he was spent. A firm grip on his elbow stopped his next movement.

"The lady says you are an engineer?" Guillermo asked, handing Mitchell a glass of water.

Mitchell sucked it down in three gulps and nodded. "Yeah, aeronautical."

"But you know things besides how they fly?" Guillermo goaded.

"Yeah, of course."

"Good. Come with me." Guillermo turned and walked away.

Keeping up with Guillermo required Mitchell to jog, and he felt winded within twenty feet. Guillermo slowed down. Mitchell sidestepped a small group of chickens that had wandered to the path. Along the side wall of the property, Guillermo's men strung razor wire and an electric fence. "I need you to help set up the solar panels so that anything or anyone coming over will not make it to the ground alive."

"If you've got big enough panels ..."

"There will be enough." Guillermo did not bother to look back as he hurried on to his next task. Mitchell felt it best to wait by the fence. One of the workers upended a bucket for him to sit on.

"Gracias." Mitchell knew even that word sounded badly pronounced. If the world was not ending but beginning and this is where a fat man from Vancouver landed, he guessed he'd better start working on learning Spanish.

Once he reached Jamestown Road, Peter hiked five miles to reach the ferry to cross the James River. He kept up a good pace, reaching the landing by 9:00 a.m., but no ferry was there.

Peter scoured the shoreline, finding an old rowboat with one good oar. He fashioned another out of river flotsam consisting of an old broom handle and a plastic detergent bottle, ruefully thinking of eight years of engineering and that this was the best he could do. The James River ran swiftly and was about a mile wide. He aimed for the far side and ended up over two miles downstream, but rowing across saved him from a sixty-mile detour to get to over the James River Bridge in Newport News.

Peter hid the boat and then walked northwest toward home. Pleasant Point Road, always a nice area along the river, was now very fashionable among the Hampton Roads commuters. His father and mother always laughed at the newcomers with their overlarge homes built too close to the water. He sighed with relief seeing his home intact, quiet. Peter banged on the door, but Soba did not answer. He went to the side yard and found the hidden key in the box beneath the willow tree. The house was empty. Most of the food was gone, but the electronics remained. Peter wanted to plop down in front of the TV and rest. Instead, he drank some water and found some old protein bars in the top cabinet.

Pulling down his bike, which hung in the garage, he headed off to the nuclear power plant. There was a hum as he neared, but it was much quieter than he remembered. There were four guards at the gate, twice the norm, and instead of sidearms, they held assault rifles at the ready. Peter laid down his bike and approached with arms up.

Almost thirty feet out, one yelled, "That's far enough!"

"I am Peter Saitou. My father is Jiromaru Saitou, the chief engineer. Can someone get a message to him?" Peter watched one guard separate himself from the others. Peter recognized the man from several years of Christmas parties. "Hello, Ed! It's good to see a familiar face!"

"We're on lockdown, so we can't let you in, but I can get a message to him." Ed nodded, and the others relaxed.

"Thanks. Just tell my father that I'm home. Do you know if Sabo—my grandmother—is in there?"

"A lot of families are here, so probably. Wait about an hour." Ed looked around the nearby woods. "They don't seem to stay out in the daylight."

Peter waited. In less than twenty minutes, a familiar head and gait approached. This time, the guards let him draw near.

"*Otousan*!" Peter felt an amazing amount of relief.

"I am glad you are safe." His father always spoke in the most formal way, but the warmth in his eyes always let Peter know that this was just a mannerism. "I and your Sabo have been watching the news, and I did not know if I was happy or sad that I asked you to come."

Peter smiled, hearing that his grandmother resided safely inside those thick walls.

"We are shutting down the reactors and should be done by tonight. After that, I may be able to get permission to let you come in. Your Sabo left some canned food hidden in a box in the guest room under the bed. We were told to bring what we could with us, and she was afraid anything we left would be looted."

Peter knew his Sabo would always think of him and looked forward to some soup and tuna after two days of subsisting on a box of Girl Scout cookies and a few packets of peanut butter crackers.

"I'll come back tomorrow, Otousan. Please give Sabo my love." They bowed to each other and parted. Peter grabbed his bike for the sixteen-mile ride home. He went slowly, especially through the small neighborhoods where he'd played with friends. Now he heard nothing but the wind through the trees. It seemed that everyone had left, gone to the plant, or hunkered down, but still, he felt suspicious eyes through many windows, but none opened a door to shout or welcome him in. The world was terrified. The little town of Surry had always been quiet, with the exception of the bustling restaurant that drew tourists and students from Williamsburg for classic Southern, home-cooked meals. The restaurant was boarded up, with no familiar line out the door. The house just past the restaurant appeared in an equal state, but the planks on one window had been pulled aside, the window behind it shattered.

The hole beckoned him. The rational voice inside Peter told him to keep going—stay in the light. Christopher Adams's mother lived in that house. Chris had earned his English degree and taught seventh grade in Richmond, so his mother would be there alone. Mrs. Adams took Peter in so often after his mother died that he knew that house as well as his own. Peter laid down his bike and knocked on the door, softly at first, then louder. There was a noise from inside, but no one responded when he called out, "Mrs. Adams, it's me, Peter. Are you OK?" Peter approached the window, pushing the board aside. He removed his jacket to finish clearing out the glass. A ranked collegiate gymnast, he had no difficulty pulling himself up and through the aperture.

Peter landed lightly on his feet and shook the glass from his coat, surveying the dark room with afternoon light filtering through the now only open window. A low smacking sound emanated from the back bedroom. Peter donned his coat for the chill that raced through him as he started down the dark hallway.

"Mrs. Adams? Are you back here?"

A grunt followed by a familiar shaved head came into the hallway.

"Chris! Man, you scared me." Peter waited, but there was no familiar reply, no "Nerd boy, what you doin' back here?" Peter took a fraction of a second too long to process that his friend was one of *them* as it bore down on him in the narrow passage.

Peter backed up but not fast enough as Chris the monster grabbed his jacket. Peter squirmed and pulled, twisting as only a gymnast can. Peter took two steps up his friend's front and landed his tennis shoe heel squarely in Chris' nose and then pushed off, forcing Chris to lose his grip. Peter fell on his back, briefly getting the wind knocked out of his lungs. Peter gasped and twisted, trying to escape from the thing with Chris's face, making it as far as the living room. Peter made a launch for the window, but Chris still had an athlete's body, lunging and pinning him to the wall and safe from the light filtering in. Chris tore at the jacket, trying to bite at any exposed flesh, teeth sinking into the back of Peter's ear.

Peter wailed both in pain and fear. Now he'd be infected. Peter's hand caught against a shard of glass still in the side of the window behind the board. He yanked it free, the adrenaline blocking him from the pain as it cut his hand. With all the force of a man who'd made it to the Olympic trials for pommel horse, Peter shoved the glass back and through the eye of what had been his best friend. The grip on the ear slackened, and Chris's body fell away.

Peter stood, dripping blood on Mrs. Adams's prized Oriental rug. The bloody hand touched the bloody ear. Peter thought of Mrs. Adams but remembered the sound from the back room and decided not to look. He grabbed a doily from the small table by the door and wrapped his wound. Peter initially thought that he needed to do better than that and then touched his ear again and realized that it wouldn't matter. It would be easier to exit the way he entered than to unboard the door, so he lifted himself, further stretching the cut and increasing the flow of blood that he now ignored.

Peter knew more eyes than ever followed him on the way home. *Let them look*, he thought. He pedaled, not bothering with anyone else. No more memory lanes for him. Peter Saitou laid the family katana on his lap in the living room as the news spilled out continuous horror upon horror. He'd spent his life running through this room, eagerly waiting for Christmas, playing video games with friends, and watching movies. He opened his college acceptance letters on this couch and chose to go to William & Mary, even though it lay just across the river.

Peter thought it odd that he heard one of his closest friend's voices and looked up to see her face, her green eyes staring straight into his.

"Do not give up hope," she told him.

He grabbed the remote and hit Rewind, watching the conference. Suddenly, the blood on the couch and his family sword meant a lot more to him. Peter cleaned his hand and ear, bandaging both well; Sabo always had plenty of bandages available, since the adventures of a teenage boy led to many minor and not-so-minor injuries. The little bottle of iodine could also purify water. If he remembered correctly from his Scouting days, it took five drops per quart and tasted nasty, but after thirty minutes, it killed any bacteria and parasite. Peter found the canned soups and other canned food and cooked the meal likely to be his last, but now he knew that there was a small chance that he could survive. He ate and felt renewed vigor and then set about securing the back room of the house.

He doubted the electricity would remain on for long, so anything requiring power tools needed to be done now. The family's mahogany dining room tabletop was sacrificed to make the inserts into the window, the legs becoming the wood needed for bracing. The engineer fitted boards inside the window frame to seal flush with the outer wall so that fingers could not pry up the edge as he'd seen at the Adamses' home. Then he cross-braced the boards from the inside and closed the window for a second layer of wood to be smooth with the inner wall with a cross bar over the interior, completing the job. Peter knew that this limited his exit. A perfect home and shelter would need fitted shutters. He lugged in gallons of water, filling every bucket, glass, vase, and anything else he could find. Peter finished his preparations when he heard an unexpected sound … the doorbell.

Peter opened the door to his healthy-appearing neighbors, Bill and Becky Chalmers, a middle-aged couple he'd known most of his life. Their kids were ten years older, and their daughter, Beth, had babysat him many times. When he'd arrived the day before, Peter had seen their house boarded up as if for a hurricane, with all the numbered panels for each window. Their eyes focused on the bandages.

"I was bitten this afternoon by Chris Adams. I'm pretty sure Mrs. Adams is dead," Peter said, surprised at the matter-of-fact tone his voice took. "I'm prepping the back room so that I can secure myself. How can I help you?"

It was Mrs. Chalmers who spoke, her voice kind. "So you saw the news, as well—the young doctor who survived."

"Yeah, she's a friend of mine from college. I'm hoping we don't just have an alma mater in common." Peter reached up and touched his ear.

"We came by to see how you were, to see if you had any plans for now. The plant is locked down." Mrs. Chalmers decided to push on with their mission, even though her husband was gripping her elbow.

"I saw my father through the gate this morning. The reactors are almost safely down, so if we survive all this"—Peter's hands waved to nowhere in particular—"we won't also be adding another Chernobyl or Fukushima to our troubles."

"We're heading out tomorrow. Our daughter lives in South Carolina. The Parris Island marine base is becoming a shelter. If you're OK, come by, and you can join us. We'll leave as soon as the sun's up."

Peter nodded, and Mr. Chalmers dragged her from the porch. The late-afternoon sun left long shadows over the lawn, and humans were quickly learning to avoid dark places. Peter withdrew inside, making sure that the tools were recharged. The door to his room was the last security measure, and he needed enough power to screw the boards in and then unscrew them in the morning. He had lots of water, an empty bucket with a lid for waste, canned food, a can opener, and Sterno if the power went out and a coffeepot if it didn't so that he could use the burner to heat up the canned food. The preps were complete.

Peter had a TV in the room. He smiled at the change in the news. Instead of stories of the infected killing and running rampant through buildings and subways, there were stories of groups of humans banding together, consolidating supplies and weapons. There were stories of more survivors, including some who claimed no fever at all, though the newsmen quickly stated that these accounts had not been verified. Finally, about four hours after being bitten, Peter secured the door, barricading himself inside. He turned off the radiator and tied himself to it, his family katana now cleaned, just within reach. He collapsed down, nodding off almost immediately in sheer exhaustion. He'd expended the energy of someone doing The Ironman that day and finally slept.

Toya regarded the hotel's storage room. When the lights came on, she and Saya heard rats screech and disperse, leaving food wrappers everywhere, bitten into confetti. The rats seemed especially fond of candy bars. Movement in one of the darker corners caught Toya's attention.

"Saya, have you ever seen rats in here before?"

Saya shook her head, poking around the boxes for anything edible. She found one untouched box of cheese and peanut butter crackers on a top shelf and several cases of soda and water.

"Our manager would have gone into fits if he saw even a mouse. Think those Zs ran 'em out of the sewers?" Saya said. She carried the case of crackers in one hand and a case of soda to the laundry cart filled with snack food and toiletries. "At least the little monsters don't care about shampoo and toothpaste. Check the top shelves. We might get lucky and find more food."

Toya had four inches on her companion, so she had a better view of the shelves. Near the noise in the dark corner, she caught sight of several more cases of something. The back end of a rat stuck out from one. The box of cereal bars next to it remained untouched. Toya pulled down the box, bringing a rat with it. The rat released the box and clamped onto her arm.

"Shit!"

She dropped the box and moved back, grabbing the rat's body behind the head, squeezing until it released. The head went sideways and limp.

"Little piece of shit!" Toya threw it on the ground and stomped on it for good measure. She picked up the box of cereal bars. Only the outer portion of the box had been chewed, so she took it out to the cart to add to the mound of toiletries in miniature bottles and AA batteries.

Saya watched the blood drip down Toya's arm. "Want me to look at that?"

Toya grabbed a rag from the back of the cart and wound it around the bite. "I'm fine. Let's go."

Some of Stokes's crew had cleared the Zs from the main bank of elevators for them. The scavenging crews were to meet in two hours. Once they unloaded their current haul into the waiting truck, they decided to start at the top and work their way down. They had better success with the vending machines than the storeroom, and when they got down to the seventh floor, they found out why. A rat was trapped, pushing down the bin cover but then could not get under it. With the light, it squealed back and forth along the plastic. Toya took her knife and killed it, its blood oozing into the bottom bin. The knife went back into its sheath, but Toya made a note to clean it thoroughly. She'd heard that dogs and pigs were getting this thing, so rats would be likely. It would also explain why the virus spread so fast. In her History of Medicine class, the bubonic plague was spread by rats through flea bites and killed roughly half of Europe. Toya scratched at the wrap on her arm. There was nothing to do about it now; she'd know soon enough.

Saya still knocked on each door, yelling, "Housekeeping!" as if expecting to find anyone alive. So far, they'd found a cowboy dead on his bed, wearing his hat, boots, and nothing else. They entered room 707 after no response. Toya noted the feet in the bathroom doorway when they started clearing the minifridge. Then the feet stirred.

"*S'il vous plait, l'eau …*" Its voice was low and gravelly.

Saya shrieked and fired into the bathroom. Toya knocked her hand up before she could fire again.

"He's alive, damn it. He could be like that woman on TV," Toya said, grabbing the gun and putting it back on the cart. She slowly moved around the door.

The man had pulled himself farther in, between the pedestal sink and the toilet. He gripped his right shoulder. Blood oozed but did not pour from between his fingers.

"It's OK, man. My friend overreacted. We thought you were dead." Toya knelt down to get a better look. He wore underwear and a T-shirt. His face was so gaunt and pale that he look like he were dead, or should be, but he spoke and was not afraid of the light.

"My name ..." His voice came out as a harsh whisper.

"Let me get you some water." Toya stood and grabbed a bottle from the cart. She twisted off the cap, flexing all her boxer's arm muscles as she handed it to him.

He released his shoulder and quickly downed the water. She handed him another and then a third. He finally nodded that he'd had enough for now.

"I'm Toya, and this is Saya. We're from Camden. It's across the bridge in Jersey."

"I am Charles Trembley. I am a science teacher from a town near Quebec City. I would shake your hand, but ..." He held up the blood-covered appendage. His accent was thick but Toya could understand most of it. The shoulder wound had almost stopped bleeding.

Toya grinned. "I'm a boxer. That amount of blood ain't nothin'. You should see a head gash. They pour blood over everything." She helped Charles to his feet. "Let's get a look at it." With some effort, they removed his shirt, which started the flow again. He sat on the bed while Saya and Toya collected some towels. Toya examined the wound track and found the bullet lodged under the skin behind his collarbone. She soaked a clean washcloth with a bottle of bourbon from the minibar and applied it. Charles sucked in his breath but did not cry out.

"This'll have to be cut out when we get him home."

"Home!" Saya seemed shocked.

"Where else do you think he's gonna go? Especially since *you're* the one who shot him."

"Stokes'll be plenty mad ..."

"Let me take care of my brother. Besides, Charles said he was a science teacher. That's probably gonna come in handy. The lights'll go out sooner than later, and he may be able to help keep some of 'em on." Charles could help some, but the demonstrations he'd done in the classroom were of the single-lightbulb scale. He kept mum.

"Get dressed. We'll meet you in the hall. We only have a few more hours of light, and it's going to take a while to get over the bridge."

Another brief argument broke out in the loading dock, but Toya was persistent. The most opposed was a young man with a bad case of the hiccups, obviously a chronic problem, since Charles realized that most of those present addressed him by that name. Toya wasn't kidding when she said the bridge would take a while. The crew manually moved cars and then came back to move the truck. After the second time, Charles examined the gearbox. It was very like the one for the combine he worked as a teen on his father's farm. He tested his shoulder; it would move enough.

"I can drive the truck," he offered when the one called Hiccup hopped in again.

"He says he can drive!" Hiccup yelled at Toya.

"Then let him!" she yelled back.

Hiccup shrugged and got down, indicating the driver's seat.

Charles climbed out and into the driver's side, realizing that they had put the cars back after moving them. He also could see the efficiency of the operation; most vehicles were stripped of batteries, doors, and other parts. After a couple of false starts, he got the feel for the truck and was able to move it forward as they cleared and sealed their barricade. Once on the other side, Charles slid over, and Hiccup drove down the narrow cleared lane. The wall of metal and debris rose on his left, close to eight feet high in some places.

"We plan on making it twelve feet with hazards stuck within. That way, no one and nothing can crawl over." Toya felt the need to explain. She'd let Stokes know that they needed hazards near the bottom, as well, to keep down the rats. He may have thought of that when it came to competing for food. Almost a half mile down, the wall was only a few feet high, except for the gate, which opened at their approach.

Stokes met them to inspect the haul. He did not expect the extra passenger. Toya could see him working his jaw muscles, the tattoos on the right side of his face rippling, and he held up her hand as she got out. She put on her biggest, sweetest smile.

"Brother, I would like you to meet my new friend. His name is Charles, he's a science teacher, and he's going to be joining us for a while."

Stokes only stood two inches taller than his sister but leaned in eye to eye, their foreheads touching. His voice was low and threatening. "You bring some fucking *cracker* to our place? Another fucking person to feed when we don't know how long—"

"Ooh, brother, he ain't no cracker; he's Canadian. French, even. Be nice to have some culture 'round here. And he knows science stuff, like how to get all those batteries recharged when the lights go out. Charles drove the truck, so he has other skills too."

Toya finally looked at Charles, and he came over. Charles decided to do what they did in the military movies. The Quebecois kept his eyes straight ahead, not down in subservience, and he did not make eye contact. Stokes's tattoos marked him a gang member. That close, Charles could see that the open dots were spearheads, the straight lines the shafts extending back to his neck. From the way everyone jumped when an order was given, Stokes was the leader. Charles knew to tread lightly but did not want to find himself someone's "bitch."

"So, Mr. Frenchman cracker, what can you do for me that I cannot already do for myself?" Stokes had moved over to him. They were the same height, but Stokes easily carried thirty more pounds of muscle over Charles's thin frame with the potbelly of the overfed and underactive. Charles diverted his eyes to the left.

"Since I do not know all of your capabilities—"

"Not an answer I was looking for. Hiccup!" Stokes turned away.

"I know how to set up solar arrays with panels and how to make solar ovens. I know how to make an electromagnet. I know how to make hydroelectric power. I know—" Charles began, his voice carrying through the group unloading the truck.

Stokes stopped and turned back. "I hope so, little Frenchman cracker. You can stay as long as you prove useful." He returned to the truck, ignoring Charles and Toya.

Toya took the Canadian's elbow. "I'll get you to Clarence; he was an army medic and can get you fixed up."

Her voice was the gentlest Charles had heard. He looked at her wrapped arm. "And for you, as well?"

"Yeah, for whatever he can do for me."

Some at the meeting the day before had talked about making quarantine and isolation rooms. They needed it now, for her.

Charlene rapped on the desk in the Elysian Heights Community Center.

"Five minutes, people!"

Her son Kevin was a medic now, and the army had sent him to school last fall to be a physician's assistant. He called that morning telling her to close the gates and enact quarantine. Anyone who'd seen the news knew that getting on the road wouldn't do any good. Charlene, former PTA president, VP of the Elysian Heights Community Association, and all around do-gooder, called for order. The walled subdivision held 380 houses, a nine-hole golf course with driving range and putting green, and a half-Olympic-size pool outside the rec center. Almost one hundred people milled around, less than a fifth of the community's original population. One person not present surprised her, Mrs. Margery Pool, an avid prepper who over the last four days had been saying, "I told you so" to anyone that would listen.

Charlene leaned over to Paul, the secretary, a fidgety man who had wanted to leave the day before but had turned back once he got to the highway and could drive no farther. His wife, Dolly, was not fit enough to walk far. Charlene knew her size-sixteen frame wouldn't make it far, either. That would change immediately.

"Where's Marge?" she asked.

Paul shrugged. "I don't know. Several people said they knocked but didn't hear anything. Her car was still there. Do you think she's got a bunker?" He sounded hopeful.

Charlene shook her head. "No, she believed in community preps. That's why she kept handing out all those storage boxes with masks and gloves and tried to get the rest of us to buy in and stock up."

"Dolly used to call her 'Crazy Marge.'" Paul gave a nervous grin.

"Well, I can't delay the meeting any longer." Charlene rapped again. "I call this emergency meeting of the Elysian Heights community to order. The first order of business is to find out who has remained and who has bugged out. I'm sending Kurt through the rows with the list. Please identify yourself as here and whether you know what's happened to your neighbors. As you do that, we'll begin to discuss quarantine and isolation."

Several hands went up. "Aren't they the same thing?"

Charlene shook her head. "Nope—quarantine is for anyone who may have been exposed; isolation is for those with symptoms. I propose we use one of the abandoned houses nearer the main gate. No one comes in without at least twelve hours of quarantine."

There was some unhappy murmuring. "What if the family comes home?"

"Then after they finish quarantine, we move it to a different house."

There was still some dissenting murmuring. Charlene put on her smile and decided to go with her slowest, sweetest Southern drawl.

"I know it feels wrong going into our neighbors' houses without their permission. It feels off to me, but the world is off. Those folks that left, well, chances are good that they won't be back for some time, and they'll be spendin' time at other folks' houses and shelters. We are talkin' about survival. We need to see what each one of us can do. Let's start with defense. How many here own guns?"

Three-quarters of the hands in the room went up.

"Now how many have practiced shooting those guns?"

Half of the hands went down.

"Well, that's a start."

"I do archery!" Claudette, a girl of twelve, stood up. "I can teach people."

"Wonderful, Claudette. That's what I need! What else?"

A man named Clark stood. "I'm a bit of a gun collector. I can let folks that know how to use them sign them out for patrol." He looked around the room. "I want them back."

"Of course, Clark." Charlene waited. "Anyone medical?"

A few hands went up, mostly women and one man. Two nurses, a paramedic, and a nurse's aide.

"Good. We'll let you set up a medical unit, probably here. Food preparation?"

One hand—Mrs. Murchins, who ran a catering company.

"We'll need to centralize food." The murmurs started again, and Charlene held her hand up. "I doubt we'll have power for long. It's easier to run one kitchen than fifty, and this way, we make sure that everything's equal." Charlene had reviewed the food issue with Marge earlier. Marge was the most vehement about centralizing the kitchen. Charlene looked around again and felt Marge's absence. Many were on their feet.

"Why do I need to share the meat I've stored up when others didn't think about it?" Mr. Parker crossed his arms, his pale face now beet red.

"Because you're gonna want Mrs. Pool to share all that lovely rice, dried potatoes, canned vegetables, and such that she has been storing away for years when you lose power and all that meat of yours spoils." Charlene kept the smile fixed to her face as Parker blanched. He collapsed back into his chair.

"You see, my friends, my neighbors, no matter what you have to eat, there are a few of us who've saved up more. Now the only way to keep us focused on surviving and not fighting each other is to get those resources together." Charlene made eye contact with angriest looking of the group, making sure they understood her.

"Who's gonna watch 'em?" Parker grunted.

"Well, sir, you and some others the town elects. Keep an eye on each other. 'Trust but verify,' as my pappy used to say." Charlene watched as the new reality struck those present. Once the murmurs quieted, she continued. "Now Paul, Kurt, and I will start working with you on getting together some work details to raise and strengthen the fence, the security detail, kitchen duty, and all those things we need to do. The only way we get through this is together."

After the meeting, as dusk descended, Charlene went to Marge's. The front door was locked, so she took out the hidden key under the mat and let herself in.

"Marge!" Charlene walked through the echoing halls. The downstairs bedroom door was open, clear plastic sheeting and duct tape pushed out. Charlene started up the stairs, drawing her pistol from its holster.

"Marge!" she called out again.

Just off the landing was the remainder of her friend's body. Charlene heard someone calling from above.

"Help! Greg's infected! He's here somewhere!"

Charlene started turning on lights as the sunlight faded.

"Turn on the lights! The news says they hate the light!" Charlene called back.

When she reached the master bedroom and turned on the light, there was a groan from the closet. Charlene turned on every lamp in the room, dispelling any shadows. She reached for the closet knob and pulled it open. The creature that was Greg, Marge's oldest son, screeched with its hands over its eyes. Charlene aimed for the head and pulled the trigger. She did not hesitate or flinch. She knew that it wasn't Greg anymore. Charlene returned to the hall.

"It's OK. It's dead!" Marge's daughter, Bernadette, emerged from a crawl space with her two daughters, Celeste and Cathy. "Are you OK?"

Bernadette smiled initially and then shook her head. She came close and whispered, "He bit me."

"How long ago?"

Bernadette checked her watch. "Six hours?"

Charlene nodded at the girls. "And them?"

Bernadette pulled them close. "They're OK."

Charlene went to the window looking over the backyard. The eight-foot back fence was part of the front wall of Elysian Heights, and four houses down was the opening to the main gate. "We'll set you up with a real quarantine, something a little sturdier than duct tape."

"Where?" Bernadette asked.

"Right here will do just fine."

Paulina landed the Bell on the soccer grounds of the fancy prep school, Raul Lara sitting by her side.

"You said there'd be fuel, if not…" Paulina shut down the rotors when she spied a small fuel truck cutting across the turf. If a groundskeeper was still in residence, he would be pretty upset.

"Where *is* that boy?" Raul Lara exited the chopper and circled, checking his watch. Then he stopped and swore as an eleven-year-old boy and a girl of likely the same age jogged across the lawn with two bags each. With the engines quiet, Paulina heard the exchange and felt sorry for them both.

"This is my friend, my best friend, Sienna. She couldn't get in touch…" The boy explained, while the girl looked away.

"I don't care if she's the president's daughter. You are coming and coming alone!" Raul Lara grabbed one of the boy's bags and began dragging him toward the helicopter. The boy dug in his heels. Lara turned and pointed the gun at Sienna.

"*No*!" The boy screamed. The girl held up her hand and slowly turned away. Paulina could not hear what she said, but was proud of how the rejected young woman held herself upright as she walked away. Paulina thought, *if that one lives, she will be a great lady one day.*

A thump on the side of the Bell let her know the refueling was complete. The boy jumped into the back seat, crossing his arms and wiping away tears while Raul Lara resumed his seat next to Paulina. Once the truck was safely away, Paulina lifted off to return to the compound and see what other errands El Padre had in store for her.

CHAPTER 5

April 15-16; Z Days 6-7

Sammy Jo got an early start. Mrs. Elvira Polk sat snugly in the sidecar with blankets tucked around. She complained about being treated like an invalid. After all, the Indian Warrior was hers, and despite recent hip surgery, she was more than capable of driving it herself. Martin lived in Seattle and wanted to protect his mother. He felt that she would be safer in the city where the military closely monitored all vehicles coming in. The panic room in his apartment could be sealed and held several days' worth of food and water.

Without traffic, the drive would take about two hours, generally less, State Highway 8 to I-5, but I-5 into Seattle was blocked by stalled cars and military roadblocks. It might take days. Instead, they'd stick to the country roads and side streets in the many towns and cities, working their way around.

State Highway 12 wound its way through the countryside and was full of its own obstacles. The sky threatened another rainstorm, and abandoned vehicles caused a lot of weaving. Elvira and Sammy Jo weren't the only ones out, but those on the road ignored each other, each too busy trying to save himself or herself to be much help. The twenty-three miles from Elma to Grand Mound took over two hours. They stopped briefly near Oakville for Mrs. Polk to stretch her legs, when a strange pair of men approached.

"Nice bike," one said from the side of the road.

Sammy Jo kept her hand on the Indian, needing to release Mrs. Polk's arm.

"Yes, it sure is," Mrs. Polk replied brightly. "I've had it almost fifty years, and it runs almost like new."

Sammy Jo groaned inside. She knew these men were looking to steal it, maybe leave them dead on the side of the road.

"But the throttle sticks sometimes and can leave you in a lurch." Sammy Jo tried to undo some of Mrs. Polk's praise.

"Nonsense," the old lady stated. "Just fire that thing up, and let them listen to the engine purr." Sammy Jo caught the glint in Mrs. Polk's eyes and realized that the lady was not as naive as she'd believed. Sammy Jo complied, straddling the bike as the motor revved. The men looked at each other, no more than ten feet away.

"Ooo-wee," one said, "why don't you let a *man*—"

His comment was cut off by the unmistakable cocking of a pistol.

Mrs. Polk held out the .38 calmly, with none of the tremor one might expect in an older woman. She gingerly stepped into the sidecar and held the gun on them.

"Now you two might not be meaning any harm, in which case, you will come to no harm, and we will be on our way."

Sammy Jo didn't need another hint and gunned the motor, getting them as fast and far along Highway 12 as they could go.

Next time they stopped, they would need to take better care and be farther off the road. The bike took care of the shaking for them. They just needed to be away. About the time the rain started in earnest, they stopped at a farmhouse on Old Route 99. A woman sold preserves, bread and mugs full of hot tea in exchange for canned food or a few ounces of gas. No one wanted money anymore. Mrs. Polk bartered her gold ring for a jar of gooseberry jam, half a loaf of bread, and some tea.

"I can't eat the ring," Mrs. Polk reasoned.

The farmer looked over the customers, gun in hand. The highwaymen wouldn't have much luck there. Sammy Jo breathed her first sigh and unrolled her neck muscles. She sipped the tea as the clouds lifted, and she could make out Mount Saint Helens in the distance, framed perfectly by the farmhouse's front window. Even without the top, it was beautiful when covered in snow.

Mrs. Polk's chatty nature won her friends among the travelers. Most had left Seattle and were heading for rural houses. Some were secretive; the term "bug out" was whispered through the room. Sammy Jo only wished them the best. Other travelers told Elvira of a place in Olympia still taking guests if they arrived before nightfall. Normally, those eighteen miles would be done in the blink of an eye; today, the journey would take hours. One group of men said they'd cleared a path along the way, so the going might be better if someone didn't mess it up. Sated, Sammy Jo and Elvira strapped on almost-useless rain gear and headed north as the next batch of clouds rolled in overhead.

They made it to the house on the outskirts of Olympia in just over two hours and locked up the Indian in the garage. The owner of the boardinghouse accepted a brooch as payment for the lodging. Sammy Jo and Mrs. Polk had their temperatures checked, and a woman gave them a stripped-down skin inspection. Once satisfied of their lack of contamination, the two were allowed into a room they'd share with six others. Shortly before dusk, the shutters were closed, and reinforced boards with slats cut to go into the wall were slid into place. Chamber pots were used for waste since the toilets were bolted closed to prevent rats from crawling in through the plumbing.

The electricity had gone out earlier in the day, but the crank radios caught them up on the news. The most consistent station was a broadcast out of Canada. The deep-voiced Alistair Breedham reported on the expansion of the outbreaks across the United States.

"The CDC and Health Canada have confirmed that rats are a major vector, spreading the virus through both bites and feces. Be wary of any food that may have come into contact with rats. I have Dr. Goodman of the CDC with me now."

"Good evening, Mr. Breedham. I'm glad I can help." Dr. Goodman had an odd lisp that caused him to whistle with the *th* sound.

"Dr. Goodman, if you could, explain what the CDC and Health Canada are doing to help contain the spread of the disease," Alistair prompted.

"Of course. With the help of Dr. O'Conner and samples from the infected, we are isolating the virus and trying to identify the origin. There are now three research facilities in the United States, one in Canada, and several in Europe and Australia still functioning and working on the virus. Right now, all we can say is to hunker down. If you develop a fever, tie yourself or have someone tie you down until it is known whether or not you are infected. Do not go out at night. Do not eat raw foods."

"Is there anything else at this time?"

"No. As soon as we have more information, we will disseminate it to the public." Dr. Goodman's voice was not overly reassuring.

"Thank you, Dr. Goodman. I turn this over to Commander Bernard Tolleson of the RCMP."

Commander Tolleson advocated against the use of firearms by those not trained to use one, advising instead the use of a bat, club, sharp stick, or other device less likely to cause accidental harm. "The smell of fresh blood agitates the Zs, especially the "zrats" and "zogs," as they are now being called, and attract them to an area. Anyone bleeding should be kept far from entrances, and any bloodied bandages need to be buried as far from habitations as can safely occur during daylight hours," the commander concluded.

Brief conversation was cut short when the boarders heard grunts from outside. Their hostess turned off the radio and the lights. "Everyone to bed. No sound," she instructed.

Sammy Jo led Mrs. Polk to their cots.

The zombie thing didn't seem to bother Mrs. Polk much. She quickly descended into snoring. Sammy Jo couldn't help but lie awake and worry.

Peter woke with a start from the screams and shots coming from next door. The room was black. There were no digital lights, and the power was out. Peter's bindings prevented him from standing. He checked his watch—3:00 a.m. The simple act of lifting his arm sent shooting pain throughout his overworked body. It had been about twelve hours since the fight with what had been Chris, and the news said that most people started with fevers within that time. Peter felt his forehead to be sure. It was cool. Then the screams stopped. Peter told himself that he couldn't have done anything soon enough to help. Shortly after the screams ended, scratching at the window began. Peter fought past his protesting body and untied himself, sitting with the sword at the ready. Where there had been one set of claws, there were now two and then many. The windows broke in the front of the house, followed by grunts in the hallway that made his skin crawl. Then he heard scratching and gnawing at the base of the door, clawing a foot or two up, and banging accompanied by growls and grunts. It would be at least three hours until dawn. The sound was relentless. There was nothing to do but wait and hope that his preparations held.

After about an hour, the noise changed, like someone trying to rip at the wood with a crowbar. Peter had not left enough space between the slats and the window frame for it to do more than scratch. Peter fought the urge to call out. He'd heard on the news that a few of the Zs were not as brain dead; some retained the ability to think and plan. One of them could be out with the others. Peter occupied himself by planning on improvements in homes to allow fortifications. Individual houses would not be practical; apartments with common space for cooking would make more sense. He imagined roll-down shutters that sealed well within the wall and roof access for defense and egress. Solar and wind would be needed within a few years.

Peter's mind became so engaged, tuning out the pounding on the door and scratching on the window boards, that he forgot time. It was quiet. His watch read 6:30 a.m. The little digital light glowed and cast a slight green tint throughout the room. It should have been dawn. Peter waited another thirty minutes to be safe and then unbarricaded the door, his body protesting every movement after the previous day's exertions. The last of the juice in his power screwdriver removed the remaining hardware securing him in the room. He held the katana to the ready as he pushed open the door.

The house was wrecked. Window glass covered the floor, and lamps had been knocked off of tables. His mother's ashes were scattered before her shrine, and shards of the beautiful porcelain urn mixed with dust. Peter blinked back tears at his error. She should have been safe in the room with him. He sorted through the waste in the bathroom and found a bottle of acetaminophen three years past its expiration date. He downed three and then started on what needed to be done. A plastic tub with a fitted lid would suffice for his mother's remains. He kissed the top of the lid as he sealed it and lowered the container to the place of honor. Peter climbed the stairs to the attic, blade in hand for any Z that may have been hiding in the dark. He needed his Scout backpack and the old camping supplies that didn't need electricity. The nuclear plant had generators with enough diesel for a few days, but if there wasn't anyone coming to resupply them, then alternate sources needed to be found.

Peter was happy that his father was safely there. It was well fortified. The plant sat on the river, so water would not be an issue. They could fish, the area near the visitor's center—currently an ornamental garden—could be converted to vegetables, and there was green space. As long as the core was safely stored, there shouldn't be any radiation issues. Peter wondered if the government might make it an evacuation center.

The door to the attic stood open, light streaming in from its one window. Peter hoped that it was enough sun to run off the remaining Zs. A quick tour confirmed that the room was empty. He dug through a pile of old gear. He added a tent, camp stove, Sterno, metal cups, and an emergency aluminum blanket to the stack he'd take. On the bottom was his old pack, which was in decent shape, though some straps needed mending.

He packed and decided to check on the Chalmerses before riding to the plant. Their door stood open. The boarded-up windows made it very dark inside, so Peter raised the katana in front of him and carried a bright LED flashlight propped under the grip with his left. Peter had done some fencing but had stuck more with gymnastics, and the katana felt very unlike the foil he had used, making bright light the primary weapon.

Peter made it to the second room when he heard the shuffling. He raised the flashlight, and the thing turned, hair already ratty and matted, smelling of urine and feces. Peter turned, catching the katana for a moment which caused him to drop the flashlight, its glow easily filling the room as the Z charged. The katana stood straight out as the Z impaled itself, reaching and clawing as the blade sank deeper into its gut. Peter turned the razor-sharp blade upward and lifted, the blade slicing up and into the chest. Peter had to move side to side as the Z relentlessly tried to grab him, but after almost a minute and with most of its life's blood spilled across the floor, it slumped to its knees and remained motionless. Peter withdrew the blade and retrieved his light.

In the kitchen, canned food remained, but anything in a bag or loose in the refrigerator was consumed, the limited remains littered across the floor. Peter returned to the hallway and crept up the stairs, his back to the wall. Thumping accompanied by grunts could be heard at the landing but did not turn him back. The remains of Bill and Becky lay on their bed, Bill's gun on the floor. Two dead Zs surrounded the bed with another struggling to get out from under an overturned table, its arms moving but not its legs. Peter dispatched it through the neck. He pulled a sheet over the unfortunate couple and took the gun. Rummaging in the closet revealed two boxes of bullets and a holster. Peter caught sight of himself in the mirror: bandaged ear, gun strapped to his side, holding a sword—a regular man for the ages.

He didn't want to call it looting, so Peter foraged through the rest of the house, finding any light survival gear and taking a few cans of tuna and beans, despite the pack already being too heavy. With the sword stuck so that the hilt peeked out from between the zippers, gun at his hip, Peter hoisted the bag on his back for the long ride to join his father and Sabo.

The trip was more nerve-racking than the day before. There were more homes with boards pulled off, less movement from behind fences. Peter imagined others like the Chalmerses and pedaled faster.

On Hogg Lane, the plant's large reactors became visible above the trees. Normally, the humming was not just heard but felt along the road, but now there was nothing. A successful shutdown. Peter's elation dimmed as he approached the gates. The guards so present the day before were no longer at their posts. A truck lay turned on its side inside the gate, bullet holes visible along the hood and windshield. The lower portion of the gate bowed out, leaving a gap large enough for Peter to push his bag through and enter.

The silence made Peter's skin crawl more than the noises had the night before. The room at home was secure. This area was assumed safe but apparently was not. Peter drew his sword, more comfortable with it than the gun. It was harder to accidentally cut someone in half than to shoot them. The visitors' center door stood open, sunlight pouring into its large windows and skylights. He swept room by room, with no one present despite its ideal daytime light. The back door, normally locked and barricaded, welcomed the world. Peter jogged across the courtyard toward the first reactor. His father's office was in that building, so he hoped the inhabitants had pulled back.

Although shut, the lock had been broken from within, as if people had to break out. Peter called up the echoing staircase without a response. The bag grew increasingly heavy, and staring up the steep, narrow stairs made the decision to stow the pack an easy one. The flashlight illuminated the dark corners. No monsters lurked, so the corner under the stairs should prove safe. He mounted the steps, never feeling so ungainly with both hands full and spread in front of him. Three stories up, he was in the hallway with his father's office. The door was the second to last on the right, Peter rapped gently, peering in through the narrow pane of smoky glass.

"Otousan?" he called in gently.

Movement came in response from behind the door.

"Peter?"

The door cracked open. His proud and always erect father could barely stand, blood running down a terrible gash in his throat. Jiromaru sank back into the only chair, the computer still blinking. Peter set down his sword to better examine his father's grave wounds. Jiromaru remained wordless at the gentle probing of the neck then the ones on his side.

"I tried to protect her, but there were too many. I finally fought them off and retreated here. I called the military, but they could not send anyone." He shook his head sadly, causing the blood to flow faster. "If the reactors were still on, they would have sent someone."

"I have some supplies in my pack. I'll head down and get them. Stay here." Peter looked for reassurance from his father.

"I could not go anywhere if I wished it. Save your supplies. They will be wasted on me." Jiromaru tried to reach for his son, but Peter retreated too fast, too determined to do what he could. Peter left the sword behind but still had the gun. The ringing of rapid feet on metal steps resonated through the building, Peter pulled on the pack to head back up. Two Zs waited at the first landing, one wearing guard blue with a gun still at his hip but not pulled, the other dressed in sanitation gray. The one in gray seemed smart, he'd kept the other back until Peter was within a few feet. Then they sprang. A shot rang from Peter's gun as they closed. Peter batted the heavy flashlight at them until he got the high ground and could take aim, getting the gray in the head as he tried to dodge back to the hall. The blue grabbed Peter's flashlight hand and started to bite down, lowering its head for the perfect bull's-eye. Peter barely flinched as the teeth gripped his thumb. He pulled the trigger, and the blue slumped forward. The guard's pockets contained another full clip, and the gun had four bullets left, safety secure. The second firearm went into Peter's waistband.

When Peter returned, the room was the same, but his father seemed even weaker than he had ten minutes before.

Jiromaru calmly watched his son wet a cloth and bathe the wounds. "I need to lie down and have a sip of water."

Peter nodded and accommodated his father, finding lab coats to soften the cold, hard floor.

"You were on lockdown. How?" Peter began, doing his best to bind the wounds.

Jiromaru nodded to the computer. "Dr. Graham at the CDC says that it does not just spread with bites; food can be contaminated, as well. Some started to get sick yesterday morning. We thought it was just food poisoning. Then the fevers became very high. Then they changed. People panicked. Many rushed to leave. Our guards shot at those trying to escape." Jiromaru turned to look at Peter. "Never assume you're safe."

"I will do everything I can to protect you." Peter touched his ear. "I was bitten and did not get sick. I am one of the immune."

Jiromaru smiled sadly. "I did not get sick, either. Being immune will not keep them from eating you." He tilted his head to the ceiling. "I need to sleep now."

"Yes, Otousan, you need your rest." Peter could barely keep his voice steady, knowing that it would be his father's last rest. The wounds to the neck, shoulder, and side had led to severe blood loss. Peter had torn through his pack looking for anything that he could use to transfuse his own blood into his father, but he had nothing. Peter barricaded the door with his father's desk and lined the furniture in a row to reach the far wall of the small office. Peter's eyes focused on the blinking computer.

The satellite maintained the Internet connection. The CDC site showed a front page full of information about the virus and Emma's bio available for the press. Peter had seen Dr. Graham with Emma on TV, so through a message to Dr. Graham, he might be able to get word to Emma. Maybe he could join her, help find a cure. His father's breathing become more labored and shallow. It wouldn't be long. The world needed to know of Jiromaru's bravery. After the e-mail blinked "Sent," Peter opened a can of beans and emptied his entire bag before realizing that he'd forgotten utensils. Fingers would have to do.

Peter adjusted himself so that his father's head rested on his lap. Raising Jiromaru's head seemed to help the breathing some, but the rhythmic sounds became slower and more shallow, followed by a series of faster ones. Jiromaru was beyond rousing. Peter heard the ding of an e-mail received but did not move for fear of causing his father any discomfort. After several gasping pauses, seven hours after Peter had arrived, his father exhaled the last from his lungs and lay still, the great man's face calm and passive. Peter let loose a wail. He didn't care if anything else heard him. He cradled his father's chest to him, rocking the body as if an infant. After the tears would no longer come, Peter dropped water to his father's lips, mimicking the ritual after his mother's death, and then covered the body with the aluminum blanket from his kit. Tomorrow at full light, he would build a pyre of old furniture and anything else that would burn.

In his mind, Peter heard Jiromaru's calm, deep voice, reminding him of the message. The e-mail was from Emma:

> Peter,
> I'm so glad you're alive! My condolences on your father. He was always so kind when I visited. I have been moved to a facility outside of Atlanta—the address is attached. Dr. Graham states that it must be memorized and the message completely deleted. The location of the facility is a secret. The only reason he is allowing me to tell you is because you are immune and because of his respect for Dr. Saitou. I am unsure of your best route to Georgia. Even the woods may be dangerous since, along with rats, dogs, coyotes, and maybe other animals carry the virus, as well. Be safe.
> *O-genki-de*,
> Emma

Even with his father's warm body so close, Peter couldn't help but smile thinking about her.

They'd met at Governor's School, a state-sponsored program for the mega-geeks across Virginia, the summer between junior and senior year of high school, becoming fast friends. At college, they took many science classes together, often choosing the same lab sections to partner up. It always seemed when one was breaking up, the other had just started a relationship, but their friendship remained solid. Emma was the standard to which Peter judged all other women, and all others came up short. At graduation, she left for medical school in Texas, and he went to graduate school at MIT. They stayed connected on Friendlynk, cheering and consoling their respective ups and downs. Knowing that Emma was alive, that she was safe, somehow made the world less dark. Peter hit Reply—"I'll meet you there. *Ai shi teru*, Peter." The computer now read 9:32 p.m., well past dark.

The movements in the hall let Peter know that he wasn't alone, but he dared not cry out again. The bonfire in the courtyard the next morning would have to suffice to bring anyone forward. The plant used to maintain a couple of powerboats to keep people away on the river side. That would be the best option of escape. The Atlantic Intracoastal Waterway stretched all the way from Norfolk to Florida, and the Savannah River went to Augusta. Though not all the way to Atlanta, it would get him closer. And gasoline might be an issue. The only Internet servers still running were the US government's. Luckily, information about states and geography answered most of his questions.

Peter dreamed that he and Emma cruised down the river, her green eyes reflecting the sparkling blue-green water. When he leaned forward to hear a question, his head snapped awake to pounding on the door and clear English.

"Doc! Let me in! Please!"

Peter jumped up and pulled the desk free, pulling the man inside and slamming the door behind him, and then pushing the desk back into place.

"Peter! Oh, God, Peter!" The man was called Butch, a big redneck in every sense of the word, who'd worked maintenance for as long as Peter could remember. A strong urine smell emanated from the man, who blubbered and thanked Peter over and over.

"Hush!" Peter grabbed Butch by the shoulders and looked into the big man's blood shot eyes. "We're in here now, you're not alone."

Butch's panicked sobs calmed as he spied the cans of food. To keep him calm and quiet, Peter opened a can of tuna and handed it over.

"No utensils," Peter said. "You'll need to use your fingers."

Butch needed no coaching and dug in, licking his fingers when he was done. The strong fish smell made Peter wish he had chosen something else, but it was too late. The beating on the door commenced, and Butch started shaking again.

"Are the hall lights working?" Peter asked to give Butch a distraction.

Butch nodded. "But some of *them* keep turning the lights off."

"That's OK. We just need light for a few minutes. Where are the switches?"

"At the top of the stairs and the end of the hall."

"The end of the hall is closer?" Peter asked.

Butch nodded.

"Good. Once I know it's daylight, I'll run for the switch and turn it on, and then both of us will make like hell for the stairs. Get down the stairs and into the light. You take the pack; I'll take my father. Let's try to get some rest. It's just a few hours now."

The katana lay over Peter's lap as he leaned back. Something told him not to let Butch know about the guns securely covered by his jacket. Later, when they didn't feel like rats in a trap, maybe, but the possibility of Butch turning on him crept through his mind, and Peter was not suspicious by nature.

A light squeak brought Peter to full alert, not the kind from an animal but the kind from furniture sliding across a linoleum floor. He must have slept for a couple of hours. Butch stood near the door with the pack already on his back.

"Is it time?" Peter asked innocuously, surreptitiously patting his waist. From the weight, he knew that the guns were still there.

"Yeah. Should be. I was getting ready." Butch's eyes had lost their fear; they looked furtive. Peter checked his watch, it was a little after six, likely still too dark.

"Why don't we eat first? It's still too dark out."

Butch looked at the sword and nodded, dropping the pack back down. They mixed beans and peas and ate in silence. Six twenty was still likely too dark, but Peter felt like Butch was ready to spring, so it was a matter of fighting Butch or fighting Zs, and Peter didn't relish either.

"Ready?" asked Peter.

Butch quickly shouldered the backpack and nodded. Peter readied his flashlight and sword. Butch opened the door, and Peter dashed down the hall toward the far end, his hands fumbling along the wall as grunts closed in behind him. For a moment, Peter thought that Butch had lied, but he found the switch and flooded the hallway. Four Zs, less than ten feet away, brought their hands up and staggered back toward open doors leading to dark rooms. Butch did not need to be told. Peter saw him tearing down the hall, bag clanking and announcing its treasures.

Peter returned to his father's office, hoisted Jiromaru's wrapped body over his shoulders, secured the katana to his side, and staggered into the hall again. As he reached the top of the stairs, the lights went dead. Peter turned them on again with his shoulder, watching the Z at the end of the hall narrow his eyes and turn them off again. Peter hit the light for the stairs and started down. They'd be on him soon. Grunting emanated from below when the light flooded the area, and then the rattling from the cans started again, getting closer, not farther away.

Butch's red and pale face met Peter's. "They're everywhere!"

"How many?" Peter kept his voice calm, even as the lights went out again.

"Thirty? I don't know—too many." Peter lowered his father's body and handed Butch the gun with the half clip from his back. Butch randomly fired below, quickly emptying the clip. Peter had taken riflery classes at summer camp, mainly target shooting with BB guns, but the principle with handguns was the same: point and shoot. He kept the flashlight down for another few seconds, hearing the Zs on the stairs approaching their prey. Peter shot the bright blue LED light up to the landing next to his father's hallway and pulled the gun from the holster, illuminating what the news was calling a "Thinker." He pulled the trigger, sending it to the ground. He took care of the other three above him on the stairs and dashed back up to illuminate the stairwell again as Butch screamed for him to come back.

The floodlight filled the area again, proving Butch right—the stairs were packed with Zs Peter once knew as people. Guards, assistants, and engineers all shrieked and grunted and pulled back, scattering away from the light like roaches, some falling from the railings and landing thirty feet below. Butch stood frozen, his jaw slack and trembling.

"Help me lift him," Peter asked, picking up the blanket around his father. Butch stared for a few seconds more and then ran full tilt down the stairs. Peter sighed and propped his father's body against the railing, positioned himself in a half kneel, and pulled himself up. After several readjustments, he attempted the journey down the steps. The lights stayed on, and the Zs kept away from it. On the last flight, the gleaming sunlight from the open door beckoned him and led to fresh air. The sun felt like freedom as stepped into the bright light of dawn. Peter walked by Butch as he cried, he understood the man's stress, but Peter needed to tend to his own grief and loss. Peter found a place in the middle of the courtyard where he could make a small pyre.

The visitors' center chairs and benches were made from as much metal as wood. Peter made his way to the boat shed. Luckily the sixteen-foot powerboat still remained tied. A quick sweep revealed that it was all clear, with the added bonus of several containers of gasoline. The gas was needed for transportation, but Peter had another priority. The paltry treated wood he'd found would not be nearly enough to cremate his father. The white lab coat would have to suffice as the funeral dress. Peter dug through his pockets. Jiromaru was a traditional man. He would want to be cremated with the six coins. A dime, a quarter, and two pennies were all Peter could find.

Lugging the gas next to the body, Peter had to force himself to talk to Butch.

"Do you have any coins?"

Butch patted his pockets reflexively, and then his eyes narrowed.

"They can be pennies or anything," Peter reassured him. Butch found a quarter and a nickel. Peter thanked him, placed all six in the lab coat pockets, and then arranged the coat's flaps right over left.

"I need some gauze from the bag," Peter instructed.

Butch pulled the pack close, almost hugging it, and then furtively opened the corner, rummaging for a minute before pulling out the sealed paper around a square of gauze. Peter thanked him and cut the gauze into small pieces with his multi-tool, placing some in his father's nose, mouth, and ears. Technically, all orifices should be blocked, but Peter could not bring himself to disrobe his father in front of Butch. Clothing would have to do.

Once the wood was soaked with gasoline, Peter asked for help placing his father on the pyre. Butch rolled his eyes, acting more annoyed than scared now, and stood, taking Jiromaru's feet. Peter arranged his father's body with head to the north and then placed tulips from the front garden around the corpse. When satisfied, Peter poured the gasoline onto his father, allowing it to soak into the clothing, and then lit the pyre.

Thick, black smoke rose and curled while the flames took hold on the jacket. There was no urn in which to place the unburned bones, picked up with ceremonial chopsticks. Dirt from the front garden, loamy and loose, would be the easiest to cover whatever remained, the reactors a permanent tombstone. Once this act was complete, Peter needed to move quickly.

The gas in the boathouse might get him as far as the Outer Banks. A motorcycle could get him farther but lacked the ability to carry extra gasoline. Eventually, Peter's protesting muscles forced him to sit. He soon found himself leaning on his side, and he drifted off in the warm April morning.

The distant sound of an engine snapped him to consciousness. Peter blinked from the midday sun. He'd managed to get a couple of hours of solid sleep. His hand cramped around the hilt of the katana, and the holster made a dent on his left elbow. Scratching his head, Peter looked around. No Butch, no backpack.

The expletive that initially came to Peter's lips could not be spoken so close to his father's pyre. The engine noise coming from the water was receding. The boat shed stood empty. The boat and several cans of gas were gone. The sound that issued forth was something primal, a combination of rage, grief and fear. Again and again, the sound rang across the emptiness until Peter sank to his knees, throat raw. Spent, Peter sobbed, swore, and wished Butch into the deepest levels of hell. And then Peter laughed with the realization that they were already there. It was time to come up with plan B. Peter considered his options as he covered Jiromaru's remaining bones with stones from the gardens.

The cafeteria and employee lounge lay two buildings back; there'd be lockers that might contain supplies. Peter moaned about the boxes of bullets in the pack. On the plus side, they were the wrong size for the gun Butch had taken, so they wouldn't do him much good except in trade. Peter surveyed his own gun. The clip held four bullets; the spare clip was empty, since he'd never bothered to reload. The guardhouse tower would have weapons and ammunition. Maybe he could find something else.

The tower door was open, the room dark and crowded behind it. The Zs snarled but jumped back with the light. Peter closed the door and jammed a metal chair leg in the handle to lock them in. He knew there were close to 150 employees with their families who likely retreated to the plant. There were maybe 400 people on the grounds initially. It didn't look like many had escaped through the front. There were normally two boats, and now both were gone. From the news, he knew that many people died from the virus, so there could be two hundred or more Zs altogether. Peter wanted a place to sit and plan.

The cafeteria had a lot of windows, but the kitchen didn't. Peter walked around outside first, surveying the area. He opened the door and called in. No sounds, no grunts, and no shuffling came from behind the doors. Peter inched through the dining room and swung the kitchen door back as fast as he could. A skylight filled the room with light. He breathed out. Canned goods covered one wall, but all were industrial sized and hard to carry. A cabinet marked "Banquet" was lined with steel pans and cans upon cans of Sterno. Those would go. The pantry revealed how the inhabitants got sick. Rats scurried over the rice, potatoes, and flour. They squealed in the light. A few ran toward Peter but turned back when hit with the sun's rays. The empty bags read "Almonds" and "Peanuts."

Inside a cabinet, he found a padlock key that opened the meat locker. Lots of meat. Peter knew from the Scouts that jerky could be made from anything if it cooked slowly and dried, but time was important. And it was time to eat: a big steak and an oversized can of green beans. The platter filled with a twenty-four-ounce steak plopped onto the cafeteria table. The sun started to show the day's age, but Peter would worry about where to hole up for the night after he'd had his fill. With the first cut of the steak, Peter heard a whimper and then a sob. Peter put down his knife and fork and unsnapped the holster. The sound repeated and came from above.

"Who's there? I'm friendly. My dad was Dr. Saitou."

The sobs burst forth in earnest, and a ceiling tile moved. A dirty, small face looked down.

"Daddy put me up here, and I can't get down." Peter holstered the gun and stood on the table, careful to move the meat away from the tiles so as not to get dust and debris on it.

"Lower yourself, and I'll get you. As you could smell, we have dinner."

The girl's hands slipped as she climbed down, and she half fell into Peter's arms. Peter observed that the ceiling was well made, and the supports would likely take his weight if needed. The girl stared at the steak as if she'd never seen food.

"Go ahead and get started," Peter said. "I'll grab another set of utensils and another plate."

She sawed pieces too big for her mouth and made happy noises; in the minute it took him to get back to the table, over a third of the steak was gone. Peter cut away a small portion as she stared at him and then started in again.

"I'm Peter. When was the last time you ate?"

"I'm Sara," she managed between mouthfuls. "My dad pushed me up there two days ago."

"How about water?"

"I had a couple of bottles at the start, and some of the pipes sweat." She shook her head. "It doesn't taste very good."

"Yeah, I imagine. Look, I'm not sure how we're going to get out of here, but I do know where to go—Atlanta. But a guy named Butch took the boat."

"He's an asshole. Dad always complained about him."

Peter grinned as she started growing more comfortable.

"Why don't we drive?"

"I don't have a car."

"I do—well, my dad … did. He …" She looked away and tears started to form. "Won't be needing it."

"I don't know how to hot-wire—"

Sara dug through her pockets and brought forth a familiar rattle. "I got the keys."

Peter grinned. "That should get us partway, at least. I can siphon some gas from the other cars and make sure that the tank's full. There are lots of abandoned cars on the freeways, but we may need to stick to back roads." Peter looked at the fading light. "We can't go tonight. It's getting too dark. I was going to rig the freezer and sleep in there, but if you know someplace better …"

She looked up. "Sometimes there are rats, but I've been able to keep them away by putting a dead rat's blood on me. I've got a couple of dead ones up there. They bit me the first night."

Peter grinned. "So you're immune!"

Sara shrugged. "I guess." Her body tensed when a branch moved outside. "They're starting to move. It's weird how they come toward the light but can't be in it."

Peter hoisted her up through the ceiling and then relocked the freezer, keeping the padlock keys. He opened the pantry and sliced open three rats before they escaped the light, collected their bodies, and grabbed a couple of bottles of water. With rat blood smeared over his legs and arms, the remainder of the rounds went quickly, and he locked every door he could find. Lights would stay on as long as there was power, keeping the Zs out of the building even if they surrounded it. He tossed the rat and the water up to Sara and hoisted himself onto the brace, securing the tile to cover the opening as best he could.

The crawl space was just that, just high enough to let Peter move through on all fours. Peter followed until they found her sleeping area with denser material under them. He calculated that they were over the kitchen with the vent nearby. The rats scuttled around but left them alone. Gnawing sounds from below kept him vigilant, but Sara's breathing deepened, and they eventually both slept from sheer exhaustion.

After the initial press conference on the steps of SAMMC, Emma sat through a series of television interviews in a commandeered office. During one of the interviews, the crowd outside became increasingly agitated, causing Esmeralda to become distracted mid-question. The conversation was terminated by Gus.

"I think this place will not qualify as safe, let's get you to the helicopter pad and see where they would like you to go." Gus led Emma by the elbow quickly through corridors and back through the hall of tents, Cory at their heels. As they went by a tent with a sign saying "Quarantine," Emma spied Andy reading on a cot.

"Wait." Emma dug in her ill-fitting heels. "He needs to come, too."

Gus nodded and motioned to Andy, staying the guard with his hand. "He's coming with us." By the time they reached the helicopter pad, Drs. Graham, Mehra and Lowe were hefting small boxes toward the Blackhawk.

"Esmeralda said you were already on the way." Dr. Graham set down a file box and stretched his neck. "They're not sure if the perimeter fence will hold for the night. We're heading to the airport, President Paulson sent a jet for us, and then off to Atlanta where we can do some real research in peace."

The transfer to the Atlanta facility went smoothly, and Dr. Miller never left Emma's side. The next morning, Emma was taken to the OR for biopsies of her kidney and liver, and a lumbar puncture for spinal fluid. Despite the soreness and bruising, she then went upstairs for interviews with the local Atlanta affiliates, a video feed from all the major networks, along with being a talking head on satellite fed roundtables on multiple twenty-four hour news networks.

Once safely at the facility, Gus's team arrived and took up quarters on each side of Emma and Dr. Miller, but Gus wondered what his team members were protecting Dr. O'Conner from. They were securely underground. The walls were lined with concrete and lead, so no zrats could get inside. The outer area was well guarded and the entrance secret. By the next morning, he realized that protection from the other doctors was needed as Gus followed Dr. Mehra into Emma's quarters. Emma was still in pain from the previous day's biopsies of almost every organ, with one vehement exception, and now the pretty young Indian doctor entered with yet another consent form.

Emma studied it and stopped. "I told you, Cavita, I'm never going to consent to a brain biopsy." She calmly handed the form back.

"Dr. Graham said that it's very important for the research to be able to get ahead—" Dr. Mehra insisted.

"Well, you will be doing that without parts of *my* head." Emma stood.

Gus noted that both of the women were not very tall, but it was Dr. O'Conner who claimed the upper hand. Dr. Mehra could not meet Emma's gaze.

"I will get Dr. Graham. I will let him explain…" Dr. Mehra started.

Emma waved her hand to shoo the other doctor away. "Get whomever you want. No one is touching the inside of my head."

Dr. Mehra scuttled out, almost running into Andrew Perdue.

"Whoa!" Andy's hands shot up as the woman rushed past him, and he focused on Emma. "Are they trying to stick more needles into you?"

Emma rolled her eyes and plopped down onto her cot, causing Cory to roll over and yank a pillow over his eyes. Emma made an annoyed face that he slept through all that and not bothered to try to take her side. "If they would try to use the functions and intellect of my brain instead of trying to destroy part of it, I may really be able to help." Emma brought her knee up and hugged it. "How about you? Have they found tasks for you?"

"Anesthetizing rats. I have to keep them unconscious while the researchers infect them, monitor them, and then kill and dissect them." Andy shrugged.

Gus had to admit that he liked Andy much better than Cory. Dr. Perdue seemed to respect Emma, the other he was not so sure about. Not that it was for him to say whose company she kept.

"I'm still tired from being poked and prodded all morning and then dressed up for interviews all afternoon." Emma combed her fingers through her hair. "And that was just the first day, from the looks of the news, we'll be sticking around for a long time."

The virus was on all inhabited continents, in all major cities, and spreading faster than anyone had imagined possible. Some countries with weak governments had already fallen. Chaos reigned in all but a few secure places, such as where they sat. Dr. Graham's sigh could be heard before the rap on the door.

"Now, Emma," Dr. Graham began in the tone one would use with a recalcitrant child.

Emma stiffened at it. "That will be Dr. O'Conner."

Andy smiled and sat back on the only chair in the room, wishing for some popcorn. Andy had witnessed Emma in the past when she "got her Irish up." She was notorious among the residents for her ability to stand up to anyone when she knew she was right. There was no backing down once something was settled in her mind.

"Dr. O'Conner," Dr. Graham corrected himself. "As you know, the research on this virus requires healthy, fresh brain tissue. A small donation on your part—"

Emma stood, chin jutted forward and face flushed crimson. "I have told you, the one absolute thing I will *not* do is allow you to touch the inside of my brain with any instrument." From the corner of her eye, she watched Gus adjust his position to stand in front of the light sconce near the door, his shadow looming even larger than his massive body, covering all those in the small space. The movement was not lost on Dr. Graham.

Dr. Graham started to say something and then stopped when the shadow shifted, covering him completely. The assistant head of emerging infections and zoonotic diseases yielded the floor.

"We can discuss this again later."

Emma felt her color calming, but the steel remained in her voice. "No, Dr. Graham, we will not."

"By the way, you have a message. Dr. Mehra will give it to you in my office." The researcher ground his back teeth for a moment and then stalked out. Emma smiled slightly at his back and then more broadly up at Gus.

"You know, I might be able to use this bodyguard thing—"

"Protective detail," Gus corrected.

"—to my advantage." Emma's grin widened. The schedule the day before demonstrated how many of her true strengths were being ignored. She possessed a bachelor's degree in biology with an emphasis on microbiology and bioengineering and a doctorate in medicine. Almost every weekend and holiday during the first two years of medical school was spent as a genetics research assistant working with virions and lab-created viruses. Smiling at cameras while arguing with someone completely ignorant of biology and being a human guinea pig were not acceptable uses of her talents. "Let's go crash a meeting," Emma announced.

"I go wherever you go," Gus replied.

Gus opened the door and to lead the way. Cory sat up in bed and asked blearily "Where's everyone going?"

Andy stood to follow. "Did you *really* sleep through all that?"

Cory shrugged. "I guess. What happened?"

Andy shook his head and hustled to follow the other two, leaving Cory to dress and figure things out for himself. Dr. Perdue caught up with Dr. O'Conner at the main office as she both squealed with delight and looked sad at the same time. She responded to the quizzical eye raises from Gus and Andy with a sad smile.

"My good friend Peter – he's immune and alive. But his father died shutting down the Surry Nuclear Plant." Emma let her eyes well up for the man she respected so much. His gentle smile that was reflected in Peter's. A smile she hoped to see again. Emma found Dr. Graham, she still wouldn't let him biopsy her brain, but in exchange for letting Peter know where she was, Emma would do more of the television interviews and allow them to draw her blood daily.

Her afternoon was spent in meetings with virologists and scientists, followed by make-up and interviews. She came to a halt when Cory found her between events. With news from Peter, she had forgotten him and their two nights together. When he bent in to kiss her, she pulled away and turned from his gaze.

"Cory, I'm sorry, we have to end this now." Emma's voice was firm.

"Why?" Cory seemed confused and went to grab her arm, stopped by Gus's movement. "Is it because I slept in this morning? I sleep, I –"

"No," Emma shook her head. "I like you; I've liked you since medical school."

"Then what's the problem?" Cory started to move in, again stopped by movement from Gus.

"That's it. I *just* like you, and I don't think it could ever be more than that. My friend Peter is alive. I've known him a lot longer, and I know it could be more than like." Emma remembered junior high, with all the girls giggling about who liked who.

"Em, give me a chance. I'm here, and this friend of yours is-" Cory insisted.

Emma knew there was no way to say it nicely. "The one I want to be with at the end of the world." Emma stepped away. "I'm late for an interview." Gus blocked the path between them and followed Dr. O'Conner to the media room.

CHAPTER 6

April 17; Z Day 8

Peter woke with a persistent poking.

"Peter, it's morning. Let's *go*!"

Peter peeked down into the kitchen and swung himself to the prep table and then grabbed her.

"We have to stock up. Breakfast, and then we load the car. I'll find some tubing I can use as a gas siphon. There were a few more gas cans in the boat shed. I'd love to get some weapons, but there's just too many Zs in the guard tower."

Virginia ham and canned peaches started the day, and then they went on to the boatshed. Sara found some flares while rummaging through supply boxes, and Peter took tubing and three almost-empty gas cans. Sara's father's Outback had a little over half a tank and thankfully took regular. Using heavy-duty kitchen utensils, they pried the tank covers open on a couple of cars and managed to fill the SUV and the cans. Around noon, they were ready. Sara found some AM stations still broadcasting. Peter stopped her when he heard a familiar voice and smiled. Emma was still OK.

Sammy Jo and Mrs. Polk abandoned the Indian three miles south of Seattle. They couldn't find any fuel, and the roads became impassable with both people and puddles. They walked along the highway, sometimes hearing shrieking inside a car where a Z couldn't free itself from a seatbelt. Other survivors trudged along with them, lining up at a military checkpoint, rain slickers snugly tied beneath their chins, some still firmly holding useless umbrellas inadequate for keeping anyone dry in the relentless rain. People signed in and then boarded the waiting trucks. Once a truck filled, it drove off. Finally, Sammy Jo and Mrs. Polk found themselves in front of a pimply teenager. His badge read, "Private Thomason."

"Name, jobs, and why you are coming to Seattle," Private Thomason stated in monotone.

"Sammy Jo Taylor, licensed practical nurse."

"Honey, you are eight credits shy of being an RN," Mrs. Polk interjected. "And I'm Elvira Polk. My son lives in the city. Maybe you've heard of him—Martin Polk, the actor?"

"Sorry, ma'am. Don't know him." The young man wrote on his clipboard. "Please climb onto the truck in front of you. One of the other privates can help you board if you need assistance." Private Thomason directed that at Mrs. Polk.

She tapped his arm. "I'm sure I can do it myself." Her tone was pleasant, and a hint of pride crept in.

The women were driven to a long, low building not far from Boeing Field. Once the pair climbed down, they found themselves in another line—temperatures checked, names clicked off, and given a cot number and a cup. If military personnel could confirm that Martin Polk still lived in the city, Mrs. Polk and Sammy Jo would be allowed to proceed. Since it was near dark, tonight would be in the shelter. The city was under a strict curfew.

Toya's fever peaked at 105. Charles and Auntie took turns giving her water and bathing her head. Charles himself recovered quickly. The bullet was close to the surface, and the stitches pulled but did not cause much pain. Once Toya was out of the woods, Charles offered to go back into Philadelphia with Stokes and his men.

Close to two thousand Zs had crossed the Benjamin Franklin Bridge the night before, and Stokes wanted to blow the path that led them from the city of 1.5 million past their door before even more crossed. For that task, he needed explosives. The Sixth District police had raided an arms dealer a few weeks earlier, with all the C-4, machine guns, and bullets going into the central evidence room. The police had apparently abandoned the city, and the Pennsylvania National Guard was setting up Pittsburgh and Harrisburg as main evacuation centers. Stokes's main worry was not the police, the FBI, or any government entity but rival gangs in Philly who had the same idea.

There had been a skirmish the day before when a group with weapons tried to climb one of the lower parts of the wall, but between hidden spikes and defenders' bullets, most of the invaders died. Then there were the Zs the night before. Charles was given five minutes of weapons training, a handgun, and a spot on the wall that was his to defend for four hours. He held his own and earned his rations and a spot on the "raiding party," as Stokes referred to it. There were three groups—the largest to enter the police station, the other two to search every hotel room, convenience store, and pharmacy in a one-mile radius of the main group. The power was out, so the shake lights they'd found in a container truck on Perry Island came in handy. Everyone carried a crowbar, a gun, and large backpack for supplies. Orders were that if a human had to be killed, so be it. Charles was pretty sure that he couldn't carry out the last order unless that person was trying to kill him, but he agreed with everyone else. His group would go to the stores and restaurants around the convention center.

Although midday, downtown Philadelphia was quiet. The panicking crowds of four days earlier were gone. Charles's group was led by Hiccup. Where Toya and Stokes were smart and careful, Hiccup was reckless. Charles also suspected that he wasn't bright enough to be leading the group, a thought shared by most from the rolling eyes when Hiccup's back was turned. It took some convincing that the search needed to be methodical, building to building, rather than just hitting the obvious spots already picked over. The professional office lunchrooms could house coffee, tea, cans of soup, sugar, salt, and often a bottle or two of booze in drawers. The area morphed into Chinatown, where packs of noodles with instructions in Mandarin filled the cabinets. Once all loaded their packs, they returned to the trucks, dropped off the goods, and continued. Two from each group traded off to defend the trucks outside the police station. It wouldn't do to have all their work go for nothing.

Stokes found the door to the district station barricaded. Using trees and rope, the group found a third-floor window unbarred, and they broke into a ladies' restroom. The Philly police hadn't abandoned the city. Stokes could only assume that the cops had realized that they were exposed and sealed themselves inside as a way to protect the public. Stokes shared the general gang mentality that the only good cop was a dead cop, and right now, that theory held double.

It was dark inside. Rotting cop corpses lined hallways and stairs, but the grunts emanating from below indicated that there were even more "alive." Stokes and his men shone the flashlights just long enough to get to the next spot and then stopped to listen. On the stairs, they met the first set of Zs. Stokes's men used their lights in unison to make the Zs in filthy uniforms back down.

Duke had drilled them back in the day. Their former leader had been in the military for almost two years until he was caught providing women and drugs to his fellow GIs just off base. Duke trained the boys like he'd been broken and rebuilt in boot camp. The only right way was his way until you proved yourself and rose in the ranks. All the men and boys now looked to Stokes to be the leader, and he'd stepped up. Now he led his team down the stairs. Stokes picked up a baton off a body and snapped it open.

"Hold on the guns. The noise will bring more too soon. We need to keep the Zs separated." Stokes raised the baton and struck the first one in the head as it lunged toward him. The other six followed Stokes's lead. The team wore thick leather jackets to protect their arms, with the collars turned up and buttoned. Until they fought in close quarters, the men had been murmuring about the heat. Now they were thankful for the protection. Once the four Zs were dead, Stokes started feeling along the corpses for weapons and bullets.

Most of the dead had guns with empty clips, but some had spare clips on their belts. The men quickly loaded their packs and moved on.

Down the stairs, Stokes was caught by surprise as a Z lunged out and tackled him. The baton came in handy again as Stokes pushed back the Z's head to give Catch a nice target, bashing its head in as he and the rest of the team turned to dispatch three more Zs in the hall. Buller slipped on the blood-slicked steps and fell down the stairs, followed by screams and grunts, as his leathers did not hold up long. The sounds reverberated through the building.

"Make sure you have full clips, get off two shots then pause. Ray, Catch, hold the flashlights—one above, one below," Stokes commanded as he rolled the Z off of him. They heard grunts from both directions, soon followed by the smell of human waste and then the hollow, hungry eyes. Stokes and Hamlet concentrated on the ones from the depths, with Malcolm and Con taking care of those from above. They stood back-to-back, and like any team that worked well together, few words needed to be said. Within a few minutes, the steps looked like they were carpeted in red, but the only movement came from the New Jersey boys.

"Weapons report," Stokes said.

There were some clicks. Most men had one and a half clips; Ray and Catch had three.

"Move down. The evidence locker should be in the basement."

They lined themselves along the railing to avoid the worst of the blood. What was left of Buller was scattered at the bottom. Catch gagged a moment and then moved on. The red glow from battery-powered emergency exit signs partly lit the way. Down two more flights and into the bowels of the building, they finally found a door that looked like it was out of every TV cop show ever made: the wire cage with the opening, the locked door behind.

Without power for magnetic locks, crowbars made quick work of the doors when four strong men heaved in unison. The next problem came when they surveyed the room: it was much bigger than they'd thought. Searching every box could take days. Stokes realized that the C-4 would likely be in its own safe. They searched the perimeter until they found the most likely candidate. It was solid steel and looked like it could hold four men. The seams were too smooth and narrow and the crowbars were too thick. It was too big to haul out.

"Fuck!" Stokes kicked it with his heel, his jaw clenching with the pain shooting through his body. The safe had an electric padlock, no power, and no key. Stokes shook his head. "Collect what guns and ammo you can. We'll head up."

He had to admit that it wasn't too bad of a haul. They picked up over two hundred guns and rifles, well over three thousand rounds of ammo, but no C-4 and no way to bring down the bridge. They broke open the main doors and stepped into the bright afternoon sunlight, the other teams waiting.

"Didja get it?" Hiccup called out. "Hic."

Stokes shook his head. "It's in a safe too big to carry out and too thick to crack."

Charles brought his head up, glancing down the street. "What is it made of?"

It took Stokes a moment to understand the man's question, and then shrugged and made a face. "What's it matter to you? I can't get it up here."

"If it is made of steel, I know a way to crack it." Charles stood and met the team. Stokes stopped and stood in front, crossing his arms. "There is a medical clinic three blocks away, they 'ad a liquid nitrogen tank that was almost full. Since even in the tank it would evaporate quickly, I did not think it worth carrying. Now, there is a reason."

Hiccup thought it funny until he had to go back with Charles and Catch to retrieve the tank. Charles made sure that all of the nozzles were tightly closed before they carried it down the two flights of stairs. The clinic had been a find with antibiotic samples, vials with unknown use that didn't need to be refrigerated, and diabetes meds for Auntie. Charles grabbed the giant drug book, as well. Hiccup insisted that it was too heavy, but Charles knew that it was the only way to know how to use their find. Pyne Poynt didn't have any surviving doctors or pharmacists.

The three followed Stokes into the precinct building and down the steps, Ray and Malcolm lighting their way. The blood had congealed enough to be more sticky than slick, but they avoided as much as they could. Charles inspected the safe. The face had a blank digital panel. He shone a flashlight along the door seam to find where the bolts went through into the frame. It had three along the side, one on the top, and one on the bottom.

"Let's lay it flat," Charles instructed. He took some of the tubing from a nebulizer kit and fit it around the nozzle for the tank and used medical tape to secure it in place. The tape and plastic would freeze, but hopefully not before the first few bolts cracked. He attached the plastic tubing to an IV catheter without the metal needle and directed the tip at the first bolt. Charles showed Catch where to turn it on. Stokes stood by with a sledgehammer.

"The door will not completely give until all five bolts are broken. Each time I back away you need to 'it the door near the bolt as 'ard as you can."

Stokes looked skeptical but nodded. Charles knelt down next to the top bolt and fit the catheter above it. He nodded, and Catch turned on the nozzle. The cool spray surrounded them, bouncing up and off the metal, turning it white. Charles held his breath as he counted to thirty. The nitrogen combining with the oxygen in the air made it hard to breathe. Once he reached thirty, Charles leaped back. The nozzle turned off, and Stokes gave a swing, the sound ringing through the room like a giant, deep bell.

Charles came back to the door and worked on the bolt on the bottom, repeating the process, then along the side. After two from the side were treated, the door was loose. Charles prayed that he had enough nitrogen to finish the job as he set himself to the last one. Stokes's expression anticipated the reward. Just before thirty, the flow stopped, Charles retreated, the gong and crack sounded, but the door did not come away completely. Ray ran back for crowbars. With three of the men heaving, the last of the bolts gave way.

Bricks of what resembled children's putty lay inside. Stokes's whoop of joy let Charles know that this was the goal. Stokes unloaded the bricks and put them in packs, and he smiled as long, white sticks and cord lay in a box, as well. Charles felt as much as saw the slight acknowledgment in his direction. In this trip, they retrieved weapons, explosives, medicine, and food, which included some smoked meats safely stored in a metal locker. They rode back into Camden on a cloud of success.

Paulina spent four days flying out with Raul Lara, returning with Palacios family members and lead henchmen. Raul Lara was under strict orders not to touch her. El Padre did not want his only good pilot deciding to take her revenge by meeting her maker in a glorious blaze. Paulina found out that Raul Lara's flying ability was limited to daytime flying in a single-engine plane. The cartel pilots had been attacked at the Mexico City airport and succumbed, making Palacios feel uncomfortably reliant on the young woman. The air force base in Santa Lucia had fallen to the infected on day five. Paulina knew that she had nowhere to go, and El Padre had access to jet fuel. The symbiosis left a sick feeling in the pit of her stomach. As soon as she could find another place, Paulina knew she would take off and never come back.

The possibility of a compound of common people had not occurred to her. Paulina assumed that survivors would be with the military or with cartels like El Padre's. Most of her flights after the first day brought men with gold, medicines, and things already becoming very valuable. Paulina flew over the coast on day seven and saw the fishing boats. Unfortunately, Raul Lara saw them too and directed the chopper to the beach. The wall made from scrap metal, old cars, and everything else and rooftops covered with solar panels marked a town full of survivors. Women with children came out of the rooms by the pools and waved at the Mexican Air Force helicopter flying their way. The compound was protected by men with guns.

Raul Lara smiled. "Fly us back to El Padre. He will want to know of the interlopers. They will need to pay a tax to stay."

Paulina bristled but said nothing, wanting to return and warn the people, but as always, Raul Lara's Walther remained pointed in her direction should she ever get an idea besides following orders.

Guillermo watched the chopper pass over. It was high enough not to see faces but not so high that he could see the passengers wore suits, not uniforms. He needed to prepare for visitors.

Charlene kicked up a pile of flour. The pantry was devastated. Zrats chewed through walls and siding to get to this bounty. The teeth scrapes showed that the monsters had tried to make their way through metal, as well. The sacks of flour were ruined. How would she feed people? How could she keep their trust? It was on her word that food was consolidated here. Charlene calmed herself. Getting angry now would not help anything and would prevent rational thought. She needed to assign zrat killers. No one would want the job. It had to be appealing, rewarding. Extra food was the obvious carrot.

The zrats had killed three people the night before and infected four more before the town could surround and kill most of the infected animals.

The doctor on the radio encouraged them to hunker down with friends, to keep hope. It was easy for her to say. Charlene watched the news before the stations went dark. It was easy to have hope when some hulking man was paid to watch over you. Charlene forced herself to focus on what was in front of her. That was what her therapist always used to say: "Why are you worrying about things that haven't happened yet? You need to deal with what is in front of you." In front of her was sixty pounds of flour made useless, along with twice as many potatoes and apples. The metal bins were slightly damaged but safe. From here on out, all food was to go into metal and glass containers—when possible, metal inside of metal or glass inside of metal.

Charlene focused on the now. Zrat killers, three or four volunteers who would get extra rations, with the top catcher each night getting extra for his or her family, as well.

"Ms. Charlene?" Paul stood with his hat in his hand, looking like he was terrified of being attacked.

Charlene raised an eyebrow.

"There's a group at the gate," he said. "They'd like to join us."

Charlene thought for a moment. As much as she hated adding mouths to feed, the community needed workers. With any luck, they might have a doctor.

There wasn't a doctor, but a handyman named Hitchins stood straight and tall with his two boys and close to twenty others.

"Ma'am." He touched his hat. "I can help you out. I can fix anything—engines, lights, pumps, pipes. Brad is a pharmacist; Ms. Lynn over there is a vet tech. We can pull our weight. Anyone that doesn't, well, we know what you'll need to do."

Charlene regarded the leader. She'd rarely seen a man so skinny. He had a long and honest face set atop a skinny neck with an Adam's apple like in a cartoon of Ichabod Crane. But it was the steady blue eyes that met hers calmly with neither submission nor threat that made her gut trust him.

"All right," she said. "Tonight, we'll get you to quarantine. Tomorrow, we'll find you lodgings."

The group smiled with relief. Ms. Lynn started to cry. Hitchins just tipped his hat. "Thank you, ma'am. You will not regret this."

CHAPTER 7

April 18-20; Z Days 9-11

Raul Lara arrived at the gate at noon with three jeeps, one mounted with a bazooka and another with a machine gun. Lara's men pointed the weapons at the opening.

"Send your leader out!" Lara stood on the back of the jeep, trying to look like one of the military dictators of Africa or South America, complete with cigar.

Guillermo swung the gate open and stepped out, his AK-47 slung across his back.

Raul Lara laughed. "I said send your leader, not a little boy!"

Raul Lara had barely said the word *boy* when Guillermo turned and hit the button in his hand, ducking down as the mines under the front two jeeps exploded, spraying jeep and body parts into the air and dirt. Guerilla fighters weren't the only ones who could use IEDs. Guillermo's men opened fire as soon as the trucks exploded, shooting at anyone who moved. After little more than a minute, Guillermo raised his hand, and the firing stopped. Guillermo was joined by Rodrigo and Sergeant Juan from what had been the Cancun tourist police. Guillermo kicked over part of a windshield to reveal a hand attached to a cigar.

Rodrigo gloated. They'd waited over three years for revenge, ever since Raul Lara killed their father, Francisco, in front of them, his mother, and three sisters. Francisco had been a good man, strong and with principles, who refused to sell drugs to tourists and others through their business offering horseback rides on the beaches south of Cancun. Rodrigo capitulated when Raul Lara turned the gun on their mother.

"Do you think we should find his head and show it to Mama?" Rodrigo asked after spitting on the arm. Guillermo shook his head. His ears still rang from the blast, and he didn't want to shout.

Instead, he turned to his men behind the gates. "Get anything usable. Drag the bodies away to burn them. If we hit the Palacios compound tonight, we'll surprise them."

Guillermo had planned it in his head so many times. He knew Palacios's estate layout, pretending to play along the wall, climbing the trees, and working as a gardener's assistant. Raul Lara had been just a midlevel henchman three years earlier when he'd killed Guillermo's father, and he'd risen in the ranks on the back of his viciousness. It was El Padre who'd ordered the action, and it was El Padre who would pay. Guillermo's men didn't like the idea of being out at night or of wasting any food for the bait, but so many of them and their families had suffered due to El Padre that they fell into line. None wanted to be left out.

Mitchell never dealt with a cartel, but the thought of a leader so close and so powerful made his skin crawl. He found Guillermo working on the plan. Mitchell helped with the IEDs. He knew explosives from summers working demolition crews outside of Calgary. The eight bricks of C-4, courtesy of the tourist police station's SWAT team, sat on the table in front of Guillermo, Rodrigo, and Juan.

"Let me come," said Mitchell. "I know how to blow the wall and keep your men safe. I can bring down the house if you need me to." He said it in a rush.

Guillermo just nodded. "Good. Now I don't have to ask you to come along. I am doing you the favor." Guillermo suddenly grinned. He didn't do that much. When he smiled, Guillermo looked like a boy instead of a leader.

They returned to the crude yet accurate map drawn on the brown butcher paper.

Once night fell, Guillermo's unit could hear the Zs coming, following the trail of meat, the last of it now tossed to the wall. Some men waited in trees, and others flanked the path. Guillermo's ground team was picked due to known or suspected immunity and had less fear than the guards above and those left to defend the resort they now called home. The Zs sniffed their surroundings, but were interested in little but the easy feed before them. Once twenty or more lined the wall, Guillermo hit the charge, bringing down part of the compound's fortification. Another charge echoed on the north side as his brother opened another breach. The C-4 had been set that afternoon, timed between passes from the guards.

The men inside yelled and began shooting. Guillermo at the west and Rodrigo to the north took their teams over the less defended walls farther down, where any warnings were drowned out by El Padre's men shooting Z's. They entered the main house. Guillermo led the way up the stairs, firing at anyone armed. Some of the servants emerged with hands raised. They were searched and allowed to pass. On the top floor, the family floor, Guillermo opened doors.

The first few were empty rooms belonging to children, but in one, a boy held a gun, protecting six children from ages two to ten behind him.

The boy was likely the same age Guillermo was when Raul Lara made him a man.

Guillermo spoke first. "I have no beef with you. If you and your siblings want to live, you will put away that gun and lead them out. I promise you shelter and food. If you stay here, you will die with your father."

"And my mother?" the boy asked.

"That will be up to her." Guillermo shrugged.

The boy looked past the entrance at the men in the hall and lowered his gun. The boy didn't care much for his father. El Padre called him stupid and weak, and he'd made Eduardo abandon Sienna.

"What's your name?" asked Guillermo.

"Eduardo."

Guillermo nodded and retreated to the hall. He indicated for two of the men to lead the children downstairs and then turned his attention to the overly quiet room down the hall. El Padre, his wife and whatever remaining henchmen would be in that room, ready. Guillermo and Rodrigo met in the hall. The brothers did not need to say anything, Guillermo nodded, and Rodrigo shot the door handle with his .45. The shot imbedded in the reinforced door. Mitchell came forward with a small gray ball and lots of wire. He imbedded the clay between the doorjamb and the door, with some in the lock. Both groups retreated in unison, mentally blocking out the crashing and growling sounds from the floor below accompanied by screams from the servants they'd allowed by. Mitchell uncoiled the wire walking backward and turned into the children's room. With a chin tilt from Guillermo, Mitchell hit the little button. The sound was muffled, but the resulting crack let them know of the success. The troop jogged back down the passage with guns drawn as two of El Padre's men jumped into the hall, going down in a rapid hail of gunfire.

Guillermo entered first, crouched, gun sweeping until he saw a woman cowering by the bed, her hands raised in supplication.

"Please, please. Your fight is not with me," she said.

Guillermo had other ideas about that. She knew what and who her husband was, as evidenced by the dark bruise under her eye. "It is not. Your children have been escorted out. We will take you. Where did he go?"

"On the balcony. He has a gun—well, three guns. He always keeps one in his sock and a little one in his pocket."

The woman babbled with relief. Two men raised her to her feet, and then a single shot came from the landing. No second shot was allowed. Guillermo's men reduced the glass to dust. The body they found was riddled with bullets, but enough of the face of the enemy remained to allow for positive ID. The man left his children orphans. His single shot had been for her betrayal. From the balcony, they saw the courtyard swarming with Zs, more than Guillermo had counted on.

Mitchell approached. "They're on the stairs. We may need to go out this way."

Guillermo surveyed the thirty-foot drop to the concrete patio below the balcony. They heard the whine of a chopper above, and suddenly, the courtyard blazed with light from the spotlight, scattering the Zs below. Rodrigo took a bead on the rotors, but Mitchell pushed up the barrel.

"It's clearing our path!" Mitchell shouted.

Guillermo looked out and nodded. His men on the grounds did not appear to need to be told as they crouched under the spotlight, shooting at the Zs they could see. The hall behind them filled with shouts.

Guillermo barked out, "Tie the sheets! We need to get down thirty feet. Secure the door as best you can."

The best way to barricade the door proved to be by placing a very large dresser where most of the door had been. Rodrigo relayed the orders to those on the stairs to get out any way they could and to help cover the courtyard then sealed the room.

Mitchell took the sheets and demonstrated how easy granny knots pulled apart and then showed them how to weave the two ends together, losing a few feet of line but allowing for many men's weight. They heard the battering at the door as the dresser began to inch forward.

"They're here. How much rope?" Guillermo's voice started to show some strain.

"One twenty-five footer, the other about eighteen," Mitchell responded.

"Two ropes will get us out of here faster than one. Tie off the twenty-five-foot one. The other will need to be held." Guillermo returned to the balcony. "Down we go!"

The men lowered themselves hand over hand. Mitchell had to be lowered, lacking the body strength to climb down. He dropped the last few feet and landed on his tailbone. A low curse stopped midsyllable when he stared up at a Z lunging for him. Guillermo's bullet dropped it at Mitchell's feet. A hand helped him up, and adrenaline got him moving. He stood back-to-back with Guillermo as the young Mexican carefully took out Z after Z. Mitchell's own aim was hindered by broken glasses, limiting far vision to one eye, but the general lack of sporting skills created more of a deficit. Mitchell did what he could and quickly improved through necessity.

Rodrigo joined them, now shooting Zs on the balcony that Mitchell could not even make out, but somehow the brothers saw well enough to protect their men until the last descended. The troop regrouped under the light and moved together as Guillermo waved and pointed toward the wall. The ladders were ready, and they scrambled over as some of the men provided cover while lying along the top, glass and wire cleared off and the remnants covered by thick pads. They retreated to the woods to waiting vehicles, the children safely stowed in one. Eduardo looked through the group approaching.

"I didn't kill your mother," Guillermo told him.

Eduardo grunted. "She was going with you?"

Guillermo nodded.

"Then Father did." It was a statement, not a question. "He was always a bastard. You made sure he was dead?"

Guillermo nodded again.

A slight smile played Eduardo's lips. "Good."

Guillermo had worried about the son plotting revenge the way he had for the last three years. From Eduardo's expression, that would not be an issue.

"Who's the pilot?" Mitchell asked.

"Father's prisoner, an air force pilot named Paulina," Eduardo answered.

Guillermo liked that, another ally, one who'd owe him a favor. "Move out!" Guillermo called.

The convoy took over an hour to weave through the abandoned cars on the highway. His men had moved several of the cars, stocking them with hidden gas to get back to the compound. Guillermo made a mental note to return for the four hybrid cars. The batteries could store a lot of energy. This foray had not been for the sole purpose of revenge. They took weapons, ammunition, and food.

The chopper flew above them, pointing the spotlight down anytime the Zs began to get too close when they stopped to clear the road. The children and a few of the servants joined them, but he'd lost seven fighters, a heavier toll than he'd bargained for. They reached the outer barricade. Guillermo stood out and gave the password, and the platform with junked cars moved back to allow them to drive in. Anyone without immunity was taken to quarantine, four separate rooms where people could be housed but kept walled off from the rest of the compound. From the paintings on the wall, it had once been a children's area so that the adults could go off and play. The chopper started back down the roadway with its light down, drawing the Zs away from the gate.

Almost thirty minutes later, they heard it circling back over the water. The pilot found the only landing spot that would be practical: on top of the administrative building. Guillermo met her on the roof.

Paulina jumped down from the Bell with two women in servant's garb and two children.

Guillermo strode forward and put out his hand. "Guillermo."

"Subteniente Paulina Esparza." She took his hand with a firm grip.

"Thank you for the assistance and hopefully for the helicopter." Guillermo suddenly felt off. There were many women around, many of them prettier than the one before him, but this one made him feel his youth.

"I doubt I have anywhere else to go." Paulina smiled. "And I brought some friends, if that's OK with you."

The women picked up a heavy clinking sack.

"We have a gift for what we hope is our new home." One of the women stated as the two set the bag in front of Guillermo.

He knelt and opened it, revealing the yellow bars within. Guillermo bowed and indicated for them to precede him. "You did not need to bring such gifts, but our little colony will appreciate what such a gift may be able to do for us. I am sure we will find room. The more, the merrier." Guillermo picked up the load, which must have been over a hundred pounds.

Paulina smiled again. She was even prettier when she smiled and made Guillermo feel even more nervous. "El Padre had more than that, but that was the only stash where Miralda knew where it was hidden."

"You clean a house for twenty years, you know where they hide things," Miralda joined in.

Guillermo had his guards show Miralda and the rest of the newcomers to quarantine, with the exception of Paulina.

"Come with me. I will introduce you to my … advisers." Guillermo turned off a hallway from the main lobby. The resort's check-in sign still hung, but the wooden counter was now gone, repurposed as part of an operating table.

Guillermo introduced Paulina to Juan, his third in command. He grunted at Paulina and looked squarely at Guillermo.

"Seven good men." Juan's tone made his mood clear.

"I know. The estate was at the outskirts of town. I did not think the population would have been so badly affected." Guillermo still felt the need to defend himself against this man. Juan was his biggest detractor and questioned him the most. Guillermo needed to prove himself over and over, never quite getting this man's approval. But Juan did not know whether he was immune and would not leave without good reason. Likely, he hoped for the day when Guillermo did not return.

"They're probably migrating to find more food. There are several farms near that estate."

Guillermo nodded. Juan was right. There was no reason to get upset.

"For that matter, we need to get out to some of the farms before the Zs get them," Guillermo said. "Trailers may be difficult to weave through the roads. We could try herding them, but that could take days." Guillermo studied the map of the region placed on the wall. "A couple of the fishing trawlers are big enough to carry a few steer, but I don't see how we could get them aboard. They can't swim that far."

Juan joined him at the map. Rodrigo and Mitchell knocked and approached. Guillermo introduced Paulina.

"The pilot?" Mitchell asked her in English.

"Yes. You are the man who kept the other from shooting down my Bell." Her English was good but strongly accented.

Guillermo brought the conversation back to the map. "Gentlemen and Lieutenant, we are trying to figure a way to get livestock from the farm area here"—Guillermo pointed to an area close to twenty miles inland—"back here." He pointed to the resort's location, dotted between hundreds of other resorts that lined the coast. "Juan pointed out that the Zs are likely migrating to find food. That area is the mother lode. We need to get to it before the main group of monsters."

Mitchell removed his glasses and stood close to the map, tapping a few spots. "If you herd them to the beach, you can probably use the resorts for shelter. If they still have swimming pools, that would give you water—probably stagnant—but it has been raining, so they should be full. Close in the main dining areas at night for shelter."

"We might find some other survivors," Rodrigo interjected.

"Or bandits," Juan snorted. Guillermo had to admit that it was more logical. The trailers weaving through traffic were not the only issue; the diesel and gas reserves were getting scarce. They'd already drained the generators at the neighboring resorts and the cars abandoned for reasons besides running out of gas or oil.

Guillermo summarized. "So we head out with a few vehicles, find horses and cattle, become gauchos, and drive them back here. The cars can carry back any fuel we find and any food that's been abandoned. If we find a farmer, he can join us, but if he wishes to be left alone, we move on to his neighbor and leave his stock alone. Warn him what's coming. We can trade with weapons and ammo, salted fish if a farmer's willing to trade."

Guillermo bent to the bag at his feet and pulled out a gold bar. "Or pay."

The room erupted. Guillermo couldn't help but smile at Paulina.

"Thank her friends," Guillermo said. "Another benefit of the destruction of our enemy."

The group nodded. Guillermo would present the plan at breakfast and reassess the skills of those present. He needed good riders, preferably immune, who could handle animals and weapons.

Meals were provided cafeteria-style, everyone getting the same thing to avoid one family getting rice and another getting potatoes and then using the energy to cook for themselves. Almost five hundred people lived in the compound now. A little over half were Mexican, and the rest were stranded tourists, like Mitchell, from all over the world. They had two doctors—one from Germany and the other from England—three nurses, a couple of engineers, and a pair of firefighters from New York. Unfortunately, most of the tourists were bankers and stockbrokers or other now-useless careers. They found new jobs, and the rule was that those who didn't work didn't eat.

The resort's original ten-foot-high fences were now bolstered by broken glass and electrical wire powered by solar panels. The walls along the beach were built from whatever materials they could find—a base of concrete from the neighboring resort's expansion with stone on top and capped by scrap metal from abandoned cars. The worry was that any summer hurricane could make quick work of their labor. Guillermo knew that it would be safer to move them inland, but getting materials and food from the sea would become more difficult. When they explored the farms, he'd need to evaluate them as possible evacuation sites.

He made the announcement the next morning in Spanish, English, French, German, and Japanese. They had a Chinese couple, but Guillermo did not speak enough Mandarin to be helpful. They spoke some English, so he hoped they understood. More women than men had experience riding, but only one had any ranching and herding knowledge. A couple of his countrymen had worked at a racetrack in the United States before being deported, and both knew how to ride. Guillermo had only a vague notion of how to herd cattle from old movies and listening to his grandfather the gaucho, who'd started the riding barn that was eventually passed on to Francisco and then Rodrigo.

Guillermo grew up working with the tourists and saddling horses from the time he was eight. Speaking their language meant more tips, so he worked at learning more every day. He would bring up chess in the trail rides and sometimes challenged the tourists to a mental match, keeping the board and all the pieces clearly in his head. Guillermo always let the visitors win. They tipped better when they won or forgot where their pieces were. Now evenings were spent playing Mitchell, and it was nice not needing to let someone else win.

After breakfast, the new gauchos braided halters and made bits as best they could. Some of the horses from the family farm had bridles and saddles. Guillermo hoped to find any needed materials on the journey. Paulina knew how to ride but needed to spend her day in quarantine per the rules.

Mitchell laughed when Guillermo invited him along. "I'm a fat black man with no sense of balance." His deep, pleasant voice carried the half chuckle. "No, I'll work on the energy grid here and see if we can get that wind turbine finished and hooked in. You can get us something to cook, and I'll make sure we've got working stoves to cook it."

More than beef, Guillermo wanted dairy cattle. The town was home to over one hundred children, and with two more on the way, they needed milk. And cheese. He already missed cheese.

The trip to the farm area went better than planned. They found a diesel tanker truck with some fuel still inside, filled the proper cans, and then marked the location to return for the rest. The first few holdings were empty—no farmers, no livestock. The families had evacuated, leaving canned goods and meat spoiling in the refrigerator. They couldn't risk an outbreak of dysentery, so the meat stayed, but Guillermo's men took the cans.

They spent the first night holed up in a house, barricading the lower floor and the stairs. They slept on the second story in shifts, but the night remained peaceful. The next day brought better luck. Abandoned livestock had wandered down to the river and were drinking along the banks. By waving their arms and walking in a unified line, they moved the cattle back to the closest farm and got them into a paddock. The cows were well fed from the open grazing, though some had sores on their legs from the thick brush and voracious flies. There were no horses in the first group. The three men with the diesel stayed and guarded the livestock, and the rest moved to the next farm.

The next place housed a farmer named Juan Carlos and his family, two boys and three girls. The mother had died at her husband's hand after exposing them all. Juan Carlos was a total immune, and all but his youngest, a toddler less than two years old, recovered from their fevers. Guillermo smiled. This confirmed that immunity was inherited. The family had had enough of being alone and had little defense with few shells left for the shotgun. The farm had four horses and eighty head of cattle, with four dairy cows. Daylight was fading too fast to move out, so they planned to send two of the motorbikes with the four horses to circle the farm. Guillermo got little signal on his walkie-talkie and couldn't communicate with his men guarding the other livestock. He sent one of the other cars back with some food and instructions to wait for the group to join them.

A few hours after nightfall, shots and neighs from those guarding the perimeter gave warning. Those on sleep duty geared back up to help the others. Almost forty Zs ambled along, making straight for the cattle. The gauchos had enough moonlight to outline their forms, picking off one after another. Guillermo saw a second group to the south and then a third. In one group, a Z slipped back and forth, making himself a harder target. Guillermo hated the smart ones and tried to get it in his sights, but it managed to move behind another Z as he fired.

Rodrigo had heard the smart ones called 'Thinkers' on the news and smiled as he opened fire with his AK-47 when the group got closer. "Try to outthink *that*!" Rodrigo shouted.

Many of the Zs walked for a minute and then started to fall, including the Thinker. Guillermo shrugged. Sometimes his brother's way of just using a mass of bullets and grenades did work better. Guillermo preferred targeting one at a time and being sure of his kill. All told, they took out over a hundred Zs that night without any losses, but they used more ammo than Guillermo thought wise, leaving them with less to trade. They would head home at first light.

By dawn, they were packed and ready. Juan Carlos kissed the grave of his wife and daughter. Since most of the children survived, he could forgive his wife, knowing that it was not her fault. The farmer did not look back once mounted up with his oldest son, his eldest daughter, and Guillermo. The eight on horseback would keep the cattle together with protection from those in the cars and on motorcycles. Juan Carlos mapped out their best route, allowing for water stops and solid ground for the vehicles. Some areas on the beach would be too narrow, he explained, so travelling fields and roads would be better.

They reached the other farm by midday, but the cattle were gone. Two men were dead and one was wounded, not by Zs but by gunfire. The wounded man would not make it through the night. They kept the cars and the diesel, but the vehicle carrying the fuel had taken heavy damage. The two men he'd sent back last night were unharmed and told the tale.

"Bandits. They came with a white flag, saying that they were farmers from close by. We asked where; we had been to most of the farms. Then someone started firing from the ground behind the one with the flag. Latcho and Henrike went down at the beginning. Paulo took the hit to the leg as we retreated behind the cars and returned fire. One of their group dropped the poles from the fence, and the cattle didn't need urging to run." Ronaldo bowed his head. "We were caught unaware. We let our guard down. I'm sorry, boss. It won't happen again."

Guillermo felt sick. He gripped the reins of his horse in one hand and reached out to clasp Ronaldo on the shoulder. "Unfortunately, it *will* happen again. We get complacent; we want to find survivors. We trust when we should not. But try to be wary. Don't let anyone drop their hands until they've been searched. When someone approaches, you must move everyone to defensive positions and protect whatever is valuable. The most valuable is life."

Ronaldo nodded.

"Let's get the diesel and get going," Guillermo continued. "We need some more distance. And everyone be on the lookout." Guillermo took the bikers to the side. "Anything that even resembles an ambush, ride back to me."

The riders nodded and roared off.

Once they reached the road, Guillermo ordered some of his men to move cars into a barricade behind them and then drive to catch up. He repeated this every two to three miles. If men on horseback followed, they would get around, but cars needed clear road. At dinner, Guillermo talked to Juan Carlos about training, so the next day, Guillermo's group with riding experience rotated with two of Juan Carlos's older children or Juan Carlos himself. Juan Carlos and his children explained how to watch the cattle for stragglers, how to move the cattle back to the group, and how to bunch them up. Bernadette, the Englishwoman watching TV with Mitchell the day Guillermo arrived at the resort, looked good in the saddle and picked up what she needed quickly.

"Where did you learn to ride?" Guillermo asked after she'd moved a straggler back to the group.

"Grew up with it, dearie. We raised Connemaras—great, feisty, smart ponies that could do anything you asked 'em to. I even saw one trained as a cutting horse in the States. They're actually an Irish breed, so my da was considered a bit odd breedin' 'em in Yorkshire, but believe me, they sold well enough. I'm glad I can finally do something useful besides gut fish."

Guillermo already knew that Bernadette had been alone on vacation to get over a bad divorce.

"What was your job before all this?" Guillermo was curious. The older woman was a feisty one herself and had pretty blue eyes under her thickened lids.

"I managed a department store in Carlisle," Bernadette answered. "Not real useful. I should have studied botany or something."

Guillermo grinned. "At least you learned how to ride." Guillermo's head snapped up as he heard the sound of approaching motorcycles. He raised his hand to call a halt.

"Ambush a little over a mile ahead. I saw a man in the bushes with a rifle. He was moving into position before he saw me. I tried to make it look like I didn't see him, but I don't know." The rider looked worried.

Guillermo dismounted and knelt on the ground next to the road, moving a few handfuls of dust onto the pavement and grabbing a stick. He made a straight line in the middle for a road, a dot for their position, and a dot for the ambush.

"I see several possibilities," Guillermo began. "It could be a straight ambush—men next to the road ready to take out who they can. It could be that the ambush is just part one, with a second group ready to come up from behind. That's more likely. Less likely is that they deliberately let us see their man and are waiting for us to divert the cattle to a side trail and are waiting there."

Rodrigo, Juan Carlos, and a few of the others studied the map and looked up and down the road for movement.

"There is an old road this way." Juan Carlos marked it on the dirt map. "It went to a resort. The resort failed since it was not on the beach."

"That could be their base." Guillermo sat back on his heels. "That gives us another option. Go there, and burn them out. When those in the ambush see the smoke, they'll retreat."

"What if it's not their base?" Rodrigo asked.

"Burning it still creates some diversion and confusion. But it will be their base." Guillermo's hunches almost always proved right. It was one of the reasons the older men and women followed him.

The gauchos moved the cattle off the road and made a corral about a hundred yards in. Four would ride horses to the old resort. That way, they could move quieter and off road. Flash-bang grenades covered by fuel-soaked cloths would catch quickly, and the noise would create enough confusion to let them get in and out. Guillermo needed to leave Rodrigo to protect the cattle and the farmer's family. He decided to take Bernadette to give them some plausible deniability if caught, Juan Carlos, who knew the way, and a good rider nicknamed "Burro" because of his laugh.

They threaded the horses through the brush and low trees, finding a game trail. The resort, such as it was, lay three miles in. Most of the other cattle were already butchered and hanging. Guillermo shook his head. There was plenty of forage, and the meat would stay fresher while on the hoof. He was beginning to feel like an old man witnessing the waste of others. Their Z proofing was limited. The door and windows appeared to have reinforcements and shutters, but he spotted no outer walls or snipers. Guillermo gestured for the others to circle. A few people were outside—some women but no children, which didn't mean there weren't any inside. He and Burro would break the back windows of the main building and throw the grenades through while Bernadette and Juan Carlos kept watch.

Guillermo secured his horse to a bush, pulling out his pistol, the two flash-bangs in a sling on his side. Burro circled and went to the opposite end of the porch. The back steps were in poor repair, so climbing along the side next to the wall proved safer. Guillermo raised his fingers for Burro to see—three, two, one. Guillermo and Burro shot the windows in unison then tossed in their grenades. In the flash before the explosion, Guillermo saw a boy of no more than four playing on the floor. The bang resounded. Screams started from everywhere, and a child's frightened sobs came from inside.

"Hell!" Guillermo whispered to himself. He jumped in, cutting himself on the glass. The boy's cries called through the heavy smoke. Guillermo grabbed him, but the child started kicking and screaming. Guillermo saw Burro's confused face in the window.

"Take him," instructed Guillermo. He handed the struggling boy out the window as all three coughed. Some furniture smoldered and created foul black smoke. Guillermo jumped back out and down to the ground, taking the boy from Burro and gesturing for Burro to follow. People ran around the building in confusion. The two interlopers dropped the boy on the ground a few feet from the building. In the chaos, Guillermo and Burro ran for the woods and rejoined the team. The structure billowed, and flames shot from the back windows. Unhooking the reins and mounting in a quick jump, Guillermo turned and led his group clear of the inevitable ruin.

When he heard noise coming from the road, Guillermo pulled the team from the path and dismounted, each rider covering his horse's nose to keep it from whinnying. Guillermo recognized one as a former resort employee who'd driven the tourists out to the farm for their trail rides. The driver would sit outside the farmhouse kitchen and flirt with Guillermo's eleven-year-old sister.

Once the group moved by, Guillermo turned on his radio and called Rodrigo. They spoke in German to prevent most others listening from understanding them. "Get the herd moving. The pass should be clear. We'll catch up."

Rodrigo knew to keep responses simple, and they'd both watched the same war movies. "Roger that."

"Let's move."

Guillermo's band wove through the trees, reaching the road in half the time it took to get to the resort in the first place, and then they galloped until they found the herd about half a mile up from its prior location. Guillermo brought himself abreast of Rodrigo, walking and waving at the cattle, stick in hand.

"We'll need to move without rest for at least ten miles," Guillermo told him.

Rodrigo looked up at the sky. It was afternoon, and the air was thick and hot. Moving three to four miles would be uncomfortable, and ten wouldn't let them rest until after dark.

"We need to set up camp before dark. In this heat, we'll be lucky to make it five miles by then," said Rodrigo.

"I know, but they'll be pissed, and once they realize what happened, they'll be after us. No ambush—straight-on attack." Guillermo preferred to see them coming, and his group had the firepower to repel the raiders.

The moving defenses were reset, and Guillermo arranged for one car and one motorcycle to the front and to stay within an eighth of a mile. Rodrigo would bring up the rear in one of the two cars, one cycle on each side of the main group, and a scouter bike to hang back and watch for followers. Everyone was on alert, weapons at hand. Before, there was talking and getting to know one another, and now there was only the sound of the herd as the cattle protested the speed and the heat. They made it almost eight miles before it was obvious that the dark would become too much to safely move through. Guillermo ordered a corral to be made next to the road, using trees and cars to secure it. He positioned sentries along the pavement, with one on top of the cab of an eighteen-wheeler. The cargo box lay open. Some unopened boxes in the back had blankets. Several layers of Mexican wool along the floor of the container gave some comfort to the little sleep they would get that night.

No one really slept, and everyone jumped as the cattle shifted and lowed. Guillermo heard a motorcycle engine just before dawn and knew that the attack was imminent. His men created a barrier across the road to act as their screen. The opposing force showed twenty men on the road, stopping a hundred yards from Guillermo's barrier. More raiders were likely trying to flank Guillermo's position, but Guillermo placed snipers around the cattle to keep them safe. Almost as soon as he thought it, a shot rang out, followed by a scream of pain.

The raiders used a bullhorn. "Surrender now, and we'll think about letting you live."

The voice was not familiar, the accent from the mountains. Guillermo had no way to answer clearly, and he certainly was not going to shout. Instead, he took his rifle. The sights were excellent. A hundred yards was an easy target for this particular model. The man with the bullhorn sat behind two layers of auto glass, which would likely deflect the bullet, but a shot would get the point across. Guillermo breathed out and fired. Juan told him in the first few days of training that Guillermo would have been a sniper if he joined the military; he had a sense of aim and balance that few could match. Through the sights, Guillermo saw the glass shatter, which prevented a view of what happened after, but when the bullhorn came on again, it was a different voice and accent.

"One good shot will not keep us from getting what we want," the new voice said, someone more local. There were more shouts and shots from the trees around them. The raiders' plan was to pen them in.

Guillermo smiled. *Not today*, he thought. He thumbed on his walkie-talkie. "It's a go."

An explosion spewed up a cloud of asphalt and dust behind the raiders, limiting their escape, and then another exploded twenty yards in front of their location. They were the ones pinned in if they stayed on the road.

Rodrigo had hung on every word from Mitchell's lips about explosives. He was not a man of nuance and control as Mitchell was, but for something like this, just a couple of big holes were all that would be needed. Guillermo shot at any of the raiders peeking around their own vehicles, knowing that these men would come after his survivors again and again. He could not let that happen. Guillermo's men advanced to within throwing range, and Rodrigo lobbed their last few grenades, blasting the raiders apart.

Once the dust settled, they waited for movement. Guillermo and his troop moved in groups of three, going around the large holes in the road. He'd shot the original one with the bullhorn in the neck. Several of the raiders were in pieces, the grenades effective. A few raiders still moaned and reached out for help. Rodrigo dispatched them quickly. Guillermo had Juan Carlos and his younger son and daughter stay back. The family would not be ready for this much carnage. Prodding through the body parts, he did not see the resort driver. Maybe the driver was in the woods, cut down by a sniper. Maybe he'd stayed behind to protect the remains of their home. Guillermo knew to watch for him but was satisfied that the immediate threat was neutralized, and he gave the signal to move on. They could make it home by nightfall.

The Seattle high-rise was the brainchild of the NSA and Secret Service. The exterior was covered in reflective, bulletproof glass. The outer thirty feet held office space for government fronts, and the interior was a modern-day fortress. It housed military communications, a weapons center with independent power, living quarters, and even a small hospital, going up thirty stories and under the earth another ten. President Paulson rubbed his eyes, trying to concentrate on what his advisers were saying.

Elsie repeated her question. "Sir, no one is questioning your authority here. But the problem remains: how do we justify sending the army into one business to protect operations and not another?"

"Like in anything else, we prioritize—food, energy, medicine, weapons. In that order. Transportation makes it even easier for the virus to spread, not that it needs any help." Despite the fatigue, his voice remained firm. "Which food and energy sources we protect first, it will depend on what's easiest to defend."

Elsie took the list of refineries to her office to think clearly in her own space. So far, they'd managed to protect ones in Linden, New Jersey, and Cheyenne, Wyoming (since they had troops already there to protect the vice president), and the Ohio National Guard was doing its best to keep the Toledo facilities up and running. The one in Galveston was struggling; though it was able to put out one-quarter of its normal production, the supply lines were drying up. The strategic reserves were in Wyoming and North Dakota, areas not severely hit by the virus—at least, not yet.

Food was more of an immediate problem. The army did not want to completely clear out store shelves in abandoned areas because they worried about survivors not being able to supply themselves, but at the same time, the quickly growing populations in the evacuation encampments set up by military bases required a lot of food. Many storage sites were already contaminated by zrats, making the quartermasters scramble for supplies. Southern farms and a growing number in the Midwest were inundated by Zs and zrats eating seed, feed corn, and the stock. Planting crops was proving impossible, both because of manpower shortages in the agricultural areas and, again, because the zrats were effective at clearing seeds, flowers and young fruit off the trees. Foods canned prior to April 1 were considered the safest, and uninfected corn and grain were being transferred into metal containers. Once they could secure transport, there was food for now, but future supplies looked grim. Finding ways to protect the animals and farms in the north and New England states where winter had not lost its grip and the zrats had yet to spread would need to be the priority.

There were eight pharmaceutical plants still in operation in the United States and close to twenty in Canada. The Canadians had already turned almost all of their manufacturing to antibiotics and major illness vaccines—including flu and measles—as well as pain meds and anesthetics for surgery. The US companies continued with business as usual. Elsie knew that she should not be surprised that the men running those companies somehow felt that all this would blow over and the world would be back to normal—and that their only concern was how to get a bigger market share. She wondered how many men really cared about medications for erectile dysfunction when their wives or sons were trying to break down the door to eat them.

Elsie gathered her findings and returned to President Paulson. He stood with newly arrived Speaker Billings. Elsie waited, but Paulson indicated for her to begin. She reviewed her findings and received the expected eye roll when explaining big pharma's reply to the president's request to change over to antibiotics and other needed medications, the exception being the plants in Groton, Connecticut, and Cambridge, Massachusetts. Their corporate headquarters had already taken a hit, and the managers on-site were running things.

"Pull 10 percent of the troops from Linden, and send them to the New England pharmaceutical plants, and send some of the guys from

Cheyenne out to the farms in Wisconsin and New England. Let's get some ammo and supplies to the ranchers in the upper Midwest—night-vision goggles, rifle mounts, whatever we can get them. Try to keep their herds safe." Paulson watched Billings stiffen.

"And Texas?" Billings asked about his home state.

Paulson shook his head. "Once you see the reports, you'll understand. Look, Will, I'm a Southerner, too, but the reality is that anything south of the Dakotas is already in bad shape. We have to preserve what we can then push back."

"I can't accept that!" Billings barked. "My constituents—"

"Are either dead, changed, or on the run," Elsie barked back, parking herself between Billings and the president. "The Dallas and San Antonio areas were hit early and hard. How long has it been since you've heard a peep from anyone but Fort Hood and Galveston? Two days? If sooner, let me know, and I'll celebrate and mark it down." Elsie held up her little permanent marker.

Billings let out a long sigh and looked away. "No, I haven't heard. I thought maybe ..."

Paulson's voice rang with sympathy. "I'm sorry, Will."

"I'll go check on my family. Jack's got strep throat. They barely let him in." Billings excused himself.

"I'll speak with General Duarte. Let him know about the redeployments, and get a report on the evacuation centers. I'll talk to James about your update and what time you'll go on the air." Elsie hiked up the stairs to the roof for some exercise and to clear her head. Her guards watched but gave her space. The steady drizzle came down harder today, with more wind. Billings's chopper made it in that morning from the way station in Minnesota, hopping along at refueling stations in the northern bases. With the wind picking up, he made it just in time. She doubted even the president's pilot could land in the current conditions.

That evening at six, broadcasting on the emergency alert system that could be picked up by all NOAA weather radios and all working US radio stations, President Paulson explained to the nation what its government was trying to do to keep them safe. At the end of his broadcast came the list of evacuation centers, mostly military bases and airports. The president already knew that his voice was not the one they listened to for reassurance but that of a man from Canada and a doctor from Texas.

Marsha McLeod listened to the president's message and hugged her girls in the cafeteria before starting her shift. She whispered a word of thanks across the ether to Gus for making sure that they had a safe place. The reports of the death tolls whispered in the halls were astounding. Not even the Civil War had caused such casualties. Marsha's size and military bearing often intimidated men, and the speed she could strip and rebuild a gun gave her a job within hours after her arrival on Elisandra Hudson's security team. The girls adapted quickly, going to classes and day care on the eighth floor of the tower while Marsha kept up with the rapid-fire Madam Secretary.

The plus and minus of such a detail was the information. She knew what was going on when the general public didn't—how little the public knew of the virus causing the infection, how little the doctors and scientists could do to stop it. Dr. Goodman spoke to the president and secretary twice a day. The researchers identified some important things. Marsha didn't understand all the genetics, but there was a virus stuck to something that allowed it to get into cells it shouldn't be able to, such as brain cells.

Marsha relieved a secret service agent named Barry for the night shift.

"She's still in the president's briefing. Should be out soon," he informed her, handing off the walkie-talkie. There weren't enough earbuds for everyone, so only the president's detail was using them. Marsha clipped it in and took sentry duty. In three hours, the second detail member, currently inside, would be relieved. Secretary Hudson exited the briefing and turned down the hall toward her office, followed by Dexter and then Marsha. Hudson always walked at double time, the only speed she knew, causing taller people to rush to keep up. From Elsie's expression entering her office, Marsha knew that it was to be a long night.

Two hours after starting, she called Marsha in, and Dexter took sentry.

"Staff Sergeant McLeod, what do you know of Parris Island?"

Marsha laughed. She'd been a drill instructor there for two years before she married Gus and became pregnant with Meagan. "Hot. The sand fleas can drive you crazy, but it's defensible. It's low country, so the swamps and water can provide plenty of food and estuary water, but good-sized desalinators can supply fresh water. The river can provide hydropower. Sunny, so there's plenty of solar."

"It's been set up for evacuees, but already it's overflowing."

"There's Hilton Head nearby. Same issues as Parris but much nicer buildings—unless the rich folk there have a problem." Marsha considered the issues. "Lots of hotels, so shelter's premade, even though no one's going to want the fifteenth floor without elevators."

"If we can eliminate the rats, that's a good choice." Elsie sat, looking more exhausted and defeated than Marsha had ever seen. "How are your girls?"

Marsha was surprised at the question; she had shooed them away when she was working the day before and had not introduced them. "Adapting quickly, as children do. Meagan is seven, and Miranda is four."

"They're big for their age," Elsie remarked.

Marsha gave a low chuckle. "Well, I'm six foot one, and I'm only up to their dad's neck, so I'm pretty sure they're going to be tall."

"Have you had a chance to talk to the colonel?" The secretary seemed truly interested.

"Briefly, yesterday, just long enough to let him know that the girls and I are safe and settled in. He's thankful the president let us come here." Marsha broke protocol and smiled.

"I, for one, am glad you're here, and so is the security team. They felt short staffed." Elsie unrolled the low country map of the Carolinas and Georgia. "Now tell me what you know of these areas."

Marsha spent the next few hours describing what she could of the different islands near Parris. Marsha had spent many off hours in a small boat, fishing and being alone, so she knew a lot of the smaller places well. After midnight, the secretary finally felt the need to head to bed.

An hour before dawn, while Marsha kept watch outside Secretary Hudson's quarters, the alarms clattered through the building. There was a breach. Jacob, who had relieved Dexter, and Marsha entered Elsie's apartment. She was up and dressing.

"Go get your girls!" Elsie barked to Marsha.

"Ma'am, my responsibility—"

"Then we'll all go get your girls."

Marsha would have said something if she were not already rushing after the secretary with Jacob trailing behind.

"Which floor?" Elsie yelled behind her.

"Twelfth!" Marsha yelled over the clamor, dodging people pouring out of their rooms.

"Stairs!" Elsie opened the door with the guards behind. The clatter above and below of stomping feet drowned out the alarms. Hudson dodged people left and right. "Coming through!"

Those who recognized her through sleep-filled eyes stood aside, causing those behind them to bump into them, but Elsie was on a mission. The door to the twelfth floor stood open as people entered the stairwell. Elsie pushed past them to exit, with Jacob and Marsha forcing their way through after her.

"Room number?"

"Twenty-three!" Marsha called over the heads of humanity.

Elsie was first in the room. Meagan was holding Miranda and saying that it would be OK.

"Your mommy's right behind me," Elsie said as she knelt in front of them.

"Where's Mrs. Walker?" Marsha asked, seeing the girls otherwise alone.

"She said to stay here so she could find out what was going on." Meagan sounded brave over the tremor of fear. Miranda rushed to her mother's arms.

"I'll leave her a message. If we don't run into her, she'll know we're OK." Marsha grabbed the lipstick tube from her table. It had been in her purse when the Secret Service showed up at the door and said to come with them. Now she wrote, "Gone with sec. of state" on the little mirror near the door.

"Let's see if we can get the executive's elevator down." Elsie pulled her pass from under her blouse and headed for the elevator. The first two were full, but the third had enough room for the group to get down to the sixth floor, the president's floor. Six was a madhouse of people rushing everywhere, a good sign that no one knew what was going on. Elsie led the family through a maze of offices and finally, with a nod from the Secret Service, to the president.

Paulson looked up, his eyes dark and even scared. "The speaker's son didn't have strep; he changed. Will tried to take the boy outside and killed a guard when one tried to stop him. Will didn't have the exit code, so he shot out the panel. When the door opened, there were hundreds of zrats and Zs in the outer building. Those things are in the lower stairwells and likely climbing."

"It will be light soon. There are connections between the inner and outer buildings on three, six, nine, and eighteen—correct?" Elsie was thinking out loud and did not expect a response, although everyone present nodded. "We need to open the connections, get people into the light. The Zs will be in the middle tower, and we can seal it off."

Paulson slowly nodded. "The army has been clearing out the old Fort Lawton buildings for another evacuation center. Even with jeeps, I don't know if we can make it in a day."

"Security will call in the vehicles from the checkpoint, stop folks from coming into the city for now, and keep them at the center south of town." Paulson ordered. "As soon as we can get the building secure, we'll start evacuating to the fort. Have Lewis-McChord send some choppers—"

"Do we get to ride in a helicopter again?" Meagan sounded excited. She had been fascinated by the noise and movement of their first helicopter trip.

Paulson smiled at her. "I will see what I can do."

Zimburg took control of the announcements, directing everyone to the bridges over to the outer building. Despite technically being past dawn, the building was still very dark, the windows looking onto an overcast day with steady, driving rain. Paulson looked down from the sixth floor to the trees below, bending and whipping with the wind, and he knew a helicopter evac was out. The men from the checkpoint said that they had been clearing roads and should be able to reach the tower in eighty to ninety minutes but would need to abandon the people at the refugee center. Duarte gave the order, deciding the temporary transfer of men during daylight would not jeopardize lives. Once the president and the selected civilians were safe, the soldiers could return to their duties.

The outer stairwells were glassed in, allowing the natural light, such as it was. When the jeeps and trucks arrived, the tower's populace was separated into groups. Duarte took the lead with the president behind, followed by his staff, security, and their families. There would not be enough space for everyone in the first wave.

"They'll be back for you," Paulson reassured those waiting under the doors, buffeted by the wind.

A senator tried to bully his way into a truck, yanking at a child seated and now screaming.

Marsha immediately stepped in, grabbing his hand. "The president said they'd be back."

"You're a nobody. You're going now." The senator snatched back his hand from the pain of her grip.

"Yes, sir, some of us need to be able to fight to protect those going. You have folks to protect you here."

The truck started to move.

Marsha leaned out for a moment and said, "We will be back for you."

The trucks moved steadily for several miles, bringing them close to the Space Needle. Marsha sat in the back and had the best view, if the dampest seat. She almost fell out when the truck came to a sliding halt. Climbing down, she saw the reason. The road ahead was flooded with several feet of rising water. The gutters and drainage, normally kept clear in all weather, were blocked by debris she would never forget, leaving the rain nowhere else to go but along the roadways. The drivers sloshed out to each other, nodded, and then returned to their cabs.

Marsha climbed back in, soaked through. "We're backing up. The road's too flooded to try. It looks like one of the drivers had an idea on how to get around it."

Elsie nodded, kissing the top of Miranda's head as she slept on the secretary's lap.

"Shouldn't we go back? Send the troops into the center of the building and wipe these things out?" One of the passengers who looked familiar to Marsha—a congressman, perhaps—spoke up, followed by general nods of assent from the group.

"I wish it were that simple. The interior is a maze of dark places where Zs can hide. It will take days to fully clear it with everyone in danger in the outer building. However, if they can't get us to a secure location, we may have to return."

The truck reversed and finally turned in the direction of the Needle, followed by another stop and start and then a stop again. Well past noon, the drivers halted for longer than before. Elsie heard her name and climbed out. Marsha indicated for the girls to stay as the executives talked.

"We have to wait for the rain to stop and dry out some," Paulson said, shaking his head, "or at least for the wind to give us enough of a break so that we can get choppers down to us." He turned his thumb to the high-rise next to them. "Offices on the lower floors and apartments above. Duarte thinks we can clear it out, seal off a couple of floors, and try again tomorrow. We'll send someone back to let the folks in the tower know that we're trapped by floodwaters."

Duarte tapped Marsha to lead the group going into the south staircase. There were four stairwells. All appeared to be normal corner placement, so windows and light would be unlikely. The flooding, along with several dead rats, invaded the building's first floor. The team slogged through foot-deep water to the stairwell. Without any electricity, they didn't have to worry about electrocution. The grunting in the stairs resonated on the metal door.

Marsha readied her rifle. "Bursts of three. We don't have a lot of ammo, so make each shot count," she instructed.

One of the Secret Service agents, still somehow managing to look put together despite the wet pant legs, pulled the door open. The Zs spilled out. Marsha's teams' shots were echoed by the ones in other halls. As the Zs fell, they reached up, grabbing onto anyone within reach. Their contaminated blood spilled through the water around them. Z bodies blocked the entrance to the stairs, which had to be cleared before the next wave could be dealt with, now clawing and pushing to get to the flesh they could smell beyond.

Zs had no fear of the bullets, their need was food in any form, and they tried to reach it even as they died. Two of the team were bitten as bodies were pulled free of the doorway. The team needn't worry about getting up the stairs to clear the monsters; they were coming to the team. Marsha fell back, dragging a Z corpse with her. The virus must have been present in the city longer than they had been led to believe. If Secretary Hudson knew, she had certainly kept it a secret. Two members retreated to resupply bullets. The carnage was similar at the other corners, the muddy water now stained red from Z-blood. Only the west stairwell team advanced upward. Marsha directed two of the men to stack the bodies as the Zs numbers diminished.

Once the stairwell appeared clear, Marsha reassessed the situation. Of her eight-member team, three had been bitten or deeply scratched. The soldiers were trying to keep their game faces, but at this point, all knew their odds. They met the west tower team on the second floor and helped finish clearing the area. One living human had barricaded herself in an office bathroom. The team instructed her to wait, and someone painted a white *L* on the bathroom door. On the third floor, another two humans had been in hiding and came out to meet the north stairwell team. By the fourth floor, all teams checked in and continued clearing up to the seventh floor, finding eight more living humans and twice as many Zs self-chained in apartments. Four more survivors shivered in the rain on the roof. The top four floors would take too long to fully clear and were sealed off.

The president and Elsie decided that the eleven soldiers who sustained injuries would be tied and locked in one office. The remainder of the fighters would be allowed to roam but would have to have their temperatures checked every hour; failure to report for the temperature check could lead to court-martial. It proved to be a good plan, since three others developed fevers overnight.

The part that bothered Marsha to the core was that she could not shield her children from the carnage. They had flown by helicopter from the mountains of North Carolina to an airport and then had taken a plane, followed by another helicopter ride, to the tower's roof. The girls had seen some news on TV and were confused why TV didn't work anymore. Now they slept fitfully while Marsha paced the halls, her temperature remaining normal. A military wife, she knew her husband would be perpetually called away for duty, but more than ever, she wanted him here, his arms surrounding her.

Before dawn, she was given permission to lie down and rest for a few hours. Duarte sat with the president and other top advisers, and they came to conclusion that Duarte should take half of the current troops to scout a safe passage to Fort Davis after clearing the rest of the building. That would provide a safe place for the president and his advisers while the troops slogged it out in the rain. The rain had let up some, but the wind had not.

By the time Marsha woke, Duarte was gone, twelve more civilians had been found on the upper floors, and seventeen Zs were destroyed. Marsha and the others in the Secret Service and security details recanvassed the apartments for food and bottled water, finding enough for the close to four hundred people for three or four meals.

The day wore on without any signs of Duarte or the troops. They collected flashlights from apartments and spread people back out into three floors to sleep. A couple of hours after dark, they heard the scurrying in the walls. Elsie and her remaining two guards, Dexter and Marsha, stopped playing with the girls and listened. A few minutes later, the screams started from above.

"I'll head upstairs. Get everyone to a central location," Dexter ordered, and Marsha complied.

Marsha grabbed the secretary by the arm, who in turn shooed Meagan and Miranda in front of them, knocking on doors as they ran.

"Everyone to the gym!" Marsha yelled. Her voice could carry through a thick forest and had no trouble penetrating the thin apartment walls. The gym was located at the end of the hall nearest the west entrance. It was a forty-by-thirty-foot room, tight for the almost two hundred people entering, but it had vaulted ceilings and only one entrance, making it highly defensible. The glow from the Space Needle lit the room in a haze, making the streets outside seem alive with life as the Zs wandered from building to building. They did not seem to like this building as much. Marsha wondered if it was because of the hundreds of dead Zs stacked below that were beginning to rot.

The room upstairs was a conference room, and the rapid increase in activity indicated that it too would become a place to make a stand. The yells from above made everyone more nervous. The president and his staff were housed in the floor below, but shouts indicated trouble there, as well. Marsha kept Elsie and the girls in the center of the room with two Washington State National Guardsmen at the door while using her police grade LED flashlight to keep her eyes on the vents above and below. The grates needed to be covered. The treadmills might work to block the lower vent if she could make the deck of one flush with the wall and secure it.

A woman started screaming, running to the door. Elsie intercepted her before Marsha could. Marsha could not see any zrats or other threats, and from the woman's panicked, unintelligible crying, Marsha could not make out what she was saying except, "It's no use. We're all gonna die!" Elsie gave the woman a slap that resounded through the room and brought a sharp halt to all other sound.

"There are children present!" Elsie hissed, although the dozen or so children, some crying softly with the woman's outburst, were all holding it together better than the recipient of the blow, who stood quiet and stunned with her hand to her cheek and eyes narrowed.

"When this is over, I'll sue you!" the woman screamed.

"Good," Elsie snorted and then quietly said, "I hope you get the chance to."

The murmurs of reassuring conversation began again as the woman returned to her spouse, who tried to be comforting. Marsha resumed her investigation of the treadmills. A young man, no more than eighteen, joined her. His sweatshirt, with the white *W* on a purple background, marked him as a local student.

"Can I help you with anything?" he asked, more politely than most teenagers Marsha knew.

"You wouldn't happen to have a wrench on you, would you?" Marsha asked.

"I have my bike tools!" The young man enthusiastically pulled forward a backpack.

Someone who might be useful, Marsha thought to herself as she longed to cut his greasy forelock.

"I'm Edgar, Edgar Allen, by the way." He held out the hand not clutching the small toolbox fished from the bag.

"Like the poet?" Marsha couldn't help but ask.

"Yeah, my dad is Dr. Allen, PhD, and a professor at the university. He specializes in virology, so they took him into the tower. Lot of good that did us, huh?"

Marsha unzipped the kit and removed the pump, handing that back, and then she pulled out the multi-tool complete with screwdrivers of different sizes and heads and an adjustable wrench. She heard scuttling in the wall behind them.

"Let's hurry this up," she said.

She loosened bolts while he finished unscrewing them. The ends of the treadmill platform stuck out too far, so the support pieces had to be removed, as well. Marsha yanked those off and then pushed the piece against the lower vent on the far wall. She moved people out of the way and got three large volunteers to press their backs against it.

"If I had nails or proper equipment, I'd screw it to the wall," Marsha explained as she lined them up. "And I'm sorry, but you can't move until morning."

Marsha turned her attention to the two upper vents, about fourteen feet off the floor. Even with her reach, they would be difficult to defend. One vent drew her attention as whiskers poked through a grate. She pushed her way to the exercise bike below the vent and balanced herself on the seat. She directed the flashlight between the slats. The zrat squealed, pulled back, and then slowly advanced again.

"Pull one of the other bikes closer. I need some clear shots," she said.

Edgar and two others complied. Marsha changed positions and then stood with one foot firmly on each bike, her hand fully extended so that she could take careful aim at the grate, firing three shots into it, resulting in more squeals and a puff of fur. Marsha repeated the process at the other upper grate. The sounds beyond stopped for a moment. Across the room, a man screamed and hopped as a zrat clung to his leg. Marsha jumped down as one of the National Guardsmen grabbed the rodent only to find his own arm the target of another zrat as several more scattered across the floor, their movement caught by the shadows cast by many flashlights. A weight stand had blocked the fourth grate. The room shifted as people pressed to the far wall, prevented from escaping down the hall by the scratching at the base of the door and the brave guard blocking the egress and certain death for many more. Marsha reloaded and shot through the opening, zrat blood splattering and scattering the remaining onslaught. Edgar Allen swung his backpack repeatedly against a wall, knocking a zrat senseless, and then he stomped on it with his sneakers and all of his 120 pounds.

The screaming woman from earlier repeatedly jumped on another zrat until its blood and insides melded into the floor. Others performed similar tasks. In all, eight zrats had entered and were destroyed, but four people in the room had been bitten. Marsha and Edgar disassembled another treadmill and positioned it over the grate, there was no difficulty obtaining volunteers to secure it. Marsha spent the night going back and forth between the upper vents, but no further intruders invaded their space.

At dawn, a round of applause erupted as the streets cleared below them and the noises outside the door receded.

Marsha's arms ached from holding flashlight and gun for so long. Her mind turned to mud with fatigue. "We can't stay here another night."

Elsie assessed the situation as she sat next to Marsha. Edgar had nodded off, his head against Marsha's shoulder.

"Where can we go?" Marsha asked, rubbing her eyes and disturbing Edgar's catnap.

"The Needle." He yawned. "It's over five hundred feet up with narrow stairs to the top that we can barricade. And there are two restaurants, so probably food."

Marsha and Elsie looked at each other.

"The Needle it is," Elsie said, nodding. She craned her neck around the west window to catch a glimpse of the top of the disc. "Let's see who else made it through the night and head out."

Elsie rolled her neck and shoulders and faced the hallway door, ready for the next challenge. Marsha roused the protesting girls, leaning on each other with a rower as a backrest. Sleep could wait until they arrived some place safe, wherever that could be.

Sammy Jo sat up with the light. Mrs. Polk already standing and looking outside. The distant sound of trucks vibrated through the window.

"They seem to be heading in toward the city," Mrs. Polk said, lowering the thin curtain.

Sammy Jo stood and joined her patient and friend. "How many of them?" Sammy Jo asked.

"All of them, I think," Mrs. Polk replied.

This seemed to rouse some of the other sleepers.

"How can it be all of them?" Sammy Jo started.

"How could you know how many ...?" queried a now-alert roommate.

"From the time we arrived at the checkpoint and into here, at the meal last evening and around the building, I counted 107 soldiers and 7 officers. I counted 136 soldiers and 11 officers loading into trucks and driving away. I think they have been ordered to abandon their post."

Mrs. Polk sounded more curious than frightened. She looked over to Sammy Jo, standing now with several others with the curtain held back, watching the trucks bounce away in the distance.

"Now, Sammy Jo, if you don't mind grabbing our things, we have a long way to go today."

Sammy Jo picked up their meager belongings, knowing better than to try to dissuade Mrs. Polk when her object was so close.

Her son's condo near the Space Needle was seven and a half miles north through pouring rain. Mrs. Polk carried her jewelry, her gun, and a box of bullets. Sammy Jo carried a backpack containing a blanket, now wet but made from microfiber fleece so that it could still keep them warm, spare socks tucked inside, a multi-tool, and the last couple of slices from the half loaf of bread.

"We'll be OK when we get to Martin's," Mrs. Polk assured her.

They sloshed through sections of knee-deep water. Mrs. Polk was determined to reach her goal despite the grimace on her face. Two hours in, close to halfway, she had to stop.

"It's a lot easier when you're driving along the highway," Mrs. Polk said. "I don't think I will ever curse a traffic jam again." She rested against the hood of a car. Shortly after stopping, they began to shiver. The air temperature was close to sixty degrees, but they were soaked through. Shivering burned as many calories as walking, and moving kept them warmer.

"Maybe if we can get inside one of these cars, we can warm up for a bit," Sammy Jo suggested.

"No need for that." Mrs. Polk sighed. "We'd only start getting cold and wet again. If we get in the car, we might not want to get out, and they don't offer much protection from those things." Her teeth chattered as she talked. "Let's get moving."

Deeper into the city, it was easier to see why the streets were flooded. The drains were blocked by debris, dead rats, and sometimes dead people, their bodies swollen from decay and rain. The beauty of the rain was that it reduced the smell of rot and death. After a brief rest at noon, they spied the Needle between the buildings.

"We're getting close!" Sammy Jo hugged Mrs. Polk.

Too tired to speak, Elvira smiled and nodded in response. She kept plodding along, one foot in front of the next. The Needle loomed before them; if the sun would ever emerge, they would have been in its very shadow when finally Mrs. Polk pointed.

"There," she said. The building was very new and modern, referred to as a "green" building, winning hundreds of awards for design and energy sustainability. On the upper floors, narrow, flexible solar panels spread out as shades over windows resembling full sets of eyelashes fluttering in the wind. The spaces between them allowed air to flow and prevented them from being blown off. Elvira and Sammy Jo walked faster across the courtyard, the shouting from a balcony twenty stories above drowned out by the wind.

The glass at the entrance was shattered, but since the building's base was raised by several feet, the lobby was dry. Sammy Jo and Mrs. Polk sighed as they took their first steps out of the wind and rain. The abandoned concierge station still had a chair, which Mrs. Polk thankfully took, tears running freely down her face as she shrugged off the wet slicker. Sammy Jo thought they were going to have to take the stairs, but the digital light above the elevator glowed green.

"There's power!" Sammy Jo clasped Mrs. Polk's hand. "I'll get the elevator." With the push of the button, the doors slid open, spilling forth seven Zs. Their vision was limited by the dim rainy day but not obliterated as it would have been with the sun. Sammy Jo screamed and jumped back, looking for any weapon she could find. Mrs. Polk stood, but her were hands too stiff and her body too wracked with chills to cock the revolver. Sammy Jo grabbed the gun and randomly shot into the group, hitting two before she was out of bullets. The chair and bits of glass became their only defense as they backed to go out into the rain. One of the Zs narrowed its eyes and lunged at them, getting around the swinging chair, grabbing Mrs. Polk and sinking its teeth into her thin shoulder. Sammy Jo felt a primeval yell issue forth as she hit its head with the chair, exposing her own back to the next Z. Her rain jacket ripped as she turned again, hearing the ding as the other elevator door opened. Initial despair turned to elation when shots rang out and human voices shouted back and forth across the lobby. Most of the Zs were herded toward the light. The one that bit Mrs. Polk made it to the stairwell, bleeding but alive.

The remaining Zs were shot, beaten, and beheaded by three men, including the handsome and famous face of Martin Polk. Elvira slumped into Martin's arms, both weeping as he inspected her shoulder. Another man tapped Sammy Jo, holding out a rag. It was only then that she realized why her arm hurt. The wound was not deep, but it sent a pain through to her heart—to get here, to get so close. There was a chance for her and Mrs. Polk, but not much. In silence, the party entered the elevator together.

When they arrived at the twentieth floor, Martin and one of the men exited first, brandishing weapons, but the floor was quiet. An electric keypad let them into the condo with sweeping views of Seattle, the Needle front and center.

"I'm Scott, by the way," said the man who gave Sammy Jo the rag as he handed over a blanket near the door. He nodded to the other man. "And that's Arthur. We normally live two floors down, but Martin thought we'd be safer if we stuck together."

When her teeth stopped chattering, Sammy Jo was able to survey the apartment. There were metal plates covering every grate, flattened tin cans making an interesting baseboard around the kitchen. Stacks of canned foods and thick plastic containers filled the dining room. One corner of the living room was taken up by something that looked like Klinger's communication station from *M*A*S*H*.

"Sammy Jo?" Martin's voice roused her from the moment of contemplation. "Could you come look at Mom's wound?"

"Sure." Sammy Jo lowered the blanket and was immediately struck by the chill in the air, and so she pulled it back up.

Scott helped her up. "It's nice to have someone with a useful skill. Martin says you're a nurse?"

Sammy Jo nodded.

"Good to have you here."

Mrs. Polk lay on Martin's king bed, looking small and in shock. She kept murmuring that he had been such a good boy. Her shoulder injury was deep but had stopped bleeding. Sammy Jo went through Martin's cabinets and found what she needed to dress the wound.

The spaghetti strap from the silk nightgown Martin had placed her in, likely left by a girlfriend, made applying the bandage easy. When done, Sammy Jo tucked her patient back under the warm covers.

"We're gonna be OK, Mrs. Polk, you hear?" Sammy Jo whispered. "You just rest."

They were not OK. In the dead of the night, Mrs. Polk's fever climbed quickly. When Martin tried to rouse Sammy Jo, her fever too was going up, though not by as much. The three men bathed the women, gave them ibuprofen and acetaminophen, and even tried packing Mrs. Polk in ice. Shortly before dawn, Mrs. Polk began to seize, foam pouring past her lips as she tried to draw breath. Scott tried to clear it with a damp cloth, and when Elvira stopped breathing, Martin pounded her chest, sending foam bits splattering across the room.

By midday, Sammy Jo's fever broke, and she woke long enough to drink some broth. By evening, she did her best to care for three ill men, each tied to their beds before they passed out. Scott and Arthur were overcome by temperatures spiking above what humans were meant to endure. As dawn lit the sky, the two fought against the light, snarling and growling at her and biting at their restraints. Sammy Jo reloaded Mrs. Polk's gun and shot the once-brave men through their heads. Martin was briefly roused by the shots and tried to get up.

Sammy Jo calmly released him, his fever almost gone. "When you're stronger, we need to remove the bodies."

She cooked up some broth as the power blinked off and on twice and then died. Through the window, movement by the Needle caught her eye. She'd let Martin know. Maybe the military folks who'd left the checkpoint were doing something there.

Emma included herself in studying how the virus entered and spread through the body. Initially, some saw her presence as intrusive, but with her ever-present guard, no one would dare touch her physically, and her abilities quickly showed her a valuable asset in the lab. Emma's level of determination was greater than almost anyone else Gus had ever known. Emma kept her promise to the president and became the main mouthpiece from the CDC in informing the public of the advances they made, but most importantly, she did it with a positive attitude, giving the world a sense that they could beat it, providing the world that feeling of hope.

Over the next two days, Emma spent every spare waking moment and some she should have been asleep, in the lab. Gus then followed her racewalk from lab to lab and then to the broadcast center. When they first arrived at the facility, over half of the interviews had used a video feed, some with an interviewer flown in. Now all were conducted by radio and in the mini studio set up in the facility, even the most intrepid reporters discouraged by the hazards of travel. The upstairs became a military headquarters with strict quarantine protocols.

The day's first interview would be with Alistair Breedham from the Canadian Broadcasting Service. Emma liked him, since he never asked the typical stupid questions. She hated questions about her love life or family. Emma hadn't heard from Peter since the initial e-mail and no word from her family. She kept hoping, but she worried that they were dead.

Dr. O'Conner sat herself in the radio chair, smiling as the chair rocked and swiveled. She pulled on the headset and adjusted the microphone, now an expert with the equipment. The CDC handlers ceased to sit with her at every interview, trusting her discretion.

"Hello, Alistair. How are you today?" Emma spoke into the microphone when given the thumbs-up that they were connected.

"As well as can be expected." The clear, soothing "Voice of Canada" replied. "I live at the studio now. It seemed safer than trying to go back and forth. Are you ready to begin?"

Most would not notice it, but Emma could hear the stress in his voice. He normally liked to chat for a few minutes, but this time, he was all business.

"Sure," Emma replied. She pulled herself forward in the chair, sitting squarely in front of the mic.

She heard Alistair begin. "Good afternoon. We are now in day nine of the omnivore encephalovirus outbreak. While some areas have effectively created safe zones, with a good response from the creation of quarantine protocols, others are seeing mass infections. Seattle is showing an uptick in the virus"—Emma noticed Gus stiffen at that—"but locals explain that the infection reached the wharf rats and is being contained."

Gus's eyes narrowed. He'd seen what happened when things were supposedly contained.

"Now for the latest on the virus research. Dr. O'Conner?"

"Good afternoon, Alistair." Emma always tried to sound professional and calm, keeping her voice and words positive, providing a constant reminder that some survived. For much of the past week, staying positive had proven to be difficult. Today, she had better news.

"We are pleased to be able to say that there is safe way to cook. Food needs to be boiled, preferably at least twenty minutes." Emma smiled at Gus's slight "ugh" behind her. "I realize that this is not the most appetizing method, but our tests have shown that it is the most consistent way to eliminate the virus."

"How about broiling?" Alistair asked.

"Any other heat or flame method has been inconsistent. Meat needs to be cooked to the point of char to consistently remove all traces of virus in tainted products. So that is even less appetizing."

"Have there been any documented cases of cows, horses, or sheep becoming infected themselves?" Alistair had asked the question before, but sometimes data changed quickly.

"No," Emma reassured the world. "If an infected person or animal is eating the meat, the virus will invade the tissue and remain until the meat rots. But if the herbivore survives, its immune system will clear the virus quickly, like we have seen in people with total immunity."

"And cats?" Alistair continued.

"Cats are odd. Most have an antibody to something similar and seem to fight off the virus. There have been a few cases of cats transmitting the virus. Typically, the cat has killed an infected rat and still has the virus in its mouth from the blood of the kill and then bites an uninfected rat or person, thus transmitting an infection. Be wary of cats for that reason, but they cannot become infected like dogs."

"Has there been any advancement with the vaccine?"

Emma's sigh carried through the microphone. "Unfortunately, not as yet. We have been isolating and working with the antibodies in my blood and that of others, but so far, no luck."

"Have you identified how it reaches the brain?"

"It's not definitive, but it appears to be using part of the transferrin receptor. Immunity occurs when people have a non-disease-causing SNP—a single nucleotide polymorphism. In the case of the omnivore encephalovirus, immune people are born with a single nucleotide change in the DNA that codes their transferrin receptor so that, at the site of viral binding, there is a curve instead of a sharp angle. Since it is not the main docking point for transferrin, people with this change do not carry any disease, but it prevents the virus from firmly attaching to and transferring into the cell. Since it can't completely attach to the receptor, the virus is left mostly in the bloodstream, allowing the immune system to respond," Emma answered. She was extremely proud of this finding: she'd helped to identify it.

"Most of those in the audience do not have degrees in bioengineering as you do. Please explain."

"Each cell has thirteen pairs of chromosomes; on each chromosome, there is one copy of each gene called an allele, meaning that you have two copies of every gene. Those genes tell the body to make proteins and other compounds that do a particular task. Transferrin is a protein that transports your iron through the blood and attaches to a receptor on all of your cells. The receptor for transferrin is in every cell in your body, including the cells of the brain. In this particular variant, if you have one copy of the protective gene, then half of your transferrin receptors will be made slightly differently. Iron gets through correctly, since that binding site is not affected, but less of the virus can get through, allowing more time for the body to respond. This does cause some illness, and how sick each person becomes varies—we call this variable penetrance—but it slows it down enough to let the immune system mount a response. In people or animals where both copies of the gene have the variation, the virus cannot invade at all, and the body simply removes it."

"So let me try to put it simply. If a person is bitten, if he has one safe gene and one not-safe gene …" Alistair began.

"In genetics, we refer to the normal gene as 'wild type,'" Emma corrected, "but we can call it a normal gene."

"OK. To go on, if a person has one safe gene and one normal gene, they will be like you and get somewhat sick but not so sick that they turn."

"For the most part. We have seen cases in the very young, the elderly, and those with certain chronic diseases or on medications that suppress the immune system, and even though they have a 'safe' gene, they can still become ill and even die. I am not sure if they turn," Emma added.

"Going on. And if you are one of the lucky to inherit two copies of the safe gene, unless you were bitten, you would never know you were exposed?"

"That is correct," Emma answered. "If a person has a brother who is completely immune or even partially immune, then that person has a much better chance of surviving than someone in the general population, although even that is not a guarantee. If both parents are part immune, then the children have a one-in-four shot of being normal instead of protected."

"Is there a test to find out if someone is immune?" Alistair sounded excited for the first time in their conversation.

"Not yet, but we'll likely have that ready before we have a vaccine," Emma responded.

"Thank you, Dr. O'Conner. We will now break for an announcement from the prime minister."

After a moment, Emma started to put down her headphones and then heard Alistair's voice.

"Emma?"

"Yes, Alistair?"

"This may be our last conversation. I was bitten this morning. One of the soundmen bluffed his way through quarantine a couple of days ago and then disappeared. He showed up changed. I helped wrestle him to the ground, and he bit through my jacket and into my arm."

Emma felt the tears well in her eyes.

"I'm so sorry. We've talked so often over the last few days that I feel we've become friends. Has anyone in your family been immune?"

Alistair's voice became distant. "No, only because I have no family. I was an only child. I never had any children I know about. I suppose I have some distant cousins somewhere."

"Are there any pictures of you? Did you do any television interviews?"

Emma heard Alistair give a short laugh. "No, my dear. My mother always said I had a face and voice for radio, and I loved it, so this is where I found my niche. If our servers are still working, there may be a photo on the radio station's website. Print a picture out for posterity. Alistair Breedham signing off."

Emma listened to dead air and lowered her headphones. The soundman said that they were done for the day. The next interview had been scheduled in Seattle and another in Boston, but they could not get through to Seattle, and in Boston, the interviewer had not shown up. With the news about the boiling and the transferrin, she'd likely be busy tomorrow. Emma focused on the virus, not on the collapse of the world. Her brain went around what Alistair had said, with the Internet servers shutting down from lack of power. Those run by Western governments were still up and running. Essential information needed to be downloaded and printed.

Gus had last spoken with his wife three days ago. Marsha and the girls were housed in a secret facility in Seattle, supposedly the safest place in North America. Now hearing that there was trouble in Seattle made Gus unusually impatient watching Dr. O'Conner sit and stare into space. He needed to talk to his wife and make sure that his family was OK. He cleared his throat, and Emma looked blankly at him.

"Are you ready to go, ma'am?"

Emma's eyebrows shot up slightly, and she stood. Gus tried to hide the concern on his face, but after a week of very close quarters, Emma read it easily.

As they walked down the hall, Rankin, Gus's younger, slightly shorter and leaner brother, took up the front. Emma glanced backward at Gus.

"Do you have family in Seattle?"

"Yes, my wife and two daughters are in a compound there." Gus's voice was low and quiet, similar to a cat's purr. "If it is OK with you, ma'am, could we stop by communications? I want to try to get a message to her."

"Of course. And Gus, as my permanent shadow, please call me Emma. The 'ma'am' thing makes me feel old, and you are at least ten years older than I am."

"Yes, m—Emma." It felt good to use her name, although he knew it was best not to get too close to the protectee.

Gus went into the small communications room covered with monitors and computer screens, everything done through satellite relays. The controller shook his head when Gus made the request.

"Sorry, sir. We have been trying to get through to the base in Seattle since late last night. Their communications are down. Some folks from Wyoming are going out to check and make sure they're OK. It's rumored that President Paulson is in Seattle, so they'll get it figured out pretty quickly."

Gus did not find any of this reassuring. He was surprised to find Emma and Rankin waiting for him in the hall.

Emma touched his arm. "Do you need to go?"

Gus longed to go, but his promise kept him rooted in place. "I can't. I'm sworn to protect you."

"Oh, bull. You have seven others here who can protect me from—I don't know—paper cuts and maybe an exploding beaker. We're over a hundred feet underground in the most reinforced place in the country next to that place in the mountains in Wyoming." Emma turned to Rankin. "You can handle walking me back and forth around the compound, right?"

Rankin grinned, turning to his brother. "Gus, we got this. You get Marsha and the kids."

"But President Paulson …" Gus began.

"… may be there, as well. We're all sworn to protect him," Rankin finished.

Gus rubbed the bristle at the back of his neck. "How would I get there?"

"Brother, you're being dense. You're a lieutenant colonel in the rangers. You tell whoever makes these things happen that you have been ordered to go wherever, and they'll do it. Orders don't get through very well. No one will question you."

Gus studied Emma. "I would feel better if you knew how to defend yourself." Gus caught his brother puffing up. "It's something all adults need to know these days."

The military personnel protecting the compound had made a firing range in the lowest level. Emma noted that it didn't look like the ones on TV. The targets were drawn onto old mattresses and then stood up against lead and concrete backing. There wasn't much left of the targets, mostly fluff and springs, but some of the targets' body parts, such as hands and legs, could still be discerned.

"Have you ever fired a gun?" Gus asked.

Emma shook her head.

"The first and most important thing is to never point a loaded gun at anything you don't want to hit. Never wave it around, and never try to use it to scare someone." Gus pulled out his service weapon and placed it on the table. "That's a .44—not a beginner's gun." Gus stooped down and pulled a second from his ankle holster. "This is a .32, so we'll start with it." He released the clip and slid the chamber back, releasing the bullet, and then he laid the gun on the table in front of them. Gus pointed to a small lever near the slide. "This is the safety. When not firing, this needs to be on."

Emma nodded.

"To load it, slap the clip into place like this."

Emma heard the smack and click as the clip slid into the gun.

"Pull back on the slide, and a bullet will load into the chamber. Flick off the safety, and you're ready to fire." Gus turned the safety back on and handed Emma the gun.

It felt heavy, the metal smelling of oil and gunpowder. She turned to the target and extended her hand, grimacing as she pulled the trigger. Nothing. The safety was on. Emma turned the gun back toward herself to look for the latch, and Gus's huge hand covered it, stopping its movement. Rule number one. When she'd turned the gun, it turned toward Gus. Her stomach twisted at her mistake.

"It's easier to feel for the safety with your thumb; that way, you don't need to take your eyes off your target." His voice remained calm and without rebuke, which made the feeling worse. "Try it again."

This time, the safety slid down easily. She breathed and fired, the gun bucking up and causing a burning sensation from her hand to the elbow. There was no explosion of fluff from the target.

"That hurt." Emma put down the gun, its barrel facing the targets, and she looked at her hand. A small drop of blood mounded up in the webbing between her thumb and index finger. Gus pulled out a handkerchief and handed it to her to staunch the bleeding. Emma was surprised that anyone still used handkerchiefs.

"I forgot to warn you about the slide. It can catch you when you're not prepared. The other thing you did was anticipate the recoil. You started to raise the muzzle prior to firing. You need to let the bullet get out of the gun first."

For the next forty-five minutes, they worked on practicing thumbing off the safety, firing until the clip was empty, thumbing on the safety, lowering, and reloading. Toward the end, she hit the midsection of the target, which gave her an oddly proud feeling.

When they left the range, Gus pulled Rankin aside. "Work with her every day. It needs to become second nature."

Rankin shook his head. "But if we're around her all the time—"

"Doc still needs to know. The world, well, there is no safety. What if the one guarding her changes?" Gus looked his brother in the eye. "What if one of *us* changes? Could she defend herself without a gun?"

Rankin chewed his inner cheek for a moment. "You've got a point. Luckily, we're not out there."

Gus stopped, his voice almost too low to hear. "Marsha and the kids are not supposed to be 'out there,' either."

"Get going. I've got the doc, and I'll tell the others. See you soon."

Rankin shook his brother's hand. There were so many years between them, their father a stern and formal man who never expressed affection or approval. Gus pulled his brother into an embrace. He would no longer fail to show the ones he loved his feelings. They'd all lost too much for that. Rankin quickly returned the hug, surprised and almost choked up by the act. Gus nodded to Emma and jogged down the hall to the stairs.

Rangers kept ready packs on hand at all times, close to a hundred pounds of gear, including a standard-issue vest he'd had to modify for his six-foot-eight frame. The improved outdoor tactical vest (IOTV) had over a dozen pockets filled with loaded clips. The bag contained a standard-issue nine millimeter. Gus had given his backup weapon to Emma, so he tucked that into his ankle holster. He hefted the SCAR, which he preferred over the M4, since it could fire either the 5.56- or 7.62-caliber rounds but required an extra eight pounds for the extra bolt and barrel, and it could more readily fix a bayonet than the standard issue. Most of the pack's weight was ammo, but he also carried three days' worth of MREs, water-purification tablets, and extra socks. Gus jogged through an array of tunnels before emerging in a suburban-appearing house, the vest already causing the quick-draw holster in his front to chafe as it rubbed back and forth under the edge of the vest's plate. He would need to get used to that feeling again.

The upper level was staged to appear like a normal, four-bedroom, three-bath, two-car-garage house. But now the interior was different. One of the bedrooms housed surveillance and more communications. The antenna arrays once kept hidden were left exposed on the roof. The windows were covered with reinforced steel.

The communications officer didn't ask any questions when he requested transport to Seattle. "The troop is meeting at Parris Island, and then you'll get your jump ship. There's little communication, but you may be parachuting in. You're the first up here. I was told there'd be eight taking the chopper."

Gus gave a neutral nod. He had no idea if the commanding officer of the group going would have an issue or not. For this kind of mission, they'd need as many good soldiers as possible. Lieutenant Godfrey poked his head in, a solid army man but no ranger. The lieutenant's eyes widened a moment when he saw Gus.

"Sir, I did not know you were coming." The lieutenant drew himself up to attention.

"At ease. They want a ranger with you. I'm it." Gus kept his face blank. This mission was his family. Lies to further the mission were admissible.

"Yes, sir!" he said to Gus and then turned to the communications officer. "The men are in position. How long?"

"Less than ten minutes out," the comm officer replied.

"Good." Godfrey looked up and down at Gus. "Make sure they can take ten."

They lined up around the empty cul-de-sac. The houses had been evacuated before Emma and her team arrived, for both the community's safety and the facility's security.

The unit loaded and flew out. Rankin was right. At every checkpoint, they just acquiesced and accommodated the ranger, most of the time thrilled to have him as part of the team. From the air, Gus saw that Parris Island teemed with survivors, most living in tents. This would work for spring, but the heat of summer might make tempers run short as people forgot the fear that brought them there. Gus understood people. For now, they were safe, but he couldn't help but worry for how much longer.

Even driving a small, four-wheel drive vehicle proved difficult. A week without work crews to clear the roads meant that abandoned cars and debris were everywhere. Peter initially estimated taking two days to get to Atlanta; it would likely take more than twice that. The plan had been to drive through the night and sleep part of the day, but with the road conditions, that was also not going to be feasible from the off-roading needed to get around the obstacles. The first night, they pulled into an old barn, using moldy hay over the car to keep down the scent of their food. Peter noticed that Sara kept scratching her leg. On the second morning, she let him look where the leg had ugly pink streaks ascending from swollen bites marks with green drainage.

Peter drove through the little towns that day, looking for pharmacies, but they'd already been cleared. By early afternoon, Sara spiked a low-grade fever, and Peter was relieved to find a gated community in Raleigh with signs that it had become an evacuation center. Peter pulled in front of the gate less than an hour before sundown, waving at the guard.

"Hey! I have a kid with a skin infection. She's immune from the virus, but the bite got infected when we couldn't clean it."

The man looked down from his perch.

"Sorry, we're full up. Not enough meds for the people we already got." The guard looked like he'd been saying that a lot.

"I'll be OK, Peter. We can go." Sara looked up, but her pallor and sweat despite the cool spring air betrayed the lie for her.

"I brought food, a carful!" Peter ran to the trunk and grabbed the hams, holding them high so that the guard could see. He was paying attention now. Most came with little more than the clothes on their backs. The guard spoke into a walkie-talkie that crackled something back. A minute later, another armed man opened the gate. For a moment, Peter thought of Butch, but this guard simply waved them in. Peter almost choked on tears of relief as he drove to the appointed spot. Another guard directed them to a low building with a swimming pool outside, a sign reading "Closed for Winter," but the top was open, and buckets lined the sides. Once parked, Peter was met by a man wearing a hazmat suit who gestured for them to follow.

Sara was too weak to stand, so Peter carried her; from behind, he heard the car being emptied of its contents. His only remaining possession was once again the katana strapped to his back. The hazmat man was met by another in matching garb. Peter could not tell the two apart, but one was a Dr. Pendler and the other a Mr. Feldman. He finally sorted out that it was Dr. Pendler who looked at Sara's leg and spoke to her softly while Mr. Feldman asked Peter about his almost healed ear and wrapped hand. Sara was taken to an isolation room made from a modified office where the partial-glass door allowed for close observation. Peter saw the doctor start an IV and hang a bag of fluids and another smaller bag of a yellow-colored liquid.

Dr. Pendler removed his helmet after he left the isolation room and met Peter.

"So I guess we'll call you her guardian?"

Peter nodded.

"Most likely a staph infection, possibly MRSA, and Lord knows what other bacteria those zrats may have in their mouths. We're starting antibiotics. We should know within twenty-four hours if it's working." Dr. Pendler scratched behind his overly hairy ears. "I don't have any equipment to do a culture, and the only blood work I can run is a blood sugar."

"I appreciate anything you can do," Peter replied.

Feldman copied his boss, breathing in deeply. As Peter was led to his cot for the night, Isaiah Feldman explained that he was from the next town over. He had been home from medical school to sit shiva for his grandmother when the outbreak occurred. By day three, the town had its first case, and by day six, he and his family were running for their lives. Isaiah arrived with his mother and younger sister; his father and brother died on the way.

Peter laid a hand on the young man's back and nodded, explaining about his trip from the northeast down to Virginia, his engineering studies and being so close to his PhD, his father, Butch, and Sara.

Isaiah wiped a hand over his eyes and forced a smile. "You're studying renewable energy? Cool. The town's trying to get a wind turbine set up. Maybe you could help tomorrow."

"How long do you think before Sara will be able to travel?" Peter asked, wanting to get back on the road as soon as possible.

"If she responds well, close to a week," Isaiah replied, pulling at the thick growth on his chin.

"I guess I might as well be useful," Peter replied.

"Good. I'll let Matt know you'll be helping." Feldman left, turning off the light. Peter stretched out on the cot with an all-too-familiar thin waffle-woven blanket seen in hospitals and grandmothers' houses everywhere. It smelled clean and helped keep off some of the night's chill. Assured of his and Sara's safety, he slept.

Charles's success in town carried a mark of respect from all but Hiccup, who regarded him as a threat to his position. Hiccup grew up feeling inferior to Toya's brains and Stokes's everything. He'd heard it whispered that it was because their ma decided to give up crack while pregnant with him and took up drinking instead.

Toya finished top of her class with high scores on her SATs, proving her brains. Stokes got his rep after a man tried to grab Toya and pull her into his van. Four days later, the man's body was found, shot through the anus and then left to die, which took twelve or more hours. The cops later identified through DNA that the deceased was the guy who'd raped at least ten girls in the Philly/Camden area. No one was sad to see him die, and Stokes jumped about two places in the gang hierarchy for creativity. Stokes said that he'd seen it in a movie once and thought the asshole needed to die that way.

Stokes went after the guy not just for revenge for Toya; it was revenge for what his own father as part of a gang did to their mother. Auntie always said that Toya was like their ma had been until she—their ma—was gang-raped at fifteen. Ma went from the top of her class to a crack whore in just a few easy steps. The cops didn't care. Only Auntie cared and tried to bring justice, but she was just one woman, and she lacked the political influence then to do much but watch "her girl" head down the rabbit hole. Stokes was the result of that gang rape and Toya from some john, but Ma claimed that it was a man farther down their street and put his name on Toya's birth certificate.

Mosha denied it, but when Ma went to prison for her third strike at age thirty, Stokes joined the gang and got Daniel to pay Mosha to tell the school that the three were living with him. Stokes kept the family together by selling himself to the gang and never looking back. That was Stokes; he never looked back. With all the shit with the Zs, Stokes focused on keeping the Zs away and making sure that the people in town got fed. Hiccup didn't think that Charles could be Stokes's friend. Charles talked of "up north" as if that frozen ground held some kind of wondrous fairyland. Stokes always focused on the present and immediate future. Hiccup had heard him say, "No black man can ever make plans past today—you never know when your number is up."

Hiccup flicked his cigarette ash toward Charles, who was looking over a detailed drawing of the Benjamin Franklin Bridge. Charles winced when he tried to wave the ash away with his left arm, which was bothering him more after his exertions the day before. Toya scowled at Hiccup. She looked drawn, but she was alive. Her survival made Hiccup feel better about his own chances.

"It will probably work better if we can get on the underside of the middle strut. That should bring down the most bridge with the least bang." Toya pointed. She'd liked physics, how everything from the smallest atom to the biggest planet affected the motion of things around it.

"If we move a lot of weight above the detonation site, that should weaken it and allow for more of the bridge to fall through." Charles tapped the point she had indicated.

"Use an X shape—blow the center at the highest point first and then the other supports shortly after. We should be able to use smaller charges and less C-4." Toya sounded excited. "We may have a couple of pounds left for later or in case we need to revise some part."

Charles smiled, bringing forth one of Toya's big grins in reply. Charles leaned in close. "We need to get rid of the cables, too, in case of zrats using them to cross."

Toya smiled even wider. Something in the way that Canadian said *zrats* put a good shiver up her spine.

Hiccup felt jealousy creep through his gut. He stalked off, looking at the bridge in the distance. He'd show them what he could do—a better plan, get rid of the big towers at the ends, that's all they needed to do. Hiccup nodded to Catch sitting on Stokes's porch.

"He in?" Hiccup asked, knowing that Stokes was supervising the last of the Philly supply runs.

"Nope." Catch didn't budge, flicking open his knife to clean under his nails. Hiccup stood for a minute. In a brief moment of caution, Hiccup realized that if things did not go as well as planned, Stokes would know who took the explosive, so he nodded and moved on. After a couple of blocks, he turned back and headed down the alley, creeping low along the last block the way the gang taught—staying under the windows, watching your step to keep from kicking stray cans or stepping on anything that might make a sound. Hiccup knew that the back porch steps creaked, so he climbed the railing and then used the old window AC unit to balance and give him a step to the second floor.

The bedroom window stood open to let in the air. Stokes took Auntie's old bedroom. Her bad knee made a first-floor room a necessity. All three knew her not-so-secret hiding place under the closet floorboards. Stokes wouldn't leave all of the bricks in one place; he never left anything of value all in one place, so Hiccup knew that some would be hidden in the room. Six little putty bricks neatly filled the space. Hiccup took four and placed the remaining two at the front so that a quick glance would look like they were still there. From all the TV shows he'd seen, four bricks looked like it would be enough for those two towers.

Hiccup had always been half-invisible, tolerated because of his siblings but generally ignored. Bernard barely even acknowledged him as he left through the front gate. The salvage teams requested that the gates stay open through the day unless the alarm sounded. They were complicated to open and close properly. The Camdenites had cleaned out everything they could use from Rutgers, and the fish from the aquarium had been stewed up or smoked for later. Hiccup circled back through the Rut–C campus and headed back toward the bridge, jogging the almost two miles. He looked at the big towers at the start and the cables above.

One brick on each tower, shoot the bricks, and the towers should tumble down like in the movies.

Hiccup had never bothered to learn anything about demolition, or science, or much besides how to roll weed, run drugs, play lookout, and look tough. Demolition didn't look that hard, but it was cool to blow shit up. He climbed down the bridge on the Philadelphia side and touched the first tower's base. The first brick became a long, skinny snake wrapped around one corner and shoved into the mortar. Hiccup repeated the process on the other side. He waited until the trucks rolled overhead, back toward Camden. Hiccup pulled his .45 and shot at the putty on the second tower, smiling—and nothing. He was sure of the hit. The putty had jumped, and there was a dent. He shot again twice, and still nothing. He stomped to the first tower, aimed carefully, and finished the clip. Nothing but neat little holes in gray clay.

"This stuff's shit!" Hiccup kicked the base of the bridge. He stormed back up and over, swearing as his shadow made his gestures appear dramatic.

Over halfway across, another group of shadows met his. Charles and Toya were pointing out places to Stokes, who nodded as they were explaining something. They stopped when Hiccup jutted his jaw and pulled out one of the C-4 bricks.

"This stuff ain't worth shit!" he yelled and threw the brick at Stokes's feet. Stokes held up his hand for the group and stooped for the gray putty.

"The stash in Auntie's room." It was not a question.

The edge to it popped Hiccup's anger like a balloon. All Hiccup could do was nod with the feeling like when he was eight and in the principal's office.

"What were you going to do with it without the detonators?" This time there was a question, though derision came through loud and clear.

Hiccup suddenly started on the habit that gave him his name. "Shoot … hic … it … hic."

The sniggering in behind Stokes came on in earnest. "Shoot it? You're a fucking idiot. Did you bring it all back?"

Hiccup ignored the second question, his ears burning from his brother calling him an idiot. "It's what … hic … they… hic … do in the movies!"

Stokes smacked the cap off Hiccup's head. "Not in the movies I've seen." He turned. "Con, Catch, go back with him and get every bit of it you can re-collect. Make him dig it out with his tongue if you have to." Stokes grabbed the back of Hiccup's shirt and brought him too close for the others to hear. "And if I *ever* find out you've gone in my room again, I will personally hang you outside on the wall by your toes for the zrats myself. Got it?"

Stokes pushed Hiccup down and away. Stokes had never treated him this way. Hiccup staggered away with Catch and Con pushing him along, making him run before it got dark. Hiccup barely kept himself from crying. It was all that cracker's fault. Stokes would never have been like that if that fucker hadn't come.

Charles scratched his head, watching Hiccup lead the other two men over the side. "If it did work – 'ow was 'e going to get out?"

Toya looked up at Stokes. "That would mean our little brother would have needed the sense to think of that. I love that boy, but …"

"I'll put him watching the river. It'll keep him away from me." Stokes looked up at the cables, bringing the subject back to the reason they were out there.

"How are we going to get them? I doubt an explosive would do much more than move them around." Stokes had spent time sitting on the walkway over the years, watching the cables move and sway in the winter winds.

"We 'ave two choices, depending on what you want to do."

Charles nodded to Toya, who brought two drawings.

"Leave the main cable attached so the bridge can be fixed someday, and take out the suspender cables where they attach to the roadway."

Stokes traced his finger along the cable still connecting the two sides of the Delaware. "The zrats can cross. Option two?"

"We need to attach explosives to the cable base on the Philadelphia side. This will retract the cables and make the bridge unstable. On our side, the blast would be big enough to damage our wall. We don't 'ave nearly enough blast cord to set it off from this side. Someone will need to set it off over there and row back if they can find a boat in the 'arbor."

"I'm glad you know that brothers can't swim," Stokes half joked as Toya ribbed him. "Why not come back across the bridge? We blow the center after they're back over here." Stokes looked down the long expanse.

"The bridge will be unstable. Losing the cables alone will eventually cause it to fall, but I'm no engineer, and I don't know if that would be in ten minutes or ten years." Charles walked to a support cable, his hand unable to reach fully around the coiled steel.

"I'll take out the cables. You show me where to put the charges. And if worst comes to worst, I can swim." Stokes looked forward to breaking the ties with the city of brotherly love that had never held any love for him.

The next day, Charles and Toya swung from ropes, setting charges as marked on the plans. They worked well as a team, signaling and tossing items, Charles's summers playing baseball and Toya's years of basketball had honed their skills as they weaved their way under the bridge, setting the C-4, securing detonators, and carefully securing the cords. Creaking from above signaled the cars moving to the center span. Once done with their X with the largest charges in the center and the corners with smaller charges between, the two moved up for one final survey.

Toya pulled out the walkie-talkie from the police station salvage mission. "Hey, big brother. We're set."

"I was wondering what was takin' so long. Now get everyone the hell off the bridge so we can have ourselves an early Fourth of July." Stokes was in a good mood. This would be fun. Charles hustled the others along. He and Toya played out the cord as long as they could. It didn't quite make it all the way to the end, with twenty feet between them and roadway that loomed over land instead of river.

"I'll take the cord. You go on back." Charles held his hand out.

"Hell, no. I'm not givin' you all the fun." Toya laid herself on the ground, detonator in hand.

Charles sighed and lay next to her, close enough to feel the heat of her thigh through his jeans. He felt himself stir and then forced his attention to the job at hand.

Toya picked up the walkie-talkie again. "Ready on this end."

The response was two distant rumbles and the vibration under their bodies. For a moment, nothing moved, and then a whistling sound followed as the bridge began to shift and the cord above pulled back through its loops.

"Three, two, one," Toya whispered, and they hit the buttons in unison.

A cracking noise close to a thousand feet in front of them rippled the pavement and then more. The yelling behind them signaled that it was time to move. Toya and Charles crab crawled backward, got to their feet, and ran as the pavement dissolved beneath them and into the Delaware below. They ran until the bridge met solid street.

The cheers buoyed them back up.

Even Hiccup forgot his anger for the moment, yelling, "That was fucking awesome!" He hugged his sister, ushering her to one side as Charles found himself moved toward the river to watch the concrete and pavement fall in along the span.

Charles felt a pang of guilt. It had been a beautiful bridge.

Charlene had to admit that within the three days of his arrival, Hitchins proved himself extremely useful. He'd already revamped the solar grids to make sure that the kitchens had enough power to cook for the rapidly growing population. The next project was to improve the water system so that for bathing, the only hot water would be at the pool house using non-potable water collected from cisterns. Each resident would get one hot shower a week based on his or her birthday and time of day and his or her initials.

The team of zrat catchers held a friendly competition each night. Charlene almost gagged at the pile the first night when the top catcher bagged over fifty. One catcher was stationed in the kitchen; the other three could roam. They wore high Wellington-style boots and thick jackets with the seams taped down. One had a golf club, another a baseball bat, and Kurt fashioned a paddle on the end of a three-foot broomstick, which made it look like an English cricket bat.

Elections were set in a few days. Charlene was running unopposed for mayor. A couple of good men were running for police chief, a position rapidly proving to be essential with the arguments over food and housing. The new arrivals often balked at the communal kitchen and water. Some even called Charlene a communist. She laughed at that, her government minor acknowledging that technically it was true, except that the work performed, not what you needed, dictated what you got. After consolidating food, the workers had a point that those doing physical labor needed more food than those who did not. There were too many residents to allow everyone to eat in the cafeteria at one time, so separating groups proved useful. The manual laborers ate at a different time and were given a few hundred calories more per day than most of the rest. Pregnant women also got an extra scoop, morning and evening. Complainers were reminded that it was still a free country and that they were free to leave at any time. Listening to the Zs around the walls at night and seeing the piles of dead zrats in the morning reminded most why they were there.

Charlene sat on her porch, sipping the weak sun tea she'd prepared without any sugar. Her attention was directed to a small honeybee on a hibiscus bush. They needed to find a beekeeper. She surmised that the honey could sweeten many a foul temper.

"Ma'am."

The voice interrupted her thoughts.

Hitchins and his son tipped their hats in unison. "There's someone at the gate."

"Fine. I'll go, but only if you accompany me."

Hitchins smiled and tipped his hat again, offering his arm as she stepped off the porch.

"I just need company, not assistance."

"Yes, ma'am," Hitchins responded.

"And I prefer you call me Ms. Charlene. The 'ma'am' thing makes me feel old." Charlene realized how old she sounded even making such a comment.

"Yes, Ms. Charlene," little Julian piped up. He put his hand in hers, swinging her arm back and forth as they walked along. Charlene ambled until a sound carried over the gate that she had not heard in a long while and worried she wouldn't again. Lowing, cattle lowing. Her steps quickened as much as the almost-fifty-out-of-shape years would take her. As she approached, the sounds of goats and chickens joined the chorus. Hitchins aided her scramble up the ladder to the watchtower. Over one hundred people with close to twice as many cattle and other farm animals spread out from the gate.

Charlene's mouth went dry, both from excitement and having no idea where she could put and protect the marvelous bounty. Hitchins read her mind.

"The golf shed," he whispered. "It won't take long to build an extra fence around the third fairway." Charlene nodded and let her eyes fix on the man who appeared the leader. He was easily seventy, paunchy but drawn. More than anything, the man looked tired, but not defeated.

"Howdy," he called up when he saw her looking at him. Leader acknowledged leader. "I'm Ralph Willis. My ranch is—was—just outside Cartersville, just over thirty miles northwest of here. The survivors are mostly from Cartersville and Atco. We held those things off for close to a week, but I lost over half the herd. Someone on the ham heard from someone else that there was a settlement here, taking in folks. I'm assumin' that'd be you."

"You can call me Ms. Charlene. You and your group are welcome. Quarantine procedures are required, and it'll be a bit crowded, but we'll find room for you and your stock if you're willing to live by the town principles."

"Which are?" Ralph was wary, humbled by his losses, not yet desperate. Charlene preferred folks not too desperate.

“We’re all in this together. Everything we do is for the good of the town to ensure its survival. We eat together, in shifts, we conserve together, we fight together. Prayer is up to each person, and there are places to do that, as well.” Charlene watched the smiles come across the face of those around him.

“Well, ma’am, that sounds fair to me.” Ralph nodded, and the gates swung open.

The horses drew a wagon with children and crates of chickens. Charlene scowled as she watched a young woman whistling at the dogs herding in the sheep and cows, which wasn’t lost on Ralph.

“It’s OK, they’re immune,” Ralph assured her. “My last two. Had to put the rest down.”

Charlene nodded; it made sense that dogs could resist the virus, as well.

A large tractor brought up the rear. Hitchins grinned ear to ear. Charlene grinned back, “I take it you have a use for that?”

“Yes, ma’am—Ms. Charlene, I most certainly do.”

CHAPTER 8

April 21-24; Z Days 12-15

Gus and the men of the unit arrived and went through a thorough physical exam and detailed account of their diet for the last few days. They were monitored for twelve hours prior to being allowed into the main part of the compound. The briefing would be at dawn.

Gus found a place to unroll his mat, and he slept better than expected. He woke over an hour before daybreak, listening to crying babies and humming mothers. Others swore at the noise, and Gus smiled. Humanity. The briefing was just that, brief. Army intelligence deduced that the compound had been overrun but not how. The rumor from a man with a radio said that many survivors retreated into Seattle proper and were holing up in the Space Needle. Good for defense, terrible for evacuation. There was no survivor count, and the information could not be confirmed. The Atlanta contingent would meet up with a troop from Cheyenne on the ground one click from the Space Needle. The president was not in Cheyenne, so he must be in Seattle. His safe extraction was the number-one priority.

The almost five-hour flight seemed an eternity. Gus normally cleared and calmed his brain before missions, focusing on the object. This time, that meant focusing on the face of his wife of eight years and his two girls. His "safe" CO and instructor duties from the most recent pre-Z assignment seemed perfect, allowing him more time to be a husband and father. Gus regretted not leaving the army two years earlier. He could be with them, protecting them. He rechecked his chute for the third time, investigating every inch and seam. One of the other airmen joked about the triple check.

"Have you ever jumped into a hot zone in a city filled with skyscrapers?" Gus asked, his deep voice carrying through the din of the engines.

"No, sir." The airman became quiet.

"I haven't, either. I'm not leaving anything to chance." Gus went back to arranging the chute into the pack; most of the men near him began reinspecting theirs, as well. Finally, the engine noise changed, and they felt themselves dropping. The intercom came on.

"Ladies and gentlemen, in nine minutes, you will be free to jump out of the cabin."

They unhooked their harnesses and clipped into the jump line.

At eight minutes, the back door lowered. In turn, each soldier unhooked, ran to the end, and jumped out, clearing the plane. The city spread out under them. At five thousand feet, they opened their parachutes and angled north of the Needle, an easy marker to guide them.

They were to aim for the wide road west of Lake Union and north of the Needle. The problem most of them noticed was that the abandoned cars lined the road, making a running landing almost impossible. Gus pointed to a couple of clear side streets—still a lot of trees, but safer than that road. With all the gear, the airmen couldn't risk a water landing. As Gus diverted, he heard some running along the top of cars, leaping while trying to bring in a chute. Gus snagged twenty feet off the ground in a large fir tree. The chute held, so he partially climbed to cut free extra cord, dangled that below him, unhooked the pack, and climbed down the rope, his gloves protecting his hands from the friction.

Gus walked up the nearby onramp, checking cars as he went. One had a changed couple locked inside, cowering from the gray light of a Seattle spring morning. He dispatched them and then assembled the men who landed safely. Gus ordered those with broken ankles and wrists from botched landings loaded into cars and told them to lock themselves in. The troop would be back, hopefully before nightfall. They waited at the appointed meeting site, but no one else was there. No planes flew above, no one from Cheyenne. Gus waited for an hour past the rendezvous time and then organized the forty remaining men into groups of five. They took parallel roads, keeping focused on the Needle. They were to eliminate any Zs found to help keep the wounded safe. Their evac site was to be the ball field. Gus hoped the Cheyenne team had come in early and that it was already at the Needle.

From the look of the streets, the last few days in Seattle had been rough. Cars were burned out and on their sides, possibly as barricades. Glass lined the abandoned city streets. Vehicles that made it to the highway could go no farther.

The mission, keep the focus on the mission, Gus told himself. It was his mantra as he and the other four men with him—one only nineteen but wearing the determined look of an older man—continued to jog down the street in fighting form. One got cover and kept a bead on the surrounding buildings while the next four advanced, and then the next in order did the same, one after another. The odor of death permeated the air, but they moved on.

Gus heard occasional shots from the next street, likely others eliminating trapped Zs. Within thirty minutes, they stood beneath the shadow of the Needle, the other thirty-five men assembled. No group from Cheyenne. Gus's men circled the large glass building. Before entering, Gus ordered all to pull down their visors and use air filters. The putrid smell wafting from the visitor's center would otherwise compromise their safety and ability to concentrate. They moved through the center, breaking up in groups of five to converge on the central tower that housed the steps and the elevators.

Movement in the darker corners caught their eye. A Z trapped in the debris flopped and twisted, more rapidly when the lights from forty rifle sights of America's finest highlighted his position. "Hold fire," Gus ordered. He grabbed a metal bar from what had been a display case and rammed it through the thing's head and stepped back. The Z Gus killed was a few feet from the entry of the stairwell—its door ajar and lower hinges broken—teeming with its fellows, so many that dead Zs blocked most of the entrance, atop which stood uncountable Zs reaching out toward the men standing in awe. Gus ordered the troops to fall back while he grabbed an information book about the tower to make his plans.

The book was written for tourists, but it did hold some important information. There were 848 stairs from basement to the top, with a banquet facility a hundred feet up. The stairwell was within the original crane used to build the tower. Up until a few years ago, those stairs were exposed to the elements. After several extremely cold winters, the metal showed signs of deterioration and the stairwell was enclosed with an insulating foam/concrete mixture, making the stairwell dark and an inviting place for Zs during daylight hours. Gus hoped the president and Marsha would be safely at the top. Gus came just close enough to get a look at the dead and the Zs on top, trying to decide the best way to clear them and gain access to the stairwell. They would need to kill the ones reaching for them to block the top of the door and then clear out a few feet of the dead, hacking and pulling from the upper part and then repeat. This was going to be the bloodiest and most dangerous breach he'd ever led.

"Keep your helmets down. Keep your hands and arms covered at all times. Groups of three will kill the ones on top, and then we'll take 'em out, in pieces if we need to. Make sure they're dead."

One of the detriments of the standard-issue M4 rifle was that it had no standard bayonet. Gus attached one to his SCAR, since it would likely be more useful than the bullets in the magazine. It took over four hours of clearing and then killing the next set before they could create an opening big enough for two men to get inside the stairwell. Normally, any breach used a five-man stacked team, but there was simply no room, and there wouldn't be unless they got eyes inside. No one in his team had a flexible optic, so human eyes it had to be. Two men climbed in to see what they could after ensuring that the mass of bodies was still. A series of shots preceded their exit.

"Sir!" The tall thin soldier's badge read "Private R. Smythe."

"Report." Gus waited, feeling even this bit of protocol to be too long.

"The stairwell spirals up, real narrow. The lower stairs and middle are covered in Zs—a couple of hundred, maybe. I think the middle ones are dead, and their bodies make a platform for the others to climb around barricades on the stairs."

Gus felt a new glimmer of hope at the word *barricades*. "Can we get to the base of the stairs?"

"A little more clearing, sir, but not as much as out here," PFC D. Sheldon commented.

Gus ordered the work to continue. The few living Zs below the second barrier were shot and killed, leaving the troop time to clear the lower stairwell. The central area around which the stairs turned resembled poorly stacked cordwood, with the exception that the upper portions, over twenty feet above, still shifted. At the first landing, there was an erected barrier across the stairs, made from car doors and scrap metal. The Zs trying to climb around fell to their deaths, and eventually enough stacked in the center well to allow the others to climb around. Gus surmised that the next few levels would have similar barricades. He sent out groups of five to advance, get into position, kill any Zs present, and then tap the next group up.

There must be thousands, Gus surmised.

It seemed like most of the turned population of Seattle must be there, along with survivors, but what brought them there? Why were they centering on the Needle? There was no available food. For hours, his men braced, pulled, cut, and shifted the central pile while trying not to drop the mass on top of themselves. They realized that they could not make it up the tower that day and that they would need to hole up. Gus had planned to use the gift shop, but when the troops stepped into the visitors' center, they understood why the Zs came. The tower had its own emergency backup lighting, and the top glowed with the Legacy Light. He'd heard Emma describing how the Zs avoided bright light because of their pupils' inability to constrict, but the primitive brain still responded to distant, flickering lights like a moth to flame. Gus heard them long before he saw them. As twilight ended, the grunting from outside reverberated off the glass, the emergency lighting barely offering a light red glow throughout the visitors' area, not enough to be a deterrent. The soldiers should not shut themselves in the tower with the shifting mass above them, but the thousands of approaching Zs left little choice.

Z body parts, most beginning to rot, were used to barricade the stairway door. The exhausted men continued to work by flashlight and glow light to clear the stairs. They disassembled and reassembled the first stairwell barricade and then rested for the first consistent time all day.

Close to midnight, one of the men started spiking a fever. Gus came close.

"Sorry," the soldier whispered. "I yanked an arm, and it came free and splashed my face shield with Z goo. I wiped it off, but I rubbed my nose a little later and some got on my lip."

Gus ordered another to stand with him. None had a thermometer, so they'd have to wait. By 4:00 a.m., he started seizing, and he was dead by dawn. Gus sighed with relief. At least he didn't turn. They'd retrieve his body when they rescued whoever was up in the Needle, if anyone survived. They could hear the Zs on the upper barrier, but none came down to investigate the troops behind.

The men started moving again at dawn, continuing their climb in five-man teams, finding the largest mass of Zs at the third barrier at the level of the banquet hall. The soldiers needed to be careful about bullets, since ricochets in the tower could injure them as easily as Zs, so they used their knives when possible. Signs for the Skyline Banquet Hall led them to a broken door. *Ding, slide, bang* repeated every fifteen to twenty seconds. Once a team cleared the room, the rest moved in to survey the space. The grand hall did not smell as badly as the rest of the building. Gus normally would have appreciated the view, but only death filled the room now. The elevator doors, also powered by the emergency generator, slid open and released a small bell-like tone as they hit the bodies lying in the way. This explained why the lowest part of the stairwell held Zs, not the elevator.

On the next level, dead Zs lay on the top of the elevators, their bodies sliding to the stairs. Floor by floor they climbed, clearing their path until the pile in the center of the stairwell finally disappeared below them, but so did the barriers on the stairs.

Gus wanted to break with every ounce of his training. He yearned to run ahead and find his family, but so many years in the army had shown him that when you break with training, people die. Instead, he focused on the door twenty feet above him. Close to the top of the tower stairs stood almost a hundred Zs, pushing against the door to the platform and restaurant entrance. The Zs turned to the new, large source of meat. Gus readied his assault rifle as the Zs closed in.

"Front four kneel and shine your lights into their eyes," he instructed. "Blind them as we're shooting them."

Gus noticed two Zs dancing back and forth across the upper part of the group. He worried about ricochets, but with the large mass, the Zs should absorb most of the bullets, and so he concentrated on those two. One had salt-and-pepper hair with a dark suit and looked horribly familiar, but what it was now made who it had been before irrelevant. Gus was impressed by the discipline of the troops. They waited, aimed, and fired. No random rapid shooting from anger or frustration, just efficient mass Z slaughter. The noise resonated throughout the tower, magnifying the sounds of thirty-five guns firing in sequence. The battle was over quickly. Some of the men wanted to toss the bodies over and into the mass pile, but Gus stopped them.

"More weight will destabilize it, and it may trap us in. I don't think we brought enough cord to rappel out of here."

Instead, the men lined the side of the stairs with the dead—after ensuring they were, in fact, dead.

"Sir." One of the women touched his arm and pointed to the man in the suit. The man who had been President Paulson now lay dead as a Z.

"Face him to the wall. The world will eventually know, but it won't be from us."

Protocol would have a private first through this door, but this should be a homecoming, not a breach. Gus approached the door at the top of the stairs more nervous than when he'd first rapped on Marsha's door all those years ago. He knocked three times, loudly. From behind the portal came a firm, clear voice.

"Who is it?"

Gus couldn't help but grin, the kind of smile that split the face in two. "Well, ma'am, me and some soldiers out here are just dropping by to check on you."

Gus's deep voice responded loudly and with a hint of pride. The sudden scraping and pulling allowed Marsha to open the entry enough to step out and wrap her arms around him as the light of the last part of day bathed the two in a rosy glow, his two girls in the doorway behind her screaming happily for their daddy. Gus had not even cried at his father's funeral; he'd been taught to be stoic and brave, but at this moment, the tears of relief ran freely in his eyes and in many of those around them, all hoping for similar happiness. Gus was pulled in by his wife and buoyed inside by his troops. Lieutenant Godfrey took over for the moment.

"Let's get inside and barricade in again for now. It's almost dark." That dampened the mood of all. The automatic lights began to glow along the outside.

Gus's large arms encompassed Marsha, Meagan, and Miranda while he surveyed the situation. Over two hundred civilian survivors, but little food remained. From the smell, little sanitation was available, though someone had found bleach, which covered the worst of the odors. The soldiers started with six MREs each; they'd eaten four over the last couple of days. Those could be combined so that everyone could eat something.

"Is there any way to turn those lights off?" Gus asked to no one in particular.

"Not that we've found," Marsha's exhausted voice answered. The only thing bigger than her body was her heart, which had been strained to every limit over the last few days. "We've tried every light switch in the place."

"It's probably someplace central farther up, but that requires the elevator," a formerly well-dressed but now bedraggled-looking man added.

Gus recognized him from press conferences as the press secretary. He added in a low voice, "You've seen the president?"

Gus nodded.

"We'll need to think of something to say to reassure the public."

Gus could not help but release a disgusted laugh. "What public?" His initial outburst brought every head up, and Gus lowered his voice. "We are all fighters now. Those of us with skills need to teach those without." He indicated his wife and daughters. "My wife can fight, as I bet you saw out there. My girls will learn. There is no winning this war; it's finding a way to survive. Everyone needs to fight to survive."

Gus's deep voice carried to every person in the room. Politicos and intelligentsia and others deemed important enough to evacuate to a secret building approached and surrounded him, looking for advise and leadership. All realized that even with the full protection of the government and military, the virus got through.

"He's right," the secretary of state joined in. "The most I ever learned was kickboxing for exercise." Elsie pulled off the remainder of her once four-inch pumps. "Start teaching me now."

Gus surveyed the dwindling water supply that they'd just added thirty-nine people to drink from but didn't want to lose the momentum of the moment.

"We'll do a brief session, and then we'll need to rest so that we can get the hell out of here tomorrow."

Gus elicited cheers from all those around. They'd already missed the evacuation from the ball field. He'd need to get a message through to the man with the radio to relay the number of survivors and that evac was needed. The walkie-talkie hadn't worked well on the stairs, but they'd been inside the main tower surrounded by concrete and steel. Now this high up with only glass, he might get lucky.

He turned on the small radio, which had been kept off to preserve the battery.

"Alpha Team Five to Seattle Radio base, do you copy? Over." Static. Gus waited a minute and repeated on the same station with the same response. He changed to the backup and tried again.

This time, a small, scared voice came on, just above a whisper. "Copy, please don't call again until daylight. They're outside." Gus immediately turned the radio off, sweat beading slightly. He'd need to be careful in the future and keep communications to daylight. Sound likely drew them in, as well.

Gus approached the group assembled in the makeshift training area. Several of the team had already disassembled guns and were reviewing gun protocols, including the rifles. The survivors watched intently. They learned to load the magazines and clips, unload and then put the clips in, and how to use the sights. None were given loaded weapons in their close confines. Gus spent fifteen minutes giving basic instructions for hand-to-hand fighting. He intended to spar with Marsha, but she shook her head and went back to the girls. Instead, Private Sheldon hammed it up and acted as the Z, coming after him with teeth bared. Gus demonstrated how to shift and use the momentum of the attacker to impale it, allowing the person to survive. For twenty minutes, the Needle group paired up to practice, alternating between playing attacker and defender.

When the sparring session was over, Gus approached Marsha and kissed her. "What's up? You love to spar with me."

Marsha's eyes twinkled at him, head slightly tilted to see his eyes. "I'm pregnant. Just over three months."

Gus forgot all the worries of the world and grinned, picking Marsha up and spinning for a minute. "Why didn't you—"

"Say anything? Well, for one thing, I know you worried enough about us as it is. This was one thing I didn't need to add until I had to." Marsha tapped his arm lightly.

Gus leaned in and kissed her softly but lingeringly.

"*Eew.*"

The little voice behind him stopped the moment of passion with both Gus and Marsha erupting in laughter.

"That's just gross." Seven-year-old Meagan stood with her hands on her hips, with her favorite, albeit battered, doll firmly in her grasp.

"Maybe I should just kiss you!" Gus swooped down and lifted Meagan in a fit of giggles, kissing her stomach until he felt another tug.

"Me, me, me!" four-year-old Miranda insisted. Gus secured Meagan in his left arm and scooped Miranda with his right, alternating kisses on each side. The moment was glorious but brief.

"Sir, I hate to interrupt." Lieutenant Godfrey stood nearby, looking uncomfortable and slightly away. He didn't question why the colonel had been added without notifying him in the first place, but now all his unasked questions were answered. "We need to plan the evacuation."

Gus nodded and lowered the girls to the floor amid many protests. "You're right. Let's find a private spot."

"The restaurant manager's office is in the back of the kitchen. Let me show you." Marsha told the girls to go play with "Aunt Elsie" and then escorted the men to the office, placing herself just inside the door before shutting it. They both looked at her. "Oddly enough, with all those leaders of the free world out there, when the shit hit the fan, they had no idea what to do. I led them here, and I had them make the barricades. They listen to me. Whatever the plan is, I need to be in on it."

Gus could not help but be proud of his wife. If anyone had the ability and the balls to get a bunch of conflicting factions to sit up and follow orders, it was her in marine corps drill instructor mode.

Lieutenant Godfrey glanced at Gus and said, "In the morning, we should be able to get a good lay of the land and see the best way out of here."

"The people need to have a clear idea of where they're going and why. Even though we're almost out of food, we've felt safe up here," Marsha responded.

"If our radio contact is still there in the morning, we should be able to get an idea of where we can go and when. Staying up here is not an option. You did not see that wall of Z bodies we had to clear to be able to get to the steps. That alone took forty men almost two days just to make a dent. And the smell is already reaching up here. Think how bad it's going to be down below," Gus replied. "The decomp will further shift the bodies. If we don't go tomorrow, we'll be trapped again."

"And anyone with open sores on their feet or skin will need to find some way to completely cover them. We have thirty-nine men now; we started on the tower with forty. The Z goo got on his lip, so masks for everyone, as well," Lieutenant Godfrey interjected.

"Boats." Marsha snapped her fingers. "There are still thirty or forty boats at the marina; you can see them from the windows. They have sails, so mobility, and we might catch some food. All those amazing ship shows say that the bigger ones have desalinators for fresh water and wind turbines for power."

"And radios." Lieutenant Godfrey smiled.

Gus pulled out the map of the city provided by the mission chief on Parris Island. The Needle was easy to find, with the harbors due west. "We'll need to get what supplies we can on the way. No dark buildings. Most stores will have been cleared out and likely dark, but the trunks of cars may have canned food, blankets, maybe even weapons they had to abandon with the vehicles."

"I'll ask who out there actually knows how to sail," Marsha added. "I don't know how far away it is, but we need to make a stop. I need to keep a promise. The government building became overrun; not everyone could leave in the first set of trucks. General Duarte went back, but there's been no word. I promised that we'd be back for them."

"How long has it been?" Gus asked.

"Five days? Time feels so off. But I promised," Marsha insisted.

"Do you have the coordinates?" Lieutenant Godfrey asked, scanning the map.

Marsha slowly shook her head. "No, but Secretary Hudson probably does."

Gus sighed. A promise was a promise. "We'll split up. Take ten men with you to check on the building. Most of the rest will protect the survivors and get our wounded to the marina. In the morning, I'll let the radio operator know the plan to see if she is close enough to join us or add any info. If she's close, I'll take a few men with me to get her."

They slept well enough considering the smell of death from under the door. There were fewer complaints about leaving with an army team as protection.

At first light, Gus used binoculars to scout the best path to the port. The wounded would not require much of a side trip along the highway, so it could be the main route. As the light grew, he watched thousands of Zs scurry into abandoned buildings near the Needle. No fog and blue sky welcomed them. The soldiers covered the feet of anyone with broken skin with plastic wrap and then the hands of those with rashes or the tendency to chew cuticles. Cloth tablecloths were cut down to become masks and then soaked in vinegar to help cover the smell.

On the third try, Gus reached the radio operator.

"This is Sammy Jo, over," she replied to his hail. "Made it through the night in a panic room. Good thing it has a manual override, else we might still be in there."

"We? How many survivors, over?" Gus asked.

"Just the two of us. Good food supply, water's running a little low. Ironic for Seattle, I know," Sammy Jo replied.

Gus heard a murmuring in the background.

"Over," she added.

Gus filled her in on the plan.

A man's voice came in. "This is Martin."

His voice was familiar, but Gus couldn't place it.

"I own one of those harbor boats," Martin continued, "and if you come get us, I'll happily bring the key and sailing experience."

Gus puffed up his chest. "Sir, I am an army ranger. I would come get you without the boat key." Gus pulled the Seattle map back out. "Where are you located? Over."

The man gave his address with directions from the Needle. Penthouse, twenty floors up. Before this month, Gus had liked having stairs. He was not so fond of them anymore. Gus signed off and then got everyone's attention.

"We'll be dividing into three teams. Ten will accompany Staff Sergeant McLeod here to the former facility to see if any other survivors made it through the last few days. Three will go with me to rescue the radio operator and her companion. Lieutenant Godfrey will lead the main contingent of twenty-five to escort you, collect the men who were wounded when dropping into Seattle, and then proceed to the marina. The soldiers will need to enter and clear all vessels before anyone else boards. Scavenge what you can en route." Gus nodded, and everyone tied on their masks.

Neither Marsha nor Gus wanted to leave their girls, but Elsie promised to keep them close and safe. For the stairs, the first trial, Meagan and Miranda and the few other children, including a slightly protesting Edgar, unhappy about being placed with "the kids," took up the middle. Half the team went in front with Gus, with the other half in the rear with Lieutenant Godfrey.

The smell caused gagging and the occasional bout of vomiting. This would not have bothered Gus as much if it didn't make the stairs even more treacherous for those behind them. They had not heard any Zs at the door overnight and did not see any new ones. Gus spoke quietly the evening before about what to do with the president's body. It was against everything in Gus's fiber to leave it. Elsie and James both convinced him to let it stay; bringing it along would attract more attention to what had happened to him. Secretary Zimburg would relay how he died bravely, defending the people. The president had been bitten while assisting others, so it wouldn't be too much of a stretch. When they reached the fallen soldier, his fellows in the rear took turns carrying him. They made a stretcher from a car hood that had been part of a barrier.

The supports the soldiers made to protect the path at the bottom of the stairs had held. Gus made the column stop so that they could clear the body barricade from inside the door, open the door, and then clear the way for the survivors. Everyone ripped the masks from their faces as they finally breathed in the relatively fresh air of the Seattle spring morning. The blue skies were already beginning to give way to low gray clouds.

"Let's split up. About a mile out, stop for a meal of whatever you can." Gus and the others rechecked their rounds and then divided up the remainder while two of the men found a better stretcher to carry the fallen soldier.

Gus gave his wife and daughters a quick kiss. "See you in a few hours, OK?"

Meagan nodded, and Miranda did not want to let go, but Marsha extricated her in expert manner.

"See if you can get back again in one piece, OK?" Marsha kissed him again as they set off in opposite directions.

The way to Sammy Jo and Martin's building was easy. The glass front of the modern, once beautiful building was shattered, allowing easy entrance. The door to the stairway was clearly marked. The unit swung in, body parts were scattered near the base, but there were no living Zs. Even for the fit, twenty flights left them winded. Before entering the hallway, they waited a minute to catch their breaths and bring rifles to ready. When quiet, the unit could hear the grunts and movement on the other side of the door.

"On my go, standard breach protocol." Gus counted to three, and the men stacked up behind the door. Private Smythe tapped Gus, who in turn tapped in front then the next two.

"Go! Go! Go!"

Private Smythe swung around and pushed open the door, swinging right with the movement as Private Sheldon swung in behind and to the left, the rest following.

The hallway was full. The phrase "fish in a barrel" came to mind as the men brought down one Z after another. They had learned to aim for the head like in all the old movies. Center mass shots would eventually take them down, but head shots stopped them faster. A Thinker hid in a doorway with too many in between to make a good enough target. The rule was not to waste ammo, since manufacturing was at a standstill. Gus heard the report of a gun down the hall and then a door slam. He hoped they got the little monster. The unit made quick work of the Zs and then reached the door, but instead of it opening, they heard screams from inside.

The team reassembled for breach, but Smythe lacked the strength to kick in the reinforced steel. Even with Gus's size, it took several hits to break the door free from its frame. The Thinker Gus had seen earlier sported a free-flowing wound in its shoulder, large aviator-style sunglasses protecting its eyes from the gray light of the apartment. It stood over a middle-aged man with his body bent at an odd angle. In that odd split second before action, Gus recognized the body as the man from a famous set of beer commercials. The Thinker turned and raised a gun, but it was riddled with bullets from the team before he could fire. When Gus retrieved the weapon, he noted that the safety was off, and he thumbed it back on. Out of curiosity, Gus patted the Thinker's pockets and found a wallet. SPD detective.

The unit surveyed the living room. There was a ham radio setup powered by solar batteries. Gus turned it on. He understood the basics; every member of a team needed to be able to work remote equipment, but these days, that typically consisted of a satellite phone. This thing looked like a relic from World War II.

"Sir?" Private Smythe brought a young woman forward. She was in her mid-twenties, above average height, brown hair, wearing a gray hoodie sweatshirt and jeans, and trying not to look at the man and the Thinker on the floor.

"If you let me. He," Sammy Jo said, tilting her head toward Martin's body, "showed me how to use it. He was going to be in a movie set in the 1950s based on if the Cuban Missile Crisis was not averted. This was part of his research. Martin joked that he'd never found a role so useful."

She sniffed for a minute and then indicated for Gus to move. He stood.

"Who did you want to contact?" she asked.

"If you can get in touch with military command in Cheyenne, that would help." Gus yielded the chair to Sammy Jo, who nodded and turned some dials after checking her watch.

"It turns out the time of day makes a big difference in how far the signals will go, so you have to adjust the channels depending on time and weather conditions."

Gus recognized when someone needed to speak to calm his or her nerves, and he let her go on uninterrupted.

"With the midlevel clouds and just past midday, with a needed range of fifteen hundred miles, I doubt we can get there. But there are some operators in Vancouver that have kept a line open with the radio station, and they can get messages to secure areas."

Gus thought of Alistair. He could get a message through to Emma and his team.

In a few minutes, Sammy Jo established the connection to the ham operator in Vancouver. "This is Lieutenant Colonel Angus McLeod of the US Army, needing assistance in communications with United States Army central command, likely in Cheyenne. Over."

"Vancouver civilian Henry Bean. Please give your message for relay. Over."

"Missed ball field evac site two days ago. Evacuating to boats from Seattle with over two hundred survivors, possibly more. Need direction. Over," Gus stated.

"Will relay. Please stand by for reply. This may take a bit."

Gus sighed. He hoped not too long. "And, Vancouver, if you can get a message to Alistair Breedham to give to Dr. O'Conner, let her know this: 'Gus made contact, unsure on return at this time.' Over."

Gus handed the mic back to Sammy Jo and walked to the window. The penthouse showed the city in all its green glory. Many of the building rooftops and spaces without buildings were green. For such a cloudy place, he was surprised at the number of solar panels. Rebuilding would require those, along with clean water and safe places to sleep.

Gus turned his attention to the piles of supplies throughout the condo. "Smythe, Sheldon. Start packing as much of this as you can get. Food, water, and batteries have highest priority." The two men started filling their packs. Gus wanted to take the radio equipment, but it was too big.

Sammy Jo brought a bag from one of the rooms. "Medical supplies," she explained. "I'm a nurse. I was taking care of Martin's mom and tried to get her here. We both got bit on the way. I survived, thanks to Martin, but she didn't. I hate leaving him here like that. Can I cover him up?"

Gus saw no harm in the request and assisted in arranging Martin's body, wrapping a sheet like a shroud. They covered the Thinker as well. He'd been a cop once and deserved the respect. So many had died or changed and would never receive a proper burial, at least here he could make a small difference, if only for Sammy Jo and his own sense of humanity.

The morning dragged on. Sammy Jo explained that when Martin heard help arriving, he went into the hall to help, only to have the Thinker rush in and grab his gun. This was the first time Gus had even heard of a Thinker using a weapon. He would add it to his report.

Gus surveyed the sky and the low clouds obscuring the sun and guessed that it was early afternoon. He needed to wait for information, but the survivors needed to put out to sea before dusk. As if on cue, the radio crackled.

"Vancouver to Colonel McLeod. Over."

Sammy Jo handed Gus the mic. "This is McLeod. Over."

"Two messages. First from US central command: 'Evac to Indian Island, Puget Sound, will arrange for pickup within forty-eight hours.' Second message from Dr. O'Conner: 'Look forward to meeting the family.' Over."

Gus grinned at that. "Thank you, Vancouver. Over."

Gus laid down the mic and turned to his men. "Let's move out!"

After helping with the wind turbine, Peter set to work on solar arrays on the roofs. By the second day, he noticed a following—a pair of men ostensibly on the crew but who seemed more interested in him than the work. This became obvious when he went to take a leak. One of the crew asked him to stow his sword, that having it there made the man nervous. Rather than rock the boat, Peter found a place to hide the katana near his room. Sara still received care and was responding well, but she would take days to recover.

Peter's suspicions rose when Sara left the hospital and immediately enrolled in the local school while he worked. The principal knew who Peter was as soon as he raced into the building.

"Mr. Saitou!"

Peter heard his name called out upon reaching the top of the stairs, his followers racing up behind him.

"So good to finally meet you! I've heard so much." The middle-aged woman with sharp hazel eyes smiled a little too broadly, glancing the way of the other men and nodding them off. "You've already meant so much to the community."

Peter was taken aback; he'd been ready to yell and make demands, but this small woman with the broad, polite smile made it difficult.

"Thank you." He took a breath, gathering the anger and outrage that brought him here. "Sara—"

"She is in placement testing. The doctors said she was bored and doing well with pills. One of the nurses brought her here for a tour, so we thought no time like the present to get things squared away."

Somehow Peter found himself walking down the hallway in the principal's wake.

"I don't know if anyone told you, but we weren't planning—" Peter finally interjected.

"Oh, I don't think there's much point in anyone planning much of anything these days, do you?" The principal smiled back up at him. "We'll just make the best of every day as it comes. Now if you'll excuse me." The principal peeled off and into an office, the door swinging shut behind her.

"Peter!" The excited voice down the hall kept him from following. Sara ran toward him, a new summer dress and sandals on her feet. He greeted her smile with his own and hugged her. "They said I'm very smart, and they're putting me with the sixth graders. Are we staying here?"

Peter caught sight of the men he now recognized as his prison guards. "I guess we are for now."

After a few days, Emma missed Gus's quiet demeanor. His brother, Rankin, could learn the value of companionable silence. Emma recognized the boredom of this assignment, but the stories of his many exploits, mostly military and sometimes sexual, were beginning to get old. Rankin did prove an excellent firearms instructor, helping her gain confidence with the handgun. He found a holster that fit in the back of her waistband and insisted that she walk around with it to feel more comfortable. Sometimes Emma forgot that it was there until she sat and the cold, hard metal pressed against her skin.

The gun felt alien at first, but when Dr. Graham insisted on bringing a live Thinker into the lab, she felt much better with it secured to her person. Rankin made sure that at least one of the security detail stayed in the lab instead of in the hall. The other scientists quickly accustomed themselves to the addition, and those who agreed with Emma on keeping out the infected were relieved by the guard's presence. Dr. Graham reassured everyone that the Thinker would be kept well sedated, and Andy assured Emma that while he was on duty, there was no way that thing would wake up.

Emma couldn't help but wonder if Gus had been on site whether or not Dr. Graham and Cory would have dared to move the Thinker in. The ranger intimidated them both. It was not simply Gus's size; he exuded a certain black-and-white morality, something he communicated without words or strong facial expressions. Putting themselves in danger put the world in danger. This facility existed because the country needed them to be there, working on answers that the assembled brains could gather and disseminate, though there were rapidly fewer places to share the information. Without Gus, the mood changed from respectful research to one that closely resembled poking a snake with a stick to see what it would do.

Emma flatly refused to be in on the surgical team to retrieve samples from the Thinker. She continued working with the antibodies, hoping to develop a vaccine that blocked the virus without making the recipient develop liver failure by also blocking iron transport. Emma and Jan looked up as Cory entered, grabbing a stool while grinning like the Cheshire cat.

"Man, you should see some of the tissue samples we got today!"

"I hope it helps the research." Emma kept her voice neutral, carrying a tray of test tubes inoculated with her most recent fragment of virus to inject into the healthy rats.

"Yeah, it will." He followed and laid a hand on her shoulder. She shrugged it away.

"I'm working," Emma replied.

"Just trying to talk. I can do that with you, right? Talk?" Cory insisted.

Emma sighed and perched herself on a stool. "About what? What have we not already said?"

"Come, on, Emma. It's been over a week, you really think—"

"As you pointed out at three days and then again at five." She started to stand, but a brief wave of dizziness forced her to sit. With all Cory's other faults, lack of observation was not one of them.

"You OK? You need some water?" His concern was genuine.

Even before the virus, they had flirted in the ER when she went to admit patients. Cory had been notorious among the nurses, never dating anyone for more than a month, so when they were working as residents, Emma left their contact in the light banter stage and steered clear of the lothario. When they evacuated to SAMMC and then to the CDC, she no longer bothered to resist his full-wattage charm and smile, finding herself in his bed and doing something she never thought she would—sleep with someone without a serious emotional bond. She hadn't even thought of her actions until Peter's e-mail. She and Cory were only together for two days, so Emma assumed as soon as she rebuffed him that he would be off to another. There were more women than men in the facility, most under forty. But Cory continued to pester her, flirt, and flatter. The only decision on which they took opposite sides was the one allowing in the Thinker. His warm hand covered hers until the moment passed.

"I'm OK. I'm probably anemic from all the blood they've drawn." Emma gave him a quick smile and covered the milder next wave of dizziness with a turn toward the bench. When she turned back, he cupped her face with his hand, but in a more medical than romantic move, he pulled down the lower lid of her eye.

"Hmm, you are pale," Cory responded critically, still with some concern.

"I'll decline blood draws for a few days and see if someone can find me some iron pills." Emma smiled slightly. "And if you don't mind, I need to get back to work."

Cory noticed Jan and winked before bowing to Emma. "As my lady wishes. See you at dinner." Cory swept out, the door banging closed behind him.

The mention of dinner made Emma's stomach turn.

"Ma'am, time to get to the radio," Jan reminded her.

Emma nodded, stored the samples, and wondered what was new in the world. Alistair had recovered; the last message from Gus was from a yacht in Puget Sound, waiting for further orders. She hoped the next message would announce his return. Emma missed having the solid rock at her back.

Guillermo marveled over how people settled into new routines. People found new topics of discussion; no longer did the TV novellas rule his mother's life. After his father died, they seemed to be the only thing that kept her alive. Now she gossiped and chatted with the other women while washing clothes in the abundant salt water, bemoaning how stiff the seawater made the fabric as it dried. If he snuck up on them, he found the conversation surrounding the girls he liked, which one they'd seen sneaking from his bedroom.

There was only one girl, or woman, that Guillermo really wanted in his bed, but she preferred spending her nights alone. The young leader initially imagined himself pure, but then night after night, a girl found a way to his bed, sometimes more than one. He discouraged anyone from visiting two nights in a row; that implied favoritism. He was not ready for any permanent attachments, unless that one indicated her interest.

Paulina and Mitchell stripped down the Bell 412 to its bare essentials, allowing more room for supplies. A tanker truck full of jet fuel from the airport provided enough gas for several runs. They'd brought in scrap metal to reinforce the lower parts of the wall to prevent zrats from digging under, weapons from an overrun military installation, solar panels, and wind generators. Guillermo was pleased by how quickly the town developed. He smiled to himself as he walked the grounds.

It had not been hard to keep people busy, and as his mother had oft quoted, "Idle hands make for the devil's work." Every night, the Zs were at the walls; plans now included sending fighters out during the day to find the daytime lairs. He wished for enough explosive to demolish some of the buildings in the outer resorts. The closer ones might still be needed for housing since more survivors joined them daily.

Guillermo's musings were cut short by the sound of rapid gunfire near the entrance. With the animals meandering, the alley near the outer walls provided the fastest route. His peripheral vision caught a shadow moving too quickly to be a friend, allowing him time to duck and spin, drawing his sabre as he turned, Juan's knife catching him along the hip. Behind his third in command stood six other men with guns leveled.

"So, my young friend." Juan smiled a little too broadly.

Guillermo's rifle was still strapped to his back, only his sabre at the ready.

"I think it is time we talked of turning over things."

"This is a coup." Guillermo's voice turned to steel, the adrenaline from anger more than fear filling his veins.

"Now, you have done a good job, I will grant you that, but it is time for more mature heads to rule," Juan continued, strolling back and forth. "If you surrender now, I will let you have a place in the unit, maybe even a sergeant, a good position for one so young."

Guillermo heard more shouts and more gunfire, and then the sounds of a rotor caused a slight spasm across Juan's face, quickly covered, but long enough for Guillermo to see it. Juan had been walking back and forth in front of his men, and that pause blocked their aim long enough.

Guillermo sprang to the side before a trigger could be pulled without hitting Juan, and he sprinted down a side alley and up the first flight of stairs. Juan and his men yelled and fired, but the concrete walls around the steps made to withstand a storm surge gave ample protection. Guillermo made it into the first room, barricading the door. It appeared to be a woman's apartment from the things dangling. The balcony stood open, revealing a sight more beautiful than a sunrise as the Bell rose from its pad. Only two in the facility could fly it, and Guillermo could not imagine a betrayal from either. With the rifle freed, Guillermo shot at the two men emerging from the alleyway. The chopper came nearer, allowing Guillermo to see Mitchell flying, Paulina on one side with a rifle and Rodrigo hanging out the other.

Determining friend or foe could not be easy. His friends shot at those in the alley. The pounding on the door stopped. Guillermo knew that they'd need to leave the stairs to return fire, but he also knew that Juan was too much a coward to make himself a target. Guillermo grabbed the emergency ladder and hooked it to the balcony railing, sliding down the sides. The screams from all around indicated that most of his people had returned to their rooms, securing themselves inside. Juan Carlos and his sons jogged from the beach side holding sticks and slings that they had made for themselves.

"Guillo, we are with you," Juan Carlos assured him, all standing under the relative protection of the Bell.

"Juan may still be back this way." Guillermo indicated the alley. He took a look at the farmers' weapons. The slings did well against the Zs, but guns intimidated humans more.

Armed men approached with rifle muzzles pointed into the air, not toward him. Guillermo recognized many of the young men he had been training. They too proved loyal. Some of them handed pistols to the farmers, and then Guillermo sent out four groups—one toward the beach, one toward the front, one to take the next alley, and one to follow him. The farmers were to stay and guard the central area. Unfortunately, no one had grabbed a walkie-talkie or any other way to communicate with the chopper. Guillermo pushed his hand up at them, and after a few gestures, Mitchell understood and took the chopper up a hundred feet for better observation.

Guillermo and his group proceeded down the alley, once trod by the feet of the well-heeled but now trod on by the barely heeled. The young men, most no more than seventeen, moved together well, proceeding slowly and as one, the way they had been drilled. With no actual enemy in sight, that was the easy part. They spun around the base of the stairs, but there was no target. They proceeded to the end of the alley, covering one another as they passed onto the small road by the fence, joining the group from the next alley. Guillermo stopped for a moment. Would Juan head toward the road or the beach? The beach had boats and no Zs on the open water. The beach it would be. The chopper whizzed down the edge then hovered. A couple of shots rang out, hitting its underbelly, but it stayed over the mark. Guillermo and his troops dogtrotted after and waved the chopper off. One slimy *serpiente* was not worth losing such a thing.

His beach team approached and pointed to a clump in a bush. Guillermo unleashed his rifle, firing in the ground in front of it.

"So, Señor Juan!" Guillermo shouted. "I do not think the town is ready for a change."

Hands slowly emerged from the bush.

"The rifle, send out the rifle."

Juan tossed it to the middle of the path.

"Good. Now keep your hands on your head, and then get on your knees. I am sure you know how, since you made many young men do that in your day."

Juan followed orders, no longer looking up.

"You must understand, Guillermo, my general, the others goaded me! They thought it would be better …" Juan began pleading.

Guillermo felt a powerful rush with this man on his knees before him. Guillermo shouldered his rifle, remembering the cut on his leg, still oozing from the movement.

"Better for who? Haven't I found us all food, shelter, weapons? Yes, now that things look good, you want control." Guillermo kept in mind Juan's mistake and stayed still, his men with clear beads on their target.

"It was my mistake, I beg of you …" Juan began again.

"Beg of me? A quick death? I'm sure that can be arranged."

Guillermo felt the words tumble forth, sounding like something from a bad movie, but the effect was euphoric. Juan cried. Not just a few tears, but bawling, his shoulders shaking. Guillermo drew his sabre, turning the grip back and forth to make the sun glint along the steel, fully intending to impale Juan and let the bastard watch his own blood flow. The plants behind Guillermo made his shadow look like he wore a strange square hat, which reminded him of Muammar Gaddafi and a conversation with Mitchell after the raid on El Padre. The two worried that into the void a dictator would emerge. Guillermo laughed and said not to worry; he couldn't stand to wear the funny hats.

The euphoria left him like a popped balloon. Guillermo now saw a pathetic, middle-aged man crying and wetting himself. He sheathed his sword.

"Bind him. Take him to the little brig near the office," Guillermo said and turned, not bothering to make sure his orders were carried out.

Mitchell found the young leader in his office, four shots of tequila in. No one worried about a drinking age anymore. Mitchell sat down across so that he could look Guillermo in the face.

"I think there needs to be a division of duties. Someone needs to lead the civil and you the military. You were distracted and blindsided," Mitchell said.

Guillermo pulled out a second glass, poured one for Mitchell, and then refreshed himself.

"You are probably right. I knew Juan was a problem from the start, but I did not keep my enemy close enough. Would you like to run the town?" Guillermo offered.

"Why don't we hold an election? Let the people decide if they want an English-speaking Canadian as their mayor. I think Juan Carlos would be a good choice. He knows farming, the people like him, and he has shown his loyalty to you." Mitchell knocked back the shot. He didn't like tequila; bourbon was more his style, but this was not a moment to bring that up.

"But I do not think Juan Carlos would sit across from me as you do, reminding me of the truth and of history." Guillermo began slurring his words.

"History?" Mitchell asked as his glass magically refilled.

"Sí." Guillermo swallowed. "Yes, I remembered I would not look good in a funny hat." Guillermo's head began to slump forward, the alcohol hitting hard and quickly.

"Why don't you rest your head for a few minutes? We can decide the town's future later." Mitchell found a couple of shirts and propped them under Guillermo's cheek as he began to snore. Mitchell exited and waved over a guard. "Guard the door. The general needs some time to think. The only ones allowed in are myself, Paulina, Rodrigo, and Juan Carlos—you know us."

"Sí! I mean, yes, sir!" The young man crossed the rifle in front of his chest and stood squarely in front of the door.

Luckily, it was Paulina who was present when Guillermo woke a few hours later with a mouth feeling like cotton. She got him some water and aspirin. As his focus returned and the pounding in his head subsided enough to allow him to hear without additional pain, he finally asked her how they knew about the coup.

"Rodrigo saw Juan and some his men going to the armory, which was odd since sunset was still hours away. He followed and saw Juan shoot the guard at the door, and then shooting started in other places. Mitchell and I were maybe a hundred yards away and were confused. Rodrigo ran up and said to grab the chopper and that he'd get us some guns. Mitchell managed to keep up pretty well, and we got to the Bell before Juan's men. Rodrigo was good to his word. Mitchell admitted that the rifle was safer in my hands, and he piloted us up. We looked for activity and saw someone shooting from a balcony. Even from that distance, Rodrigo recognized you."

The story brought some clarity to Guillermo. He sipped the water, trying to keep his stomach from lurching. The aspirin helped the head. "We need to convene a court-martial. Try to figure out everyone involved." Guillermo rubbed his temple. "But not today. The bodies—"

"Already taken care of. We carted them a couple of miles away. Most of the women are bleaching the sites where bleeding occurred," Paulina informed him.

"Good. Let's sleep. It's likely to be a busy night." Guillermo stood, wincing and sucking in his breath as the laceration on his leg pulled open again.

Paulina looked down at the deep cut. "That needs stitches. You can sleep in medical."

Guillermo refused the hand of assistance. This was not the time to appear weak.

The night was almost as bad as Guillermo imagined. The onshore breeze had blown the smell of blood far and wide, bringing the zrats and zogs in droves, followed by the Zs. Mitchell wondered if somehow they communicated or if instinct alone told the Zs to follow the zrats to food. Wave after wave approached the walls. Normally, the smell of dead Z kept them back, but now the smell of human blood was too powerful of a draw. The southern compound was breached, and Mitchell heard the chopper respond to the area, the bright light forcing them back while the newly pared-down militia kept up a heavy barrage of fire, creating a wall of dead Zs to replace their own wall.

Guillermo fought, fired, cajoled, and inspired his troops and the civilians through the night. Mitchell marveled at Guillermo's focus and drive. He possessed the energy of youth, the focus of a man, and an intellect that—as much as it pained Mitchell to admit it—surpassed his own. Before dawn, fewer Zs approached the wall, and as the sun broke over the water, a great cheer grew through the town. They had survived to a new day. The men of the militia drew lots for their shifts, the civilians took charge of body disposal. The south compound would need to be quarantined that evening, so anyone on the body-disposal duty would stay there.

It wouldn't be until after another night of fighting—fewer Zs this time—that the issue of Juan and his men could be decided. A jury of nine soldiers was established by lot. There was a lawyer and a senior law student among the survivors in camp. Again by lot, the lawyer drew to defend and the student to prosecute Juan and his men. Juan had recruited close to fifty fighters they knew of, most killed in the coup by Guillermo's men before word went out that they were to face trial. The trial would begin in two days.

Guillermo took Mitchell aside. "I have not forgotten our conversation. You are right. I need someone to lead the civilians. I will call for volunteers to stand in the election. I hope you will add your name."

"I will be honored." Mitchell grasped Guillermo's hand. It felt good to look to the future.

Charlene smiled and accepted the congratulations of all those around her. There would be music before dark, and any booze they could find was opened and shared. Charlene donated most of Al's supply, except for a special bottle of thirty-year-old scotch, which she secured in her room. That would await his return. Chief Hillier toasted to her health and shook hands with Mr. Parker for a good, close race. The smiles and momentary ease on everyone's faces made her imagine that someday, life may be able to get back to normal. Then she realized that *this* was normal.

To keep the peace and folks happy, evenings like tonight would need to be a routine. Humans needed music, company, and time to let one's hair down and dance. Alcohol was almost gone, which was probably a good thing in keeping folks civil, but they could have fun.

Thirty minutes before dusk, Charlene took the stage to a roomful of cheers.

"All right, now. If you folks would indulge me. I want to take a moment and pray." The room grew quiet. "Dear Lord, thank you for every precious moment we have here. Thank you for all those present, whether they believe in God, Allah, Jehovah, or choose not to believe. We are here to help each other survive this trial, in the spirit of humanity. I believe you have gathered us here, under this roof, for a purpose I do not yet understand, but I will be here to answer your call and your command. Amen."

The responding amens joined in around the room.

"I would like to thank everyone for their service thus far and their help in the coming days. No one knows how long it will take to rid this world of the Zs, zrats, and other infected creatures. But as long as communities like this can come together, humans—and humanity—will survive.

That is what I call on us to do: remember humanity. A single human might survive, but for humanity to survive, it takes community, love of one's neighbor, respect for human life. Thank you for your votes, and I will turn the stage back over to our band to finish out the night!"

The crowds cheered her off. For now, people smiled and laughed. She hoped they could continue to do so.

Hiccup's fiasco sent him to organizing the groups doing the lowly jobs of collecting scrap metal and items to shore up the wall and firewood and other combustibles for the fires, spending the hours after sunset prowling for zrats, and feeding the rooftop pigeons in the tenement building. When he stopped grousing, he realized that he was not that unhappy, but admitting anything like that would be to lose face, especially now that Charles spent most of his days planning with Stokes and Toya. Auntie let him sit and gripe and then would pat his hand.

"Different jobs are for different folks, Arnold. They have heads for plannin' and such. The good Lord blessed you with a good back. You just do your work the way you should, and you'll be all right." Auntie rose, returning to the kitchen. She sat on a high stool that allowed her to chop the vegetables and supervise the others cooking. Auntie had been poor her whole life, and she knew how to stretch supplies in ways no one thought possible and still make the food taste good.

Hiccup stalked back to the tenement. It had taken some time to clear out the rats and zrats—not that anyone could tell the difference—but folks could move in since the crew monitoring the building hadn't heard anything for a couple of days. The ceiling tiles had been removed to give anyone a good look at the crawl spaces and clear aim if one showed up. Hiccup walked up the fourteen flights to the roof, opening one of the pigeon cages to pet his favorite bird.

The thick wire of the cages had kept the zrats from making them a meal and had given Toya an idea for making gardens. The salvage crews were instructed to look for any kind of wire and wire fencing. They'd brought back seeds from a hardware and grocery store not far out of town, and Toya longed to get them started. Hiccup thought that maybe if he helped Toya with the gardens, Stokes would forgive him. He released his pigeon and watched it fly, make an arc, and then return to the top of the cages. Stokes said that pigeons always came home from wherever they were released. If they found another town, they could trade birds and communicate.

Hiccup saw movement along the road near East Camden. There was a gate on the little bridge, the river deep enough this spring not to need an addition to the wall yet, but since that area often froze in winter, Stokes thought they might need to build one in the fall. Hiccup didn't have binoculars, but he could make out a small group with backpacks and a horse. The strangers waved at the guard. Hiccup knew that Stokes would come, and he was curious. Hiccup hightailed it down the steps and came up breathless, jogging over to the bridge. Stokes was already there, with his white shadow, talking to the group. Catch opened the mechanism, and three of the group walked in. The opening was too low for the horse, so Con crossed the bridge—and Hiccup assumed that he was leading them to the front entrance. The three coming in were men—two white and one guy darker. Hispanic, Hiccup assumed.

Stokes jumped down from the observation tower, Charles moving more gingerly behind, favoring his shoulder.

Stokes noticed Hiccup and waved him over. "Dr. Austin Draeger, surgeon from Cherry Hill, and his brother Trevor." The men appeared to be in their thirties, both now sporting full beards. "And Mateo Peron. He and the lady who's taking the horse around are from Cinnaminson. There's room in the tower. Take 'em up to five to drop their stuff and then bring 'em back to the church to meet Auntie."

Although Stokes ran everything, it was Auntie that had the final say on who could move in.

Auntie made tea as she chatted up the four. Austin was the clear head of the group.

"What brings you from Cherry Hill? You'd think you would be evacuated into some beautiful tower with plenty of food." Auntie handed out the tea in china cups and the little packages of cookies from the vending machines.

Austin grunted. "No such place. The refugee camp in Fort Dix was overrun. We couldn't get into the quarantine in time. Olivia there"—Austin nodded to the sandy-haired woman in her forties—"showed us how to smear the zrat blood on to keep the Zs away. After a few days, we gave up trying at Fort Dix and decided to try our luck back home, but the Zs were still bad there. Last night, we saw your lights and thought what the hell and to see if we could join you."

"You're a doctor?" Auntie prodded.

"Yes, a general surgeon. I finished my residency two years ago," Austin confirmed.

"And your brother?" Auntie asked over her tea.

"I'm a lawyer." Trevor snorted. "Don't think there's much use for me right now, but maybe when things settle. I'm fit, and I can work."

"Can you shoot?" Stokes added.

"Not really, but I can learn." Trevor looked down at his hands.

Auntie turned her attention on the other two. The woman spoke with a slight lilt. "I ran a riding school in Cinnaminson. Mateo was the head groom. The horse is Gamesman. He's an Irish Warmblood I was training as an eventer." Her eyes locked with Auntie's. "And if my staying means giving him over as food, I will leave right now."

Auntie's teeth clacked for a moment. "I'm sure he can be made useful without needing to do that." Her eyes met Stokes's, making it clear that no one was to harm the horse. "There's a small park near the school. You can stable him there."

Olivia leaned back. She had a gentle smile when she relaxed and then turned for a moment as a tear sprang forth.

"Thank you. You do not know how much I have worried I would lose him. It must seem stupid to you." Suddenly, the woman whose calm forcefulness made her conviction known melted into sudden tears of relief. Auntie patted her hand, and the men in her party choked up, as well.

"Thank you." Austin rubbed his neck while releasing a long-held breath. "We've been wandering, and I didn't realize how scared we'd been until now. I suddenly feel as safe as I'm going to."

"Welcome to Camden." Stokes held out his hand to each, followed by Charles. Austin clasped Charles's shoulder, who winced.

Austin stopped and started to probe the shoulder through the shirt fabric. "Bullet wound," Charles explained. "Ten days ago, I think"

"I have my first patient—if you have any kind of medical clinic set up you can show me," Austin offered.

"After he sees to Charles, we should probably have a formal quarantine," Auntie said. "In the school, the principal's office has a glass door and a nurse's station. Have them stay there tonight. After that, we can let them settle in the tower." Auntie nicely called the tenement "the tower." It did sound nicer.

After they left, Auntie had another cup of tea and checked her blood sugar—213, a little high but not too bad. She smiled out the window. Who'd have thought some high-and-mighty Cherry Hill surgeon and his brother would need to seek refuge in Camden, with some fancy-ass horse prancing around the schoolyard? The world had definitely changed.

CHAPTER 9

April 25-28; Z Days 16-19

Sara continued to improve, and was almost done with the antibiotics, but the town found excuse after excuse for the engineer not to leave. Peter had an escort, morning and night, and he was never left alone long enough to sneak out. Sara attended school daily and was allowed to wander. She explored every inch of the compound, reporting her finds back to Peter as they ate their evening meal. The old jail housed all the guns confiscated when people entered the town and was under heavy guard, so Peter knew that there would be no additional weapons to the katana if they found the chance to bolt.

Day sixteen started the same way as had any other over the previous ten days. The crank radios were set up and working, AM stations carried the news. Ireland's Father Patrick had cleared Killarney and was working his way across the island. The immune priest felt called by God to eliminate the scourge from the green paradise as Saint Patrick had driven out the snakes. Listening to the news gave the community something to discuss besides the food; today's breakfast was oatmeal with prunes. They were out of raisins, sugar, syrup, and most anything else that was sweet. But they had food. Some of the other shelter sites they were in contact with were running out and needing to go farther afield to resupply. Parris Island was overpopulated, diverting everyone to Hilton Head and Savannah, and those there could not spare any supplies.

Later in the morning, everyone was surprised when the watch called out about trucks in the distance. "Military convoy, from the look of it!" someone shouted from the observation deck.

Peter felt hope rise and worked out his options. Maybe they could help him get to Atlanta. But if they needed an engineer, he could find himself in the same situation. Leave Sara to the safety of the community and slip out by himself when the convoy entered? Or retrieve his sword, collect her from school, and both sneak away? Peter shook his head. This was not something he could decide for her; Sara needed to decide that for herself. Maybe they could find a car and supplies on the road. It was morning; they might be able to get a good distance before their absence was noticed. While most people, including Peter's "companions," stood trying to get a look over the wall, Peter found the school. It seemed every child had his or her face plastered to the upper windows, but he didn't see Sara's.

Peter found the girl sitting in the hall reading a book. She looked up as he came in alone. "Do we get to leave now?"

Peter quickly looked around and nodded. Sara smiled and stood, securing the book. They jogged back to their room and wrapped the katana in a blanket, making it less obvious as it protruded from the backpack. Sara slipped on a pair of jeans, and each threw in a spare pair of socks and underwear. No one paid attention to the engineer and his companion as the army entered through wide-open gates. The men looked spent, their uniforms loose and dirty. They smiled and waved at the cheering townsfolk. Peter and Sara melted to the back of the crowd, the citizens trying to reach up to their new saviors. Once in the rear, they ensured that all eyes were on the convoy and then dropped down in the high grass and snuck around the wall, running for the woods in the nearby park. The pair escaped supplied with one blanket, the clothes on their backs, one set of extra underwear, socks, one sword, two water bottles, and one copy of *Harry Potter and the Prisoner of Azkaban* by J. K. Rowling. Peter began to second-guess himself and considered going back when he heard the gunshots and screams.

Peter jumped up but stayed in the woods with Sara's hand on his arm. "What can you do?" she whispered, her voice quavering and face pale. "They have guns."

Peter's stomach turned, remembering the good people in the town who helped Sara. Even if they tried to trap him there, they didn't deserve this fate. His gun and those of so many more were in the small armory in the compound.

"And now they have more. Let's get as much distance as we can," Peter said as he shouldered the backpack.

Peter admitted that Sara was a trooper. After walking and jogging over five miles, she did not ask to stop. He called for a rest, and she did not protest, collapsing down on the ground for a minute. Peter pulled out their water bottles. They'd been heading due south and needed to get southwest to get to Atlanta, and they needed transportation.

Sara looked at her bottle. "Do you think they're OK?"

Peter thought about telling a lie, but she knew the truth already. "Probably not. Those men will take what they want. I hope it's just food and supplies and that then they'll just leave to loot the next place."

"Why do they do that?" Sara asked, lying back for a minute with her eyes shaded.

Peter considered all the sociological aspects from the class on government breakdown Emma had talked him into taking. "Because they can," was his final reply. "You OK to get going again?"

Sara nodded.

They set off at a slower pace but kept to the smaller roads. About twelve miles out, they came across the town of Apex. The deserted North Salem Street still had flyers in the store windows announcing "Peakfest! Reserve your booths now!" Peter saw the sign for the police station and gestured for Sara to follow. Something about the empty streets and rustle of wind made him want to keep quiet.

Like everything else, the police station was abandoned. In the back was a one-wheeled motorcycle lying on its side in the small garage. Peter dug around and found the wheel and a spare tire and then rigged a couple of charged car batteries to power the air compressor to inflate the tire. Only one-quarter tank of gas. He found some tubing and a bulb for a siphon. Sara sat and watched quietly.

"You're good at all that. You'll need to show me," she piped up.

"I promise. But right now, I need you to find some clean paper or cloths." Peter smiled down at her.

"OK. What for?"

Peter picked up the adult helmet by the bike. "So you can wear this and still see."

She giggled. "You think of everything." Her stomach rumbled, causing embarrassed giggles, knowing that there'd been no lunch and maybe no dinner.

"Well, if we hurry up, maybe I can think of something to do about all that growling!" Peter smiled, only partly forced. He did not want to imagine what might have happened if he had left his charge in town. Peter promised himself that Sara would stay with him. With that thought, the bike came to life with a beautiful low growl.

His bike at home was little more than a moped for getting to and from school; this thing was a monster made for speed. Sara's helmet still rolled down over her eyes despite the padding, making them both smile.

"I guess you won't need to see much, anyway. You'll have to wear the backpack and hang on tight, OK?"

Sara nodded, the helmet rolling back and forth.

It was late afternoon, and they wouldn't get much farther before needing to stop for the night. A house with garage door still down, front door on hinges, and most windows intact would be the object. They found an older home with solid wooden shutters still open, allowing in the day's light, so it was less likely to house as many Zs. The front door sat slightly ajar, and it was swollen and stiff as Peter pushed it open. He and Sara called out, but only silence responded. They explored, starting at the top and going all the way to the basement—no Zs in residence. Peter pulled the bike into the front hall and then showed Sara how to secure the shutters from inside as well as out. They locked the doors and then used furniture to barricade them, including the door to the basement. Peter took a deep breath and braved opening the refrigerator and was rewarded with a molding block of cheddar and bottled water. By candlelight, he cut away the mold, revealing several ounces in good condition. Sara found some well-sealed crackers in the pantry, and they picnicked in the living room, saving half for breakfast.

Sara propped herself against him and promptly slept. Peter lay back against the couch. The people in the compound were good people. Staying would not have helped, he rationalized, but the sense of guilt prevented sleep. Instead, Peter's brain recalled the area. There were several abandoned cars on the street outside. Atlanta was about four hundred miles from where he sat. Three weeks ago, those four hundred miles would have taken less than a workday. If they could find open road, they could do it in less than two days with a stop to secure themselves for the night and refuel at least twice. Pushing harder than that would get them into trouble.

The night was blissfully uneventful. The radio announcer had said that blood attracted Zs, so most in the area had likely been drawn to Raleigh. After another repast of cheese, crackers, and water, they weaved along a hundred miles of secondary roads before the torrential rains drove them to seek shelter. The town of Mount Pleasant, North Carolina, would have to do for the night. Peter and Sara decided to avoid the main highways, especially with the fake military convoy somewhere out there. Most smaller towns had evacuated, which made scavenging easier. Peter stopped feeling guilty about taking supplies, food, and leftover gas in garages meant for a lawnmower or in a car parked in a garage. Breaking into businesses was now something one just did to find what one needed to survive. For the moment, holing up in an auto parts store just off of NC-49 would do. If the day did not lighten much, they would need to get into town for better nighttime security.

"Peter! Bingo!"

Peter heard a crash as he propped the bike in the back. In the main lobby, Sara happily stood with a crowbar propped against a snack machine, sweeping glass out of the way with her sneakers as she reached in for bags of chips and candy. The part of him that wanted to be a father someday cringed, but the part that was still a kid almost danced with joy at the sight of peanut butter cups. Sugar, fat, and salt—just what exhausted travelers needed. The soda machine required some muscle to pry open. It held bottled water, as well, he justified to himself.

In Raleigh, food was rationed to around thirteen hundred calories per day. Within minutes, their stomachs were the most full since the steak they'd eaten in Virginia. They sat on plastic benches staring through the big front window at the darkened sky unleashing its deluge. Lightning flashed, and the thunder roared.

"Do you think they come out in this?" Sara asked as she crunched another chip.

"Biologically, they're still human. I doubt Zs appreciate being wet any more than we do." Peter let the chocolate dissolve on his tongue, savoring it as never before, never knowing that he needed to.

"Do you think they're scared?" she persisted.

"The smart ones, maybe." Peter tilted his head back to stretch his neck. "The other ones don't seem to have enough brain left to be scared."

"Why are there smart ones?"

Peter grinned and ruffled her brown hair. "That is likely a question for my friend Emma when we find her." Peter stood. "Let's see if they have saddlebags for the bike so we can take a lot of this stuff." They found the bags and took some spark plugs and other small portable parts that he might need later. The rain lightened, but the sky continued to be dark, especially to the south. Peter checked his watch. So much for making it to Spartanburg, let alone Charlotte today.

"It looks like we'll be here for the night."

Sara looked skeptically out of the large window. "What if—"

"We'll head into town to see if we can find a house with an easy-to-secure attic." Peter imagined that would be the easiest to defend, and one with a roof access hatch was even better. Peter added roof access to his mental design of the Z-proof building.

Not far away was a small complex of duplexes near the middle school that met most of their needs, including attic stairs that retracted to the ceiling. The bedding in the home was intact, and the garage held a midsize car with three-quarters of a tank of gas. Whoever lived here either was dead or had bugged out with friends. They planned to take full advantage of the situation.

Sara's ability to cover her nose with her upper lip and excellent breath-holding technique when opening refrigerators also scored them more bottled water and some single-slice packaged cheese that looked like it would be good until the dinosaurs returned. When they pulled the ladder up after them, they felt as secure as anyone could in the circumstances. Peter knew that he'd feel even better if the rain stopped. Overnight, the thunderstorms cleared but left behind heavy clouds that continued a steady drizzle too heavy to ride a bike in, especially with a ten-year-old girl holding on behind.

Peter considered taking the car, but it lacked the maneuverability of the bike, and this one was strictly rear-wheel drive, which was more likely to get stuck in the mud trying to go around any obstacle on the road. With Sara's agreement, they'd wait out the rain. The extra day allowed for exploring the neighborhood houses for further restocking. A lot of people in the area must have had kids. They found pounds of processed cheese, canned spaghetti products, and baked beans. One closet on a high shelf held the item Peter had wanted to find: a handgun with a couple of boxes of bullets. If they came across a nest, or hive, or herd—groups of Zs had been called several things—he needed a weapon that could down many at a distance. The sword was a wonderful weapon, but it was not much defense if they were surrounded.

After scavenging and eating, Peter and Sara practiced using the katana. He showed her how to swing, thrust, and move with it. It was much too big for her, but she managed the basics. A sharp kitchen knife that she could tuck into her belt loop made a more practical weapon.

By evening, the rain finally slacked off as they tucked themselves into the attic. The night proved less restful, as banging and grunting permeated the house. There were Zs below, but since Peter brought the attic hook with him, a Thinker couldn't reach the ring to get into their space. The crash when the bike fell over made Peter cringe, but he knew there was no use going down. During the day, the house had been pretty light even with the rain, so he imagined a bright, sunny day would prevent the Zs from remaining in the house after dawn. Sara shivered from fear more than cold, but the noise eventually abated.

Once it had been quiet for a while, they dared to talk.

"Why did they know to come here?" she whispered.

Peter had been considering it. "Probably cooking the food." They'd cooked the beans and spaghetti Boy Scout–style with the cans opened and set into the coals of the fireplace.

"I'll eat it cold tomorrow," Sara replied.

"Me too." Peter pulled the pack with the gun and sword that much closer, and Sara fingered her knife. With no further sounds, they nodded off for a few hours. A bright dawn beckoned them downstairs, not opening any doors in case of dark spaces in the rooms. The bike was on its side but unharmed. Peter filled the tank with siphoned gas from the car, and they loaded up, ready for the day.

Jan reported that there were thunderstorms above. Emma sighed. She loved to sit on her back porch at home and watch the lightning, tea in hand, counting the time from the strike until the crash of thunder. She hadn't had a breath of fresh air in two weeks, and she longed for the smell of ozone after the storms.

"Any chance I could go above for a few minutes?" Emma asked. The answer was Jan's dour look.

"Sorry, up top ..." Jan started to explain.

"There's one down here now too," Emma grumbled, her normally positive disposition beginning to wear thin.

"Believe me, we know," Jan replied.

The team was not happy about the monster housed in the facility. At the briefing, Rankin had pointed out some serious holes in the security measures and had been working with the facilities' security force to shore them up. In Jan's mind's eye, she could see the colonel returning, taking one look at the Thinker, blowing off its head, and dumping the body outside.

"What are you thinking about?" Emma asked at Jan's sly smile.

"The colonel taking out the trash."

Emma's own grin lit her face. "Gus is going to throw such a fit when he sees that thing."

"No further word?" Jan asked.

Emma shook her head. "You know I'd tell you as soon as I heard. They were going to Bowen Island near Vancouver. The Canadian prime minister was allowing the group to join one of theirs."

Emma had looked up the area. Officially, the island had fishing villages and retirement homes. Unofficially, she wondered if the facility was more like this one. Hopefully, without a Thinker in residence.

"And how are my favorite ladies?" Andy swept in; his normally easy grin seemed forced.

"Well, thanks," Emma replied carefully, watching the grin dance between that and a grimace. "What's wrong?"

"I'm not supposed to be telling you this." Andy glanced in the hall and then pulled the door closed. Jan took her cue and stepped in front of the door. "They're going to do an fMRI today."

Emma felt the blood drain from her face and almost fell to the floor, but Andy caught her arm and helped her to a chair. Jan stepped forward for a moment and then returned to her post. Andy brought Emma a glass of water.

"Cory said you didn't look good the other day. You've been taking your iron?" Andy hovered.

"Yeah, probably the lack of sun." She glared at Jan. Emma sipped the water, letting the world come back into place, and then looked at Andy. "They can't wake it up. Dr. Graham promised."

"Well, I was excused from my shift two hours early and overheard them readying for the test," Andy explained. "You should know, maybe your people …"

Emma nodded, too vigorously at first, and then focused on Jan. "Tell Rankin that they're waking up the Thinker. They're going to do a test on its brain called a functional MRI."

Jan looked conflicted. "I can't leave your side, ma'am."

Emma stood, steadier now. "Then we'll all go."

Less than five minutes later, they found Rankin standing with Lieutenant Borland, the security chief, looking over blueprints. He looked startled to see them.

"What's wrong?" he asked.

"They're waking the Thinker." Andy chose to speak up.

Lieutenant Borland stiffened. "When? Where did you hear that?" Borland insisted.

Andy explained as he had before. Borland did not speak another word but turned on his heel, heading for the stairs and down three levels to the one with highest security where the live virus and the Thinker were housed. The only one technically without clearance was Jan, but since she packed the rifle, no one questioned her.

The thumping of the MRI was distinctive and drew them down the corridor. Emma, Andy, and Borland entered the observation room and stood in front of Dr. Graham, watching the monitors with Dr. Mehra and Cory. The already crowded room became claustrophobic. The large window showed the machine, the Thinker's hands flexing and opening in the restraints, its fingers feeling the edge of the straps.

Emma stood before Dr. Graham, her own hands clenching and releasing. She wanted to punch his smug little grin but held back. "You promised when the others agreed to bring him here. He'd *never* be awake."

“Dr. O’Conner, you have to understand, the only way to see how the brain works is to see it in action.” Graham turned his hand to the monitors, scrolling through the pictures of the brain highlighted in blues and reds. “You see, when it’s shown pictures of children, the brain response is the same as if we show it *meat*.”

“Hell, if you ever watch those things, you’d know that,” Andy scoffed.

“Look at what’s destroyed—the prefrontal cortex, parts of the limbic system … and look, the pars opercularis; that explains the deficient language. They can understand our words, but they can’t talk to us or understand our facial expressions.” Emma knew that the pars opercularis was part of the Broca’s brain for speech, causing problems for stroke patients and an area often underdeveloped in people with autism. What she did not see was how this improved their understanding of the virus and how to stop it.

“So you woke it up, endangering us all, to find out that it can’t talk to us. Great. Thanks. I’m sure you’ll get a Nobel or something.” Emma felt furious, turning red from her collar to her hairline. She pulled open the door. “Let’s go. If they want to play with fire, I want to be as far away from the flames as possible.”

Cory ran out behind her. “Come on, Em. This is groundbreaking! How their brains function! Now if we could get a regular Z and compare—”

Emma glared at him and then spun and marched down the hall. Cory returned to the room where a heated discussion between Dr. Graham and Borland raged. Rankin looked at the door to the MRI room, fingering his service weapon. Borland’s argument was stronger, and the lieutenant sounded like he would not back down from the medical director. Rankin caught up with Emma and Jan. His smile faded a few strides later when the lights cut out, plunging them in complete darkness, without even a glow from the emergency lights to guide them.

Rankin ran into Jan, who had stumbled into Emma. They found the wall and each other’s hands. “The storms must have knocked out the generators,” Jan commented. Rankin held his breath in the dark, listening to the complaints and yells behind them.

“I take it you don’t have your night scope with you?” Rankin asked Jan.

“No. Didn’t think about it,” she replied.

“Let’s feel along the wall until we get to the stairs,” Rankin suggested. He’d left his small penlight/pointer in the security office and cursed himself. They heard a door open behind them.

Cory's voice called out, "To keep from running into each other, we'll need to play Marco Polo. I'll start. Marco!"

Jan called back, "Polo!"

A moment later, they heard Cory again. "Marco!"

If it hadn't been so eerie, Emma would have found it fun.

"Polo!" she and Jan shouted together, a little too loud for the now silent hallway.

A few more times and Cory stood with them.

"Dr. Graham and Lieutenant Borland went in to check on Bob," Cory explained.

"You guys named him?" Jan's derision carried through the dark.

"Calling him 'the Thinker' all the time sounded like a comic book character or artwork. Take your pick," Cory explained. "Andy and Cavita are staying in the MRI control room with the tech."

"At least someone's being smart." Rankin sighed. "Jan, go and make sure that Dr. Graham's not trying to untie the thing until the backups to the backup generators come on." Rankin kept a firm grip on Emma's hand. "Let's get you back upstairs."

Emma linked hands with Cory as the two men kept one hand on the wall and one firmly on Emma. There had been several doors between the stairs and the MRI, but none remembered how many, so they checked each door as they went along. Three more doors down, shouts rang from behind them, along with gunfire from an automatic weapon.

"Keep moving," Rankin whispered, speeding up the process, hoping the power outage would weaken the magnet enough for him to force open the door to the stairs. They heard a door open, and a smell hit Emma's nostrils that made her gag, followed by sounds of snarling.

"Run." Rankin gripped Emma tighter and forced her in front of him.

Emma lost grip on Cory but ran with Rankin's pushing. The bestial noise came closer, and Cory screamed. Emma turned and tried to head back, which caused Rankin to stumble, taking them both to the ground. Rankin's arms protected her head, but the cracking noise accompanied by his grunt could only be made by bones breaking. Then the snarls were there, a few feet away.

A weight came down, and Emma heard it snuffling and chewing at Rankin's jacket. The thing moved down, and Rankin cried out as his cotton khakis were rent by insistent teeth. He tried to shift, but his right arm could not cooperate. Rankin twisted his left leg to secure the Thinker and keep him back. Emma squirmed, getting her right hand to pull the weapon pushing into her back. In one motion as instructed, she pulled it free and flipped off the safety, and when steel met teeth, the face of hope fired. And fired. And fired with the strobe effect filling the hall with smoke and thunder until the clip was empty. After several seconds with only the hollow sound of the trigger reverberating in the darkness, Rankin twisted his body and covered the gun with his left hand. He pushed the remainder of the Thinker off and rolled, sucking in a breath with every movement of his arm. The only thing keeping Emma from shaking was Rankin's weight; without it, she felt like every fiber would vibrate apart.

A low hum filled the hall, followed by a pink glow as emergency lighting finally kicked in. The Thinker lay against the wall, missing the upper half of its head, but it was the blood pool forming a few feet down the hall that grabbed Emma's attention. Regrouping into doctor mode, she rose up and headed to Cory. His arm pumped blood from just below the elbow. Emma shucked off her jacket and her shirt, making a tourniquet from the thin fabric.

"A few hours ago, I fantasized about you ripping your shirt off like that," Cory said weakly.

"Hush. We'll get you up to the surgical unit." Emma looked up to Rankin holding his own right arm, the right wrist and forearm at an odd angle.

"I don't think you need …" Cory tried to say as his head went forward. His pulse was weak and over 120.

"I'll check on the others." Rankin pulled his arm close and jogged down the long hall. The MRI room was a bloodbath. Dr. Graham and Borland were beyond help, and Jan sputtered blood from a gunshot wound to the chest and would join them in a few minutes. Rankin saw Cavita and Andy looking through the glass.

"It's dead," he told them. "Go help Dr. O'Conner get Dr. Miller to surgery."

"The doc?" Jan whispered.

"She's OK. Not a scratch. For that matter, she was the one to kill it," Rankin reassured her.

"Good. All that training …" Jan gulped for a minute.

"May have saved us all," Rankin replied. He didn't mention being bitten and definitely was not going to mention where. "You can rest now."

Jan gasped a few more times and was quiet.

When Rankin reentered the hallway, he could see the group at the far end. The three were carrying Cory as best they could and had made it to the Exit sign by the stairs. Rankin mentally put his own pain aside and jogged back to join them.

"Help me get him over my shoulder," Rankin commanded.

Once secured, Emma punched in her code, and the door to the stairs opened. She led the way up two flights to the surgical suite. Rankin and Andy lowered Cory onto a gurney as others crowded around, confused, full of questions but ready to act.

Dr. Lowe was the most experienced surgeon of those in the facility and rushed in when called. Emma had already scrubbed and prepped the arm, Andy securing Cory's airway. They worked for three hours to repair the artery and most of the damage. No one asked if it would help. They were doctors; their first order of business was the present patient. Once out of surgery, they could worry about immunity.

Emma stayed with him through recovery. When Cory woke, he found her hand on his.

"I wish things had been different," he whispered.

"How so?" Emma replied, gripping his hand.

"That I'd been more persistent before. That I'd had a chance to get you to more than 'like' me."

Emma blushed as she gripped his hand and turned away slightly. "I thought we got to know each other pretty well."

"Not in the way I wanted to, not in the way that really matters." Cory sounded tired and withdrawn. "If it's a boy, name him Alexander. If a girl, then Catherine. With you as the mother, our child will have no choice but to be great."

Emma stiffened and tried to pull away, but he gripped her hand with more strength than she thought possible. "I did something unethical. Call it the ER training—you know, any female from eleven to fifty with vague complaints get a pregnancy test. I ran the blood you had drawn that day when you were so dizzy in the lab. I was going to wait until you knew."

Emma couldn't help but let her free hand flit down to her lower abdomen, realizing now the reason for the dizziness, the change in appetite, why things smelled odd.

"Why tell me now?" She dreaded the answer.

"Your blood wasn't the only off-books test I did. I checked myself for the gene. I don't have it. In a few hours, I'll spike a fever, and a few hours after that, someone—likely from your guard—will make sure that I'm not a threat."

"The test isn't perfect. You could have—"

Cory shook his head. "No. You came up with it, so I'm sure it's as close to perfect as any test out there. I wish you hadn't spent so many resources on me. It'll be a waste." He settled his head back on the pillow. "But I'm glad we got to talk. I hope your Peter finds you."

The conversation had taken its toll, and his eyes drifted shut. Emma choked back a sob and found Rankin watching her.

His right arm sported a new bright-blue cast from elbow to fingers. "I'm heading down to isolation. They'll be moving him, as well." Rankin indicated Cory. "You'll need to stay up here. Pat will be in charge until I'm cleared."

Emma was glad that at least he was thinking positively. Andy and Pat entered behind him.

"I know the last few hours have been rough, but you need to eat something. I think they have rice in chicken broth today." Andy touched Emma's arm and she rose, releasing Cory's hand.

"Isn't that what we had yesterday?" Emma murmured, trying to choke back the tears welling up.

"Haven't had any new supplies in a week. It's why the secondary generators took so long to kick in; the fuel for them had been diverted to the main generators," Pat explained. "We're waiting for word from central command."

"Don't you mean the government?" Emma asked as they stepped out, casting one last glance to Cory.

"I don't think there is a government anymore," Pat replied.

The road between Coosawhatchie to Ridgeland became the military staging area and quarantine before people could be transferred to Parris and Hilton Head Islands. It's also where Gus and Godfrey decided to commandeer a jeep to head back to Atlanta. One look at the silver leaf on Gus's shoulder, and no questions were asked. The Canadian air force commander that flew them back contacted Alistair. There had been no contact with the Atlanta facility in almost twenty-four hours, and Gus felt something rare: doubt. Without him on the mission, his wife and daughters would likely be dead. If something happened to Emma, he would never forgive himself. The area had been rocked by storms, they reminded him, and communications problems were likely out from that.

The sergeant in charge of the vehicles informed them that one lane of I-20 had been cleared. Once they reached that part of the highway, they should be OK, but the roads near the staging site were clogged with people escaping after trying to hole up as long as they could. The now four-man team was given ammo and a couple of MREs each. Gus was happy for anything; he could see that resources were stretched past capacity. The team set out before anyone else asked questions or decided that a jeep was too valuable of a commodity.

They bounced along the sides of the road. People reached up, hunger and desperation written on their faces. "You're almost there," Godfrey or one of the men would call out to them. Some of the refugees barely bothered to get out of the way, trudging, carrying what little they had left that held meaning. All his life, Gus had seen those escaping from war in Africa, Asia, and the Middle East. He never thought he'd see it here.

The team barely made it to the military holding in Allendale by dusk. The army set up a protected area at the airport. Most of the runway was covered with pitched tents, surrounded by walls made of concrete road barriers four high. The rule was that they would protect anyone who made it inside the barriers by dusk. After that, the thick iron gates were shut, and those outside were on their own. The military had a separate walled-off area that included the airplane hangar, which acted as their barracks. To enter that side meant a twenty-four-hour quarantine. Towers erected along the perimeter housed the soldiers who kept the hordes back at night.

Every night, the Zs streamed around, attracted by the smells and sounds of human habitation and the domestic animals that were so much easier to catch and kill than the wild ones. Packs of zogs sniffed and dug at the gates whose poles extended several feet into the ground, holes that had to be filled and packed every morning. Lieutenant Drake was in charge. Gus presented himself at the wall less than thirty minutes before dusk. They could stay in the outer yard between quarantine and the outer wall. Some of the men inside threw them a few blankets with instructions to leave them at the entrance.

As soon as the sun set, they could hear the new sounds of the night. Unlike in the Needle, where the noise came from one direction—the stairs—here, the sound was everywhere as the Zs shuffled and grunted and threw themselves against the barriers, sometimes causing an edge to shift or move. Any time they concentrated too much on one spot, the snipers in the towers began to shoot down those causing the threat. The noise continued all night and did not abate until the first hint of dawn. No one slept until then.

Gus and his team took a few hours' sleep, while those stationed there donned hazmat suits and cleared the dead Zs from the gates and the road.

A giant pit a few hundred yards from the compound surrounded by giant earth mounds told the story better than any individual. Gus felt for those stationed at this place of death, trying to protect those moving through and clinging to life. Lieutenant Godfrey checked the map and was sure that they could make Atlanta by dusk.

Elberton provided their last stop before Atlanta, or so Peter hoped. A granite showroom, of which there appeared to be several, had an attic storage area for pictures and small sample squares and provided the safest place to rest for the night. If they didn't cook food and foraged in the morning, they attracted less attention from the local Zs. The Atlanta metropolitan area had a previous population of over five million, so there were a lot more Zs to attract. It didn't allow for much sleep.

Peter found that vending machines with protein bars were his favorite targets. He could at least pretend that he was supplying Sara with the nutrients a growing girl needed, and they definitely did not require cooking. Houses near schools provided convenience foods. Sara found a trove of toaster tarts in one refrigerator that were still untouched by the zrats. The aluminum packaging protected the contents from the decaying stench of everything else in the closed container. Peter felt elated that day; their journey should end well before nightfall. He looked over his shoulder and shot Sara a quick smile and then revved the bike's motor, turning onto the state highway. A road sign read "Atlanta—110 miles."

Emma couldn't sleep, and despite Rankin's instructions, she headed down to quarantine with Pat and Decker in tow. She stood outside the glassed observation area, watching Cory writhe and seize, strapped firmly to the gurney. Emma recognized the nurse in her rubberized protective clothing as Melanie.

Emma tapped on the glass. "How high?" she asked.

"It's 110," Melanie answered, her voice flat and withdrawn.

Emma wondered if Melanie and Cory had a history, as well. Emma could only nod and walked to the next window.

Rankin appeared to be sleeping, his nurse sitting in a chair near him, blankly staring at monitors. Emma asked the same question.

"It's 105.4," came the reassuring response.

It had been close to sixteen hours since the bite. He would be OK. Emma smiled for a moment. If Rankin was part immune, it improved Gus's chances for immunity to at least fifty-fifty. Emma thought about what Cory had said—that soon one of her guards would do what needed to be done. Emma didn't want any more blood. Cory was part of the reason she was still alive and the face of hope.

The med cart stood in the hallway, and she put in her code without thinking. The needed vial was kept on the top shelf, and Emma drew up the required dose. Pat and Decker watched but remained silent as Emma stepped into Cory's room. Melanie stood back as Emma connected the syringe into the IV, injecting potassium chloride into the saline solution as it fed into Cory's body. He tensed for a moment and then went slack as the monitors flat lined. Melanie turned them off and covered Cory with a sheet. Emma lay down the syringe and stepped into the hall. She had remained focused and calm throughout her task. Emma had not loved him, but he had been a friend when she needed one. Now Emma braced her hand against the wall, sobs rolling out as she began to drop, caught by Decker, and then was finally lifted and carried back to her room.

Almost an hour later, Andy entered, bringing a tray with weak tea and oatmeal almost as thin as the tea. Emma sat and stared at the tray, letting the oatmeal dribble off the spoon and back to the bowl.

"Not very appetizing, but it's breakfast, and Dr. Perdue is instructing you to eat."

Emma really looked at him for the first time since their arrival. Andy was never heavy, but there was an extra punch in his belt and gaunt pockets beneath his eyes. Emma looked up at Pat, who showed a similar level of weight loss. "There's a meeting in thirty minutes in the conference room," Andy said, watching Emma closely. "We've been asked to be there."

Emma nodded and choked down a few bites of the oatmeal, her stomach turning as soon as the gruel hit. She barely made it to the bathroom with Andy in the way and then lost what she'd choked down, tasting even worse mixed with the bile from her stomach. Andy rubbed her back until the retching subsided and she could stand.

He sat her on the dressing chair and unhooked the partial bun of hair that had become unraveled since the early hours of the morning. Emma hadn't cared to look in the mirror. Andy picked up her brush and worked it gently through the snarls of hair until smooth.

"I have three sisters—well, my older sister is a full sister, and the two much younger ones are halves. They loved it when I brushed their hair and told them fairy tales of handsome princes in grand carriages." He started making a French braid, pulling it snug and smooth.

"Have you heard from them?"

Andy shook his head, securing the end of the braid with a hair tie. "No. They're in Dallas. The city was hit shortly after San Antonio. Last I heard, they made Love airport an evacuation center. I'm putting them firmly in my mind's eye as being safely there. It's partly how I keep myself going."

Emma sighed, wondering about her mother and siblings, tears filling her eyes. "How else? You said partly."

Andy looked over the top of Emma's head and made eye contact in the mirror. "Knowing that humans will survive. Maybe I'll even be one of the lucky ones—but if I'm not, some of my friends are." He smiled as her eyes cleared. "Now I can go make myself presentable. See you in a few?"

Emma nodded and grabbed her makeup, smoothing on some base to bring color back to her face, mascara, a little eyeliner. She sipped some tea and stood, steady again.

The conference room was packed, but one of the security sergeants gave up his seat for her. Drs. Lowe and Mehra entered and stood in the front of the room. Andy snuck in behind them and made his way to stand near Emma. When Dr. Lowe cleared his throat, the room became silent.

"I have been in contact with Dr. Goodman in Cheyenne. Central command can no longer supply two facilities." Many started talking at once, too many to clearly hear anyone, and Lowe held up his hand. "No more food or fuel is coming."

Several stood and shouted. Again, Lowe held up his hand, and the din quieted.

"Choppers are arriving today to evacuate us. They will be here by noon. Take only what you need. There will be no way to return. As you know, the facility has a failsafe. If generators do not kick in within four hours, a bomb will be set off to destroy all the dangerous samples stored here. We cannot take the samples. If the vaccine work can be safely stored for transport, then it can come along, but no live viruses, toxins, or other potentially dangerous material can be transported. Each of you can bring forty pounds of materials and possessions with you. Go pack; you have four hours."

Emma turned to Andy. "My printouts—before the Internet went out. How to make penicillin and sulfa drugs, evidence-based herbal therapies … I have over three hundred pounds of paper."

"Em, I don't have any clothes worth keeping. You can have my forty pounds. Let's pack."

Andy and Pat led the way through the throng. Decker and the rest of the crew met her outside.

Decker spoke up. "Rankin's fever broke; they'll be able to release him in time. I'll get his and Gus's gear."

For the next few hours, tempers flared as fights over what could go and what couldn't, but by noon, the facility was empty of its over four hundred inhabitants. As the sun summited the sky, the Chinooks landed, ready for loading. Emma stood with her group, thinking of Peter and no way to leave word. She remembered college and the dorms, their dinner group ... and if someone needed something, they'd leave a sticky note inside a cabinet door.

Emma stood stock still, watching the next chopper approach. *The kitchen—I could leave a message there.* She forced her way between Pat and Decker, jogging between those in line and moving back to the house. It had been a normal-looking house from the outside, and it held a kitchen. Emma didn't have a pen or paper. Pulling out drawers, she found a paring knife. She opened a cabinet and began to carve.

"Doc, we gotta go! They're loading!" Pat and Decker stood in the doorway, horrified how they'd let her slip away from them for even a minute.

"Just a second! I have to leave a message for Peter." Thus far, she'd carved P—CHEYE, but Decker grabbed her off the counter and threw her over his shoulder. Emma flailed and dropped the knife. "Wait! It's not—" but they were running from the house and past the people in line. Decker half lowered and half tossed his charge into the helicopter next to Andy and then stepped in himself, keeping a hand under her arm until they were well above the ground. *I couldn't warn him about the bomb*, Emma fretted as they flew over what was Atlanta.

Peter and Sara heard the helicopters when they stopped for lunch less than ten miles from Atlanta. More and more areas were blocked with cars, and some areas looked like deliberate barricades that no longer served a purpose. Even getting the bike through could be tricky at times. Peter had to rely on his almost eidetic memory to reach their destination, but not all roads still bore signs. He watched the choppers and wondered if he should be following them, the goose bumps on his arms telling him that they were a bad sign. Refueling would have to wait. They should have enough to find the facility; he'd worry about gas when he got there.

The house was in a suburb near the botanical gardens. Once they reached the city, Peter realized that the helicopters were gone, and he felt his stomach tighten. In midafternoon, they found the house. Empty. The doors were open, and it was obvious that a military group had been there. Base wires for communications and computers covered several of the second-story walls. In the basement was a door with a coded keypad, now blank and black. They pounded just in case but didn't hear a sound. Sara started foraging in the kitchen.

"Peter," she called.

He smiled at the uneven scratch marks on the inside of the cabinet door. Even doing this, her handwriting was terrible, but he could decipher the letters. Emma had remembered their college dinner club.

"Where do you think *Cheye* is?"

"Cheyenne, most likely," came a deep voice behind them. Peter turned and drew his pistol. He'd been practicing and was a fast draw, but there was not a chance against the three rifles pointed at him by men in uniform. Memories of the fake army made his jaw clench.

"Sara, get behind me," Peter ordered.

"But, Peter, I think these are *real* army men," Sara piped up. "Their shirts are tucked in." Peter realized that she was right. These four looked tired, with dirt on their clothes and sweat, but they were neat, their hair slicked down or close cropped, their shirts tucked in and boots wiped down. What they'd seen of the fake army had looked dirty and slovenly.

"Emma's Peter?" the big man with the deep voice asked.

Peter smiled and lowered his gun, and the three with the rifles did the same. Peter liked being thought of as "Emma's Peter."

"Well, it looks like they bugged out, but I'll be happy to get you to her." Gus extended his hand. "Angus McLeod—just call me Gus."

Peter clapped it, and Sara held out her own.

"And I'm Sara."

Gus smiled and shook her hand, as well.

Godfrey cleared his throat. "Sir, we don't know how much time—-"

Gus nodded. "Come on. We have to find a place to settle in for the night." Gus gestured for them to follow.

"Why don't we stay here? There's a good attic space," Peter pointed out.

"Because some time in the next minutes to hours, this building and all beneath it will explode, leaving a crater the size of a football field," Gus explained as he ushered them out.

"Oh." Peter picked up his pace, guiding Sara in front of him.

"Sorry, ma'am, there were just too many in there." Hitchins seemed embarrassed.

Charlene knew the huge warehouse store was a long shot, either picked over or infested, but she'd hoped. The worst part was that three of the group members were bitten.

"If we can get in there, there are still aisles of canned food, gardening supplies, paper, pens. We did get some batteries near the entrance."

"Thank you for trying. We'll need to look elsewhere for supplies." Charlene sat on her porch, her unofficial mayoral office, looking out at those wanting to talk to her.

The neighboring housing complexes and all stores within ten miles were picked clean. They hadn't seen a squirrel in a week, and where deer used to come up to porches for food, they were nowhere to be found. Elysian Heights now held over three thousand five hundred people, and it had a dwindling food supply. Some of the other nearby minitowns had withdrawn to the coast, where the military shelters were set up. At least on the coast, people could get seaweed and fish. Charlene raised her brow and looked at the next person.

"Mayor Dillon, I just want to start by sayin' how much we appreciate you takin' us in. We couldn't have made it to the coast, not with Pa's heart." The woman in her thirties looked vaguely familiar.

"I'm just glad I can be here to help." Charlene smiled back. The smile had become a little more forced of late, but she did her duty and put it on. "How can I help you now?"

"I've been to Brad the pharmacist already, and they don't have any more diuretics—the medicines that makes Pa, well, pee, so that it puts less pressure on his heart. Are any of the searchers looking for medicines or just food?" The woman looked uncomfortable asking, like she wanted too much.

"They look for everything. But I'll make sure they look for …?" Charlene prompted.

"Furosemide. They give it to horses too, so you might find it in a tack shop." The woman smiled in relief, her request delivered.

Most of the people who came to the porch were like this woman, asking if Charlene was aware of some medicine, some supply needed for a family member. Sometimes Charlene felt overwhelmed by it all, but she understood their need to ask. Every day was a miracle, and they looked for one more. She wondered at herself sitting in this position, trying to protect people from the terror the world had become. *If not me, then who?* she asked herself, waving up the next person.

Dr. Draeger's new clinic took up most of the first floor of the house next to the church. Auntie insisted that Austin, Trevor, and Clarence room above it because it was better for emergencies. Austin knew as soon as he looked at Charles that the wound needed to be reopened, and he gave Charles an antibiotic to take until all the needed equipment could be found or modified. Clarence did a good job getting the bullet out of Charles's shoulder, but a bit of something must have remained to allow it to fester. They lacked any anesthetic, and no one had seen any beer or liquor for days, so Charles would need to literally bite the bullet for pain. A clean plastic handle would have to do.

Austin opened the wound tract while his brother pinned Charles to the table. There was some drainage, mildly purulent with some odor, but left much longer, it likely would have eaten into the bone.

"Turn over; I need to look at the other side," the doctor commanded.

Charles's eyes swam and did as he was asked, taking a few deep breaths before again biting down on the plastic, already lined with his teeth marks. The skin had mostly healed, forcing Austin to open it back up with his knife. He rinsed the wound with rubbing alcohol and discovered the problem—a small piece of fabric still in the bullet tract. The vials no one recognized the names of from the doctor's office in Philadelphia proved to be gold, as Austin put it. Ceftriaxone and clindamycin, potent antibiotics he would use on the man responsible for finding them.

Charles passed out before the procedure was finished. Once Austin confirmed that the packing went all the way through, he sewed up one side. When Charles woke, Austin sat so that the two men could look eye to eye.

"I know you need to be useful," Austin said, "but you need to keep that arm still for the next three to four days for it to start to heal. You're to come back every day for me to look at it and for your antibiotics. Understood?"

Charles tasted plastic bits in his mouth, which felt like parchment. "*Oui*," he replied and nodded, beginning to sit up.

"French, that's the accent!" Trevor gave Charles a hand.

"Canadian—Quebecois." Charles felt the need to correct them.

"I am sure at some point we will get the story on how you ended up here. But it looks like I've got a line of patients waiting."

Toya met Charles in the waiting room and helped him to the street and into the sun.

"You look almost as bad as when you got here." Toya's strong body moved him along and back toward the house with his room. It took a minute to realize where they were heading.

Charles forced them to stop. "No, I promised Stokes—"

"I'll let him know what you've been through. I'm sure he'll give you a day." Toya urged him along.

Charles wouldn't budge, his shoulder aching but his head clearing as the intensity reduced to a throbbing. He had become used to the pain and could tolerate it if he had to. "No, if I lie in bed, I'll 'urt more. Stokes will 'elp distract me, I'll let 'im know what Dr. Draeger said about not moving my arm for three or four days and let 'im decide."

"Ugh!" Toya pulled away. "Why do men always need to be so damn stubborn!"

Charles tried to shrug and stopped. "We are what we 'ave to be."

Toya narrowed her eyes and took up his right arm, more roughly this time, turning toward the church where Stokes and Auntie had their "office."

"Fine, but I'm staying until you tell him." Charles was grateful for the support.

Auntie and Stokes had similar responses to Toya's original one, convincing Charles that he did indeed look like shit.

"I can be weak and 'elpless in my room or weak and 'elpful 'ere. Please allow me to be 'elpful." He thankfully sank onto one of the pews.

Stokes looked him over for a moment and then grinned. "Hell, I'll let you do the paperwork. Duty rosters for later this week. Last week's are in this notebook. The list of the new people and what they may be able to do is folded in the back of it. Auntie will let you know who shouldn't work together. Toya, let's see those lobster cages the retrieval team found and see what we can do with them."

Charles moved to the office and sat on the chair, careful not to lean on his left arm. He opened the notebook and laid out the pages before him, names swimming together until he rubbed his eyes and let them settle. Stokes had surprisingly neat handwriting, small block letters typical of a draftsman.

"He was going to be an architect," Auntie commented over her sewing, her arthritic hands still nimble enough to repair the tears in someone's shirt.

"Pardon?" Charles looked up. He'd never thought of Stokes as anything but a smart gang member, something he had never realized could exist until he was here and living among them. The main difference between Stokes's life and his own was the acceptance of violence, both in its commission by you and against you.

"Before his ma had her third strike and went back to prison for good, he would be on the computers at school learning how to design and build things. When she went upstate, he put away his drawings and notebooks and went to talk to Duke. It near broke his math teacher's heart when Stokes quit school to join the gang. Broke mine too, but I knew why he done it." Auntie broke into a mischievous smile.

"And what is the smile about?" Charles asked, rearranging the papers into an order he could use.

"Two things. It took the world going crazy for my Stokes to go from being a destroyer to being a builder of worlds." Auntie started humming "He's Got the Whole World in His Hands."

"And the second?" Charles prompted.

"Now that that boy's got you doin' them rosters, he ain't never touchin' them again." Auntie went back to humming but looked at Charles over her sewing.

Charles groaned and started to write.

Elsie breathed a sigh as the Chinook hovered above the Cheyenne site. She'd appreciated the Canadian hospitality, but she needed to be on home soil where she could make a difference. Marsha had a difficult time keeping the girls settled. In their excitement, Meagan kept leaning over Press Secretary Zimburg, who seemed uncomfortable around children. Although he never said a word, his face betrayed his feelings. This final leg had been the hardest, flying over abandoned towns, burned fields, and desperate people waving at them, hoping for rescue.

They landed on the elevated pad protected by thick wire on top of stone walls. The greeter was a pleasant woman in army fatigues. With the noise from the rotors, she waved them along and down a flight of steps to an open hallway.

"Good afternoon. I'm Sergeant LeStrange, and I will be coordinating your quarantine and then room assignments. You will be taken in groups of three to medical, where you will be examined and given a quarantine tag. There are absolutely no exceptions to quarantine; I do not care if you have been bitten three times and survived. If you have a fever or a bite, you will be placed in an isolation room instead of the group rooms. Men and women will be separated; children under twelve can stay with a parent of opposite gender. Any questions?" Hearing none, she looked down at a clipboard and held a pen ready. "As I say your name, please step forward. Secretary Elisandra Hudson, Secretary James Zimburg, Staff Sergeant Marsha McLeod."

The three stepped forward as asked, Miranda and Meagan holding Marsha's hands. LeStrange looked down.

"Ah, they must be Miranda McLeod and Meagan McLeod."

Marsha nodded.

"I guess the five of you can proceed to medical."

Another armed woman in fatigues with a sewn-on badge reading "Private A. Alfonse" gestured, and they followed down another white hall. Behind them, LeStrange's voice bellowed out, "Sammy Jo Taylor, Edgar Allen, Bob Dickson."

Marsha and her girls were ushered into a small, clinical room and given examination gowns.

"You will need to remove all clothing for the examination," Private Alfonse instructed. The door shut, and Marsha got the girls undressed and then herself. The harried woman who entered wore the requisite white coat, asked minimal questions, and examined every inch of their skin. The girls couldn't help giggling through most of it. When she looked at Marsha's lower stomach, she looked up. Marsha simply nodded, and the doctor continued.

"Good." The doctor seemed satisfied and handed Marsha three small blue cards. "Get dressed and then open the door. You will be escorted to the women's quarantine." The doctor exited and closed the door behind her.

"Will there be books and toys there?" Miranda asked.

"I don't know," Marsha answered, helping her with her shoelaces.

Once dressed, they were led to a large room with twenty bunks and a window above them. Stairs were built along the far wall ending in a solid-looking door at the top. Elsie waved them over, and they settled in. Miranda found a box with books and carried one over to Meagan to read to her. Marsha circled the room, realizing that she was acting like a she-wolf examining the den. All vents were made of tight, thick steel, securely sealed into the wall. Tapping on the walls produced a solid thud all around, likely plaster backed onto stone or brick. The door seals were tight. Satisfied, she returned to her cot where Elsie had watched the proceedings with interest.

"Are we secure, Staff Sergeant?"

Marsha appreciated that Elsie refrained from any sarcasm. "We are, Madam Secretary," Marsha replied.

"Good. Relax, and get some real sleep," Elsie commanded.

"I will when—" Marsha realized that the girls had already nodded off in each other's arms, book falling to the side. Like a good mother, she picked up a blanket and spread it over them and then removed her shoes and lay in her own cot, toes over the edge.

"Not made for tall folks like you," Elsie observed, stretching out her five-seven frame.

"Not much is." Marsha yawned. "It's even worse for Gus. He hates to fly on commercial planes, so when we do get a chance to take a vacation, it's mostly car trips."

"My parents used to drive to the national parks. According to my official parks passport, I have been to forty-three of the fifty-nine national parks, and since Pinnacles was added long after I left home, I shouldn't have to count it." Elsie wished she knew where that passport was now. It held no actual value, but a memory went with every stamp. Elsie would have continued, but she realized by Marsha's breathing that she already slept.

Everyone woke when they heard a sharp click. A slot opened near the base of a door, and little boxes were pushed in. Each box contained a hard-boiled egg and a small boiled potato. No one turned down the meal. Elsie wondered if the room was in perpetual low light, but when her watch indicated that they had been in for a full day, the lights brightened, and an announcement came on.

"Please proceed to the stairs. Once in the hallway, there will be a table with your room assignments." Marsha found the table marked M–P. An envelope gave them a room number and a small map on how to get there.

As they turned down another hall, they saw Sergeant LeStrange with another clipboard. She spoke to another sergeant next to her. "The Atlanta contingent should be arriving soon."

Marsha heard. Atlanta meant Gus, if he'd had time to get there.

The trial took most of the day. The law student, Miguel, did an excellent job presenting the evidence, and Michelina, the defense attorney, looked like she was at least trying. But even so, the jury took less than thirty minutes to find Juan and the three companions guilty. Juan was sentenced to death; the other three would be turned out, immediately. The three watched the sun creep down in the sky, all begging to stay for the night and to leave in the morning. There was no sign of sympathy as the convicts were handed a knife and their packs with a couple of cans of tuna and beans and a blanket. They were forced past the outer gate by gunpoint. No one cringed when distant screams rang through the air after sunset.

Shortly after dawn, Juan was marched to the wall, where his original attack on Guillermo took place. "A jury has convicted you to die for treason. Have you any last words?" Guillermo asked.

Juan swallowed, looking around those assembled. He tried to speak but could not; his mouth too dry. Guillermo placed a hood over Juan's head and stepped away, raising his sword. The firing squad stood in attention. "Ready!" The rifles came up. "Aim!" The rifles were cocked. "Fire!" Guillermo said, dropping his sword. Juan's body jerked and flailed, falling onto the sheets of plastic spread under and around him. Those on the sides moved in to raise the plastic edges and keep the blood from falling to the ground—Mitchell's idea. They could roll him and all his blood up in one nice package to take far from the compound.

Mitchell himself was in town, smiling and running for mayor. He would face Juan Carlos and a woman from Chichimila named Carlita. Carlita had been suspicious of Guillermo's army doing so much and had become increasingly hostile to Guillermo over the last few days. Guillermo appreciated her candor in some ways, but he knew that she would prove difficult to work with, so he quietly let it be known that he preferred the other two. Speeches were given later in the afternoon. Mitchell rose to the podium first.

"*Mi español es mal*," he began, to many laughs and cheers. "*Sino mi corazón es pura*."

Guillermo had to give it to the engineer for trying, and in his native language, Mitchell could prove an eloquent speaker, but his Spanish made native speakers cringe. Juan Carlos followed. He spoke simply, as a farmer, as a survivor who has lost a spouse and a child, bringing cheers and tears to the eyes of many. Carlita was fiery, talking of reclaiming their lands, but the people were still too scared. She received only mild applause.

Election day was made a feast day. They had butchered a cow three days earlier, collecting the blood and all the parts. Miralda made blood pudding, and the meat was aged under close observation for a few days to tenderize. It would still mostly be for stew, but the candidates, Guillermo, and a few others who had shown bravery in the coup would get a small steak, as well. Music played through the day as, one by one, all those age twelve and up were checked off on the census and given a ballot. By 3:00 p.m., all votes had been cast, and by 5:00 p.m., all votes had been tallied and recounted to be sure. Guillermo stood by the central fountain with the three candidates. He thanked Carlita for her service; she had come in third. Guillermo was surprised at how close the count was between the other two, and he had underestimated the engineer's popularity, but it was Juan Carlos by seventeen votes who carried the day.

The farmer wept and thanked everyone. He turned to Mitchell and immediately put him in charge of energy.

"I know nothing of how to make the lights work," Juan Carlos explained in broken English and in Spanish, which made those nearby cheer as he and Mitchell shook hands. Guillermo suddenly felt a load lifted from his back. Food and energy were no longer his problems. He smiled and danced with a dozen girls around the square.

CHAPTER 10

April 29–May 1; Z Days 20–22

"Ma'am, jeep approaching."

Charlene looked up and followed Kurt to the wall and up the observation tower ladder. Three weeks ago, she would have had to stop and catch her breath, her knees in revolt. Now the climb was easy. The forced diet and exercise had dropped almost twenty-five pounds from her once plump, forty-eight-year-old frame. She took the binoculars from Kurt and looked at the approaching vehicles: a jeep with four men, a child, and a man on a motorcycle. The men in the jeep were wearing fatigues; the one on the bike was in jeans and a jacket. They stopped a hundred feet from the gate, turning off their engines. The biggest of the army men, who sported a silver leaf on his shoulder, got out and stood in front of the jeep, hands out.

"Hello. We just need safe lodging for the night." Gus's deep voice carried across the lawn and up.

"What have you got to trade?" Charlene answered. She was certainly not giving anything away these days.

"I'm afraid—" Gus began.

The young one on the bike suddenly jumped in. "We've got canned tuna, some of these"—he fanned out four very familiar-looking candy bar wrappers—"and coffee."

Charlene found her visceral response to seeing chocolate and coffee to be the closest thing she'd had to an orgasm in over a month.

"OK. We have a contained guesthouse. You won't be free to move around the town, and you'll need to surrender your weapons. You have my word that you'll have them back when you leave tomorrow," Charlene replied, her mouth already watering over the chocolate.

Lieutenant Godfrey straightened up. "We can't—"

Gus gestured him silent. "I will accept your word," Gus replied.

Kurt hit a button, and the gate opened.

"You have power?" Peter called up to her.

"For essential things, yes." Charlene replied. "Turn the jeep to the left, and go down five houses. Sylvia will meet you there."

Gus and company did as told, handing the chocolate and coffee over to Sylvia, who then let them into the house. Cots with blankets had been set up throughout the ground floor. The windows were shuttered on both sides, and a young man collected their weapons, placed them into large plastic containers, and duct taped them closed. Peter made a sound when they took the katana, but he allowed it. On pieces of tape on the tops and sides of the containers, the young man wrote their names. He did a quick search, checking them for concealed weapons and knives over four inches long, taking Sara's kitchen knife.

The young man nodded to the kitchen. "There are beans and rice kept in double bins. We think we've gotten all the zrats, but just in case, please return all food to their storage boxes. There are extra bins to use for your own food while you're here; please do not take any of ours with you. In the bathroom, there are instructions on using the composting toilet. Clean water is in the kitchen in the covered buckets; please use the ladle to take it out. The stove is gas and does work; please use it sparingly, and cook in only one pot. If you cook the rice first, then put the beans in the last five minutes or so—that works best. There are clean rags in the bathroom and some water you can use to wash up. It's not purified, so don't try to drink it. I'll be back in the morning to let you out."

Gus thanked him. The young man went to the door, knocked, waited while a peephole opened, and spoke briefly to the person on the other side. The door opened, and the young man slipped out, and then they heard the lock behind him. Gus realized that he'd never heard the young man's name.

"Coffee and chocolate—who'd have thought those things could become the most valuable of trade goods?" Godfrey sat down on a cot and stretched his neck.

"When I saw them and realized how much I missed them," Peter replied. "The candy bars are also great energy bars."

"You wouldn't happen to have any soda, would you?" Private Smythe asked longingly. He was about nineteen and thin as a rail, probably even before all this.

"Naw, too heavy, too much jostling. Some of the best places to forage now are vending machines in waiting rooms—car showrooms, mechanics, even some doctors' offices. Grocery and convenience stores are already pretty cleared out." Peter grinned at Sara. "And if you can hold your breath against the smell, some foods that don't really require refrigeration are OK too."

Gus regarded the two and was reminded of how easy he'd had it since the outbreak. He'd gotten a cushy assignment protecting the doc, and though he'd had less food than normal, he had never needed to miss a meal.

Peter found himself as the cook. There weren't any spices, so he pulled some salt and pepper packets they'd picked up along the way. In looking at the food, it would likely be breakfast, as well. He found some cornmeal in a bin in the back and thought he could make tortillas, so at least the beans and rice could be packaged differently. Peter was not going to complain and would hit anyone over the head with a frying pan, including the big guy, who did.

"Better than the MREs," Private Sheldon spoke up, cleaning the bottom of his plate. Peter cooked; he would not clean up, as well.

"Unfortunately, Mr. Saitou, you have already proven yourself too good of a cook with few ingredients for anyone else to attempt it," Gus complimented as best he knew.

"I'm OK with the cooking, as long as I don't have to do the dishes." Peter smiled in his reply. Gus only needed to jerk his chin to the privates and indicate the kitchen, and they promptly jumped up and took care of that, not that there was much left to clean. Peter heard the grunts starting outside, followed by rifle reports, and jerked around.

"It seems they have the pattern down," Godfrey reassured him. "We saw something similar along the route at an old airport. If the Zs or Thinkers concentrate too much on one spot, they'll gun them down. Not enough ammo to kill them all, so they keep them at bay all night."

Peter nodded, understanding but not completely reassured. He'd had a decent look at the defenses, and they appeared to do a good job. Better than the community in Raleigh.

"The problem comes when it's not Zs, but raiders made to look like the army," Peter said.

Gus stiffened. "There are people pretending to be—" He stopped and looked at Sara. "That's what you meant when you said I was a *real* army man. You've seen them."

Peter and Sara nodded and explained what happened in Raleigh. Godfrey and Gus became visibly upset.

"This will completely undermine the peoples' trust—what's left of it." Godfrey swore as they heard gunfire to the north.

"We'll warn this group and anyone else we see," Gus said. "When we can get to a radio, we'll need to get a message out. This group is very organized; they may have radios we can use and let Cheyenne know we're OK."

When dawn arrived, it was the woman from the wall who greeted them through the slat in the door, introducing herself. She heard their request and accepted another two candy bars in trade for the message. Gus wondered how many Peter had tucked away in that saddlebag.

"Have your breakfast. I'll see if I can get a response," Charlene instructed, and the slat closed.

Peter doubted that any Mexican would have accepted his version of tortillas, but they came out better than expected, loaded with rice, beans, and a side of tuna. While the privates cleaned up, the door to town opened. Charlene stood with a wagon loaded with their bins of weapons next to her.

"Arm yourselves, and get up the tower. I need you to see something," she directed. Charlene did not turn to make sure; she simply assumed the others would obey. The men tore off the tape and grabbed their guns, Peter tucked the katana into its normal spot in the backpack, and Sara secured her knife and followed. Charlene had mounted a small telescope, pointed toward I-75. She indicated the scope, and Gus stooped down to take a look. He saw jeeps, trucks with brown tarps, and some cars. The men in the trucks wore ratty fatigues. Gus's jaw clenched.

"No real army band would set up a convoy like that." Gus glowered at the distance, not able to see with the naked eye.

Sara stood on tiptoe and looked through the finder. Her voice tried to sound brave, but the quaver gave away her fear. "That's them," she confirmed.

Peter took his turn. Staring at the lines, he stopped, finding one particular man in the truck.

"*Butch.*" Peter spat the name out like a curse word.

"You know one of them?" Charlene spoke before Gus could.

"Bastard stole my pack and my getaway boat in Virginia. I might have made it to Atlanta in time if it weren't for him." Peter ground his teeth, and then he saw Sara looking at the ground, about to sneak away. Peter caught her shoulder. "*His* fault, not yours." He didn't let go until she made eye contact and gave a half smile.

"What was their plan before?" Gus asked.

Peter and Sara described how the town greeted them, opening the gates, and what they heard after. Gus nodded and looked at Charlene.

"We can use that, but you won't like it." Gus outlined his plan. He was right; Charlene didn't like it, but with the firepower of that group, she couldn't see an alternative. The alarm bells would tip off the raiders, so Kurt organized getting the message from house to house. Charlene directed that the children and elderly should wait in the storm cellars, and everyone else should grab a gun and hide it.

"How well can you shoot?" Gus asked Peter.

"I earned a medal at summer camp with the pellet rifle. I've gotten used to this thing." Peter patted his revolver. "I've shot a bunch of Zs and a couple of Thinkers."

"Have you ever shot another human?" Gus asked.

Peter shook his head and thought back to Raleigh. "No, but with this group, I can start."

That was good enough for Gus. He couldn't risk this Butch recognizing Peter in the crowd, so Gus placed Peter lying in a tower as a sniper with Godfrey. He, Smythe, and Sheldon were distributed around the main entrance, also lying in wait. Sara would go to the cellars with the other children.

"Don't come out until the shooting stops," Peter instructed her as Charlene led her down the ladder and into the little "town." Peter went to his assigned tower, taking in what he could. The subdivision was built around a driving range, putting green, and nine-hole golf course with a pond and a large building next to a large swimming pool. Overall, it was bigger than he'd thought. The golf course was divided for sheep grazing, cow grazing, and wheat. There were gardens in almost all the green spaces, with homemade chicken coops in the yards that he could see. In Raleigh, people had set up to wait for rescue; here, they had renewed civilization. He rightly guessed they had a town council.

Peter watched the main tower folks start shouting as the convoy approached, whooping and hollering as if they felt relieved. The outer gates opened, and the convoy started in. The "army" had to turn to travel to the inner gate, eight houses down, which stayed closed, a truck across the entrance. The people poured out of the small side gate, cheering and waving, guns carefully tucked behind jackets on this warm morning.

Charlene stepped up to the main tower, smiling her warmest Southern belle smile and waving herself with a small fan in her best Scarlett O'Hara impersonation. "Good morning, gentlemen! Are y'all a sight for sore eyes!"

One of the raiders stood in the fifth jeep, wearing a lieutenant's silver bar, and called back to Charlene. "Yes, well, ma'am. We need you to move that truck so we can come in. These men have been battling the Zs and need some refreshment and rest, if you could be so obliged?" He affected a Southern accent but sounded more like someone from a bad Western or pretending to be Chuck Yeager.

"Well, sir, your men are welcome in town; they just need to come through these side gates. Your vehicles need to stay out here. We have children and livestock in the streets and would not like you to accidentally harm one." Charlene smiled her warm smile back at him, fanning just a little faster.

"Ma'am," the "lieutenant" said a little more stiffly. "I'm afraid I must *insist*." The tarp came off of one of the trucks as a man spun a high-powered Minimi assault rifle. Gus recognized the weapon and knew it could fire up to one thousand rounds per minute. He didn't let the gunner get off a single shot. Gus's rifle report echoed through the camp. The townspeople drew their weapons, and another twenty raiders went down. The vehicles in the back threw into reverse too late as the gates slammed shut, effectively boxing them in.

Charlene kept her pistol's bead on the "lieutenant" and smiled. "Now, do you boys just want to put down your weapons, or do all of you want to die?"

The head of the raiders looked at the towers, now with snipers evident with weapons pointed at him and his men. He held his hands to his side and slowly unclipped his pistol, taking it out and laying it on the ground before kneeling with hands on his head. The townsfolk swooped in to the men, tying them with anything available, pulling guns out of reach. Charlene kept her smile fixed in place and glanced down at Gus.

"Well, we have them captured. What do we do with them?"

Gus stood, securing his rifle. "I have no idea," he replied.

The defenders of Elysian Heights wasted no time in finding rope and other ways to tie their captives, lining them up in the midway between the walls and removing the weapons and vehicles. Peter made sure that Butch could see him with rifle in plain view.

"I dare you to give me an excuse," Peter whispered to himself, but he already felt his anger abating. It wasn't in his nature to kill in cold blood or simply for revenge. When some of the captives started to move and one jumped up to run, Peter planted rounds in front of him, and he quickly dropped back to the ground. Smythe took out the runner.

A few hours later, Gus returned. He brought water, a toaster tart—likely from Peter's own saddlebag—and news. "Command is sending a colonel from Fort Knox to take custody. The town gets to keep half the food, fuel, and vehicles and a third of the weapons and ammo. We're to go along as part of the escort and then will make our way from there to Saint Louis, where they're sending supplies up to Cheyenne. We should be able to get a transport from there. I did not mention that two of the group would be civilians."

"Will that be a problem?" Peter looked across the town at Sara playing with some other children. He was relieved that for a few hours she could be a kid.

"I don't know yet. I promised to get you to Emma, and I will. If it means we strike out on our own, so be it. Just try to keep quiet, and let me do the talking," Gus advised.

"What time?" Peter asked, looking at the early afternoon sun.

"Later this afternoon, but it means another night here. Charlene and the town council are deciding where to put the prisoners. A lot just want to leave them where they are, some want to put them in the quarantine house, but that's hard to supervise and may be needed for the colonel's men." As it was, the prisoners below had been yelling for a bathroom, food, and water. The day was heating up into the mid-eighties, and it was humid. Peter and the others told them to piss where they sat. No matter what they had done, Charlene would not torture them and Peter knew someone would need to bring them water soon. As if on cue, a group of men with buckets and ladles proceeded from the gate. One ladle of water over the head, the other held to the mouth. From the glare in the townsfolks' eyes, the fake army men knew better than to ask anything more. Peter turned his back on the men below and instead looked over the town. With places like this, the world could survive. His vision ranged to the hills and beyond. They needed thicker walls, but two sets with some way to quarantine between had been a good idea.

They needed more sources of power. The town had some solar panels and a couple of small wind turbines. Somewhere they must have propane tanks to supply the stoves and a couple of electric generators powered by diesel or gasoline. He'd read about a horizontal windmill being built in France a few years ago that could power twenty or more houses and the smaller Archimedes-style out of Rotterdam could produce enough for another four or five. Suddenly, Peter realized that Gus was snapping his fingers in front of his face.

"Sorry, I was thinking about how to get more power, make it safer, better in some ways."

"I was saying that you can take a break. Walk around; the town has some great ideas we can bring to others, and if you can improve on them, even better." Gus took over the spot on the tower, nodding his dismissal.

Peter caught Charlene as much as found her behind a house with a sign marking it as Town Council. She dragged on a cigarette.

"I quit twenty-seven years ago when I was pregnant with Kevin, my oldest. I found a pack clearing out one of the houses, tucked under a loose floorboard. Probably some teenager's. I opened the pack and lit one like I'd never quit. I've been hoarding the few in it, and after this morning, I needed one." She took one last puff and blew the smoke out slowly, watching it rise before dropping the butt and snuffing it out with her boot. "How can I help you?"

"I'd like a tour. I'm an engineer; I even specialize in alternative energy sources, and I wanted to see if I could trade ideas. You've done an amazing job. For humans to survive, we need to replicate it, get people supplied with the knowledge of how to sustain themselves." Peter allowed his respect and appreciation to show in his face and voice.

Charlene lapped it up like a kitten and practically purred out her response. "Well, it wasn't just me. We have a no-work-no-eat policy. I did remember something from all those Colonial history classes my children and I took. Even the oldest help make rope or chop vegetables in the kitchen."

They went to the kitchen first. What had once been the community clubhouse was now the community kitchen, cafeteria, and general meeting area. A schedule was posted on the door as to when people were to come for meals. Breakfast appeared open, but lunch and dinner had shifts based on the type of work.

"This way, the laborers get a little more food without the others seeing the disparity. Some of the teachers and others think it's unfair that a person who's building and carrying rocks and other heavy materials all day should get more food." Charlene shook her head.

They headed into the kitchen, which held two industrial-sized stoves with additional tubing connected to the wall, with a similar configuration for one of the wall ovens, all now at work making bread. It smelled wonderful, but it made Peter mindful of the zrats.

"We boil the dough first and then bake it. Everything comes out more like bagels that way, but after the first couple of days, no one complained. The bread is dense and fills you up."

"How do you power them?" Peter noted that they looked to be gas appliances.

"Ah." Charlene grinned. "Sometimes, the oldest ways are best."

Just outside the kitchen stood a huge pile of logs and an unusual double-barreled contraption. Peter's jaw dropped. They'd built an industrial-sized gasifier. Four men worked with the wood and coals, keeping things running smoothly.

"Hitchins, our guy that built it, was part of a project in DeKalb County to produce gas from waste; he's working on incorporating that into the design. He'll be around somewhere."

They moved on to the houses, most converted into dorm-style sleeping quarters. If the families that owned the houses had stayed, they kept a floor to themselves.

"How many people are here?" Peter already realized that there were more than he'd thought.

"Without your friends and the prisoners? Three thousand, six hundred and eighty-four with three women ready to go into labor at any time." Charlene kept her voice even.

Peter couldn't help but whistle and turn toward the fields where the golf course was.

"Yeah, I know." Charlene kept her voice down. "We won't have enough resources to get all the way through summer, let alone winter. We have foragers and hunters, but they're going farther afield and starting to meet up with other towns like this. We know there are food warehouses nearer the city, but they are dark and crawling with zrats and Zs. Anything not in cans would be compromised, but what's in those cans could get us through the winter."

"For the long run, you need farming." Peter looked around.

"And a way to protect the fields. We tried to plant outside the walls a week ago, and those damn zrats ate up every seed we put in the ground." Charlene felt disgusted at the waste. "We've been using the small field inside the walls to set up fodder for the cows and sheep. Grass can grow until November around here, but even with short winters, we'll need something."

Peter's mind went back to the stairwell at the power plant. "To get into the warehouse, you need to light the interior really brightly. If you can find a way to power and transport floodlights, that would force them back and give you a way to get in and out." Peter started working through an idea, stringing car halogen headlights together. "Let me talk to your Hitchins guy tonight and run some ideas by him."

Charlene checked her watch. "I'll make sure I introduce you. The other group should be getting here soon. I'll be at the gate." She turned and left.

"Peter!" a familiar squealing voice called out. She ran to him, taking his hand and twirling underneath it, showing off the sundress someone found for her. "They have a real library and bikes. They're nicer here than that other place." Sara smiled, swinging his arm.

"That other place took us in and gave you medicine. Always be thankful for that," Peter reminded her.

"Yeah, I am." Sara looked down at her sneakers. "And I am sad about what happened to them. But they did try to make you stay, and they made me go to the school where I already knew that stuff. I saw the chalkboard here, and they were being taught how to set up a solar oven."

That made Peter smile. Charlene even made the schoolwork practical. Though he needed to move on, he felt a pull to stay. He looked down at Sara.

"Would you like to stay?" Peter asked slowly.

"Only if you do." She let go of his hand and stared up at him.

"You know I won't be," Peter reminded her.

"Then I'm going too." She grabbed his hand again, and they walked back to the tower. Peter climbed up next to Gus and sat, Sara tucking in between them despite the day's heat.

"Ideas?" Gus asked.

"Several. They've got a gasogene engine—also called a gasifier. It takes wood and makes it into carbon gas for cooking and heating."

"Will that work in other places?" Gus sounded interested.

"If they have a good source of wood. Look at Easter Island; once you clear a forest, it doesn't come back very easily. It does give a good temporary source while other stuff is being built." Peter smiled. "The problem is getting people to see that they need to build the next stage while the first one is still there."

Gus snorted. "That requires people to think ahead."

Peter became more solemn. "The only way to see this through is to think ahead. The world is a game of chess, and we must anticipate the problems to be able to solve them before they arise."

"But unlike chess, the world does not have any set rules." Gus looked down at the prisoners tied in the line. Those without hats were getting sunburned. They had stopped bothering to call out. Some moaned. When the wind hit wrong, the stench of human waste was already nauseating.

"Well, there's physics, and no one gets to break those laws." Peter grinned and then saw that Gus didn't get the joke. "And there's human nature. We've seen the bad"—he gestured to the men below—"and the good." He gestured to those behind him in town. "And bad is often easier to predict. Their goals are more direct and tangible." His eyes lit on Butch, leaning against the man next to him. "We just need to recognize the bad and not somehow think he'll change or have some miraculous epiphany."

"You have a very negative view of humanity." Gus looked at Peter more closely. He'd thought Peter would be more like Emma, eternally optimistic, but instead he saw a pragmatist, and someone beginning to tend toward the cynical. The man had already covered over eight hundred miles and would need to cover two thousand more to get to his goal.

Peter kept his eyes on Butch. "Yeah, it got that way a few weeks ago."

Gus thought of Marsha and the girls. How his daughters would grow up in this world. He'd had fears of "bad men" before. Child molesters, rapists, terrorists. Now the world was dividing as Peter pointed out. How would he keep his girls among the good? He'd seen the bad, and he never wanted to see the ugly, the way Sara heard the people in Raleigh the week before. Gus was also glad that Peter and Sara had escaped, not just for their sakes but for the sake of those behind him. He rubbed the top of her head.

"Hey!" She laughed and pushed his hand away—or tried to since the hand was half as big as her entire head.

"Look!" Peter called out as those in the other towers did the same. A speck in the sky in the distance and a low rumbling sound came closer. Charlene called from the tower in the front that held the telescope, and Gus nodded.

"Someone will relieve you at six," Gus told Peter as he headed down the ladder.

"He looked sad," Sara observed.

"He was thinking about his family," Peter answered.

"At least he still has family." Sara looked in the distance, bringing up her knees. She'd been strong, stronger than anyone would expect of a ten-year-old. Peter drew her to him, keeping his eyes on the men below, some looking at them curiously, especially Butch.

"I'm your family now, and I'm not going anywhere without you," Peter whispered to her.

"No one can promise that." She looked up at him, her eyes serious.

"I know, but I'll do everything I can to keep it." Peter meant every word. Emma would have to understand.

"I know." Sara smiled and stood to watch the approaching chopper. "It's *huge*." She cupped her hands around her eyes. "It must be a Chinook," she said with authority.

"You must know your helicopters." Peter sounded impressed and took her word for it. The flying hulk approaching had two giant rotors on top and was a third of the length of a football field. He had never realized a helicopter could be that big. And the wind it whipped up outside the wall made everyone dive down for cover until the rotors slowed and finally halted.

"Cool!" Sara scrambled down the ladder to make a run for the entrance. Peter longed to follow her, but he had a task. The prisoners sat upright, jaws jutting out. Butch watched him defiantly. Twenty well-armed men in fatigues exited the Chinook and stood before the gate. Peter couldn't hear what was said, but in a moment, the gate opened, and they entered. The men took up positions around their thirty-three prisoners. Gus and the man who must be the colonel talked, walking down the line of the fake army guarded by the real thing. The senior officers picked fifteen men, including the "lieutenant." These men were untied and rebound in handcuffs and then led out to the Chinook. Five of the army guard got in, as well, and a moment later, the rotors whirled, and the helicopter lifted off.

Sara climbed back up to the tower, breathless with her excitement. "They're taking them to Arnold Air Force Base!" She plopped down next to Peter. "They have a hangar they can use as a prison there. We follow with the rest of them tomorrow. And it *was* a Chinook." Sara was the happiest Peter had ever seen her, even happier than finding the candy bars. Who knew? Give the girl a helicopter, and she'd be thrilled.

Promptly at six, two men climbed the tower to relieve Peter. There were still a couple of hours of daylight, and he needed to eat and find this Hitchins fellow. Peter saw Charlene talking to an extremely thin man wearing a cowboy hat.

"It was hardest getting them to give up the spare batteries, but we allowed them to take a couple more guns. Believe me, Charlene, it will be worth it."

"It sounds like you made a good deal," Peter butted in.

Charlene smiled. "Just the man I was telling you about. Peter Saitou, meet Steven Hitchins." Peter grinned at the thin man and held out his hand. Hitchins had a solid, gripping style of shaking hands, demonstrating that his size masked strength.

Peter launched into ways to get the food and supplies from the warehouses. "If you line five to six car headlights into cages with a charged battery, they would likely stay on for over an hour, four or five such cages would allow enough light to fill the section being cleared to keep the Zs and zrats and any other infected creatures at bay."

"And now we have enough fuel to get us there and back." Hitchins nodded. "I like the idea." He turned back to Charlene. "So do we get to keep him as part of the bargain?"

Peter started, and his face fell.

"No, unfortunately, Mr. Saitou has someplace he needs to be, and it is not here."

Peter felt embarrassed at the sigh of relief that came out.

"Please know you will always be welcome. And you won't need to bring any candy bars next time." Charlene smiled in a truly warm fashion.

Peter took her hand and bowed with a flourish. "Ms. Charlene, you are the truest lady I think I have ever met. I hope we meet again under better circumstances."

Charlene felt her color rise. At her age, it was unusual to be made to blush, and she liked the feeling. She nodded to Peter and Hitchins and left to find Gus and Colonel Pearce. They had to figure what to do with the remaining eighteen prisoners tonight. Bringing them into town would create a stir, but leaving them as Z bait between the walls would be cruel. The Zs themselves could be kept behind the main wall, but the zrats were a different story. Charlene found Kurt giving the colonels a tour of possible places to house the prisoners, but all had obvious problems … too hard to observe them at a safe distance, locals too close by, easy access to something that could burn. They finally agreed on the playground.

It was outdoors, which was a bit of a problem, but a couple of zrat killers would be there to knock down anything approaching. They had been able to get the in-town zrat population down dramatically, but new ones still managed to chew and dig their way in. The military and town guards would surround the prisoners and keep them tied in place. Once the zrat killers caught a few, they could smear the blood onto the guards' boots and clothes to deter any others, but those clothes would need to be collected and boiled in the morning. No one liked the idea of handling the virus in any form, but keeping from being bit was paramount. Pearce agreed, and Charlene said she could find spare pants and shoes for the men if needed until theirs were ready.

The zrat catchers preferred being called zrat killers. Within days of that job starting, people felt comfortable sleeping on the floor and with their beds closer to the wall. Charlene could never get the mental picture of zrats trying to climb the now metal posts of her bed and continued to sleep in the middle of her room and nowhere near a vent. Peter mentioned building a concrete and stone wall starting six to eight feet underground to help limit the access for all types of Zs. With the right resources, they could do it.

Once the town's children were safely away, about thirty minutes before dusk, the prisoners were marched in and seated in a circle. Peter,

Gus, and Sara watched from farther back and then retreated to dinner—chicken with rice and dumplings. Peter smiled at another way to boil dough. Spinach with onions completed the meal. Peter checked Sara in the corner of his eye, and she ate the spinach without complaint. Even the children learned that food was food and that there was none to be wasted.

Colonel Pearce joined them. "So you're my witnesses?"

Peter nodded. "We saw them come into Raleigh. I recognize some of them, including the lieutenant. When the men arrived, Sara and I snuck out since the town had been forcing us to stay because I'm an engineer. We didn't know what they really were at first; we thought like the town did—the army coming to the rescue. Sara and I were maybe a couple of hundred yards away when we heard the shots."

"And the screams," Sara whispered, her fingers playing with the tines on the fork.

"Young lady, those men will pay for every one of those screams." Pearce looked at her until she looked into his eyes. "Good. We should be starting about an hour after its light. I'm going to check on my men and get some shut-eye."

"We'll do the same," Gus answered. He turned to Peter once Pearce left. "We'll be staying with Charlene tonight. She said there'll be music. Some of the townspeople have a band, and they'll start right after dinner. We can stay for a little while, if you'd like." Sara looked at Peter and nodded vigorously.

"I'd like to hear a few songs, at least," Peter agreed.

It wasn't long before the tables were folded and the band came out, consisting of a fiddle, a guitar, a singer, a sax player, and a drummer. They immediately struck up a very modern version of "Yankee Doodle"

The zombie virus came to town
Blazin through my body
It struck my sister first of all
And then my brother, Donny

Chorus: Yankee Doodle keep it up
Yankee Doodle dandy,
Defend the gates and wreck the steps
And with your knife be handy

Father and I went down to camp
Along with Captain Goodin'
And there we saw the Zs stacked up
Like cord wood for the burnin'

Chorus:

There was a captain at the walls
A barkin' out his orders
Killin' zombies left and right
While firing off the mortars

Chorus

The crowd sang along loudly with the last verse, and by the final chorus, Peter, Sara, and Gus added their voices. They stayed longer than planned and might have stayed even later, but a cacophony of gunfire resounded from every wall around the compound.

The music came to a halt, and all present scrambled as the warning sirens blared. The town had drilled for every emergency, and everyone knew their jobs. Peter grabbed Sara. "I'll take her to Charlene's and then get to the wall."

"I'll be near the main gate," Gus called back as he rushed out with the locals.

Sara gripped Peter's hand as they ran through town and past the playground, the prisoners sitting and watching closely. Charlene's house was dark, but the door was open. "Go upstairs, and secure yourself into a room—the attic if you can get to it."

"Don't leave me!" Her eyes were already wet, and her body started to shake. Peter bent and hugged her tightly.

"It'll be OK. I'll be back as soon as I can." Peter felt Sara's trembling continue, so he took her into the house and up the dark steps. He unhooked the flashlight from his belt, lighting the way to the attic. The attic door had a lock inside. "Go in and lock the door. Find some things you can place along the stairs. You'll be OK. I'll be OK." He handed her the flashlight.

Sara finally nodded reluctantly and stepped inside. Peter closed the door and did not move until he heard the lock firmly click into place.

Back downstairs and out the door, Peter found empty streets. He heard almost constant gunfire ahead. Even in shadows, Gus's hulking form was distinctive in the crowd standing on the tower to the left of the main gate. The tower was crowded with riflemen, and the ladder covered with those helping to reload. Peter secured the katana in his pack and climbed the side. When his head popped over the top of the wall, he almost let go in shock.

He'd never seen so many. It looked like the National Mall in Washington DC on the Fourth of July. Zs pushed against what he had considered an impervious gate and strong stone wall. Zrats and small zogs in the midway scampered in the blood-soaked earth of the battle, and some dug at the ground below them, trying to get under the interior wall. The blood. The smell of blood and death brought them. The town had laid the fake soldiers' dead bodies outside the gate but had not burned them. The only thing that could stop this group would be daylight. Or any bright light.

"Light!" Peter shouted. When Gus and the few near him turned, Peter repeated, "We need light! Floodlights, car lights, lights from a stadium—whatever we can find!"

Gus realized that he was right. There were not nearly enough bullets in the town to save it.

"Where's Charlene?" Peter yelled. Someone pointed to the next tower.

Peter scrambled down and up to her perch. "Charlene!" he called.

Someone thought he was crazy and grabbed him. Peter shook off the hand and saw Hitchins.

"Floodlights!" Peter yelled at him. Hitchens looked confused for a minute, and then the realization hit his overwhelmed brain. The thin man forced his way to Peter.

"The barn ... well, the workshop and storage shed. We have the floodlights from the community center. We took them down to save on power."

With the ladder blocked, Hitchins swung himself easily over the side next to Peter. They climbed down and ran full tilt. Hitchins may not have been a young man, but he was fit and fast, and Peter had to work to keep up with him.

"When you talked about the food warehouse, I figured I finally had a job for these babies." The classic floodlights were already mostly in a cage, but the huge rectangle of thirty by twenty-four lights was too concentrated; they needed smaller groups. "If we can space each light about ten feet apart, they should light up the midway and get some light past the wall. Outlets on the outside of the houses should give us enough power."

They heard screams and a flurry of rapid gunfire.

"We don't have much time. Let's get some near the entrance gates and then work our way around from there."

Peter was already picking up tools and wiring. Hitchins just nodded and did the same. He yanked a tarp off a mound in the back, revealing four golf carts, and he started loading. Peter and Hitchins pulled apart the light cages and freed the individual floodlights.

Hitchins tossed Peter some electrician's gloves. "You're gonna need these. We can't turn off the power while we wire them in. I have a few guys that can help if we can find them."

The handyman drove toward the gate with Peter behind. Hitchins pointed out the wiring near the house by the town gate and pulled off to set up by the main entrance. The men had never stripped wires and attached into a system so fast. The main gate lit up just a few seconds before the inner town gate. They heard screeching from the zrats and former humans, and cheers went up as the Zs moved back. Peter knew that it would be seconds before the creatures would move farther down the wall. He ran to his next spot, cursing as he stepped on a zrat that scuttled after him. It had managed to dig under the gate before the lights hit.

"Ugh!" a zrat killer behind him sounded as his large, flat bat hit across its back. "You bit?" he paused to ask as the bat came down on several more scurrying over the ground.

"Don't think so. I'm immune, anyway." Peter took a breath. "Thanks."

"Hmph," the zrat killer grunted and moved on to refill the hole and add rocks to where the creatures had dug under the fence. Peter moved on. Halfway through hooking in his next set of lamps, he saw two lights come up. Hitchins had found help.

After Peter left, Gus and Godfrey went for the Minimi, currently loaded on a truck in the midway. It had been years since Gus had needed to fire anything like it, but with something that fast, the main idea was aim over the wall and into the hordes. Godfrey moved the truck along so that it stayed just inside the light cone as the outside of the town lit up. The distant lights might attract more Zs, but Gus had no idea how since it seemed that all of the infected of Georgia must be at their gate. Now he could only hope that the generators would last the night as more lights came on. He fired steady bursts of ten and paused, creating a regular rhythm. As he loaded the next belt, he felt movement in his pant leg. Gus's hand moved too slowly and felt the sharp teeth pierce his skin and begin tearing through the flesh.

He grabbed the zrat through the thin fabric, crushed it, and then pulled the body free and threw it to the ground. In the few seconds on his body, it had torn a hole almost the size of a baseball into the back of his calf. Gus cut off his pant leg with a knife, secured a bandage to stem the free flow of blood, and then returned to the job at hand. If worst came to worst, he would have twelve hours to help out. He thought of Marsha, Meagan, and Miranda. He would see more than one night. He'd see them again. Gus started his ten shell bursts again.

By midnight, his arms ached, and there were only seven ammunition boxes left. He saved some for the times when one of the lights flared out. They drove to the area and covered it until the bulb could be changed. The lights were working. Zs approached the wall and then grunted with hands over their eyes and stepped back. Gus kept himself awake remembering every soldier in his first command and heard Godfrey singing below him.

Gus grinned and half joined in on the chorus. "*Defend the gates and wreck the steps And with your knife be handy*"

On night watches, Gus learned that you could feel the dawn before you saw the light. Something in the air felt different. He heard retreating movement beyond the walls and realized that the Zs had that sense, as well. No one knew where Zs went in the daytime … likely into the abandoned, boarded-up houses in nearby subdivisions or in stairwells of larger buildings and school hallways. As the first hint of light, the town erupted in cheers. Gus stood, and his wound screamed pain into his brain. He steeled himself and knocked on the roof of the truck cab. Godfrey's embarrassed look told that he had finally nodded off.

"Let's get back to the front gate."

Gus saw Godfrey nod, and the engine fired up.

When Gus lowered himself from the truck, the townspeople cheered and clapped. Their second victory in a row. Peter found him, and the gymnast's grip and concerned look showed that he'd seen the bandage. Gus nodded and continued to thank the people for thanking him. Peter disappeared for a few minutes, and Charlene's overly happy voice cleared a path to him.

"You just let our heroes through here." She smiled, and her brief glance to his leg and no change in facial expression told Gus that she knew. "Of course, everyone in this town is a hero today. We'll see if the cooks have any energy left to get us a special feast." Charlene took Gus's arm, playfully reaching up to pat his shoulder. "But for now, you are going to let my guest get some rest." From murmurings, Gus knew that others had seen the bandage, but the path was clear. They passed the community center and the playground and headed to Charlene's home. Peter stopped at the playground and then ran to catch up.

"Where did you move the prisoners?" He stopped in front of Charlene on her porch steps.

"I haven't moved them anywhere. You go ask your other army people where they took them." Charlene kept her smile but glanced at Gus's leg.

Peter almost protested since he was not one of the "army people," but he kept his mouth shut and started running up the stairs. Charlene led Gus to the solarium, where a cot was situated near a bolt with chain.

"When were you bitten?" she asked kindly, seating him on the cot.

"Around midnight," Gus replied, fatigue seeping through him.

"So about five or six hours before we'll see a fever," Charlene calculated.

Gus lay on his abdomen, his legs extending well past the end of the bed. She fetched a bucket of water from the kitchen and soaked off the bandage.

"Zrats are nasty little things," Charlene said. "They seem to eat anything. We haven't seen any possums. They're probably eaten or staying high in the trees. We've had some success in poisoning the zrats, but it takes cyanide. Even the potent rat poisons with brodifacoum don't seem to do much to them." She packed and bandaged the wound. "I'll get you something to eat."

Peter ran into the room panting and half in a panic. "Sara's not in the attic. The door's been kicked in."

They heard yelling and screaming a few blocks away. Peter didn't wait and sprinted toward the sound.

Peter pulled up with his heart pounding more from fear than exertion. Several children stood with knives at their necks, held there by the former prisoners. Peter didn't wait to be seen and hopped a fence into a garden and moved along the side. Sara glared ahead with her jaw and fists clenched as the tip of a butcher knife sat millimeters below her pounding carotid. The men and their captives were lined up near the back gate, only three feet wide and now used for livestock to go out one at a time to graze the midway.

The midway wall was fifteen feet high. The side fence he stood behind now was eight feet high and ten feet from the midway fence. He couldn't scale the fence and get around them on the midway without being seen and without help. Peter loosened the fabric around the katana. He hadn't had a chance to properly clean off the zrat blood from last night. After mounting and wiring the lights, Peter had helped kill the zrats that made it into town. Now the blade shimmered with the morning light. He secured it in his pack, ready to be drawn.

Peter peered between the fence slats at the men, debating his next move, when he heard shouting and a woman's voice.

"I am sure we can come to some agreement," Charlene said in her overly sweet voice. "Those are just children you have there, and I am sure you do not want any harm to come to them."

"We want our food and our guns, and then we'll be on our way." Peter didn't recognize the one talking. The man held a young boy of about seven or eight by the shoulder. From the expression on Hitchins's face, it must have been his son.

"Well, gentlemen." Charlene brought herself to the center of their attention. "As I'm sure you heard last night, we had a bit of trouble. And although we may be able to return some of the weapons, the ammunition may be another thing altogether. As to the food, well, I'm sure some provisions for your journey could be made available."

Peter's mouth went dry. She was negotiating with them. These things were less than the Zs—men who turned on their own kind.

"You seem to think we're kidding here, ma'am," the less-than-man was saying. He turned to a compatriot. "I think we need to give them a demonstration of how serious we are." The other man grabbed Sara's arm and turned her, holding the blade flat against her throat.

Peter's world went hot white. He backed up to the other side of the yard and ran up the eight-foot fence, vaulting over the top while twisting in a double somersault, landing behind the man holding Sara while drawing his sword. The tip of the katana wet itself between the man's spine and left shoulder blade. Sara jumped away as the knife and then the man fell forward, the sword's tip withdrawn as Peter turned to two of the other prisoners now converging on him. Time became very slow as three shots hit the speaker, the one behind Peter, and another prisoner with single bullet wounds to their foreheads. Peter had the strange feeling that the dead men must now be Hindi since they had gotten their third eyes. Peter twisted from one side to the next, forcing himself to cut off the exhausted laughter that tried to escape from his lips. Gus tackled another man closing on Peter before he could whip the blade around, pulling it back before hurting his friend. Then Sara's arms were around him, and he vaguely saw Charlene holstering her pistol. Then time returned to normal.

A man from town pounded on his back. "I'll make you a proper sheath for that beautiful blade."

Hitchins was gripping his sobbing son as if he could never let go. Peter felt spent, the adrenaline of the night and that moment gone.

Gus gripped his shoulder and by force of size and power moved them back to Charlene's. "So are you some kind of ninja?" Gus asked quietly.

Peter shook his head. "Gymnast. The sword's an inheritance from way back—from my many-great-grandfather who was samurai. I've been learning to use it along the road."

"He's teaching me too," Sara claimed proudly.

"Good. I have a feeling swords will be back in vogue." Gus smiled.

Colonel Pearce caught up with them. "The prisoners managed to make a break during the confusion and overwhelmed my men. The four that guarded the prisoners are dead. We're too exhausted to leave, and with that horde out there, we may need helicopter evac rather than risk the road."

Gus nodded and pointed to his leg. "We'll know by tomorrow morning if I'll be joining you or not."

Pearce looked Gus up and down then at Charlene. "I can help guard—"

Charlene took Colonel Pearce's arm. "Now you don't have to worry yourself about that. If his temperature goes above 109 degrees, he won't have a chance to turn. My assistants and I will see to that ourselves."

Pearce had missed the scene by the back gate, so he did not realize how capable this Southern lady could be.

"Don't worry, Gus. You're like us." Sara swung Peter's hand. "Your bite might get infected like mine did, but not by the virus. Just regular stuff." Sara sounded so confident that it made Gus smile.

"And how do you know this?" Gus asked.

Sara shrugged. "I just know." Sara did prove to have some sixth sense.

After a good breakfast, Gus was bound to the cot with a chair to prop his feet. He slept until sunset, waking refreshed. Kurt sat in the room reading a book and checked his watch when Gus stirred.

"I'll check with Charlene, but I think you are among the truly lucky. You never went above 99, and that was likely 'cause the room got hot." Kurt returned a few minutes later with the key. "We need to be able to give something out that shows you're immune. A new way to attract the ladies."

Gus rubbed his wrist. He couldn't wait to tell Marsha that the girls would be safe. And their new one. Stretching the leg reminded him of the cause of the confinement. He looked down. The bandage oozed some clear liquid, and the area was slightly swollen and tender, but there were no red streaks.

"Well, don't you look dashing?" Charlene commented as she set down a tray. Gus seriously doubted that *dashing* was the proper word, but he was too much of a gentleman to correct a lady. He did appreciate the smell from the bowl she'd brought, which contained beef stew with onions, carrots, and potatoes, rich with a thick bread for dipping.

"Thank you, Ms. Charlene." He waited, feeling his mouth water.

"Now don't you wait for me. You dig in. Once you're done, you can meet me by the front gate. We don't know how many will be back." She turned to leave.

"And the prisoners?" Gus wanted to make sure that there was no chance of a repeat of the morning's debacle.

"Tried, all but two convicted and hung. The remaining two could show that they were not in Raleigh and that they'd joined after. They were also in hiding for this morning's events, not participating, so the town was more inclined to show mercy. We'll burn the convicts' bodies tomorrow well away from town. The other two are securely tied. We will give them a pack with two days' rations and water tomorrow after dawn." Charlene left.

Gus watched her go and dug into the stew, which tasted as good as it smelled. Gus hadn't woken to any cheers or revelry.

"She didn't make it public." Peter joined him and perched on the almost elevated side of the cot. "It could have been; there were enough people calling for blood. It was Hitchins who made sure that it was private, and he didn't go watch, either. He said his boy had had enough bad things in his brain and didn't need to see men hang. They screened one of the towers with a big tarp and hung them there."

"Pearce?" Gus asked between mouthfuls.

"He was the judge. He and Charlene even made sure that they had a defense attorney. Not that there was much he could say. He did get the two off, one of which was Butch. The son of a bitch didn't join until after Raleigh and hid near the main gate after the group broke free. Didn't have a drop of blood on him, so they couldn't pin the guards' deaths on him, either. The trial took less than an hour. Sara and I said our piece about Raleigh and this morning. A few others testified about last night and today. The jury talked about five minutes and had their verdict, and the men were marched to the tower." Peter shook his head. "Frontier justice. In this instance, probably a good thing, but I know it could go bad pretty fast."

"Is Pearce still here?" Gus qualified his earlier question. He wanted to put those men far out of his mind and had no intention of giving them another thought.

"Yeah, he has a sat phone and says the chopper will pick us up tomorrow morning. Sara is ecstatic about riding in a helicopter."

Gus rose after finishing the last of his stew.

"You're going to be OK to walk around?" Peter glanced at the slight ooze from the bandage.

"Yeah, I've had worse."

With the last light, they made their way to the main gate, the ring of lights blazing on. The horde was moving in, but not nearly as many as the previous night. They could manage. Elysian Heights would be OK.

Camden's, and many other communities', hardest week came when the drugs ran out. A lot of the addicts had squirrelled away their favorite habit, but with the last of those stashes empty, the doc was seeing some serious withdrawals. The alcoholics went through the roughest time, and two died from DTs. This was followed by those hooked on benzodiazepines, such as alprazolam, who experienced severe seizures. The others were having everything from mood swings to vomiting and sweats, depending on their drug of choice. Stokes was glad when that was over. On the bright side, he found that some people weren't stupid, just high, a form of stupid he very rarely participated in.

His lack of interest in the drugs he dealt was part of why Duke and Daniel tapped him as a possible leader in the ranks of the Shujaa gang. Daniel couldn't have someone who liked to use the product handling much of it. Stokes appreciated Daniel's advice; the gang leader had been the only father figure in his life. Early in the gang, Stokes watched over users in the safe house, places they could get high on gang-provided drugs and be given a heads-up if the cops started closing in. There was not much incentive to emulate the users, although other members did it. Daniel said that it was because they failed to see "the big picture," a talent Stokes held that Daniel admired.

Now Stokes watched the river. Some folks still sailed, looking for some safe place to call home. With over two thousand people already, he couldn't take any more, despite how much Auntie pushed him. He let them sail on by. Petty Island sat across a narrow waterway from Pyne Poynt, which once housed a container yard and an oil depot for some big oil company. His people had found a container full of flashlights that had to be shaken to charge instead of a battery, which let them scavenge without worrying about carrying spare batteries. Transporting the fuel to Cooper and Pyne Poynt required abandoned boats and lots of portable containers. Stokes had the guns, and no one in his crew had any qualms about using them, so no one dared confront the Camden survivors. Even Auntie held her tongue when he drove off any other scavengers. No, this was now survival of the fittest—Darwinian, as Toya and Charles would say.

Stokes smiled a little when he thought of the funny French way the man pronounced his name. He was a geek, no question, but not a wimp. There was a hardness to him that circumstances brought out. Charles was efficient and smart, and he quickly proved loyal. When placed in charge of the duty roster, he reorganized the town into three crews for getting needed food and materials. Now only the immune were allowed to leave the walls; that way, no one could bring the virus back with them. Those within the town had jobs regardless of prior profession.

"Sir, the Cape May Lighthouse reported Coast Guard boats looking for survivors." Charles puffed some after climbing the eight flights to the lookout. Doc Draeger probably wouldn't want him stressing his shoulder, but that was between the Frenchman and the doc.

Stokes shook his head. The government never did them any good before, and he didn't see them helping now. "Did they say anything?"

"I do not think so." Charles looked troubled.

"Have everyone report back. Keep down and out of sight."

Stokes considered putting some defenders onto Perry Island, but they had cleared almost everything worth having from the place, so he didn't think it would be worth it. In a few hours, the first of the small cutters sailed up the Delaware. He saw their binoculars out, so he sank down under the edge of the balcony. The sun was behind him, so he didn't need to worry about anything reflecting and revealing his location. They looked legit, initially pulling over near the USS *New Jersey*. Stokes and company had stripped anything useful from the hulk and cleared out the nearby aquarium. The wall and river marked the boundary of his town, so Stokes readied himself for the visitors.

Along the water, his defenses weren't as good as they were by land. Plans included a wall along the river one day, sunk deep enough to keep out the river zrats, but other pressing items took priority. Stokes willed the Coast Guard ship to turn around, but they moved on after checking out the *New Jersey*. The sailors carefully navigated the bridge debris, keeping the engines slow at the wall, and then they moved past, eventually pulling into the marina by one of the scrap yards near the point. Stokes sighed. He'd need to meet up with them.

He jogged down the steps to his bike and revved the engine for the five-minute ride. Three of his men stood mute as they watched the Coast Guard come ashore. They didn't say anything but effectively created a small human wall on the road to their town that opened to Stokes. They took in the five-foot-nine, lean frame wearing tattered jeans and a leather jacket with short-cropped hair. He had a pair of scars on his lip and forehead, not bad enough to be disfiguring but easy to see. It was his bearing that marked Stokes as the leader, erect with his shoulders back, eyes wary but his face calm. Stokes needed to hear what they had to say; he didn't plan on alienating them from first impression.

In turn, the sailors kept their weapons at their sides, none drawn. They wore military uniforms, mainly Coast Guard, but a couple may have been army. One held his hands out to his sides and indicated that he must be the one in charge.

"Good afternoon. I'm Lieutenant Bradley. We're just checking to see how people are doing."

"You gonna bring us food? Weapons?" Stokes asked. He was careful with his voice; history had shown that his tone could piss people off in about a tenth of a second.

"Eventually, maybe. We're trying to find secure places to take survivors so that we can rebuild. Get an idea of the remaining population." Bradley looked at the park behind them, the horse grazing and ignoring the activity.

"We got about two thousand folks. We doin' OK for now, but if you want to bring us some zrat traps, some ammunition, some fresh food, that'd be good." Stokes had stopped about thirty feet from the men. Close enough for them to see that they weren't going to be allowed any closer.

Bradley looked at the remnants of the bridge. "The bridge?"

"Too many Zs and zrats coming over." Stokes kept it simple.

Bradley nodded. "If anything comes available, we'll let you know." Bradley turned back to his men who proceeded to their boats. "We're not your enemy. We're Americans and survivors, as well. It's up to all of us to help out so more can survive. Keep your radio to AM 1100; we're broadcasting twice a day—oh seven hundred and nineteen hundred hours. Seven in the morning and seven in the evening. There'll be information on where to pick up food, evacuation points, how to make a zrat-proof garden. Stay safe." Bradley nodded once more and waved for his men to move on.

Stokes wondered where they'd find a place to sleep. Maybe somewhere else farther up the river or on the boats, but that would be tight.

Stokes grinned. Toya had already figured out the gardening bit; it would be cool to see how close her design came to what they described. Stokes turned to his men.

"You checked the nets?"

They glanced at each other and finally shook their heads.

"Lazy asses. The nets are there—might as well check them while you were waitin'."

The men jogged to the water's edge and started pulling up lines. A few shad and a bass wriggled in the net, good to add to tonight's stew. Stokes carried them back to the kitchen. He knew he'd find Charles and Toya there, heads close. It was fun to spook them, act like he didn't approve. In reality, Charles treated his sister as his queen, and Stokes could ask for no better than that. The two were too chummy with the Cherry Hill contingent, but if it helped the new group to be useful, then what the hell.

He found them as expected, Toya pulled close, whispering something in Charles's ear that made him smile until he saw Stokes. Toya whirled around with that mean "I'll get you later, big brother" look on her face. Stokes plopped the bag of freshly killed fish onto the table, and the kids and old folks who were the cooks descended to get to work.

"The shad are really starting to run. We should eat good for a couple of weeks." Betty smacked her false teeth against each other. "I hadn't seen no one fish in so long I didn't think we still knew how to catch 'em."

They had started fishing with string and safety pins for hooks like someone had seen on a survival show. Olivia knew how to repair an old fishing net they'd scavenged and now put to good use. She was helping mend more that washed up so that they could get a steady supply of fish. Charles had set up supplies for a smoker, which he'd seen how to do on a cooking show.

"The men on the boat? Coast Guard?" Charles was staring over his shoulder, watching the fish getting cleaned and gutted.

"Yeah, census or somethin'—tryin' to find the survivors. Doubt they'll be back—looked to be in a hurry to get goin'." Stokes took a sidelong look at Charles. He should have had him go to the water; seeing a white face may have made them more likely to bring aid. "They said to set the radios to AM 1100 … there'd be news."

Charles's head jerked up. Trevor set up a ham-type set, and they had their first communications with Cape May over the last couple of days.

That in itself lifted everyone's spirits. Getting news from beyond would be a celebration. The last broadcast they'd heard was nine days ago, when the main stations from New York went dark. Dr. Emma and Alistair Breedham somehow managed to make people think that the world could be OK, and then they seemed to be gone as well. Charles watched the fish being diced and tossed into pots of boiling water. Nothing was OK. But if they were still broadcasting, it would be nice to hear a voice from home. He jumped when he felt his butt squeezed as Toya came around, now with her arms crossed.

"So we just gonna stand here and watch people work?" Her eyebrows rose up and into her bangs, the haircut that had looked like the former First Lady's beginning to kink up at the roots and extend out. No one dared to tell her that she looked like she'd stuck a finger in a light socket.

"You got anything better to do?" Stokes asked his sister. The affectionate tap on Charles did not go unnoticed.

Toya slid to Charles's side, who in turn kept his gaze dead ahead. "Oh, I can think of a few things. Let's check the perimeter." Toya turned to Charles more fully, her full mouth just slightly turned up in the barest hint of smile.

"Good idea." Charles turned to Stokes. "Unless you need ..."

Stokes shook his head and waved them away. Stokes found Auntie holding court on one of the pews. The church housed the biggest kitchen and seating area in the Poynt, and the yard out back made it easy for people to grab food and stand outside talking. Each person had to bring his or her own bowl and spoon. They got three bowls per day of whatever could be scrounged and cooked, even if that was ketchup on rice. If you complained, you got an earful from Auntie or one of her minions, so you learned to say thank you and move on. They'd built a stage in the back, and after someone said grace, the line could start to move through the kitchen. People played music or rapped, and one guy even did a comedy routine when the mood struck him. Some nights were more somber, and no one was in the mood. If weather was blowing through, folks would take their bowls and hurry home.

"Auntie, you know where the radio got to?" Stokes asked when she had a break in her conversation. Stokes was technically the one in charge, but in reality, it was Auntie's force of nature that kept everyone working together.

"What you need that for? Nothing's been on for a week or more." She said it louder than needed, making sure that anyone in the large room could hear.

"A few Coast Guard came by—no food or nothin'—but said to turn on the radio every day at seven and seven for news. Thought I'd hook it up so folks could hear tonight." Stokes always felt off talking to Auntie. With everyone else, it was Stokes who projected that sense of command, making those around nervous about what he had to say.

"Check in the deacon's office; it may need batteries. Those you'll find in the kitchen."

Auntie sounded more curious now. It was only five thirty. Dinner would be ready by six, and the line outside was already forming. Stokes wanted it set and ready. Bringing the world back to the Poynt felt important.

The old radio was where she'd said it would be. Who knew that such old stuff would be so important again? The working MP3 players let them listen to music, batteries recharged when the cars went out on runs. Charles had set up some solar panels grabbed in Philly. He wanted more, but the high-rises on which they sat housed the Zs during the day, and Stokes couldn't see himself risking his men for them. A small windmill and a waterwheel stuck in the river provided electrical power for the stoves and emergency lights; that would have to do for now.

Stokes fiddled and found channel AM 1100. Instead of static, it let out that long blast of sound he'd grown up hearing, normally followed by "This is a test of the emergency broadcast system." Now it said "Please stand by until 7:00 p.m. EST for important information" followed by three loud blares. Stokes quickly tuned it off when he drew a crowd. "It says 7:00 p.m. No use listening to that racket until then." Word moved fast that they'd hear from elsewhere tonight. The weather was nice, with clear skies and a breeze, so everyone was in a good mood when Stokes turned the radio on a few minutes before seven.

"Good evening to all." Alistair's voice carried well, but even at full volume, the little radio only carried the sound twenty to thirty feet through the crowd, and not at all as soon as everyone cheered the now familiar voice. "As promised, Dr. Emma O'Conner rejoins the broadcast this evening after her evacuation. We will get to her in a few moments after news from the rest of the world. In Ireland, Father Patrick continues to move slowly across the island, clearing all before him of the virus. He states that destroying all buildings and crops is necessary for the greater good; no zrat, zog, or Z can survive without shelter from the sun. His people live on what the sea can provide and claim that they are the healthiest of men. In Chechnya, the leaders have continued to expose everyone to the virus so that those 'not fit' can be destroyed and let those with a chance live on. The world leaders that can be found for comment have universally condemned the tactics. Here in Canada, the warmer weather has allowed greater virus activity. It has been contained on Prince Edward Island, and most of Newfoundland is clear. Vancouver has established strict quarantines on several of the islands in the sound, but the city itself is not doing well. Montreal was silent today. Here in Toronto, we seem to be through the worst of it, though new cases are still reported daily as they work to eliminate the rat and zrat populations. All citizens are advised to avoid the underground walkways. Now to Dr. O'Conner."

Charles and Toya had snuck in close, and Charles couldn't help but smile.

"Good evening, Alistair. It's great to be back." Emma's voice sounded happy. It bounded back and lifted the mood of all those close, which in turn lifted those farther back.

"You sound happy with your new place," Alistair commented.

"Not so much the new place—it's a bit cramped—but happy news. A good friend was back in touch earlier today. He is alive. We missed meeting up in Atlanta, but he is on his way to where I am now." From the tone of voice, anyone in hearing could tell that this person was not just a "friend" in her heart.

"*Ah.*" Alistair extended the sound knowingly. "It's wonderful for any of us to be reunited with friends and others we love." Alistair's tone returned to factual and newsman's gravitas. "Now, tell us what else we need to know."

"Local military bases of all service branches are combing the country to find where our pockets of survivors are located. This will help distribute emergency information and supplies. We are reminding all to do any butchering away from your settlement and to extinguish or cover all lights at night to minimize attracting the Zs."

Stokes snorted. They burned old tires on the riverfront and laughed while they watched the Zs go into the Delaware and drown. The zrats were too small to see, but sometimes they could hear them screeching in the water. No way they were stopping that. Killing more of those things was a public service.

Emma continued, "We have been trying to identify sounds that might deter the Zs, but any we have found are also irritating to humans, and we have confirmed that loud noises also attract Zs."

"Any new insights on a vaccine?" Alistair asked hopefully.

"We have a few possibilities that we will be testing on dogs in the coming week. We have found it difficult to distinguish between zrat Thinkers and regular zrats, which are important distinctions with the vaccines. It's easier to tell if they're zog Thinkers or zogs," Emma concluded.

"Thank you, Dr. O'Conner. Due to communication issues, our segment on zrat proof gardening will need to wait until the morning. Until then, keep safe. Alistair Breedham signing off." The sharp sound afterward pierced through the early evening as the crowd erupted in cheers. Even those too far back to hear the broadcast breathed a sigh of relief. They weren't alone.

The night crew went to light the tires. Stokes pulled Charles aside.

"Find us some speakers to get the sound to everyone. They need this."

Charles nodded. One of the apartments had a wicked setup. It would take some convincing for the current inhabitant to part with it, but he was sure something could be worked out.

The tanker was almost empty of its jet fuel, and they needed to make the trip up the coast to refill it or lose use of the Bell. Guillermo developed an intricate pathway laid out along the highway. By locking the brakes on most of the cars but not on a select few, his men could move those cars out of the way, allowing the tanker to move through, and then they could block the path again. The thirty-four miles took over three hours. The airport was deserted as before except for some sounds inside the buildings. The access to turn on the pump was in the service hanger—a large, dark place when the doors were closed. They brought a truck with a generator and spare fuel to run the pump.

"On three, open the doors," Guillermo commanded.

They had closed the doors and left them unlocked the last time since rust would ruin the pipes and dials. Screeching from what must have been close to twenty Zs began as the portal flew open. The Zs blinked and huddled as some attempted to hide in the shadows beneath the three small planes inside. Paulina and the men drew their guns and methodically shot one after the next, carefully avoiding the planes and several barrels. One of the Zs ducked behind the oil drums.

"Damn Thinkers." Guillermo went to the back of the jeep and pulled out a net.

He and Rodrigo grabbed an end and started walking toward the drums. The Thinker saw them coming and made a dash for it. As soon as he was clear, Ronaldo got a clear shot, and the Thinker went down. Paulina retrieved the glasses it wore, a habit she and Guillermo had developed in trying to find another pair for Mitchell. The man was currently sporting a pair with small, teal colored frames. The three put on their plastic coveralls and protective gear and then methodically hauled out the twenty bodies, scooped out some fuel from the barrels, lit the bodies, and then returned to the job at hand.

Rodrigo found the pump and switched it on, but no sound came forth. Guillermo and Ronaldo found the backup generator and checked it. It was out of fuel and needed oil for the pump. They filled it and then turned it on with a resounding roar to life. Paulina straddled the top of the tanker, wrestling the hose into position, while Rodrigo and Ronaldo made wiseass remarks.

"Yeah, boys, I don't see any of you competing with the nine hundred horsepower of the Bell, so knock it off." She considered turning the fuel nozzle onto them and decided against it. The fuel was too precious, and they couldn't be sure how much longer it would last.

The group loaded back up and returned to the compound about an hour to sunset. For some reason the trip made Paulina see the town with new eyes. She looked over the resorts that had become a refuge for over two thousand souls. The town felt surreal. People smiled and waved at her as they cleaned fish, and others fanned themselves on balconies to cool off in the steamy evening. The pool water in the ornate infinity pool was green and murky, now used as the drinking water after it was boiled. They had a clinic, a small school, a laundry, and the kitchen with dining area to the back. The inner walls were lined with hammered and reclaimed metal from cars and pushed down several feet into the dirt, providing another barrier for the zrats. On the beach side, another wall was built with a gate to the sea, now open and revealing the last of the fishing boats coming in for the day, their catch feeding most of those present. The shallow areas farther down the beach allowed them to collect seaweed to feed the cows and for the stew. The cow and chicken barn were in what was likely the children's area when it was a resort, cartoon characters still proudly painted on the walls. Paulina smiled looking at her balcony with the tomato plant hanging down covered with small green fruit.

Paulina shook her head in disbelief. Her people weren't just surviving; they were thriving. She thought of hurricanes and prayed, *not this year*. She felt proud of supporting Guillermo in preventing the coup. The creation of this town was miraculous. Guillermo found those to help, including Mitchell and Juan Carlos. Paulina smiled when she thought of Mitchell, but going that next step was not a good idea, not with how Guillermo looked at her. That look, and the way some of the women ribbed her about their leader, might become dangerous. Paulina could not think of Guillermo as anything but leader, not as a boy. But if she chose Mitchell, it could send a rift between the two, and she had no intention of being a cause of anything that could jeopardize the town.

Thinking of the devil, Mitchell came up to greet her with a platonic peck on the cheek. His deep voice that seemed to always carry a smile within it rumbled forth.

"They caught a nice haul of red snapper today. I was heading down for dinner—care to join?"

Paulina rolled her eyes since he'd spoken in English. She and Guillermo were trying to get him to say more in Spanish, even with them.

"I will if you say it in Spanish," Paulina challenged him.

Mitchell groaned. "*Yo quiero su compania por la comida.*"

Paulina shook her head. "Close enough."

Mitchell saw Guillermo and waved him toward them.

"*La comida*!" Mitchell grinned at the two.

"*Bueno*!" Guillermo replied and clapped his friend on the shoulder. "*Estoy con hambre*!"

The three leaders proceeded, while those along the way quietly parted for them.

CHAPTER 11

May 2-4; Z Days 23-25

"Sorry, sir, we're going to have to set down." The comment was directed toward Lieutenant Colonel McLeod.

"Fuck!" Peter slammed his hand down.

The last couple of days had gone too well, and he knew it. Sara looked worried and covered his hand. In the time they'd been traveling, she'd never heard Peter swear. Her father swore all the time, but Peter just gritted his teeth and moved on. The Blackhawk had been buffeted all afternoon, fighting rising winds, and it was going to run out of fuel long before reaching Cheyenne almost a hundred miles to the north.

"We'll set down in the town of Fort Morgan. They may be OK." Erik, the pilot, gave them a thumbs-up.

Sara was well aware of how long it could take to find a safe place for the night, and she squeezed Peter's hand harder. He felt chagrinned at his outburst. Jiromaru did not allow swearing in the house. He so felt self-conscious when something slipped.

"Some of the towns up here haven't seen as many Zs," Peter said as he smiled at Sara, not quite convincing himself, either.

They landed near the railroad station, the parking lot packed and the cars developing a film of dust. The country station was a simple brick, one-story building, its small windows broken out and too dark to risk exploring. The pilot secured the chopper and headed down the street with them, past several buildings likely boarded up before the Zs struck. A couple of streets away was Main, once like most other Main Streets with hardware and furniture stores.

Peter and Sara were the experts at finding shelter on the run, but none of the places they saw looked likely to have attics. One building, however, next to the Humane Society Thrift Store, had big windows on the first and second floors. As soon as they stopped, the thrift store door opened, letting out an older, lean, and active-looking woman accompanied by a pack of six dogs of all shapes and sizes with happily wagging tails and tongues lolling. Sara giggled as she busily tried to pet them all as they crowded around, licking.

"Hey," the woman said, taking them in with her steady gaze. She concentrated on Gus and Erik in uniform. "Headin' to Cheyenne?"

Gus nodded. "Lieutenant Colonel Angus McLeod." He held out his hand.

The woman shifted the sealed bucket and took it firmly.

"Hazel. Problem with your chopper?" she asked.

"Almost out of fuel," Erik responded.

"Can't help you there, but I can offer food and shelter." Peter glanced upstairs. "Not up there; can't defend the stairs well enough. Nope. Got a good place down the street a bit."

"Thank you," Peter answered. He realized that asking if she was alone might seem threatening, and he held his tongue. Hazel knew what was coming next.

"Some folks stuck it out a couple weeks, but they've moved on—some to Denver, some up to Cheyenne. I couldn't leave my fellas, so we stayed." She scratched the neck of the largest, a Newfoundland mix by the look of him. "This boy here's even immune. Too bad he's been fixed."

The Newfie leaned into her, enjoying the attention. Peter thought of the two herd dogs in Elysian Heights. Those and this pack were the only ones he'd seen. Most people put theirs down as soon as they realized that dogs could turn. The hounds jumped around Sara and the others, accepting the neck rubs.

"I was making my rounds before dinner, picking up some food for them." She shook the bucket, and the dogs ears perked up. "Then I was headed to the café to cook. The owners kept their freezer on a generator; you have to out here since we can lose power for days at a time. They left me the frozen stuff since they couldn't take it. I use it for general storage since the seals and the cold keep out the zrats, and the triple locks have kept out the Zs. There'll be enough." Hazel led the way to a small restaurant, well lit and airy with a skylight, six small tables, and a counter. The kitchen was small and wide enough for two at most.

Peter went in to help. The pork chops' packaging date were pre–Z virus. The news had shown that the pig farms had been wiped out in the first few days. Pigs died from the virus at a much higher rate than people did, and none seemed immune. Peter thought that he had seen the last bacon in his lifetime and almost shed a tear. Hazel pulled out some frozen broccoli, and even though cheese should not be frozen, under the circumstances, it was necessary. A line of frozen water jugs, each two-thirds full, took up the bottom shelves. Hazel grabbed one to thaw and a box with tea bags.

They took the haul out to the road and set it on the warm pavement to thaw. Hazel snapped her fingers and said, "Leave it," and every dog lay, head on its paws, watching the bounty as if it would move. Gus grabbed some chairs from inside and set them in the parking lot, enjoying the spring sun. If any bird came close, the dogs jumped up and chased it away and then went back to their spots.

"They're well trained," Gus observed.

"Should be—haven't had much else to do the last couple of weeks. We walk a little farther out each day, looking for what folks left. Bits of gas for the generator, tea bags, coffee bags. A few folks even had those emergency rations they touted on the end-of-the-world shows. You have to add boiling water to 'em—a little hard without power."

"What did you do before?" Peter stretched out on the warm ground with his back to a tree.

"Taught math at the middle school and volunteered at the animal shelter. The manager was puttin' 'em all down, and I snuck these guys out. Bob"—she nodded to the Newfoundland—"saved my life."

Bob got up and padded to her, leaning in. She scratched him fondly as he plopped down at her feet. Peter got up and turned the meat over to better thaw, and then shook the water jug. "Here. Put a few of the tea bags in." Hazel stretched her hand out, not getting up with the eighty-pound dog now sprawled across her legs.

Peter did as asked, smiling at the rapid coloring of the water. Tea, pork chops, and broccoli with cheese. If they could find some applesauce, life could be complete. It only took about thirty minutes for the sun to do its magic.

Peter and Hazel gathered up the food, leaving the tea to steep. She had a burner and a coffeepot. She dumped the broccoli into the coffeepot and turned on the burner.

"Turn every minute or two," Hazel instructed, while heating up a cast-iron skillet.

The sizzling got everyone's attention as the pork hit the pan. She appeared to be an expert, flipping at the right moment for perfect brown. Hazel touched the side of the pot and nodded to add the shredded cheese.

"Don't mix now," she warned, turning off the heat. The cheese quickly melted along the heads and spears.

They feasted al fresco, tables moved outside by Erik and Gus. They shared stories of their families. Peter spoke mostly of his grandmother and of how she'd come to live with them when his mother died. Gus talked of his girls and his siblings, and Hazel was single and no children, but she was proud of her nieces and nephews. One of each was safely in Denver and had tried to get her to evacuate when communications were still clear. Gus asked for their names to get a message to them that she was still safe. With less than an hour of sun remaining, the humans cleaned up while the dogs enjoyed a bone each with their regular food.

"I don't let food in the shelter," explained Hazel. "We attract them enough as it is. Smells like tonight will bring a bunch, which is why I eat here and shelter about a mile away, so we'd best get going."

The walk was brisk, but all were now fit with forced exercise. In a yard by the train tracks sat the perfect shelter.

A metal container, the kind used to transfer almost all goods known to man, sat on a cement slab that was once used for an RV. One foot from the top of the container was a line of small openings a half-inch wide and about two inches long, allowing ventilation. The doors were currently closed with a crossbar. The dogs went to the side to do their business and then padded back as Hazel opened the door.

"You folks may want to take a cue from the dogs. I go to the left over that way." Hazel pointed to a line of shrubs. "So why don't you boys go to the right?" After they finished and reassembled, Hazel let them in. The container was forty feet long, eight feet wide, and eight feet high. Her own bunk, neatly made with a folded blanket, would have passed any army inspection. A stack of folded cots were to the left of the entrance. They unfolded the ones they'd need, leaving two unused.

"I have a bucket in the back if anyone can't hold it until morning," said Hazel. "I will admit that I generally need to use it, so move my bunk farthest back."

"You're prepared." Gus admired the neat and orderly way the container was arranged. She'd built shelves for the blankets and sheets and another for books. He suddenly realized what was missing. Hazel had artwork around but no photos. Maybe some preferred not to remember what it was like before.

As the sun sank to just a few degrees above the horizon, Hazel closed them in. The inner doors had two crossbars and bolts that went through the bottom and into the cement and another two that went into the roof. Peter walked the corners, going over bunks and admiring how the container was secured into the cement slab. He climbed and put his fingers through the ventilation holes and peered out. Hazel watched him closely in the fading light.

"If I put the slats closer to the roof, the zrats could get in. As it is, sometimes the Zs stick their fingers through. I've cut a few digits off, though I swear the fingers grow back. I know that's crazy, but most of those Zs are locals; many were my students. Maybe that's why so many people left—they couldn't stand the thought of killing a friend or neighbor." Hazel sighed and sat on her bunk. "I prefer no light since it seems to bring them closer."

"That's OK," Sara said, sitting on a bunk next to Hazel and immediately surrounded by three of the dogs. The young girl fell asleep soon after dark, her happy cuddling noises with the dogs quickly receding into the deep, even breathing of sleep. They heard the grunts and shuffles, the nudges against the containers, but the Zs did not seem too interested in the container once they determined that the normal measures were in place. The building did not budge; they could not get in, and so they moved on.

Peter finally settled down, though he jumped every time he heard something across the roof or against the walls. Sometime in the middle of the night, he heard Hazel rise, and a minute later, they heard a click and urine hitting a plastic bucket, then a click again.

Hazel must have heard him move, since she whispered, "And by the way, if you need to use the bucket, don't forget to lift the lid."

Her cot creaked as she settled back down. Peter heard Gus turning, and the box that supported his feet moved against the floor. Peter finally managed a few hours of decent sleep after that, rising at dawn with Hazel sitting cross-legged on the floor reading a book, surrounded by dogs. She smiled as Peter joined her, debating on using the bucket or the great outdoors.

"It may be a bit before they wake," Hazel whispered.

Peter looked over Sara sprawled on her cot, still in deep slumber, and Gus who looked about the same. Erik started to place a hand over his eyes, trying to keep out the filtered light of dawn. Peter took the opportunity to be first at the bucket, followed shortly by their bleary-eyed pilot.

Within a half hour, roused by the sounds of the others, all were up and ready to see what the day would bring. They walked back toward the café for breakfast. Peter felt the need to get more information on why this woman was so willing to stay on her own.

"Do you know if you're immune?" Peter asked.

"I don't want to find out unless I absolutely have to. I know the odds are against me." Hazel shook her head. "We need to stop by the coop first and get the eggs."

The "coop" was a chicken coop that looked like her own shelter. There were two layers of chicken wire surrounding it and the small field next to it, including wire over the top. "The wire goes two feet under the ground. The zrats and zogs sometimes manage to dig under, and I'll find them trapped in here in the morning. That's how Bob saved me; he caught a zog as it lunged, held it down, and tore out its throat. You'd never think he'd be capable of something like that."

She opened the first door, went down a short way, and then opened the second. As they got closer, the clucking and noise from inside grew clamorous.

"All right, girls," Hazel said as she unlocked and opened the slat.

Hens fought their way through and down the ramp, and a rooster stuck its head through then finally the rest of its body, its comb erect and red. He began to crow as soon as his feet hit the board. Hazel led the stranded group to the other side and a narrow door cut into the back secured in three places by locks. It was only wide enough for Hazel, Sara, and Peter, who entered slipping sideways. Hazel lit her flashlight, revealing two rows of nests, and then she untucked a bag from her waist.

"Lay them in gently," Hazel instructed.

The three worked quickly, gathering forty eggs. They slipped back through the entrance, securing it. Gus looked in the bag and whistled.

"Good protein," he commented.

"Yup. They keep the dogs and me well fed."

Without another word, she led them out of the chicken corral and on to the café. Hazel shooed her guests outside as she prepared their meals. Within minutes, a smell filled the air like a siren and her song—bacon. They couldn't resist the temptation to peek in to see if they could "help," and Hazel chased them back out with a snap of her towel and then again proved herself the ultimate hostess. Coffee, eggs, bacon, and a kind of drop biscuit made in the pan with the bacon grease were loaded onto the plates Sara that carried into the dining room.

Two of the tables that had been OK the day before were now cracked.

"They were in here last night." Gus remarked, righting a table.

Peter looked around, but there were no dark corners in the small building in which the Zs could hide. The only room with the door still on it was the freezer, and that was triple locked.

Once everyone had their fill, Gus asked about a map of the area so that they could make it to Cheyenne.

"Well ..." Hazel wiped her mouth and laid down the napkin. "You'll need to head west on I-76, then northwest on 34, and then north on I-85. When you hit I-85, you'll likely be in with a bunch of ... I don't know what to call them ... refugees?"

"How about 'the displaced'?" Peter thought about the term used in World War II and the Great Depression.

"I guess that will work. It's about 110 miles to Cheyenne along the roads, but it will be better than trying to go the eighty or ninety over land. It's dry—no shelter, no water. Along the roads will be towns, way stations set up by the army once you get to I-85. One of the houses in town has bicycles in decent shape." Hazel looked at Gus. "I don't know about you, though."

Gus shrugged and stood, picking up the plates and laying them along his long arm. "I'll manage." Riding a bike, even one too small, sounded a lot better than walking to Cheyenne. Before setting out, Hazel explained that she left the garage doors open in the places she'd explored.

"Leaves them fewer places to hide," she explained as they walked into the residential parts of town.

This neighborhood had larger houses and yards than the ones near the café. They saw some cars.

"I already took all the gas," Hazel added.

One garage had kayaks and bikes suspended from hooks. Spare tires hung by size, and a small portable pump and some replacement spokes and other tools were scattered on the workbench. A fine layer of dirt and dust covered it all, and the metal was starting to rust, but everything was in good shape. The adult male bike was set for someone around six foot one, and the seat could be raised a few more inches, so Gus shouldn't be any more miserable than Peter, the shortest of the men and therefore relegated to the boy's bike. Sara's fit her perfectly. She quickly went out into the street doing figure eights, the dogs chasing her and running into each other.

Gus assembled what he and Peter deemed they might need, found a hiking pack, and then returned to the café. Hazel loaded them up with water and preserved supplies.

"Why don't you come with us?" Sara asked of her new friend.

"Because someone's gotta be here to help strangers who become friends." Hazel gave Sara a quick hug.

Gus shook her hand. "If you change your mind, ask for me. We'll find a place for you," he promised.

"Since you can't promise a place for my fellas here, I'll have to pass, but I'll keep it in mind." Hazel embraced him and then Peter and Erik, and then she pointed them to the highway. A few of the dogs tried to follow after, but she whistled them back.

Hazel warned them the first real town they'd hit was over thirty miles away, and even pushing it, she doubted they could safely make it by nightfall. The better bet was stopping at the Yardly ranch between the reservoirs. Before the virus, it was a place for tourists, and if they were still there, the Yardlys she knew would be hunkered down for the long haul. The group was to tell them that Hazel had sent them.

Gus had no trouble finding it. The "Welcome to Yardlys' working and dude ranch—come for a day or a month, and you'll never lack for something to do" sign led them down the right road. Gus smiled at the ad aimed at families desperately trying not to let technology take over their lives.

Once they made it down the ranch's gravel road, the entry no longer looked so friendly. A man lay on the tower over the front gate with his rifle pointed at Gus.

"Halt," the gunman instructed. "We ain't takin' no more guests."

It was Sara who spoke first. "But Hazel told us to come here."

"Hazel who?" Neither the voice nor the gun wavered.

Sara gave an exaggerated sigh. "Hazel in Fort Morgan. She used to be a math teacher, and now she takes care of the dogs since everyone else wants to kill them."

The gun briefly went down, and they heard the click of a walkie-talkie and a murmur. A moment later, a voice with static could be heard. "Let them in."

"Roger," the guard replied. He disappeared for a moment, and they heard him land on the other side of the gate. The door swung open to usher them in, closing the gate behind. "Keep heading up the road, past the pool and to the main house. You'll go through a second gate, but they've been told you're coming."

Cows grazed by the roadside. The immediate fence was a combination of wood and triple layers of barbed and chicken wire with bits of dead Z, creating the odd aroma that they all noticed when riding up. The second gate opened, and they rode over the cattle guards and past the pool, now covered, and could not miss the main house, whose solar panels reflected the late-afternoon sun. A large man who looked like he'd walked out of central casting for the grizzled rancher stood on the porch, waiting.

Gus led the way after propping their bikes by the porch.

"Joe Yardly," the rancher introduced himself.

Gus presented the group, and all shook hands. Joe bowed to Sara, who laughed and curtsied.

"You can take the bikes over to the barn and then come on in. We'll have some fresh water for you to wash up before supper," Joe said and then retreated into the house.

With the bikes secured a couple of buildings down, they returned to the house and were greeted by an older woman.

"Howdy. I'm Betty Yardly. Let me show you your rooms." She smiled down at Sara. "I even found you a dress that will look very pretty."

Peter and Erik would share a room, with Gus the next floor up, two doors down from the Yardlys, and Sara between in a room decorated completely in pink and frills.

"This was our daughter's room and then our granddaughters' when they visited," Betty said.

"Are they OK?" Sara whispered, even though she knew it was impolite to ask.

"Yes, thank the Lord. We've been keeping communication with the old ham radio. I used to laugh at Joe tinkering with that thing; now I bless it almost every day." Betty smiled as she opened the closet, eyeing Sara. "This should fit."

It was covered with sunflowers and had a bow in the back.

"You can wash your face in the basin. There's some fresh soap, and a brush for your hair. The chamber pot is under the bed."

Sara no longer needed to ask what one was. This one looked authentic, made of porcelain and decorated.

"Supper should be ready in thirty minutes."

The group reassembled in the main dining room. The last of the day lit the room. Peter examined the windows—an outer set of shutters, then the window, and an inner "door" to cover the window from inside with additional bracing at the ready. The front door had a shutter as well with three braces across. Once all was secure, the lamps were lit, giving an odd odor.

"Beef tallow," Betty said as she and some other women carried in food. "My momma taught me to do it when I was girl, and I never thought I'd need to use the skill, but here we are."

Two tables were set up in the large room, each setting twelve people. The men assembled at the first, the women at the second. Sara looked at Peter when Betty called.

"Come sit next to me." Betty gestured, locking eyes with Peter to let him know not to complain. Peter nodded and sent her over.

"Let us say grace," Joe's voiced boomed over the group as he took the head of the table. "Dear Lord, thank you for another day in these troubled times. Thank you for our guests tonight, and please allow them to continue their journey in safety. Thank you for your blessings. We understand the meaning of your curse. It is a time to rebuild this world as you intended it to be, a world that fears you and blesses you in all things, creating a world that adheres to your word and your laws."

Peter almost choked biting down on his tongue, but he kept his head down in obeisance.

"In the name of the Lord, amen," Joe finished.

Everyone, including Peter, murmured, "Amen." He would not insult his host or risk the group being turned out into the night. Everyone sat as if on cue.

The food was passed around the men's table first, and then Betty or one of the other women took it to the women's table, sometimes with little left on the plate or in the bowl. The women kept their voices low, and Sara was quickly reminded to lower her voice with a word from Betty after receiving a look from Joe. The head of the house liked to proselytize throughout the meal, inviting few comments from those gathered. Those at his table, eating his food, were expected to nod and agree, no matter what outrageous or bigoted words shot from his mouth. Peter caught Gus's calm expression but saw that his ears were turning a livid red. Peter himself used every Zen breathing and distraction technique he could think of to make himself not jump up and call the man out for what he was. Joe turned his gaze to Peter as the meal almost finished.

"So what church do you go to?" Joe's smile spread a little too wide.

"Unitarian," Peter promptly responded.

In second and third grade, the Bible Bus parked just off school grounds, and once a week, the students "voluntarily" took Bible class during recess. Peter begged his mother not to make him go, but she did not want him singled out. The summer before second grade, every Sunday, they took the ferry across the James River and went to the UU Church in Williamsburg, so when he was asked that same question, Peter would have an honest answer. He'd been back twice since the third grade, and the Bible Bus ended, but it was still his stock reply on the rare occasion it was needed.

Joe snorted but accepted the answer. To be polite, he asked the same of Gus, who was Presbyterian, and the pilot, who was Catholic.

"As it says in Luke," Joe began, "if we are all the Children of God in Christ—"

Peter couldn't stop himself; he had to correct the man about something. "Galatians."

Joe stopped, not accustomed to being interrupted.

"Galatians 3:26. 'For ye are all the Children of God by faith in Christ Jesus.'" Peter felt Gus's firm kick and practically yelped. "But I'm sure it says similar things in other books, as well." An almost eidetic memory could get you into trouble sometimes.

"And a Bible scholar. I should have known since you were named for an apostle." Joe nodded comfortably, sitting back in his chair.

Peter inwardly sighed. He was actually named after Peter Higgs, the man who formulated the existence of the Higgs boson, otherwise known as the "God particle." Peter decided not to correct him again and made it through the rest of the meal without note.

After supper, Gus asked to use the ham radio to contact Cheyenne, and Joe agreed.

Twenty minutes later, Peter heard a tap at the door. Gus must have used a fingertip since the door didn't rattle its hinges.

"They say it's not safe to go along the highway; they'll send a chopper for us in the morning. It'll pick us up back on the road."

Peter was happy to hear that they would have limited interaction with Joe tomorrow; he might not stand up to another round of scrutiny.

Andy was decidedly jealous of Emma's apartment. He whistled and plopped onto the couch. The TV had a working DVD player—not that either of them had anything to play. The cartoon video left in it indicated the age of some of the prior inhabitants.

"Man, you even get your own bathroom!"

Emma sat next to him and then leaned back to look at the industrial tile ceiling. "I share it with six guards," Emma reminded him, "who take up the spare bedroom."

"Em, really, you have your own bedroom. I'm in a bunk room with seven other guys who skipped their last bath day. I think you win." Andy settled into the couch, letting himself mold into the cushions. "Maybe I'll just stay here."

Emma smiled. "I might even let you if it's OK with Peter when he gets here."

"Oh, I knew I should have gone for the love interest." Andy elbowed her.

"Ow!" Emma rubbed her arm.

"Sorry. Want to watch the cartoon again?" Andy seemed hopeful.

"I don't think I'm ready for a singing fish three times in one day. Besides, there's a meeting with the senior advisers in about an hour, and they invited me to attend." Emma brushed down her sweat- and dirt-stained shirt that no amount of bar soap and rubbing managed to clean.

"I saw the secretary of state go into a room a few doors down. She's taller but about your size; she might have some clothes," Andy said.

As always, Andy read the odd things that distressed her. Emma could deal with Zs. Talking to however many survivors over the radio? No problem. Being inundated with questions at every meal she could handle with aplomb. But showing herself to the new president in a dirty shirt made her stomach tighten and feel embarrassed.

"I feel odd asking her," Emma started, touching the stain on her sleeve.

"I'll go with you." Andy stood and helped her up.

As they opened the door, they came to an abrupt stop as Press Secretary Zimburg stood next to Pat chatting with a small wardrobe hanging on a rack.

"Oh, good." James smiled. "Just who I was looking for. We need to get you dressed; there will be photos and video today."

The press secretary and Andy wrestled the rack into the room.

"He's probably going to make you surgeon general since God only knows what happened to the one before. That will make you official," James said.

Emma was taken aback at the news. She was twenty-eight and hadn't quite finished her residency. There were so many doctors present with so much more experience.

"B-but Dr. Goodman—" Emma finally stuttered out.

"Lovely man," James said. Holding up a light pink blouse, he glanced at Andy's screwed-up face and shook his head. "You're right; terrible color for her." He grabbed the light blue one that Andy held out. "Much better. But, yes, Dr. Goodman is lovely, but the man cannot speak in public—or should I say, others can't *listen* to him speaking in public." A gray jacket and pencil skirt soon met with both men's approval. "No, this is definitely the right decision. The public knows you, trusts you, and—if I may say—loves and adores you. In a few years, they won't remember you weren't already surgeon general before the whole thing started."

Emma hooked the ensemble over her elbow and went to change, stopped short by a quick whistle. Andy held out a pair of nice black pumps.

"Ooh, perfect." James almost clapped.

Emma slipped into her bedroom while the two men chatted—or flirted, more like. When she reemerged, Emma felt like she was interrupting something special.

"Excellent!" James declared as he pulled away from Andy. "Take anything off the rack that will fit and then leave it in the hall." Secretary Zimburg waved as he left, more to Andy than to her.

"You found a friend?" Emma teased.

"Maybe." Andy smiled. "Now let's see to your hair."

At the appointed time, Emma entered the hall and met with Secretary Hudson emerging from her rooms, flanked by two guards—one a woman who could only be described as Amazonian with her height, broad shoulders, and military carriage, and the other was shorter, darker, and—from the looks of his nose—likely a former boxer.

"Dr. O'Conner, I'm glad we get to meet before the rest of the council gets together." Secretary Hudson moved lightly and quickly in her heels, almost outpacing her guard.

"The pleasure is all mine, Madam Secretary."

Emma had always been impressed by the energetic woman who never let a foreign leader or congressman get the better of her. Elsie didn't always win her fights, but she always fought for what she believed in. As they walked, Emma felt the burning eyes of the Amazon woman behind her. Emma had become accustomed to being watched; she had to accept it as a normal part of life, but this woman's interest was somehow different. They descended another four levels to the most secure area with a room decorated as an exact replica of the Oval Office.

Elsie led them past that room and down a hall to a large conference room. The decor was definitely late '60s or early '70s with dark wood paneling. The TV monitors and central computer console seemed the only modern redecorating to be attempted. The large oval table had place cards. Emma sat near the far end, Elsie at the president's right hand. The rest of the group continued their muted conversation as the women took their places. A man wearing a military uniform covered with medals took the chair to the president's left, and James sat next to Emma. With the sound of a throat clearing, they all rose as the president entered. He nodded and took his seat without further ceremony.

"Thank you for coming. I am glad to see the numbers expanding as we locate more leaders to help our great nation navigate the crisis." His attention took everyone in turn. "I am sure there is no need to remind you that what we say now is considered top secret. Things that we can discuss with others will be given to you in a folder." His gaze turned to Emma and James. "This is especially true for the two of you. You are the most often in the public eye. We need to keep the public informed but not add to their fear." Emma and the press secretary simply nodded. "Justin, if you can give us the update on survivors."

Interior Secretary Justin Marshall cleared his throat. "We have continued to explore waterways, since they appear safest way to travel, and have found many survivor outposts. The ones with the best defenses are on islands, including Tangier Island in Virginia, and those on peninsulas that can close themselves off. Some of the reports include the destruction of major bridges to keep the Zs from crossing. We will provide a full list of towns and their rating during tomorrow's meeting."

"How many citizens can we account for?" Elsie asked.

"So far, between the estimates from the towns and the military-led refugee camps, close to 47 million," Justin responded. The murmur that erupted in the room took several minutes to quell. Emma couldn't help let out a gasp. Before the outbreak, there had been over 315 million people in the United States. "I am sure we will find many more; we just started exploring and tracking surviving citizens."

The president wiped his brow and nodded. "And communications?"

"We have completed twenty radio towers with solar-powered transmitters in the last five days. We have five protected Army Corps of Engineers crews working along both coasts, and then they will cut across the country. Most of the time, they have been able to repurpose existing towers to the new radio frequencies and scavenge solar panels. The goal for each crew is to get a tower operational in two days."

"Good. Gabriella, anything back from the Nelsons?" The president turned to the secretary of energy.

Gabriella Monteverdi cleared her throat. "They want to be paid in gold." Gabriella grimaced as the room turned from upset at the loss of life to outrage at the greed. Emma felt confused.

James leaned toward her and whispered, "The Nelson brothers have four of the remaining six operational oil refineries, including the only one with jet fuel—refineries that are being protected by the US military and the National Guard." Emma felt her pressure rise with the others.

President Solis rolled his shoulders. "They have us. We need the fuel to find our people and move essential goods and personnel. If we pull out our troops from their protection, we don't get any fuel, but we can use military guards and weapons as a bargaining chip. Negotiate hard, and remind them of patriotism."

Gabriella nodded.

The president turned to Secretary of Agriculture Walter Branch. "Food?"

"We're helping some of the larger ranches move their herds onto islands in the Great Lakes, and for those not close, we're building triple-concrete barrier walls around the animals. As to mass food production, the zrats ate the flowers from the fruit trees; we didn't get a chance to wall them off. We'll try to secure fields for rice and grain production in time to get at least a few small crops in, and the botanists and engineers have come up with some elevated grow boxes we talked about this morning, so folks can make mobile container gardens."

"Elsie, anything new internationally?" Solis sounded hopeful.

"We were able to raise a few members of the Italian parliament on the sat phone. They have retreated into the Southern Alps. They say the Zs are not moving past the snow line, which we've also heard from Canada. The Russians are trying to systematically destroy them, but the colonel we spoke with says they're running out of ammo faster than they are killing the Zs. Most of their government has retreated up to Siberia. Iceland, Finland, Sweden, and Norway are taking in survivors from all over, probably more in population than they have lost to the virus, but their food and fuel reserves are running low. We lost contact with Chechnya." Elsie still felt revolted when she thought of their leaders' tactic of exposing everyone.

"Any ideas why these creatures won't go into the cold?" the president asked.

"Homeostasis," Emma replied without thinking. It was the pimping-type question she was used to on rounds. Everyone looked at her.

"Go on," President Solis prompted.

Emma felt her color rise but forced herself to speak slowly, lecturing, "The Zs run at a body temperature hotter than humans. We noted that with the first few victims. Where we maintain at 98, give or take a degree, they run about 101–102. With the need to run at an even higher temperature, they have higher fuel needs. The greater the difference in temperature, the higher the caloric need to maintain their bodies in their normal working state—homeostasis."

"So for the Zs, the warmer, the better." The president rubbed his chin. "Thank you, all of you. We will adjourn for now and reconvene in two days. You'll be given your packets on the way out."

"Good job." James grabbed her shoulder as they stood. "I need to talk to you about Colonel McLeod. I'm finishing the details on a story we'll report tonight on how he rescued some of us from the Space Needle. I need a few details of how he went from protecting you to getting us out three thousand miles away."

Emma shrugged. "He lost contact with his wife, who had been evacuated to Seattle. I didn't think I was going anywhere, and she and their daughters needed him more than I did. Rescuing the rest of you was just a bonus."

James grinned, his glance taking in Elsie's Amazon security woman, whose gaze softened some as she overheard the comment. "Let me introduce you to someone. Dr. Emma O'Conner, meet Gunnery Sergeant Marsha McLeod."

The two women clasped hands.

"I'm pleased to meet you." Emma tried not to grimace from Marsha's grip.

"It's good to know the woman my husband was pulled away to protect was worth the effort." Emma was shocked by the bluntness but realized no malice was in the comment. After a moment, she realized that it was a compliment.

"Thank you," Emma replied, and Marsha released her hand. James gestured for Emma to follow. "I will see you again soon." With that, the women parted.

"You are *not* allowed to transfer to her security detail," Elsie half joked.

"I would not dream of it." Marsha held the door for the secretary and breathed a sigh of relief. The doctor was definitely not Gus's type. Marsha knew it could have been the pregnancy causing the green monster to invade her thoughts, but seeing Emma's fine features, pale skin, and eyes, Marsha knew that she had nothing to worry about as the tawny muscles beneath her shirt rippled.

Charlene was sad to see Gus and his friends go. Peter helped improve the electrical system, getting the solar panels wired in a way to boost the power. Colonel Pearce said that he'd make sure Elysian Heights would be on the survivors list, so as the government got a handle on the situation, more aid would come through. Charlene could only hope for help by winter. Hitchins planned the food warehouse run in the morning. He'd use the trucks and fuel that the "army" had left. There was a gas station at the warehouse, as well—likely sucked dry but worth a shot since they'd have a generator with them. After a great debate, the army took the Minimi. There wasn't enough ammunition left for it to be useful, and in exchange, Elysian Heights could keep ten more rifles.

Gus had diagrammed out how to make their own bullets using spent shell casings, gunpowder from fireworks, and scrap metal. He showed them how to remove gunpowder from an active shell so that they could make the mold. During the day, Charlene sent out crews to pick up as many casings as they could find. Like everything except fight Zs, humans had done it before and could do it again. The farmer and his daughter, Clarisse, showed several of the townsfolk how to shear the sheep, and now some of the others were going through Mrs. Pool's books on how to make wool. They were in the process of washing it. Hitchins had laundry soap on the supply list.

A natural spring fed the grass for the golf course, and if they needed water, the Chattahoochee River sat just four miles to the east and Altoona Lake about the same to the northwest. They'd need to start making nets to supplement their food; catching with a line wouldn't provide much. Cisterns and the pool supplied most of their day-to-day needs, and with the steady spring rains, water was not currently a big worry.

She knew the Dobbins Air Reserve Base had been abandoned and scavenged, but maybe copper wire, large tubs, or vats or other supplies could be salvaged. The fear was that the large, dark buildings could hold hundreds of Zs, so thus far, they avoided much exploration. Charlene rolled her neck and tried not to think of her children or Al. When she remembered her family, a dark pit began in her stomach and soon threatened to overwhelm her. Normally, she worked herself through the day, but even then, Charlene could find herself waking in the night, feeling alone and small in the dark. She wanted to wake up and find that it had all been a dream, but each morning dawned with the fortified fence surrounding the Heights, with cows grazing on the rough.

The sound of feet pounding made her look up from the porch.

"Madam Mayor! Charlene!" Kurt held his side, sucking in air hard and fast from his run. "You have a message from your son!"

Charlene was at his side without remembering standing or coming down the stairs.

"On the ham! Just came through!"

Charlene was already jogging in the direction of the clubhouse when Kurt caught up, shoving a piece of paper in her hand. Charlene stopped to read.

MOM, GOT WORD FROM TYBEE—KRISTINA AND CONNER ARE SAFE. NO WORD ABOUT DAD. LOVE, KEVIN.

Charlene cried, hugging Kurt, twirling with the note from sheer joy. Her daughter, her son, and her grandson were alive. She found herself kissing the note and holding it to her heart as if it were one of her family. All of the trials, all of the fighting, all of this was now worth it. Charlene carefully took the note inside to dry before folding it, not wanting the letters to smear. It was her only tangible proof. Her living room displayed a painting of the Madonna with the baby Jesus, a replica of a famous painting bought on a trip to Italy. She fell to her knees and clasped her hands before the sacred lady.

"Thank you, with all of my heart, I thank you." Charlene realized that next to the days her children and grandson were born, today was the best day of her life.

Toya hated waiting for the seeds to sprout. From the packets, she knew it could take weeks. The metal and glass cold frame, created from a picture Toya found in a gardening magazine, fit snugly over her large square pots made of several layers of wire of slightly enlarging size, allowing for drainage, but keeping the zrats from getting to the tender roots from the underside. The raised garden situated near the river allowed for irrigation, though the glass top did not let in the day's rain; that would need some modification. The last couple of days had been solid and gray with little wind and a steady spring rain that felt good at first but then penetrated through the skin, causing a deep chill. Toya secured her MP3 player under her shirt to keep it as dry as she could, singing hip-hop while checking the progress of each bed. She smiled at the beans, already sending up their first little leaves.

Hiccup waved to Toya on his way to his main zrat-watching station; between the Delaware and Cooper Rivers seemed to be a hot spot. He set up a light before dark to bring them in and then *thwack!* with his baseball bat. Even as gray as the day had been, he figured that it was about an hour before sundown—time to set up shop, baseball bat in hand. Hiccup would be whistling if he knew how. He had found his calling. The town hadn't seen a zrat in days, not since Charles put Hiccup in charge of the zrat-killing team. Hiccup was still pissed at Charles and would get even at the first chance, but he felt less like killing the little Frenchman and more like pounding him into the dirt for all to see.

Movement along the river stopped Hiccup in his tracks. A person climbed onto the riverbank while Toya remained oblivious, singing over her seedlings.

There was something wrong in the man's thick sunglasses on a dark, gray day. Hiccup broke into a run, shouting and waving his arms. Toya caught the movement and initially smiled but then turned at his gestures in time to see the wet man coming toward her. She couldn't stop the scream that erupted as the man lunged, trapping her by the seedling beds. From his peripheral vision, Hiccup caught sight of Charles running, but he was too far away. Hiccup wished he were watching some terrible horror movie, yelling some smart-ass remark at the characters, but instead it was his sister, trapped with only a trowel and her fists for her defense.

The man bit at Toya, who punched and jabbed with her gardening tool in her right and her fist with her left, but he was too close for her to get much power behind the hits. Hiccup picked up speed and cocked his zrat bat. As the man turned and raised his hand to block the blow, Hiccup swung for the fences, hearing a welcome crunch from the bones of the man's left forearm. The man barely grunted and used his right arm to pull Hiccup closer, keeping the bat from being readied for a second blow. His mouth clamped through Hiccup's T-shirt, tearing at the flesh. Toya's scream changed from one of fear to one of fury as she stabbed at the man's back with the trowel. The man pushed back, shoving her against the glass, shattering the cover as she lost her balance. This freed Hiccup to land a blow on the man's head, throwing askew the sunglasses and making him stagger. Toya grabbed one of the metal support bars from the now broken frame and pointed it forward like a lance at full run, burying the tip into the man's chest. The man pushed her back by the face, ripping out the metal stake. Blood flowed around him, but he stood, righting the glasses as Hiccup took another swing, breaking the man's other arm as it raised to ward off the blow. Now Hiccup could swing at the head again and again, leaving it less than melon pulp by the time Charles arrived.

Charles took Toya in his arms, her hands and back covered in small cuts, but none looked serious.

"I saw his eyes." Toya's own held fear. Like most, she had become complacent behind the wall and in the light of day. "He was one of those *things*."

Charles swallowed. He hadn't thought of a Thinker going for a swim in daylight, but it remembered enough to wear sunglasses. By the time anyone else arrived, there was only a bloody mass where the monster's body used to be.

Stokes's arrival finally calmed Hiccup enough to stop his stomping and swearing. The torn T-shirt with the open sore told a tale all its own, and no one had been willing to approach Hiccup in his rage. Toya, from knowing that he needed to burn himself out, held Charles back, and most of the others kept their distance from fear of what that bite signaled. Stokes took the bat and placed it on the ground, taking his brother into a hug as Hiccup's tears burst forth.

"He was going to get Toya, *hic*" Hiccup choked. "He came out of the river, but it's day—*hic*" his sobs came forth again. The crowd turned away under Charles's and Toya's direction, trying to give Hiccup some space.

"Ya did good, Arnold. I'm proud of you." Stokes hugged Hiccup again. "Let's take you to Doc and let someone else get this thing's body cleaned up."

"Yeah, I pulverized it." Hiccup's tears dried as his smile broke out, turning to Charles. "This time tommara, you'll be puttin' me on the outside crew." Hiccup left with a cocky swagger, already enhancing the story.

Stokes should have taken Hiccup to the isolation room at the school, but he brought him to the room that had been Auntie's and was now his. Something about being able to sleep in his big brother's bed made Hiccup proud.

Before dawn, the fever started, climbing quickly. By 10:00 a.m., Toya and the doc knew that he wouldn't be among the immune, but Stokes refused to let anyone touch his brother. Hiccup seized and recovered, sweat poured from him with the fever. By nightfall, the temperature lowered, but his irises were lost to the huge pupils. Hiccup growled and lunged at anyone in the room, straining against the handcuffs that bound him to the bed.

Toya touched Stokes on the shoulder, who shrugged her away. "Would you ... I can get Catch or—"

"*No*!" Stokes roared back at her. "It has to be me."

Hiccup's Glock sat on the dresser, loaded, ready for what must be done. Charles took Toya's hand. Stokes turned and glared at him. Charles knew that Stokes blamed him—whether for the zrat duty or not being the one with Toya, he didn't know—but the feeling of not belonging shot through Stokes's gaze as much as if he'd been told to go away and never return. Toya's hand kept Charles from retreating down the stairs. Stokes walked back and forth in the narrow little hallway, beginning to sweat. He pulled off his jacket and threw it to the floor and then kicked it out of the way.

Ready, Stokes shut the door to the room. Stokes remembered giving the pistol to his brother, telling Hiccup that he was a real man now. Daniel rebuked him, saying that a real man didn't need a gun; he needed his wits. The gun was just a tool. Stokes had to talk Daniel into taking Hiccup. It was the only way Stokes could keep an eye on his brother, keep him from getting into real trouble. Hiccup was fast, so when a cop showed up, there wasn't much worry about him getting caught, though others would have liked it if he could spot a cop before one pulled out the badge.

Stokes sat on the end of the bed, hot tears running down his cheeks, watching his brother lunge, the eyes empty turning away from the single candle in the room. He couldn't remember the last time he'd cried. Stokes felt a need to do something, to know something. He looked at his brother again and then offered his arm.

The strong teeth and jaws of a seventeen-year-old clamped down and through the flesh. Stokes pulled away, stunned by what he'd done. Did he think his brother was still in there? This proved that Hiccup—Arnold, he corrected himself—was gone. In a day, he'd know the truth about himself. Stokes stood, and a few seconds later, he fired three shots into his brother—chest, chest, head. Toya jumped, hearing each one, tears running freely as she sank to her knees. Stokes opened the door, wrapping a shirt around his arm, which caused Toya to weep even more.

Charles noted the blood seeping through the cloth and stepped aside, allowing Stokes access to the stairs.

"I'm getting a blanket. Help me with his body," Stokes said without turning.

Charles knew that it was directed at him. The blame had shifted to another useless place.

Outside, the people of Pyne and Cooper Poynts lined the street. Catch and Con bridged the body in the procession. The rain had let up in the afternoon, allowing them to light the tire fires along the river. Hamlet found a board to lay Hiccup across a set of four tires, and Stokes soaked the shrouded body in kerosene. Toya and Stokes each took a torch, placing them on the corpse, the body erupting in acrid-smelling flames. The town stood, feet shifting, and Auntie led them in "Amazing Grace," since that's what one should always sing at a funeral.

Reverend Curtis cleared his throat. "Let us bow our heads, remembering Hiccup—"

"Arnold!" Stokes yelled out. "His name was Arnold! None of you remembered that!"

"Then let us remember Arnold," Charles began. His voice was low, but it carried through the silence following Stokes's outburst. "'e was very good at killing zrats." There were several claps and low cheer to that.

"And he saved my life," Toya added, her tears flowing again.

"And he never tired of talking about his big brother," Catch added, clasping Stokes on the shoulder.

“So, yes,” Reverend Curtis began again, “let us remember Arnold and what he meant to us, how he helped our survival, how his memory will live in us all.”

The vigil lasted most of the night. Toya led Stokes back to her little apartment down the street from Auntie’s. Toya washed the wound and checked his temperature. It was 101. She watched him as he fell asleep.

In midmorning, she and Charles determined that it was safe for her take a break since the fever never climbed above 104.

When Stokes woke that evening, it was Charles who sat vigil. “Toya was too exhausted. I sent ’er to bed.”

“Thanks.” Stokes took the bottle of water Charles offered, draining it quickly.

“The people would never follow me the way they do you. Why?” Charles had to ask and thought that if he did not do it now, he never would.

Stokes shrugged. “I needed to know. If I don’t have to live in as much fear of them, maybe I become more useful.”

“And if you died?”

“I wouldn’t care anymore. You and Toya are smart; you’d figure out how to get by without me.” Stokes adjusted his pillow. “Now let me sleep. I’m tired. And don’t sit there and watch me; that creeps me out.”

Charles grinned and nodded, leaving Stokes to his rest.

Guillermo adjusted his binoculars. No doubt about it—a cruise ship adrift. Their supplies would be gone, and a ship that size used too much fuel to be an effective getaway ship, but his curiosity pulled at him. Thiago, the fishing boat captain, waited for orders. “Take us closer. We’ll see how desperate they are.”

“They could have good radio gear—better than what we have here,” Paulina pointed out.

“And if we can haul it closer, a really nice desalinator, generators, diesel engine parts, linens,” Mitchell added.

“More people to fight the Zs, build walls. Maybe another doctor.” Guillermo had no concern about his population. The sea was providing plenty of food, so long as people were OK with fish and seaweed stew. If anyone complained about the diet, it was pointed out that no one made them stay and that they were welcome to leave when they liked. No one volunteered to go. “Maybe they’ll greet us as liberators.” Guillermo grinned at Mitchell.

“Not my president. I’m Canadian,” Mitchell reminded him.

Guillermo laughed and slapped his back. "I know, but I like pulling your leg. Let's show them our friendly faces."

That meant more European-looking ones less likely to scare those on board. It was why Beatrice joined them, although boats were obviously not her preferred method of travel, as she hugged the rail the entire way out and groaned more once Thiago gunned the engine.

Roughly twenty wet people, from the ragged clothing crew and passengers alike, lined the promenade deck of the *Glory of the Atlantic*, with makeshift bows and a few guns in evidence. The ship had seen better days. It was dinged and dented all over. The flapping tarps and cloths on deck indicated where most lived. The faces that looked over the sides were dirty enough to cover their ethnicities.

Mitchell waved. "Ahoy! We're friendlies!"

Those in hearing distance cheered but were quickly shushed.

"We've created a village on shore. You're welcome to join us," Mitchell said.

One of the men on deck nodded, and a crewmember threw a rope to Thiago, who attached it to the trawler. A ladder was clipped onto the side of the promenade, allowing Guillermo, Paulina, and a fitter Mitchell to climb aboard. The passengers and crew parted for a man in a relatively clean uniform who introduced himself as Navigator Samuelson, acting captain. The promenade was as clean a place as any, and they sat on lounge chairs as Samuelson and some of the passengers relayed their tale.

They had been on a transatlantic cruise when it all started. Despite stories of the outbreak, they finally had to dock for supplies in the Azores. The crew searched far and wide for food and fuel and were gone past dark. They brought back the virus, as well: zrats in the supply boxes and their droppings in some of the food. A couple of the scavenging crew were bitten. Within days, over half of those on the ship were sick, and the uninfected took no mercy. Anyone with a fever over 106 was immediately terminated and thrown overboard. The zrats were relentlessly tracked down. So many European towns were burning that they'd had no choice but to turn back to North America. They siphoned fuel from an abandoned tanker adrift and then planned to go to Miami, but it, too, was in flames. The people in the Keys waved them off and kept them from landing by force. They planned on Playa del Carmen or Cozumel, and they spent the last of their fuel near Cozumel, only to hear the Zs on the shore in the night. They had drifted in the Gulf for the last three days.

As Samuelson spoke, more people joined them. All told, just over two hundred souls remained aboard on a ship that could easily carry four thousand. Some of the survivors wiped away tears, and another woman brought them weak sun tea, likely made with the last of their fresh water.

"We will be happy to join you," Samuelson said. "We have no other choice."

"I doubt we have enough fuel to move the ship close enough, but we can ferry the people back on fishing boats. We'll need to strip some parts from the ship, but that will take a couple of days," Mitchell told Samuelson.

Guillermo nodded in agreement. Navigator Samuelson did not blink at the man looking askance of the boy; he'd seen much stranger things over the past month.

"That makes sense. I stay with the ship. When you're done with her, I'll go with ya." Samuelson squinted at the waves and the sun and then looked over those on board. "How many can you take now? A few are very weak and won't last much longer."

Guillermo leaned over and shouted to Thiago, who answered back. "Twenty if we stay aboard for now. I'll go and bring the other boats. We can get close to a hundred off today, carry a few supplies for tonight, and get the rest tomorrow."

Samuelson and the woman who had brought the tea, now introduced as Assistant Cruise Director Violet from Australia, selected nineteen of the older and weaker members now on the promenade. Samuelson roped them in for the climb down to the fishing boat, which proved a lifesaving precaution for an elderly gentleman, and then Thiago and Guillermo threw back the line and headed for shore.

Mitchell and Paulina stayed and toured the boat, looking over the equipment and deciding what would be helpful for the town. A few hours later, Guillermo returned with food, Thiago, and four other boats to load more survivors. Guillermo headed back to make sure that all quarantine procedures were being adhered to. With such a large group, he wanted to be sure.

"The boy is your leader?" Samuelson asked as they climbed the stairs to the bridge.

"Yes, but I wouldn't call him a boy anymore," Paulina answered.

"He hasn't been a boy for years, long before all this." Mitchell gave Samuelson and Violet a sketch of Guillermo's life, starting with the murder of his father to now. "So now that he's had his revenge, his energy is focused on helping others survive, trying to make himself as different from El Padre as possible."

"He must be smart." Samuelson looked out over the water, watching the trawlers bounce through the waves.

"Brilliant," Mitchell and Paulina answered together.

Samuelson checked his watch, stood, and tinkered with the radio, turning up the volume.

"Good evening, North America," said the voice on the radio.

"That's Alistair Breedham!" Mitchell felt a lurch of happiness. "He's still broadcasting!"

Samuelson put a finger to his lips, he wanted to hear.

"I am sorry to say it has been a difficult day. Quebec City has been forced to evacuate all remaining survivors. The consensus is that those beautiful older buildings, such as those along the Place Royale, have too many places for zrats and other small infected creatures to survive, spreading the contagion in an unfortunately efficient manner. They are considering using demolition crews to bring down some of those buildings that harbor the highest concentration of infected beings. On the Pacific coast, most of the remaining survivors in Vancouver have evacuated to Bowen and Gambier Islands. In Edmonton, a group of stalwart citizens are refusing to leave the city and have secured the Skyreach Centre for evacuees. We have no news from Europe. Now I turn to Dr. O'Conner in the United States."

"Good evening, Alistair. I am so sorry to hear about Quebec City; it and Montreal have always been on my list of places that I wanted to visit." Emma's voice conveyed her warm sympathy.

Mitchell wondered if it came naturally or if she had been coached.

"Now would not be the time." Alistair's voice kept the firm gravitas, but somehow Emma knew he was trying to make a joke.

"I'm a little preoccupied, anyway," Emma replied. "I do have some better news. Communications towers are going up both coasts, which will be able to transmit multiple frequencies. Using waterways, we will be starting a limited mail system, so surviving family members can find each other. In addition, thousands of Super 8 reel-to-reel projectors with manual-crank backups, left over from the Cold War, will be distributed to towns that we have identified. We will be including instructional videos that review some of the information that has been discussed on this broadcast. I wish I had news that could help Quebec City."

"Will any of these projectors be coming north?" Alistair asked.

"Yes, President Solis has allocated three hundred to be given to Canadian authorities to distribute as they can."

"Thank you, Dr. O'Conner. Now we turn to Dr. Zovitch on part two of our water-purification series."

Mitchell grabbed some paper to take notes. Most of the conveyed information he knew, but there were a few options he had not considered.

After the fifteen minutes discussing water, Alistair returned. "Until tomorrow, stay safe. Alistair Breedham signing off."

"They're on every night?" Paulina asked.

"Alistair is on morning and evening. The morning is shorter, but they often have more news from Europe. The radio frequencies travel better and further at night to gather that information. In the evening, the doctor comes on, and then they have information to help survivors." Samuelson clicked off the radio as the emergency broadcast sound came on.

"We need to find a way to take the antenna." Mitchell looked up.

"It's under the radome on top. Getting to the wiring will be more of a challenge if you need it." Samuelson stood and stretched. "Time for my rounds."

After dark, Samuelson paced the deck. Mitchell went below and examined the giant desalination system. Without natural light or onboard power, the flashlights from the last fishing boat provided his only way to get a good look. The tubing would come apart, and the generators seemed in decent shape but would be difficult to offload without a crane. Some sections of PVC tubing were close to four feet in diameter and might be better suited to making raised beds than to try to heat and cool large volumes of water. After measuring the doors to the room and the equipment, only the middle and smaller sections of tubing could make it out. Two of the desalination generators would fit, as well.

Guillermo didn't want to scuttle the ship, but a hurricane could throw the ship on land, crushing their village. Once all useful items were offloaded, the ship would go down. It took too much fuel to be useful for an evacuation. Mitchell made sure that he stripped as much wire as possible. Paulina returned to get the Bell. The generators would have to be flown home. The radio equipment could be broken down and placed on board one of the fishing boats. Mitchell looked forward to the news more than he ever did at home.

After three days, Samuelson and Mitchell boarded the fishing boat and hit the button. A rumble below deck caused a second wave, and the trawler pulled away. The *Glory of the Atlantic* began to list and then groan as her hull ripped open, and then she turned in a storm of bubbles and froth. In minutes, she sank below the waves as if she'd never been.

CHAPTER 12

May 5-10; Z Days 26-31

Emma paced. Yesterday, when Peter didn't arrive, she'd felt almost in a panic and could barely keep herself together for the news. Luckily, everything was written, and she forced herself to read off the script instead of using it as a guide. When the message came through the night before that they were all safe, she'd wept with joy. Emma forced herself not to think who this "Sara" might be. All she knew was that "Sara" had also been in Raleigh and spoke as a witness against the fake army. They were to arrive at noon today and then spend the required night in quarantine.

The early morning senior staff briefing felt like the longest on record. She tried to say as little as possible, hoping that would move things along. Once the helicopter left Cheyenne, Emma joined Marsha and her two girls on the observation deck. Rankin hugged them all.

"I know it's crazy; you live down the hall, and I still barely get to see you." Rankin rubbed Meagan's hair with his good hand, the other still in a cast. Technically, he shouldn't be on duty, but with the tight staffing, he'd stayed on Emma's protection detail. When she protested the need, Rankin reminded her of what had happened the last time they'd thought she was safe. "Meagan, Miranda, I would like you to meet Dr. Emma O'Conner. I know you and Marsha have already met. Doc, this is Gus's family."

Emma extended her hand to the two girls. Meagan couldn't have been more than ten, and she already reached Emma's shoulder. They were polite and watched their mother. Marsha smiled, and the two women kept up small talk while Rankin watched the growing crowd below, intermittently teasing his nieces and joining in on the women's conversation.

After another eternal hour, Emma held the sight she'd been waiting almost a month to see. His hair was longer, but his smile was the same. She pounded on the window and waved. Peter raised his hand, as did the child next to him.

Emma smiled at Gus and mouthed the *thank you* she wished he could hear, but Gus's eyes were on Marsha and his girls. After a while, other duties called, and the group dispersed, happy in the knowledge that their loved ones were safely there.

Since arriving, Emma had taken shifts at the clinic and worked on her vaccine research. The lab was much less advanced than the one at the

CDC, though some of her work and that of the others could continue. The Cheyenne site housed a large fuel reservoir that could keep the lights on for some time to come, but the memory of the sound and smell in the black hallway still haunted her. Once again, she was stuck far underground. She sat on the council with General Loran, Dr. Goodman, President Solis, and some of the prior White House staff that had arrived a few days earlier, part of the group that Gus had saved in Seattle. Gus didn't know the hero status that he enjoyed in the local surroundings.

Emma greeted Sammy Jo at the clinic, another welcome arrival from Seattle, a good nurse with OB experience. Sammy Jo smiled in response and gave her the rundown of the patients waiting: a three-year-old with constipation, an older man whose gout was flaring (where he got food rich enough to make his gout flare was the first thing Emma wondered), a woman with headaches, and a young man with anxiety. The few doses of anxiolytics remaining were restricted to extreme hospitalized cases only. She'd have to leave him for last, since teaching the breathing techniques to relieve anxiety took about fifteen to twenty minutes. A few more patients trickled in as Emma worked through the afternoon, records typed on a word-processing program and printed in case the computers stopped working.

The gatherers were asked to bring back food and medicine as a priority, but office supplies for printer ink, paper, and pens were in short supply, so they brought back what could be carried of those items, as well. Almost all manufacturing had come to a halt. There were a few oil refineries in Canada and the northern United States still running and a clothing mill in Maine where the employees built a wall that sank several feet below ground to keep out the zrats. Alistair was keeping a close tally on what businesses were operating and which were closed. The biggest concern was farming. When areas were systematically cleared, there were likely enough canned goods for survivors for a year or more, but without food production, he feared for the future. The newsman maintained many contacts and developed hundreds more by the day, and he reported to her the highlights of the information gathered before their daily interview, which she in turn relayed to the council.

Emma had to be ready in the studio by 4:30 p.m. daily, and she spoke live for each coast's broadcast. It was the most fun part of the day. Albeit limited, she even received fan mail with the resumption of some mail services. Emma heard a throat clear.

"Are you done with the chart, Doc? I wanted to get it filed, since I promised to help on the OB ward this evening." Sammy Jo stood politely near the desk.

Emma blushed at her daydreaming and signed the chart, handing it over and then following the nurse out. It was almost showtime. The studio was set up for TV, as well, so the president in the undisclosed location could give speeches and interviews. Since there weren't any TV stations broadcasting, the cameras were covered, and only the large microphones were on display. The other benefit of radio was that she didn't need to worry about makeup. Water was severely rationed, so the extra needed to wash off the day was discouraged. She felt like a pro these days, getting the mic and the settings done. The soundman stopped in to check on her and then was off to work the incoming messages. He'd taught Rankin and Pat how to run the equipment and do most of the troubleshooting, and they knew where to find him if needed.

Rankin sat in the sound booth, trying to dig into his cast to scratch while Pat took up position by the door. The green light came on, and Alistair's voice made her smile.

"Any word?" he asked.

"Peter's here in quarantine, along with Gus and a young girl and their pilot." Emma's relief rushed from her.

"Thank God, or whatever you believe in," Alistair responded. "I'm happy for you. I know it's been a hard month."

Emma couldn't stop the almost hysterical laughter that issued forth. "A hard month? The world just fell apart, we are only beginning to get an idea of how much of the population has survived so far, and *I've* had a hard month?"

Alistair kept his voice calm. "Yes, we all have, but you have been forced to do it with a smile. I didn't realize how much until last night. And I'm glad you have a chance at some happiness."

Emma forced her breathing to slow, unconsciously reaching below the table to touch her lower stomach. She had no idea how much this little one might affect that chance. "I'm sorry I overreacted."

"Oh, don't apologize. I think you've earned a bit of emotional outburst. It's fairly refreshing, actually. You should hear me swear at everyone from the sound engineers to our remaining janitor when even the smallest thing is out of place. And the absolute *stink* outside if I leave a window open that no one else seems to notice."

Emma stiffened. "A bad odor you can't identify—a cross between sour, overly sweet, and skunk?"

"Yes!" Alistair sounded delighted. "What *is* that?"

"I think it's Z," Rankin butted in, one ear to a headphone and holding the mic open.

"Who was that?" Alistair asked.

"Rankin, Gus's brother, one of my guards." Emma sounded distracted. It was the smell from the hallway and the smell her research rats gave off when they were injected with the virus and started to spike a fever before being sacrificed. "And I think he's right. All three of us fought off the virus. Maybe it gives off an odor you only smell if you've been exposed."

"Maybe that's why they don't eat each other," Alistair mused. "They smell too bad."

"Maybe," Emma whispered.

"Ah, showtime." Alistair broke in.

Part of Emma's presentation now was announcing the identified communities of survivors, letting them know that they'd been recognized and mapped. The map in the council office showed more pins every day as the Coast Guard went up rivers and tributaries where they could and the air force flew their helicopters low over cities and towns, looking for signs of life. Scattered small groups that wanted to be brought in were taken to government shelters and camps. Some places wanted to be left alone and were marked with a black pin. Emma did her presentation each time with the energy and enthusiasm she was known for. Tonight, she wanted to rush away and look at Peter again, needing to reassure herself that he was really there. By the end of the last presentation, Emma was out of her seat, hand over the off switch.

"Good night, Alistair," she said before receiving his reply. Over a thousand miles away, Alistair saw the switch go red and smiled.

"Go get him, and Godspeed," he murmured to the universe in general. Once Alistair signed off, he rose stiffly and made his way to his rooms on the top floor. The reassuring upward glance showed that ceiling tiles had been removed to prevent crawl spaces for the zrats. Getting out of the building was almost impossible, since the lower four floors of stairs had been removed and supports set in their place. Food was brought in during the day and raised on pulleys, and waste was lowered in buckets. Elevators were shut down on the bottom floor. The building generated its own power with solar panels and a small windmill to provide electricity for the antennas and equipment. For not the last time, Alistair was glad that he had no family to worry over; it was enough to worry over his friends. He and six employees shared what had been office space in the penthouse.

An old mattress on the floor provided difficult sleeping arrangements for a man of his age, but he managed. The windows were rebuilt since the old ones did not open, and the warming afternoon air would be stifling if they had no circulation. This evening was almost pleasant as he listened to the night sounds of Zs grunting against doors and then distant gunfire as the city's security troops wound through the streets, eliminating any Zs they found. Alistair never imagined that he'd find the sound of gunfire reassuring.

Emma asked to be excused from the morning briefing, but Elsie asked her to stay. More tacks went onto the board. Settlements in Saint Charles, Arkansas, and Camden, New Jersey, were added to the board, both with the dark blue pin for "appear to be holding their own." The highest level was the green pin for "thriving," then the blue, then yellow for "will likely need assistance soon" to red for "likely needs evacuation—imminent threat of collapse/starvation." The few green pins and most of the blues lined major waterways with access to fish as a source of food. Yellows dotted areas where power was needed for irrigation, and red lined interior plains and the desert southwest where power was needed to pump the much-needed water and where most food from the ground was being consumed by the infected.

Emma's eyes always strayed to Virginia, where the city of Chesapeake carried one of the rare green pins, and to Texas, mostly bordered by red to the west, with blues near Austin, New Braunfels, and Baytown, and a yellow in Galveston, which had no fresh water supply of its own and relied on desalination. San Antonio had been evacuated; there had been too many infected too early on. The government/military camps were marked with white pins and scattered across the country, from Alcatraz to Martha's Vineyard and down to Parris and Hilton Head Islands.

Emma paid little attention to the presentations. She was thinking of the smell, that people were regrouping, about communications, and then she suddenly realized that the meeting was ending. Elsie and James would let her know what she needed to say that evening. With too little sleep the last two nights, Emma had trouble focusing. Andy would cover her shift in clinic later in the day.

People made way for her in the hallway that headed to quarantine, smiling and nodding, but for once, hers was not the face they sought out. Gus would be embarrassed by the deserved hero worship. Emma jogged up the steps to the observation area, already crowded with onlookers. Rankin helped to make way to the window where Emma found Marsha and her girls. They smiled to each other in greeting, both more intent on the men below. Gus and Peter stood near the bottom of the steps, grinning and appearing to have a lively conversation going. Sara stood behind them, looking at her shoes. When one said something, she'd look up and give a nervous smile and then return to studying the floor instead of the crowd gathered above. The minutes ticked by, and security cleared away all but Emma, her guard, and Marsha and her girls.

A buzzer sounded, and the door below opened. Peter ducked under Gus's arm and raced up the stairs, Gus on his heels, taking three steps at a time. Peter burst through the door and into Emma's arms, almost knocking her into the glass. Her laugh was stopped by his mouth on hers. They had never kissed beyond the quick peck on the cheek that could be shared by friends. This was a kiss of passion and repressed longing. When they stopped for a moment to catch their breaths, Emma felt the blush rising in her cheeks.

"It's good to see you too," she said softly, smiling into his warm brown eyes.

Peter's hand caressed the back of her neck, sending a delicious chill along her spine that sparked her desire even more.

"I love you. I've wanted to say that for so long, long before all this," Peter started in a rush, his arms pulling her into his chest. "I feel stupid realizing that it took the world going to shit to make me say it."

"I love you too." Emma's response almost couldn't leave her lips since they were buried in his shirt.

He released her for a moment, laughing.

"Let's go someplace more private to talk," she suggested.

"Why not here?" Peter asked in the now almost empty observation area.

Emma realized that the noise was not just the buzzing inside her head but a roar from below as the people greeted Gus, their hero. James had broadcast the story of how Gus continued the rescue mission despite being told that it was too dangerous and that the second patrol from Cheyenne would not be coming (not true, but when did political spin rely on truth?). How he led his men through the Z- and zrat-infested city, dug through the bodies of Zs, and led his men fighting up the Needle's steps to rescue the citizens trapped there. How he miraculously found his wife and daughters who were supposed to be elsewhere, and how he led them out and to safety. Hearing Alistair's deep, rich voice relay the tale gave Emma goose bumps. Secretary Zimburg took an old newspaperman's advice and wrote the legend.

Peter turned as a small voice cleared her throat. He grimaced slightly in embarrassment. For a moment, he'd forgotten Sara. "Sara, come meet Emma."

Sara slowly held her hand out.

"I'm pleased to meet you, Sara." Emma shook her hand formally.

"Nice to meet you too." Her tone was more sullen than Peter had heard before.

"There are a lot of things to do here. There's school, and books, and others your age," Emma added.

"And Zs?" she asked quietly.

"They have kept them out so far," Emma reassured her. "And we have an entire army here to protect us."

Sara shrugged. "I'm not that scared of them. I want to learn how to kill them."

Peter started at the comment, but it did not seem to cause Emma any problems.

"Good. Everyone is required to take classes using weapons." She grinned at Peter. "Gus suggested it in Seattle, and Elsie—um, Elisandra Hudson, the secretary of state—has implemented the rule here."

Emma realized that Peter had noticed Rankin, who stood quietly near the wall, and had turned so that he could see Emma and Peter in his peripheral vision and look down the stairs into the main hallway. "And Peter, Sara, this is Rankin McLeod, Gus's brother. He's part of my protection detail."

Peter looked worried. "I thought you said we were safe here. Why do have a protection—"

Emma grinned and kissed him. "A holdover from President Paulson. In San Antonio, the president instructed Gus to form a protection detail for me and to continue it until he was given the direct order to disband it. The order could only come from the president."

"And since President Paulson is dead—" Peter continued.

"No one has bothered to disband it. I thought about requesting it," she said as Rankin looked down at her and then at his right arm cast, "but it turns out to be useful once in a while. Let me show you two around your new home."

Emma hooked her elbow into Peter's, and his free hand took Sara's. Rankin led the way, the hall downstairs cleared out after greeting Gus. She showed them the commissary, explained how people earned points by doing different jobs, and then could buy clothes, shoes, and toiletries with the points. Peter noted that there was no food or candy. In the cafeteria, Emma explained that people were given a time based on the floor they lived on and that they needed to come through on time or miss their meal. The cafeteria was the only place where food was to be consumed.

Peter wasn't so sure. The sergeant inspecting his bag prior to entering quarantine determined that the candy packages had no holes, and he was happy to accept one in exchange for letting Peter keep the remaining three. He imagined that others brought in food the same way. Peter decided not to tell Emma about his contraband in front of the imposing mute guard of hers.

They continued on to the school, which included a gym where some children about Sara's age were learning the important points to thrusting a knife. Sara's interest piqued immediately. The instructor stopped for a minute and waved them over.

"Hey, Doc. Who's this young lady?"

"I'm Sara," she said, speaking up for herself.

"She's my adopted daughter," Peter added, noticing Sara's grin widen. "I'm Peter Saitou."

"Hank Daughtry."

The men shook hands.

Hank noted the sword sheath poking from Peter's pack and whistled. "From that grip, I know that's a true samurai katana."

Peter pulled it free. "Family heirloom."

Hank took it and watched the light along the blade. The kids were now standing around in wonder.

"He used it to kill a man who was going to kill me." Sara sounded proud.

The other children looked at her with respect.

"I'll find you a proper whetstone for it. I know we have them for the bayonets," Hank offered. "It looks like it's taken some recent dings."

Peter nodded. "It's seen more use in the last month than in the last two hundred years. I've been hoping to find a good whetstone."

Hank handed it back, nodded, and returned to his class. Sara looked longingly after them.

"Yes, you can go." Peter yelled after Hank, "What time do you finish?"

"Three thirty," Hank answered.

"I'll meet you here at three thirty."

Sara grinned and ran to join the class.

Peter and Emma continued to walk arm in arm. His referring to Sara as his adopted daughter made what she had to tell him a bit easier. A knot stayed in her throat, left over from last night's dream where he became angry and called her a whore, stalking out. Peter never used language like that, but her news could change the way he felt. Emma needed a few minutes more of him not knowing.

Emma had been given a family suite, consisting of three rooms and a bathroom—two as bedrooms and a communal room—a palatial amount of space for the compound. When Emma unlocked the door, she felt herself lifted from her feet as Peter carried her over the threshold, kicking the door closed behind, blocking any chance of Rankin following. Peter lowered her onto the little couch while his mouth found hers again.

Emma considered waiting, but she knew if she was to tell him, it had to be now. "Peter, wait. Please."

He stopped, looking a bit confused.

"There are things I need to tell you that you need to know before we go any further," she said.

Peter looked around the room, the size of it. "Is there someone else?" Jealousy crept into his voice.

"No!" Emma stopped. "There *was*." She paused. "Kind of."

Peter tried to pull his hand away, but she gripped it. "Let me start from the beginning."

Peter felt a knife in his gut turning, followed by a harsh hum in his ears and the need to leave. Somehow, her tears stayed him for a moment. He had traveled so far; he could hear her out. Emma started in San Antonio with her bite and then flying to Atlanta with the fellow doctors that saved her. Then she explained about Cory and how she needed someone close and how that changed when she received his e-mail.

"Ask Gus. He was there; he'll tell you." Emma felt so desperate, but Peter listened.

His jaw relaxed, and he finally sat instead of standing over her, ready to head out the door. Emma told of the Thinker, and what Cory told her … and how he died, how she'd killed him. Emma felt Peter's hand along her back as she turned away. She spoke of the evacuation and how she needed to get him a message. Peter felt his lips turn a slight smile, thinking of the bad handwriting. Then she stopped, and he realized that she was crying in earnest.

Peter knew that the next few seconds would decide their destiny. How could he criticize her? Mentally, he knew that they were not together and that he had no right to be jealous of something that happened before Emma knew that he was still alive. The jealousy was there, but Peter couldn't let it control him.

"As you know, I adopted Sara—well, technically, if not legally. She needs a mother. If you can see your way to being her mother, I can see myself the father of this little one." Peter let his hand settle on Emma's stomach, still so flat and thin.

Emma's tears somehow flowed harder, leaning into his chest as his arms surrounded her, supporting her. Peter released the auburn hair from its bun, letting it cascade down her back. He tilted her chin back and kissed her softly, drinking in the subtle smell of coffee.

Peter grinned and reached into his pack and rooted around in it for a minute. He pulled out a battered but distinctive foil package. He kneeled before her as she sat on the couch looking at him in surprise and consternation.

"I do not have a proper ring, but right now I think most would value this gift over diamonds. Doctor Emma O'Conner, will you marry me?"

Emma began to laugh as she took the mint patty in one hand and his hand in the other. She pulled him forward until their lips met.

"Yes," she whispered.

He leaned back, dragging her on top of him. Peter's hands played through her long hair, his tongue flitting into her mouth. Emma sat up and placed the patty on the couch then pulled off her blouse and bra. Her small, firm breasts hung over him. He partially sat, taking one in his mouth while fondling the other. Peter sat fully and grabbed a leg, removing her boots and socks, kissing each toe, and then unhooked her belt, allowing Emma to shimmy out of the rest of her clothes. She reached up, and his shirt hit the floor next to hers, followed by the belt. They heard a sound by the door. Emma grabbed his hand and pulled Peter to the bedroom. By the time he landed on the bed, Peter's own disrobement was complete. Emma ran her hand along his length and guided him to her. They pulsed together as two heartbeats now in the rhythm of one synchronized in the harmony of the ages, coming to fulfillment.

They lay together after, not quite believing that the other was there, their hands entwined, watching the other's face. "My engagement present's in the other room. If I don't get it before Pat or one of the others, it will be gone."

Peter grinned. "I didn't just carry it fifteen hundred miles for it to be consumed by someone other than you."

He stood, his body lean and strong, his muscles well defined and moving with catlike grace across the floor. He winked at her and peeked out of the door. Seeing no one, he flung it open and took two steps back. Emma laughed into the sheets. She'd never missed a home meet and knew his preparation. Two long, bounding strides and a pair of front handsprings brought him up to the couch. Peter grabbed the prize and strode back to the room, leaving the ring as a victor, closing the door, and handing her the silver-foil package.

Emma unwrapped it, poking out the center with her nail and putting her ring finger through it. Peter smiled.

"See, it even fits!" Emma giggled and fed him the center piece and then started nibbling the edges. She raised her eyebrows, and he joined her, alternating their little bites until it was too thin and either had to be eaten or saved.

Emma removed it and set it back into the packaging, folding the foil around it gently to keep it from being broken. "I'll save it for later." She kissed him.

He returned the kiss, engulfing her in his arms. "Until I get the nonedible type."

Emma laughed again. "I don't know; the edible type was pretty nice."

They lay entwined as long as possible until it was time to get Sara.

Most of the citizens of Camden sat cross-legged on blankets and some on chairs they'd brought, circling the old church. Burt and Clarence managed to rig speakers around the building to carry the broadcasts. The morning news was brief and included regional weather forecasts, but the evening news was the main event. Promptly at seven, the tune played, and everyone became silent, stopping in midsentence.

"Good evening, North America," Alistair's voice rang throughout the yard. "This is Alistair Breedham, and I hope all our listeners have had a safe day. Here in Canada, the remaining parliament members met in the recently cleared Prince Edward Island. They have removed the connecting bridge; anyone entering the island must go through quarantine at the old ferry terminal prior to crossing. Only those with permission are allowed access to the island, so no one can joyride over. The Mounties have set up cannon and long-range weapons to destroy any unapproved watercraft or aircraft approaching the island. They have created two new havens for the public safety—one in Corner Brook, Newfoundland Island, and the second in Gull Harbor in Lake Winnipeg. Please bring as many blankets and as much nonperishable food and medical supplies as you can carry. Roads are only passable by foot, bicycle, horse, or motorcycle. There have been spikes in the outbreaks in Toronto, Montreal, and Edmonton. Warmer weather allows more Z activity, so as the spring progresses into summer, we must remain vigilant. The government would like to remind you to secure yourselves in upper floors at night, line floors and walls with metal to prevent zrats from chewing through, and limit light that escapes through windows. Now, for what I know to be more positive news, I turn to Dr. O'Conner."

"Thank you, Alistair." Emma's voice bounced through the speakers in cadence with the upbeat rhythm of her style of speaking. "I hope they can contain the recent surge in cases. Within the United States, we continue to locate communities that are surviving, and we hope to begin to bring more assistance to those most in need over the next few weeks, so please hold on. We know that those in coastal and riverfront areas are doing the best. Access to fresh water, fish, and other seafood appears to be key to survival."

"Like the earliest settlements," Alistair commented.

"Exactly. Using flowing water, many have created electricity, which gives those areas another advantage."

As Emma listed the communities discovered and their status, Charles had a US map out and a pen, marking all the announced locations. The town cheered when they heard Camden announced and that it was getting a "blue." Charles was pleased by the recognition of how well they were surviving, but mildly concerned. In the days of social media he avoided saying when he would be out of town to prevent being the victim of someone wanting to break in. He realized that the map in front of him could just as easily lead raiders to settlements worth attacking.

"Tonight will be part three on water purification—using a sand filter—discussed by Dr. Zovitch. We are working to confirm that the smell of Z and zrat repels the infected. If you have recently dead Zs and zrats near your community, you may wish to wait a day or so on burying them in order to repel Zs. We do not recommend applying blood or other material to one's person due to the risk of infection."

"Before I let you go, I understand your 'friend' is now safely with you and through quarantine," Alistair prodded, the gentle teasing present in his voice.

"I suppose you can refer to him as something else. He is my friend and has been for ten years, but he is now also my fiancé."

The crowd cheered for her. Charles grinned as Toya nudged him.

"Your girlfriend's been taken."

Charles felt a little shy. "She was never my girlfriend. But you are." Somehow in the moment, he found the courage that he'd lacked almost since the moment he'd met her crouching over him in a hotel bathroom. "Toya, *je t'aime*. I love you."

Toya grinned back at him, her fingers gently playing with his earlobe. "And what would you like to do about that?" she teased.

Charles took a breath. He dropped to one knee and grabbed her hand. "I would like to marry you."

Charles had never seen Toya speechless; she had a remark or comeback to everyone and every situation. She slowly smiled and dropped to her knee to look him eye to eye, not releasing his hand.

"You sure? You make it back to Quebec and I won't just be some little fling?" Her voice was huskier than normal, her eyes searching his face, looking for the joke.

"I 'ave never been more certain. We will survive this and 'elp make this new world." Charles clenched her hands slightly tighter, worried that she would pull away.

Toya's smile became wider, gradually exposing her perfect white teeth and reaching her eyes. "Then, you beautiful little Frenchman, hell yeah!"

Catch jabbed Stokes and indicated the couple, but Stokes had been watching from the corner of his eye, and from Charles's position and her response, he knew that only one thing could have occurred. A slight smile curled his lips. He was happy for his sister, and he might even let her know it.

Charlene sat in the dining hall hearing the news. She stood and raised her glass of tea. "To Peter!"

"To Peter!" the crowd shouted back.

She sat down, thinking of all the cans of food now in storage, and she looked around to all the couples kissing, some in earnest conversation. More than anything else, she realized what that announcement meant. They *would* survive. There would be love. There would be marriage, children, and a *future*. She just wished Al were here to see it with her. Charlene felt the bench move and looked up at Hitchins.

He leaned his glass forward to clink with hers. "To the future."

His eyes were full of meaning, but she couldn't do it, not just yet. Peter making it to Emma reawakened a hope inside her.

"But never forgetting the past," Charlene replied.

Hitchins nodded in understanding. Charlene noticed the farmer's daughter, Clarisse, chatting with some young men, but her eyes constantly strayed over to Hitchins. Charlene leaned forward. "Your time may be better spent in another's company."

Hitchins looked up as Clarisse's eyes met his and widened for a second, and he saw her blush and look back down.

"You'll be OK here?" Hitchins asked to be polite, already standing.

"Of course." Charlene smiled at him as she watched him make his way across the room, the young men melting away from Clarisse as soon as she made it obvious that there was only one person she wanted. "Best wishes," Charlene whispered as the two heads came closer, and Hitchins's slightly high-pitched laugh rolled through the room.

CHAPTER 13

June 9-14; Z Days 61-66

Emma and Peter wanted a small ceremony officiated by Father Nicholas the week after their engagement. This was immediately usurped by Press Secretary Zimburg. He, Elsie, and the president decided that the country needed a morale boost, and next to the birth of a child, there was nothing more beautiful or more filled with promise than a wedding. The ceremony would be broadcast live via radio, and then the film could follow. Emma doubted that anyone would want to see her wedding video, but Elsie reminded her of the viewership for royal weddings.

"I don't think I quite qualify as a 'royal' anything," Emma griped.

Elsie just smiled and patted her hand. "Honey, you are by far the closest thing we have to a celebrity. Everyone will be thrilled to watch it."

Emma would have retorted, but her stomach lurched, and she had to excuse herself. Morning sickness was a misnomer; it could hit at any time. Most seemed to chalk her frequent bathroom breaks to wedding jitters, but Emma knew that Gus suspected the truth. She was going to tell him, but Peter convinced her not to say anything until after the wedding.

The wedding would take place in the Cathedral of Saint Mary's in Cheyenne with the reception a couple of miles away at the Cheyenne Botanic Gardens at Sloan Lake. The workers moved heaven and earth to clear the area and fix the windows and benches torn apart for firewood and weapons. James hounded Emma to find who would walk her down the aisle, so she only half jokingly asked if her guard would do, but the press secretary did not find it so amusing. He also shook his head when she planned to walk by herself. James insisted that this be about having a sense of something almost normal but spectacular. Emma finally had the courage to ask Alistair if there was any way he could make it.

"I had been hoping you'd ask," was all he could say. The Mounties promised to get him there safely a couple of days before the big day and insisted on being part of his guard.

Andy found himself assisting with flowers, seating, and the reception. He finally threw up his hands and said, "Just because I'm gay does *not* mean that I automatically know something about planning weddings." He wasn't so annoyed when James confessed that it was a ploy for them to be closer.

Emma was proud of how the country came back together. They received letters identifying more communities, Andy found his step-mother and two of his sisters, twelve more members of Congress had been located, and Emma discovered an aunt and a cousin. As the radio towers went up, the chatter became excessive, so regulations went into effect to mandate certain hours and channels to be used by military and government only.

The next hurdle to be addressed was transportation. Planes and helicopters used too much fuel, and roads needed too much manpower to maintain and build, leaving trains the only thing that made sense. Throughout the northeast, passenger rail lines were plentiful, less so to the west, but cargo rail crisscrossed the entire United States, already in place and easier to maintain than roads. Peter knew that hybrid engines for trains existed, so he worked with the engineers to develop a working prototype to lower fuel use and expand fuel types. Peter felt happy to be busy. He saw Emma and Sara a couple of hours a day before Emma went on the air and had some time with Sara listening to the news, then a break between broadcasts, and then together again as they readied for bed.

During the broadcast, T minus four days to the wedding, Gus pulled Peter aside, leaving Sara with Marsha and his girls.

"I wasn't sure what to do with this," Gus began, "but there have been too many to ignore, and I can't bring myself to show Dr. O'Conner."

Peter felt a crawling sense of dread. "Show her what?"

"These." Gus removed a stack of about twenty letters from a sack. "There are more, but these are among the worst."

Peter sat as he and Gus unfolded them. Block letters but different handwriting, they all conveyed a similar message.

> *Luke 13:5: I tell you, nay: but, except ye repent, ye shall all likewise perish.*
> Until you repent and cast out your false God of Science, you are damned. Our way to salvation is through Jesus alone. If you continue to preach the false Gospel, you shall be torn from this earth.

By the time he reached the end of the first letter, Peter found his hand shaking in a mixture of anger and fear for his beloved. "Who else knows?"

Gus began to fold them back up. "The general, Press Secretary Zimburg, and a few others. Most of the letters that come for her are from adoring fans, thanking her for giving them the strength to survive. There are always a few who need to vocally disagree."

"The wedding will need—" Peter paced, unsure of what to do the violent energy that coursed through his body.

"—to proceed. When you are above ground, there will be hundreds of guards—closer to a thousand from the cathedral and in and around the park," Gus reassured him.

"Then why bother to show me?" Peter felt his anger directed toward his best friend.

"For one, you need to know, because in your shoes, I would want to know. Secondly, Dr. O'Conner can be impulsive. You may be able to keep her from putting herself in harm's way." Gus put his hand on Peter's shoulder. "Emma's safety is my responsibility. I won't let anything happen to her."

"Her safety is my—" Peter started, but Gus wouldn't let him finish, gripping the shoulder tighter.

"Her *happiness* is your responsibility, as much as it can be placed upon another. Her *safety* is mine. I swore an oath to it." Gus finally released Peter when he nodded.

Peter shrugged his shoulder, grimacing slightly, and then he checked his watch. "It'll be close to her break. I'd better get going."

In the lounge, Peter heard Emma's chipper voice.

"With the addition of almost three hundred thousand Alaskans, it brings the total US population up to sixty-one million known survivors. There are still many remote areas we have not been able to get to, so the hope is to find at least another five to six million."

Although overall the news seemed dire, it was far better than the count a month earlier.

Alistair responded, "The Canadian minister of citizenship reports our current population to be at eighteen million; with several major cities now either abandoned or stabilized, we seem to be through the worst of the outbreak. How have the vaccine trials been coming along?"

"Unfortunately, even though the antibody response was strong in the most recent vaccine, the dogs became Thinkers, which in turn is giving us an idea of how those occur in the first place. We have identified a breed trend for the immune canines. Dogs with close wolf DNA, such as malamutes, and those not that close, such as Newfoundlands and Cavalier King Charles spaniels, have a higher rate of immunity, close to 25 percent. Australian shepherds and border collies are close to 10 percent. Unfortunately, the overall rate for dogs is close to that of humans. For the safety of all, the consensus at this time is that only dogs with total immunity should be kept;

even partials should be put down. I have to admit that my love of dogs made me a dissenter; I recommended the partials be kept and spayed or neutered, but I understand the reasoning."

"It's good to know the breed trends; that may help those decide when an animal is bitten what to do. Thank you, Dr. O'Conner. I look forward to meeting you in a few days. Now we will be going to Ms. Alma Fried on cheese making."

Emma removed her headphones, her smile warm when she saw Peter through the glass in the lounge.

"What makes you look so dour?" she asked after their kiss.

"The weight of the world." Peter kissed her again. "And that of developing a more efficient hybrid locomotive engine. The breaking energy transfers well into the batteries, but we need to be able to recapture more to really make this work."

"So you can't transfer some of that swinging motion of the big beams that connect the wheels?" Emma offered as Peter took her arm for their evening stroll through the halls.

"Those are just on the engines, so not enough kinetic energy to do much, and likely the device would create drag." He paused a moment. "But the pivot and leaf spring, if we could capture the compression energy of the leaf spring as it goes over bumps. Hang on a minute." Peter harassed several people until he found a couple with some scrap paper and pen. "If I could put a small compressor here and here, using the kinetic energy to compress the air with the energy released to a small flywheel in with copper wire and a magnetic coil attached to the undercarriage ..." Peter held his breath for a minute. "That could be it!" He kissed Emma again, the letters a memory for now. He handed the pen back to the couple and looked sheepishly at Emma, who stood with her eyes dancing in mischief.

"Go on. Go see if you can get something to work. I may see you before morning." Emma smiled and shooed him along and then turned, almost bumping into Gus. "Oh! You were not the guard on duty when we started our walk."

Gus shook his head. "No, Rankin was supposed to be on this evening, but he's in physical therapy for his hand. He'll take over in a bit."

"It's not just that. I'm half your size, and I couldn't sneak up on a deaf man. I just don't know how you walk so quietly."

Gus gave it a moment of serious thought. "Practice," was his best reply. "After you." He indicated the hall back toward the studio.

Emma checked her watch. "I still have time for a walk."

"Yes, which we can do. And Marsha, the girls, and Sara are sitting in the lounge listening to a woman wax poetic about how to make cheese. I am sure this is very important information for some, but I do not see any of those four finding it particularly interesting." Gus raised his eyebrows.

"So it's really a rescue mission." Emma still felt Peter's energy at his discovery.

"It is indeed," Gus agreed.

Emma whistled a bit as she walked briskly down the hall, challenging Gus to move quietly at that speed. She felt on top of the world with a sense of happiness she could barely contain. Emma skipped, which did force Gus to jog, causing some rattling of equipment.

Joe Yardly handed Rich the rifle and scope.

"That doctor is leading this country down the wrong path," Yardly said. "We need to wrest the power now, before it's too late. My nephew knows the area and has been assigned as a perimeter guard, so you can get onto the grounds but not too close. She'll be surrounded, so you'll only get one shot."

Rich nodded. "I've only ever needed one shot." He checked the Dan .338 sniper rifle. "But I need to know the weapon. Is there somewhere I can target?"

Joe nodded toward the back of the house. "You can set up on the roof. We're about to clear Z parts from the outer fences. You'll likely be two hundred to three hundred yards from the party; the fence is about that distance."

Rich headed up the back stairs. Joe sat in his front room and opened his Bible to Revelation 17:1–14. The gunfire reverberated through the house.

Yes, the harlot must die, Joe thought as he closed the book.

Paulina stiffened when Guillermo approached, feeling the ghost of his hand on her thigh as they flew back the desalinators. She avoided him for days altogether, avoiding Mitchell, as well, and trying not to get her friend onto their leader's bad side. Guillermo thought it was his imagination at first. After all, how could anyone not want to be around him? He was the leader who'd fought off multiple attacks from Zs, cartels, and raiders, but as soon as Guillermo approached, Paulina said, "The tomatoes on my balcony are getting blossom-end rot. Beatrice is meeting me to show me what to do," and she practically ran away. Guillermo couldn't understand why it made him so angry.

He could force Paulina to come to his room. His men would bring her and make her part her legs for him, and then she would hate him forever. Guillermo sat on the roof with the last of his beer. His father would be proud of all he had done, but that act was not the act of a man; it was the act of a beast like El Padre or his henchmen. Guillermo remembered Francisco telling Rodrigo that if he ever wanted a woman, he needed to convince the woman to want him. If there was no convincing her, she was not the one for him and to let it go. Guillermo thought that it would be easy. Thinking about Paulina made his groin stir and his mouth dry, but the thought of her hating him was worse than the thought of never being with her. Guillermo stood. He was a man and would behave like it.

Guillermo made it down the stairs. At this time of day, he'd find Mitchell with Juan Carlos, planning and designing improvements for the town. They smiled and waved him over.

"We've come up with a plan for the hurricane wall." Mitchell sounded excited. "By my calculations, we should be able to withstand a ten- or even a twelve-foot surge. We need to create curves and channels."

"But so many walls, my friend. I don't know." Juan Carlos still appeared skeptical.

"The areas between can be grazing grounds most of the time, along with roadways. I'll do a mock-up and have it ready in a few days." Mitchell's excitement grew by the minute.

Hurricane season was starting, and the monster storms would hit where they would. No amount of prayer could divert those winds. Mitchell's eyes met Guillermo's. Guillermo did not seem to share the enthusiasm. For that matter, he seemed sad.

"Why don't we walk, and I'll give you the tour of what I have in mind," Mitchell suggested.

Guillermo nodded and followed Mitchell to the walkway.

Since the coup, Guillermo never traveled without guards, who kept a respectful distance ahead and behind to allow privacy but were always within easy reach.

"So what's up? You've been after me all month to come up with a hurricane plan."

"Paulina." Guillermo's heavy sigh told it all.

"Women have been a mystery to me my entire life. The ones you like often won't give you the time of day; the ones that like you always want to change you for some reason. One day, I will like one who likes me back for *me*—that's the hope, at any rate. Unless she's already a Z, then that may prove a problem." Mitchell elicited a chuckle for that one.

"You like Paulina too." Guillermo's comment hit more like an accusation.

"Sure. What's not to like? She's confident, she handles anything with a motor like a pro, she's not afraid of grease and dirt, and she's smart. If she only liked me back, I might be safe." Mitchell shrugged.

"She is relaxed around you. She smiles and laughs when you joke with her." Guillermo sounded more like the surly teen than the leader of a community now numbering close to six thousand.

"I've never tried to come on to her. I've stayed in what a lot of us geeky guys call 'the friend zone.' Most women like her will shut down when a guy like me comes on to her. So I stay in the periphery, the friend they can rely on, and sometimes we end up like Peter on the news and the girl he's loved for years does love him back, and in a few days they'll be married."

Mitchell grinned at the clear blue sky, the sweat pouring off in the humidity of the afternoon. The radio equipment from *The Glory of the Atlantic* let them pick up the news from the United States and Canada, and they sometimes listened in on radio messages running back and forth.

"They've been friends for ten years. That's a long time," said Guillermo.

The two found themselves facing the beach.

"If someone else comes along, you don't leave your life on hold; you move on with that one and remain friends with the first. Win-win." Mitchell felt so wise and pragmatic. If it were ever that simple. "Now, let's go over the surge walls."

Charlene sat on the porch, the letter from California in her hand. It wasn't Al's writing, and she couldn't open it. Her daughter and grandson played on the steps below, waiting. Finally, she tore it open. The writing had nice loops and circles above the i's.

> Dear Mrs. Dillon,
> I know this is not the letter you wanted to get. I saw your husband Al's picture on the correspondence board at our compound in LAX and knew I had to write. You likely already know what a brave man your husband was …

Charlene could make it no further. The low wail that issued from her heart brought Kristina to her side and caused Conner to cry. It was news she knew to expect, but there had always been hope, the thin hope, that he would also be OK. She should have known that no one in this world would be that lucky.

Kristina picked up the letter as Charlene's sobs dissipated.

> There were not that many guards, and even with piling what we could over every entrance at night, the Zs got in. He and some others fought the Zs back so the rest of us could retreat into an upstairs area we could seal off better. He would not back off until he knew the rest of us were safe. He didn't return. If it is OK with you, I kept his picture so I could show my son when he is older what the man who saved us looked like. God bless you.
> Antoinette Howard.

"Like Dad to be the hero." Kristina wiped back tears and set the porch swing in motion, her son and mother to each side.

Charlene nodded. "He would put the safety of others before himself. It's one of the things I loved about him." The tears flowed too fast to bother wiping.

Townsfolk approached but stepped back in understanding. Kristina shook them off and then led her mother into the house and made tea, wiping her tears onto her sleeve until Hitchins arrived, taking the teapot and doing kitchen work so that the two women could mourn together. In times past, people would bring food, but since that was strictly centralized, they arrived with mop buckets and dusting cloths. Not that Charlene's home was ever dirty, but it became the cleanest it had been since the day it was built. No dust mote could withstand the cleaning force that day.

Over the next few days, Charlene forced herself to do more, focusing on the now and on what she had. Everyone was more deferential than normal; she knew that would pass, as well. No one had loved her like Al, and she had loved no one else like she'd loved him. Al would've wanted her to refocus on the living, and his memory deserved no less.

Charles marveled at the twinkling lights along the pews from so many strands of Christmas decorations, the silk flowers cascading along the benches and on the arch he stood beneath, modified from one of her raised beds. Originally, they would have done the wedding in the church, but too many wanted to attend, so they held it outside in the late afternoon. Charles was a man accustomed to wearing suits, and he felt proud waiting at the front, Catch standing as his best man. The church kept enough recorded music, and Burt happily acted as DJ as all waited for the bride. In a moment, the music struck its chord, and the piece by Wagner everyone knew as "Here Comes the Bride" brought all in attendance to their feet.

Toya was no less than radiant. Another mystery was where they found all that white taffeta. Her dress cascaded around her in glory. Stokes walked her down the aisle, looking, Charles had to say, happy. And then she was there, her hands in his. The reverend spoke some words, but Charles could only see her eyes and her smile. With a squeeze from her hands, he said, "I do." More words were said, and she repeated, "I do." Then Charles heard the most wonderful thing. "I pronounce you man and wife. You may kiss the bride." And Charles did, with cheers all around.

The reception was the evening meal, the normal fish stew with some potatoes provided by the last government drop. Charles also received word back from his brother, happy to hear of his survival and his impending nuptials. Their mother had not survived, but their father was the source of immunity and was doing well, sending his regards. The family farm was now host to over five hundred survivors, which required a lot of work. Charles snorted. *Try organizing six times that with fewer resources.*

The evening festivities were briefly on hold during the news, and with those willing to learn about cheese huddling near the speakers, the rest chatted and mingled, all dressed in the finest clothes they could find. Then they danced. Charles already knew that Toya did not like to follow, and this carried over to dancing. They laughed after the official first dance.

"Maybe I should let you lead," Charles admitted.

"Maybe you should," Toya agreed. They decided to alternate and did much better.

At the end of the evening, they were able to retire to their apartment on a low floor of the tower. There could be no honeymoon, no exotic locale to fly off to. But they would have each other. Both Charles and Toya decided that that was damned good in and of itself.

Emma had to admit that Alistair was right; he had a face for radio. A man in his late fifties, he looked closer to seventy, with long jowls and droopy eyes reminding her of a basset hound, but his voice in person managed to resonate even more than it did over the airwaves. They broadcast the show on the night before the wedding from the booth Emma considered her second home. Their banter was lighter than normal, and when the West Coast broadcast was finished, Alistair grasped her hands.

"My dear, you are even prettier than when all this began. You seem to radiate light and hope. I think marriage will suit you well." Alistair drew back and stood. "But I am an old man, and tomorrow looks to be a long day."

"Our paths go together, since you are staying with Elsie and her family. They are a couple of doors down from mine." Emma linked her arm in Alistair's, and Rankin took the lead with the Mounties behind. Emma felt slightly ashamed to think that they would be in bright-red uniforms, but she was informed that, for most duties, they wore much more somber attire. Tomorrow, however, they would be in their traditional glorious red.

"So where is Peter this evening?" Alistair asked as they strolled.

"Finishing a way to make the train engines more efficient. Tonight he will be staying with Gus and his family. They have young daughters, so I told him he couldn't be out late."

"Hmm, so no seeing the bride—"

"It's a silly superstition, but we decided to keep it."

"What should I call you at the next broadcast?"

"What?" Emma felt perplexed.

"Dr. O'Conner, Dr. Saitou, some combination?"

"Oh!" Emma finally understood. "Peter and I discussed it. We felt, with fewer people, we needed to be more casual and personal. So simply 'Dr. Emma' or 'Emma' will be fine."

"Hmm. Should I be Alistair only?"

"What you call yourself will be up to you. Alistair, Breedham, Ali B., " Emma beamed up at him with mischief.

Alistair rolled his eyes. "I do not need to reinvent myself as a postapocalyptic rapper."

Rankin stopped at Emma's door. Alistair released her.

"Until tomorrow, then," he said before parting.

Emma entered her apartment after Rankin to find Sara sulking on the couch.

"What's wrong?" Emma felt the little cloud cover her happiness.

"Nothin'." Sara turned to stare at a book.

Emma sighed and sat on the edge of the couch, the only room the child would let her. "Are you angry about the wedding? About your dress?"

"You're going away!" Sara bit her lip and turned away even farther. Emma could hear the quaver in her breathing.

"I don't think anyone's letting *me* go—" Emma stopped as Rankin cleared his throat.

"I heard Peter and Gus and Marsha talking. You're all—"

A quick knock let in Peter, who grinned sheepishly. "The walls are too thin. We're *all* going away ... for two weeks."

Emma jumped up and kissed and then hugged him. Sara hopped from one foot to the next.

"Where?" Emma and Sara called out in unison.

"Me to know, and you to find out." Peter pecked Sara on the head and then left a soft and lingering kiss on Emma's bow of a mouth. "But, with luck, there will be sunshine. Now I'm off to bed. I have the happiest day of my life tomorrow." He parted without allowing Emma another touch.

"And I guess we need to pack." Emma hugged Sara.

"That won't take long," Sara pointed out.

Emma thought of the closet back in San Antonio where she couldn't quite close the door due to the amount of stuff. The clothing here could fit into a carry-on. The only possession from her past she truly missed was a photo from her older sister's wedding, with everyone dressed in their finest and her younger brother making faces while pulling at his suit. That photo was firmly in her mind, but she worried that the image would fade with time. Emma never received word from any of her siblings, and that loss filled her for a moment, shooing Sara out.

"You are quite right. Let's try to get some sleep," Emma said, and then she collapsed on her bed with thoughts of how her family would react to Peter, finally sleeping a couple of hours before dawn.

Elsie woke her early, rushing to do her hair and her makeup and then finally buttoning her in to *the* dress. Emma marveled at the intricate embroidery, the colorful hummingbirds and honeysuckle vines across the bodice and down the side and then incorporated into the ten-foot satin train. Her headdress was a golden tiara studded with small garnets and other gems. She finally stood before the mirror and could not believe it as she looked at herself, half expecting a flock of animated bluebirds to whisk in and start singing. With the exception of the tiniest bulge in her lower abdomen, Emma looked like a princess in an animated movie. She started to giggle and then laugh at the sheer ridiculousness of it all.

"Careful you don't start tearing up. We don't want to redo your makeup," Elsie advised, opening the door for James.

The press secretary beamed. "You are going to look great on camera." He handed her a mixed bouquet, including branches with small, white flowers.

"I don't know if I want to walk down the aisle carrying hemlock." Emma eyed the dangerous little buds.

"Unfortunately, it's one of the few things blooming that's not edible." James took a turn around Emma. "Very nice. Now we just need to get you to the church on time."

James started to hum as he ushered them out. Andy met them at the door and took up the job of page, draping the long fabric over his arm. During the ceremony, several of the young children, including Miranda, would do that honor. Sara and Meagan would be flower girls, Elsie her matron of honor, with Marsha and Cavita as attendants. Gus was to stand as Peter's best man, with Andy and a fellow engineer named Douglas as groomsmen.

Emma felt her excitement rise in the elevator. Not only would she marry her love, she would finally see the sun for the first time in over a month. The sky was almost too much. Her existence as a troglodyte made her feel almost as uncomfortable as the Zs as she blinked and almost winced at the illumination of midday. She felt a pleasant prickling in her skin as the warmth filled her, allowing all her worries to burn away.

Then there was the camera. She blushed and waved as the carriage pulled up. It was more of a surrey, complete with a fringe on the top. The pair of Clydesdales sported dappled coats and carefully brushed "feathers" of glowing white hair above their hooves. Rankin handed her in and then took the seat beside the driver. Two of her other guards, wearing suits but sporting rifles slung around their backs, took positions ahead and behind.

The streets were filled along the route to the cathedral; people brandished cards with doves and roses drawn on them, cheering her along. Emma could not understand why the guards looked so tense. How could any of those faces harbor any malice? Why would any human wish to harm her? Emma could only imagine that Gus took his job very seriously.

Alistair met her at the church, assisting her down and to the waiting area.

Marsha smiled and touched the intricate hairpiece, saying, "They certainly went all out." Her own emerald-green gown with its empire waist hid her second trimester pregnancy and thigh holster well.

Elsie made sure that the flower girls' "petals," made from scrap fabric, were ready in their baskets. Rankin tapped at the door, and they nodded in readiness. The strains of Pachelbel's Canon in D filled the air, and Marsha regally walked out, followed by Cavita. Elsie gave instructions to Meagan, Sara, and pages and exited with a smile. Emma nodded to the flower girls, who laughed, three years in age between them but of the same height, both of whom had a tendency to be rambunctious and preferred play fighting over anything else. But here they behaved and exited in their most graceful manner, though not without Meagan sticking out her tongue prior to leaving first.

Alistair took Emma's arm. They both smiled at the camera and waited near the door for the opening strains of the Prince of Denmark's March, the trumpets filling the cathedral, bringing Emma and Alistair into the church aisle. Despite all the familiar faces and some new, only Peter's mattered. She heard the murmurs of those remarking at her gown, the occasional tug as a page fell behind the others, but Peter's smile of wonder pulled her along. Emma wanted to run to him, show her eagerness, but the long train would have been an impediment. After what felt an eternity but could have been no more than a couple of minutes, Peter's hands clasped hers.

They each spoke their vows clearly for all to hear. The proper ring was a lovely platinum-and-diamond band, with Peter's a simple band of platinum, all chosen by the good Secretary Zimburg. Then they kissed, and all cheered. For the recessional, Emma insisted on a modern folk band's upbeat love song, which begged for dancing. Andy and Douglas took care of the train while Gus and Marsha watched the crowd as they exited. Gus's greatest fear was the route from the cathedral to the lake. He'd placed snipers on every other building and watchers on the street, but again, all those present seemed happy for the couple, and some cheered for him, as well.

In the small room in the conservatory, Emma was finally unleashed from the unwieldy train. "This thing is amazingly heavy." She fingered the fine satin. "But how beautiful."

Peter could only grin. "Not as beautiful as you." He snuck in a kiss.

"You might be rewarded for that line." Emma grinned.

"Even better. Shall we get through the never-ending line of guests?" Peter took her arm. James set the reception line by the lake, a better backdrop for the cameras. Emma had done eighteen-hour shifts in the hospital but never felt so tired as when she finally sat to eat the wedding feast—beef stew with dumplings and boiled greens. James wanted a feast with old-fashioned steak and barbeque, another area Emma and Peter overruled; having that kind of meal while so many struggled would have been like rubbing their faces in the tragedy. No, the wedding meal would be like that of most of the country.

June days were long, and they would take advantage with dancing as the band rolled out. Peter and Emma twirled and danced on the crowded floor. Emma saw an opening and raced to the nearby garden, Peter at her heels.

"Emma! Keep close." Peter sounded frightened.

"We'll have to go in soon. I want to see the sky. I want a moment with my love." Emma kissed him as he reached her. "And let him know I will always love him."

"Now, you've got you're shot!" Bill hissed. Joe's nephew had found a spot with good cover but almost no view of the reception itself. The harlot had been behind others all day, until now.

"I know my job," Rich answered, finger over the trigger as he breathed out.

Peter could hear some of the guards approaching; he smiled and knelt before Emma, kissing her lower stomach.

"I promise to love you too," Peter whispered.

"What are you doing?" Bill became agitated, his voice beginning to carry as Rich folded up his tripod, the devil woman still smiling across the grass.

"There's a special place in hell for anyone who murders a child or a pregnant woman, and that woman's pregnant." Rich efficiently secured the rifle and tripod into a bag and started sliding backward through the grass, guards beginning to close in on Bill's sound and movement. "If you don't want to get caught, I suggest you shut up and move."

Emma laughed and bent over Peter. "I would kneel too, but I think this dress is too heavy to let me get up again."

Peter stood and took her arm, glancing at the patch of tall grass a hundred yards away that was now getting a lot of attention from the guards as Rankin took up his place behind and Gus in front, both looking upset. Peter thought of the letters and tightened his grip, leading her back to the safety of numbers. Her smile never wavered as the face of hope looked into her future.

End of Book I

Zapocalyps: Pathogen Character List:

Al Dillon– Charlene's husband – Los Angeles

Alistair Breedham – voice of Canada - Toronto

Angus McLeod (Gus) – Lt. Colonel in the Rangers, heads Emma's protection detail

Antonio – research assistant- Mexico

Arthur – Martin Polk's neighbor - Seattle

Auntie – leader – Camden

Barry – Secret Service Agent – Seattle, etc.

Beatrice – Middle-aged Englishwoman trapped on vacation

Belinda- research assistant – Mexico

Bernadette – Margery Pool's daughter – Elysian Heights

Bernard – Camden guard – Camden

Betty Yardly – rancher – Fort Morgan

Bill – ranch hand - Cheyenne

Bill & Becky Chalmers – Peter's neighbors – Surry

Bob the Newfoundland – immune dog of Hazel's – Fort Morgan

Brad – pharmacist – Elysian Heights

Buller – Shujaa gang member – Camden

Burro – one of Guillermo's men – Playa del Carmen

Burt – motorcycle mechanic - Camden

Busayo – New York cab driver

Butch – maintenance man at Surry Nuclear Plant – Surry, etc.

Carlita – Mayoral candidate – Playa del Carmen

Catch – Stokes' best friend and fellow Shujaa gang member - Camden

Cathy – Bernadette's younger daughter – Elysian Heights

Celeste – Bernadette's older daughter - Elysian Heights

Chantal – teacher from Quebec – Philadelphia

Charlene Dillon– mayor of Elysian Heights - Marietta

Charles Tremblay – science teacher from Quebec – Camden

Chief Hillier – Police Chief – Elysian Heights

Chris Adams – Peter's childhood best friend – Surry

Clarence – former army medic – Camden

Clark – gun collector – Elysian Heights

Clarisse Willis – farmer's daughter – Elysian Heights

Claudette – twelve-year-old archer – Elysian Heights

Colonel Pearce – commanding officer at Fort Knox – Elysian Heights

Con – Shujaa gang member – Camden

Conner – Charlene's grandson – Elysian Heights

Damilola – Busayo's wife – New York

Daniel – founder and chief of the Shujaa gang

Decker – Army MP and part of Emma's protection detail – Atlanta, etc.

Detective Morales – San Antonio Police Department – San Antonio

Detective Williams – San Antonio Police Department – San Antonio

Dexter – Secret Service agent - Seattle

Dr. Anderson – senior researcher – Mexico

Dr. Andrew Perdue (Andy) – Anesthesia Resident – San Antonio, etc.

Dr. Austin Draeger – surgeon - Camden

Dr. Broadwell – general surgeon – San Antonio, etc.

Dr. Brown – Family Medicine Attending – San Antonio

Dr. Cavita Mehra – CDC investigator – San Antonio, etc.

Dr. Cory Miller – Emergency Medicine Resident – San Antonio, etc.

Dr. Emma O'Conner – the face of Hope – San Antonio, etc.

Dr. Goodman – head of the CDC – Washington DC, etc.

Dr. John Lowe – CDC researcher and surgeon – San Antonio, etc.

Dr. Pendler – community doctor - Raleigh

Dr. Thomas Graham – Zoonotic and Emerging Diseases Div. of the CDC .

Dr. Zovitch – water purification expert - Cheyenne

Dolly – Paul's wife (not in good health) – Elysian Heights

Duke – 2nd in charge of the Shujaa gang – recruiter and trainer

Dulce – girlfriend of Raul Lara – Mexico

Ed – gate guard for Surry Nuclear Power Plant – Surry

Edgar Allen – nerd teenager - Seattle

Eduardo Palacios – son of El Padre – Playa del Carmen

Elisandra Hudson (Elsie) – Secretary of State – Washington DC, etc.

El Padre Palacios – head of the Palacios family cartel – Mexico

Elvira Polk – mother to Martin Polk – Seattle

Erik – helicopter pilot - Cheyenne

Ernesto – infected person – New York

Esmeralda Garcia – news anchor – San Antonio

Father Nicholas – catholic priest - Cheyenne

Father Patrick – Catholic Priest ridding Ireland of the scourge

Femi – cab driver/ Busayo's cousin – New York

Francisco – Guillermo and Rodrigo's father

Gamesman – Irish warmblood - Camden

Gehler – Chief of Staff – Washington DC

General Duarte – General of the Army – four star – Washington, DC

General Loran – Secretary of Defense - Cheyenne

Greg Pool – Margery Pool's son – Elysian Heights

Guillermo – fourteen-year-old leader of the Playa del Carmen compound – Playa del Carmen

Hamlet – Shujaa gang member – Camden

Hank Daughtry – phys ed and defense instructor - Cheyenne

Hazel – survivor/dog lady – Fort Morgan

Henry Bean – radio operator- Vancouver

Hiccup/Arnold – Stokes and Toya's younger brother – Camden

Hitchins – handyman – Elysian Heights

Hugo – research assistant – Mexico

Isaiah Feldman – medical student - Raleigh

Jacob – Secret Service Agent – Seattle

Jan – Marine on Emma's security detail - Atlanta

James Zimburg – Press Secretary – Washington DC, etc.

Javier – Guillermo's friend – Playa del Carmen

Jiromaru Saitou/Otousan – nuclear engineer/Peter's father - Surry

Joanna – nurse at San Antonio General – San Antonio

Joe Yardly – rancher near Fort Morgan

Josette – teacher from Quebec – Philadelphia

Juan – former Sergeant in the Cancun tourist police – Playa del Carmen

Juan Carlos – farmer – Playa del Carmen

Julian – Hitchins older son – Elysian Heights

Justo – research assistant – Mexico

Kevin Dillon– Charlene's oldest son, army medic and physician assistant student – varies

Kristina – Charlene's daughter – Elysian Heights

Kurt – Charlene's assistant – Elysian Heights

Lieutenant Borland – head of CDC facility security – Atlanta

Lieutenant Bradley – Coast Guard – Camden, etc.

Lieutenant Drake – commander at Allendale transfer facility - Georgia

Lieutenant Godfrey – Army officer – Atlanta, etc.

Lupita – nurse at San Antonio General – San Antonio

Malcolm – Shujaa gang member - Camden

Margery Pool – prepper – Elysian Heights

Maria Castaneda – research assistant – Mexico

Marsh McLeod – former Marine Staff Sergeant, Gus's wife – Seattle, etc.

Martin Polk – actor, son of Elvira Polk – Seattle

Mateo Peron – groom - Camden

Meagan McLeod – Gus & Marsha's older daughter

Melanie, LVN – nurse at San Antonio General, San Antonio, etc.

Michelina – lawyer – Playa del Carmen

Miguel – law student – Playa del Carmen

Miralda – El Padre's housekeeper – Playa del Carmen

Miranda Mcleod – Gus and Marsha's younger daughter

Mitchell – aeronautical engineer trapped on vacation - Playa del Carmen

Mosha – Toya's biological father

Mr. Ortiz – patient Alpha - San Antonio

Mr. Parker – citizen of Elysian Heights – Elysian Heights

Mr. Velez – patient Beta – San Antonio

Mrs. Murchins – caterer/cook – Elysian Heights

Ms. Lynn – vet tech – Elysian Heights

Navigator Samuelson – acting Captain of the Glory of the Atlantic – Playa del Carmen

Nelson brothers – owners of most remaining oil refineries – Rhode Island

Olivia – horse trainer - Camden

Pat – Army Military Police Officer on Emma's security detail- Atlanta

Paul – Secretary of the Elysian Heights Community Council – Elysian Heights

Paulina Esparza– Lieutenant in the Mexican Air Force – Playa del Carmen

Peter Saitou – engineer, Emma's friend from college – on the road

President Paulson – US President – Washington DC, etc

Private A. Alfonse – assists in quarantine in Cheyenne - Cheyenne

Private D. Sheldon – Army private – Seattle, etc.

Private R. Smythe – Army private – Seattle, etc.

Private Thomason – gate security – Seattle

Ralph Willis – farmer – Elysian Heights

Rankin McLeod – Navy Seal/ Gus's younger brother – Atlanta, etc.

Raul Lara – henchman to El Padre – Mexico

Ray – Shujaa gang member - Camden

Reverend Curtis – minister – Camden

Rich – sniper - Cheyenne

Rodrigo – Guillermo's older brother – Playa del Carmen

Ronaldo – soldier for Guillermo – Playa del Carmen

Sabo – Peter's Grandmother – Surry

Sammy Jo Taylor – nurse taking care of Elvira Polk - Seattle

Sara – ten-year-old girl rescued by Peter – Surry, etc.

Saya – Toya's friend and hotel housekeeper – Camden

Scott – Martin Polk's neighbor – Seattle

Secretary of Agriculture – Walter Branch - Cheyenne

Secretary of Energy – Gabriella Monteverdi - Cheyenne

Secretary of the Interior Justin Marshall - Cheyenne

Sergeant. LeStrange – coordinates intake in Cheyenne – Cheyenne

Sienna – friend of Eduardo Palacios- Mexico

Stokes – Shujaa gang 3rd in command, leader – Camden

Sylvia – Kurt's mother, runs the quarantine house – Elysian Heights

Thiago – fishing boat captain – Playa del Carmen

Toya – boxer, Stokes' sister - Camden

Trevor Draeger – Austin's brother - Camden

Veronica – Emma's roommate – San Antonio

Vice President Solis – US Vice President – Cheyenne

Violet – assistant Cruise director of the Glory of the Atlantic – Playa del Carmen

Will Billings – Speaker of the House - Seattle

Acknowledgements:

Kathleen Eaton-Robb, Mary Eaton and Suzan Eaton – my wonderful sisters who helped edit and gave unwavering support throughout the creation of this book.

John Nowinski – my loving and supportive husband, who gave up many evenings and weekends of togetherness for my reawakened passion for writing

Anthony Villa – who helped make the military areas feel real

Laura Ferguson – my best friend, who's insights on story flow helped to make this book come to life

CPSIA information can be obtained
at www.ICGtesting.com
Printed in the USA
FSOW01n0839250915
11505FS

9 781457 534355